THE REDEMPTION CENTER IS CLOSED ON SUNDAYS

ALSO BY ANDREA HAIRSTON

Master of Poisons

Redwood and Wildfire

Will Do Magic for Small Change

Archangels of Funk

Mindscape

THE REDEMPTION CENTER IS CLOSED ON SUNDAYS

ANDREA HAIRSTON

TOR PUBLISHING GROUP
NEW YORK

THE REDEMPTION CENTER IS CLOSED ON SUNDAYS

Interior illustration by Pan Morigan

A Tor Book
Published by Tom Doherty Associates / Tor Publishing Group
120 Broadway
New York, NY 10271

www.torpublishinggroup.com

EU Representative: Macmillan Publishers Ireland Ltd., 1st Floor, The Liffey Trust Centre, 117–126 Sheriff Street Upper, Dublin 1, D01 YC43

The Library of Congress Cataloging-in-Publication Data is available upon request.

ISBN 978-1-250-80731-1 (hardcover)
ISBN 978-1-250-80733-5 (ebook)

First Edition: 2026

Printed in the United States of America

10 9 8 7 6 5 4 3 2

Dedicated to Bruce Berkow (1948–2025)—
Friend and Visionary

Yo,
I believe
in gravity.
I feel the stars
calling.

BOOK I

YESTERDAY AND TODAY

JOURNAL ENTRY:

---

*The haunted houseboat gathers Strangers, Ancient Enemies, and Lost Souls then waits to see what they will do, if they can survive themselves . . . An improv on their heartbeats.**

STORM MUSINGS:

---

*Later, something kills me. In the meantime, I live happy.**

* Captions from the Iris Library's International Trickster Exhibition

T O D A Y

PAULA—*Clues*

Any random group of people have much more in common than they realize. Not just 99 percent of the same genes, not just sharing this particular moment in history, this unique traverse of the Earth and Sun through vast darkness. Everybody is entangled in miracles and mysteries. . . .

Contemplating cosmic connections with strangers on a hot Monday morning in August, Paula B. Queenie avoided spewing nasty slop she'd regret at the new tenant from across the hall (who said his name way too fast) and at Karl, her upstairs neighbor (who was sweaty and disgusting after a workout). Standing by a rickety banister in the flickering shadows of a busted fluorescent, they yelled about America circling the drain. Mostly Karl yelled.

Two women had gone missing in the last six months, then turned up dead. Unprecedented in this necklace of picturesque New England towns around the university. The cops found one victim yesterday, a few blocks over, a rich lady celebrity according to internet chat. Actually the dog found her sticking out of an RC recycling bin in the borderlands between a good neighborhood and the dodgy section.

No real leads yet, so Karl ranted about corrupt cops with dirty secrets who *could give a shit about our side of the map.* The new tenant, a defiant middle-aged athlete in running togs, raced away from Karl's blather, singing a Bulgarian folk song. Paula quivered at this latest horror and wondered, who drew the maps? Who consigned their five-story, cement-block apartment building to the shadowlands, where a killer might lurk in a crowd and pass for harmless, where everyone was suspect: Upstairs Karl, the new tenant, even Paula. Mapmakers, man!

Why would Paula kidnap some rich child then dump them in the recycling with shredded documents and a burnt turkey (that even the dog didn't want)? Why would anybody mix trash like that? Paula swallowed a curse. She probably shared (secret) impulses with the kidnapper, the killer, and the victim. Of course, Paula beating up a Mercedes-Benz with a sledgehammer wasn't as bad as beating a person to death . . . She had to think on this tonight, when she had more clues.

"Fuckin' banana republic!" Karl yelled into the stairwell as the new tenant escaped out the main door. Karl had a bathroom leak and called five plumbers. Nobody was available before this evening when he had to work. "Stupid-ass unions."

"What about the landlord?" Paula ventured.

"That shitbag's office put me on hold then hung up," Karl replied.

Instead of letting him wait, instead of coming home to a flood or reports that socialists were sabotaging American infrastructure, Paula clomped up warped, uneven stairs to fix the leak for free, if she could; turn off the water if not. Karl hovered over her, fascinated, clueless, and funky. A raggedy towel from his gym job stuck to his neck: PUMP IT UP! BE THE BEST YOU! Paula showed him a rusty joint and nasty blockage then suggested that whatever he put down the drain on a regular basis, he should dispose of somewhere more appropriate.

Karl almost broke into tears, relieved that the socialists hadn't found him yet. He huffed and flexed. "I'm ready for 'em though."

A big guy and a weight lifter, Karl shaved his body hair so as not to obscure the tattoos or muscles. Only bushy, dyed-blond eyebrows remained—a scary look for social media, hashtag Survivalists-Forever. He'd been in training for the apocalypse since he was twenty-five, ten years and some change. His shallow closets were jammed with neatly stacked canned goods and survival gear. Oil lanterns, ancient weapons, paper maps, and tools hung on the walls of his otherwise spartan apartment. Paula liked to be prepared for anything too, but seriously. She started to leave, and Karl blocked the front door, pleading with her to reset the Wi-Fi while she was up.

Instead of saying no, she left a voice message at today's cleaning job. "An'qwenique, I have a mission—might be running late." She'd have to race to make the 7:30 AM bus. "Oops, almost forgot." She opened the valve to let Karl's water through again.

"At least I'm not stuffing bodies down my pipes." Karl laughed. Paula didn't. He was keeping something from her. He dragged her to the spaghetti junction by his router. She switched it off then on. No problem.

He shoved his phone in her face and scrolled multiple sites. Supposedly the cops put out a call on social media and everywhere to find the owner of a goofy St. Berdoodle (St. Bernard / poodle mix). Why would cops do that? Every image was blurry, refusing to resolve: a haze of curly silver hair except lopsided black ears and black masks over slitted eyes. Social media hype, but Paula recognized the dog immediately. They'd met when Paula cleaned out the dog's cage at the Pet and Wild Animal Rescue. Paula deep-cleaned the Rescue every Thursday. Always an adventure.

"Police tried to take that dog in for questioning yesterday. She escaped." Karl scowled. "I can't believe you haven't seen these." He was one of the average Americans who checked his phone 144 times a day. Paula had trained herself out of that. (Worse than kicking heroin.) She wasn't letting Karl or anybody drag her back. "A dog like that walked you home from the bus one night, right?" Many nights.

She squinted at an image. "You think that stray is the dog cops are looking for?"

"I don't know. You tell me," Karl replied. "She's your friend."

Few animals stayed long enough at the Animal Rescue for

Paula to make friends. The Rescue's mission was to release everybody back into the wild or find a good people-home ASAP. The St. Berdoodle was there maybe four weeks. She broke out of her cage to follow Paula around while she cleaned or sometimes to go on a midnight stroll. Nobody figured how the dog got loose. Paula asked her point blank once, *What's your secret?* She jumped up, put soggy paws on Paula's chest, and licked her nose.

The landlord's no-pets-just-service-animals policy prevented Paula from adopting the big fluffball. Good prospects took the St. B home and returned her a few days later till last October. Paula was surprised how sad the empty cage felt. By Halloween, she knew the dog had found a home and wasn't coming back, and good for her. Then, one Monday night in November, the St. B showed up at the bus stop. Instead of turning her in for bad behavior, Paula gave her a cheese bun. They'd been meeting ever since, no questions asked. Paula refused to check the collar for an owner.

"I can't tell these stray-hounds apart," Paula lied.

Karl didn't notice. "Give up anything you know. The cops could use some help." He raged on about the idiot police allowing a major suspect to chase after the dog and poof, they were both smoke. This was not mere incompetence. This was part of the plot to destroy capitalism: recycle or die! "RC's Disposal—their motto is '**DUMP IT ALL AND START DOING BETTER!**'" Karl shook his head. "That ain't random, that's new-age code. We're supposedly so messed up, we gotta dump everything American and—"

"Right." Paula never knew what to say when Karl spun these theories. She wiped flecks of spit from his screen. The St. Berdoodle was magic. Forget trying to lock her up.

"You claimed the dog could Houdini her way out of San Quentin!" Karl interrupted his own rant.

"Your Wi-Fi was fine, right?" Paula sidestepped.

He hugged his bare chest, sheepish. "You're my one friend in this building."

She was the only person who listened to him for more than thirty seconds. Did that make them friends? Paula could talk to anybody, one of her superpowers. Karl wanted to talk about murder, mystery dogs, and that suspicious character, a burly Black man, who claimed the dog wasn't his. Exactly, *this dog belonged to herself.* According to the trash-talking disinformation-nuts Karl mainlined, the Black man walked away from the crime scene and nobody had seen him since. He was a serial killer sex addict, an anti-fascist terrorist, or both. The internet, man!

"OK," Paula said carefully. Challenging disinfo-teers in possession of flimsy camera evidence was almost impossible. "Black Mystery Guy is more likely an innocent bystander, a later victim, or even an alien with unknown powers."

"Alien?" Karl looked offended. "I'm being serious." So were the other disinfo-teers.

"According to your sources, Black Mystery Man walked into the brush following the dog, then both of them literally disappeared on the security cameras. The police and the Feds combed the entire area and found nothing. Disappearing is a difficult trick for us Earth beings. And how'd the Feds get there so quickly?"

"OK, maybe not the Feds." Karl pouted, furry eyebrows wiggling. "Guys checking out the scene saw shit."

"Did they understand what they saw?"

The Norse gods on Karl's chest became agitated. "But an alien? No way."

Paula sighed. "I clean a building over there, Cloud Heights Enterprises, a cutting-edge tech firm. Their security cameras are no joke. Nobody's disappearing on that rig."

"Calling nine-one-one then disappearing is this guy's how-to-get-away-with-murder plan."

"Not the optimum plan for a burly Black man," she countered.

"I'm not being racist," he insisted. His jaw and hands clenched.

"Uh-huh," she replied, weary. Karl sputtered. He expected her to argue. Why? People believed in the world they wanted to believe in and ignored evidence of other worlds. Karl, his disinfo-teers, and Paula too, lived in a multiverse while insisting it was one world. What could anybody do about that besides despair? Paula refused despair, however she had yet to come up with anything better.

Karl squirmed. "You got me wrong. I just mean, we are all suspects."

Paula startled at her earlier thought in Karl's mouth. She narrowed her eyes at him. "Tattooed, burly, bald white dude, with a hint of a southern accent . . . Alabama?"

He nodded. "Tuskegee, but from New England, mostly."

"I don't imagine you murdering anybody," she said gently.

He licked his lips, excited by her faith in him, yet still unsure. "I don't think of you like that either."

"How sweet of you." Hard to predict what she might do. Beating up that Benz was a total surprise. Anger and violence crackled under her breath, snuck across her skin.

"I've seen someone disappear, live, on stage," Karl said. "What you need is the right setup. Dude at the gym says you can even fool cameras. Deepfake 'em."

"Deepfake? Not this particular horror show. The clues don't fit," Paula declared.

Karl's eyebrows went up. "Oh yeah?"

Especially the St. Berdoodle bit. The dog walked Paula in and out of some nasty mess on High Street several times. Saved her butt down by the river too—when she got lost in a tunnel and a maze of trails. A rescue dog! Burly Black Man was probably the dog's friend. She led him into a dangerous situation and when it got dicey with the cops, she helped him disappear.

Paula had seen the dog disappear before, at the Mooseberry Mall that night last spring when half the county lost power. The St. Berdoodle blinked out like the lights. The other time, they were walking by the Maple Street fire station and the alarm went off. Engine after engine screeched into the street. The dog growled at tones Paula couldn't hear. Her tail was a blade and her silver hair shimmered like it was full of tiny sparks. She leapt over the fire hydrant and was gone.

Both times Paula refused to trust her eyes and concocted crap explanations about sudden dark, sensitive dog ears, and mad dashes that explained nothing. This allowed her to ignore uncomfortable, inexplicable possibilities. She refrained from mentioning any of this to Karl.

"Deepfake or not, the dog is key." He was right about that.

"Yeah. OK, but I can't be late for work." Paula patted Karl's arm. "I have dust and pollen patrol for An'qwenique."

He nodded. "Your rich lady writer."

Paula slipped toward the door. "An'qwenique thinks she's middle class."

"That's rich." He smirked. "Ignore my rant. Tell the cops where the clues take you. I maybe rag on them too much, but they didn't do squat for Melody."

"Similar case." Paula shuddered. "Except Melody was sticking out of a car wreck with a dead otter."

Karl shuddered too. "Nobody cares about a mouthy waitress." He loved sparring with Melody over a hot mocha, and Melody liked it too, or so Paula thought. "Don't sit on what you know." Karl was adamant. "Hand over info about dogs and danger-mysteries to professionals."

"Uh-huh." What did Paula have to tell the professionals? Admitting to herself that the dog was magic or alien was hard enough. "Update me tonight with what else you dig up on this murder mystery."

"Sure thing." Karl was thrilled by the prospect.

Paula escaped into the hall as he mulled over his assignment.

Half the wonky fluorescents winked out. The landlord would wait till it was pitch black to replace burnouts. Paula stumbled down uneven stairs not thinking about the treacherous dark. Because—

What was the St. Berdoodle up to?

YESTERDAY

OONA—*Secret Life*

Sunday morning before Oona found the body started like a typical day.

The St. Berdoodle covered a lot of territory on this side and the others. Her maps had no fixed borders, just the routes she discovered and enjoyed. All the worlds were accessible, a vast realm to be appreciated and defended. Searching for her lost carnival crew, Oona had gotten to know half of everybody in the small towns around the State Forest and people from everywhere at the Redemption Center. A good thing. She had a big heart and more energy than most, which meant big fun and big trouble too.

Oona didn't know it, but she was a great detective dog.

Sunday was Zsuzsu Marlene Hönig's day. Her name and address could be found inside Oona's collar. Zsuzsu slept late, then rain, shine, or sleet wheeled down the back ramp of her old farmhouse to the garden that bordered the State Forest. Using a cane, Zsuzsu walked ten steps to the red mulberry, her favorite tree. She wobbled, yet Oona didn't run over and brace her. Instead, she wagged her tail for encouragement.

Zsuzsu was muscular and tall, with tight, cinnamon curls cut close to her head. Gauzy green garments hugged a wiry form, *the airy-fairy athlete*, according to Oona's running buddy. *Two Zoos full of mischief and spirit, marmalade and honey*, Paula claimed.

Zsuzsu laid her cheek on the crinkled gray bark of the mulberry, mumbled about elephant skin, cried a bit and laughed too. Eighteen minutes standing in gravity! Every day since her July birthday she added thirty seconds of resisting Earth's mighty tug, then back to the chair and up the ramp for breakfast. Even if Zsuzsu smelled frustrated, her muscles and bones thanked her. Oona felt that for sure.

This Sunday the resident star was a hazy red disk. Wildfires burned somewhere, blowing ash and smoke everywhere. "Red sky in the morning, sailors take warning," Zsuzsu said when she caught Oona jumping the neighbor's honeysuckle hedge. A pot holder dangled from Oona's mouth. The faint taste of jollof rice was a comfort. "Where have you been?"

Jarred by Zsuzsu's sharp tone, Oona dropped the pot holder in the wildflowers. She had a full program. Friends, duties, meals, and toys were scattered miles apart. There were always unexpected adventures and sometimes dangerous escapades. Although it was still Sunday morning, and Oona wouldn't discover the body till Sunday evening.

"I know that guilty look," Zsuzsu said.

Oona couldn't help herself. Going the distance was in her blood. And she had a carnival crew to find. What would their act be without Oona?

"I need a higher fence." Zsuzsu bit her bottom lip. Concern wafted from her skin. "I'm stuck in a chair and you're supposed to be on a leash or behind bars. You don't get to roam the streets. This is the world. We don't have to like it, but it is what it is."

Oona put her paws in Zsuzsu's lap and licked her salty chin.

"Cut that out." Zsuzsu wiped her face. "Your mama was a one-hundred-fifty-pound St. Bernard, or your daddy. You're too big for anybody's lap." Oona put her head on Zsuzsu's shoulder and nuzzled till the woman almost laughed. Oona licked her again. "You're breaking the law!" Zsuzsu hugged her. "I like the law. What am I supposed to do?"

Zsuzsu went off for hours every day to work at Cloud Heights Enterprises. She left Oona in the yard—an acre and a half surrounding an old farmhouse, plus a barn full of fun: squeaky toys, a crows' nest with hatchlings, old farm equipment, and goat and horse aromas. On hot days the barn was cool and shadowy, perfect for naps or to escape the rain. A chute on a timer filled Oona's bowl for evening meals. The crows feasted if Oona missed dinner. They knew the schedule. Beyond the barn was adventure among the hemlock, birch, and sugar maples on the vast State Forest.

"What were you doing next door?" Zsuzsu squinted at the neighbors' honeysuckle.

Last night Oona and the neighbor mutt prowled the woods to the Redemption Center, a surprise around every corner. On return, opening the neighbors' gate was a trick. But Oona was a carnival dog, raised by a musician, a magician, and a clown. She was fed tricks with her puppy chow. After leading the mutt home this morning, Oona banged the latch closed from the inside and jumped the honeysuckle hedge.

"The Cloud Heights geeks don't really want me to bring you to work. Hypocrites—saving coral reefs and exotic birds, but they don't do anything hard. They do nothing for the folks right outside their door." Zsuzsu's heart pounded and anxiety flavored her breath. "I can't afford to get mad." She scratched Oona's itchy ear. "You like anybody. I don't. Most people are bullshit, so disappointing, including me." Suddenly sad, she set Oona's paws in the clover and rolled up the zigzag ramp toward the porch.

"You'd hate being cooped up on the fourth floor. I do. Video conferencing from home is impossible right now. They've done studies: in-person is more productive, and I can't look weak." She was a jumble of conflicting scents. Oona raced up to her. "The Pet Rescue people said you needed a job, fun. What fun am I?"

Zsuzsu came home late every night, too tired for words. She fell asleep streaming a thriller or chef show. When Oona had completed her nighttime rounds, she slipped into the house, woke Zsuzsu up, and made her go to bed.

"It's selfish. Leaving you here with nothing to do. Of course," she tapped Oona's nose, "I know you're up to something."

Oona spent much time looking for her carnival family. She lost them last September during an early snow. She was an excellent tracker. Finding anyone else took a day or two at most. It never occurred to Oona that her carnival family might have gone farther than her nose would take her. So, whenever she caught a whiff of their favorite food—jollof rice or dodo (fried plantains)—she raced off to find them. No luck yet. The pot holder was a yummy toy though.

"Small towns, everyone's in your business. Nobody wants me living alone. Melody from Haven Bagels lived alone. Partially deaf . . . She taught me to sign my order." Zsuzsu signed, *pretzel bagel with goat cheese and jasmine tea.* "I'm much more aggravating than Melody. Why take her out instead of me?" Tears welled. "Don't tell anyone, but I miss the tea witch." Oona licked the tears away. "After they found Melody stuffed naked in a car wreck at the Mooseberry Mall, I lied on the wellness forms, said you were a trained caretaker." She choked out a giggle. "You waking the neighbors when somebody torched paint in their garage—that made everyone believe me. The fire could have jumped to my roof or into the State Forest." Zsuzsu looked around before whispering, "How did you break into Pete and Cal's house?"

Oona wagged her tail and ran to the kitchen's sliding glass door. She needed food and a nap, fortification for their Sunday-afternoon adventures.

"Acting innocent, sweet, like you can't open that door. Lügen haben kurze Beine. *Lies have short legs*. My Oma used to say that. She was Bavarian. What'd she know?"

Oona nudged Zsuzsu's wheelchair toward the kitchen.

"What are you, four, five years old? So sure you can take care of yourself." Zsuzsu sighed. "My other grandma was from Queens. *Quit whining*, she'd say. *Shit or get off the pot.*" Zsuzsu gazed at the mob of trees beyond the barn. The State Forest was acres of protected land. "People say these woods are haunted or cursed or Nipmuc sacred ground. I say all three. That's why I stick to the path and let you bushwhack. And I always feed the spirits."

A network of boardwalks crisscrossed the woods and wetlands behind the house, broad enough for two wheelchairs and a person walking, although Zsuzsu had no visitors recently. *Scared most her friends away*, according to neighbor Pete. *What would Zsuzsu do without you?* Pete asked Oona this every day. His wife, Cal, answered, *Get lost,* and they laughed. But they were wrong. Most people had a hard time staying on Oona's maps except the mutt next door, Zsuzsu, and Paula. They crossed over without fussing, as if they barely noticed the border static. The boardwalk across the marsh led to the Redemption Center Sunday's adventure.

"You know the secret trails to avoid tourists." Zsuzsu looked up at the orange sky. "Dave the weatherman says the air is poison today. Bad news for our walk."

Oona pawed the latch to the sliding door. Zsuzsu slid it open.

"Hungry?" Oona raced back to the wildflowers and picked up the pot holder. "You wallow in anything. Bring the hose before we go in."

Hose was a great game. Oona deposited the pot holder mitt in Zsuzsu's lap and dragged the green water dragon from under a table. It had blue marble eyes and a gaping mouth with a red tongue and silver teeth. Zsuzsu opened the gasket and doused Oona, who feinted one direction then another, as if she hated getting wet.

Zsuzsu aimed the frothy spray at Oona's butt. "Who's my water girl?"

Oona leapt into her wading pond and splashed water everywhere. Nobody would believe the fun she had with Zsuzsu. Oona was too much for most people, leading a secret life. That's why other folks returned her to the Pet Rescue. Inside the house, Zsuzsu wrapped the 135-pound dog in a giant beach towel and they cuddled on the couch.

"If something happened to you, I don't know . . . Who else can put up with me?" She sounded sad and scared. "Don't let me catch you sneaking around. Don't let anyone catch you." Oona *could Houdini her way out of anywhere*, according to Paula. Zsuzsu didn't know that, yet. "Like you ever listen to me. Like you even know what I'm saying."

Forgoing the cane and moving on unsteady feet, Zsuzsu filled Oona's dish with her favorite morning treats—a medley of chicken, barley, and carrots. She set this by the glass door. A bowl of granola and fruit sat on a nearby table. They ate outside whenever the weather cooperated. Not today.

"Dave says smoke is squatting over the whole of New England," Zsuzsu muttered. "Bad air from Canadian forests burning up, not ours, thank God," Zsuzsu muttered, then sighed. "The trees are all ours, the fires too."

Oona gobbled her bowl and licked it clean. Her routine at any safe-smelling dish.

Zsuzsu sat back in the wheelchair and held up the pot holder. "This is beautiful. A covered bridge by a waterfall." She sniffed it. "Tomato sauce and cloves. Yum." Oona was glad Zsuzsu liked jollof rice.

Outside, a fast-moving thunderstorm washed down the wildfire haze. The clouds fled and the sun was a yellow burst. "Is this happening?" Thrilled, Zsuzsu grabbed her phone to check. "Dave the weatherman says the air is clearing up, then a hailstorm on Monday. It'll be hot but we can do our Sunday walk. Now that's good luck. And it's cooler in the woods." Zsuzsu patted Oona's head, in a grand mood, using her fun voice. "We both love the Redemption Center. We do, we do! Don't we?"

Oona woofed and wagged her tail.

"That spooky old mansion always manages to surprise us. Melody used to say: *The giant sundial is out of this world. You have to see it to believe it!*" Zsuzsu sighed. "Did I tell her about the Redemption Center or did she tell me?" Oona cocked her head at the intensity in Zsuzsu's voice. "Who cares. It's somewhere to escape myself."

Since the phone was on, Zsuzsu scrolled through text messages, email, and social media. Oona fell asleep at her feet. After a few moments, they were both snoring. A morning nap—Because who wanted to feel tired on their Sunday-afternoon adventure to the Redemption Center!

T O D A Y

PAULA—*Hidden Connections*

Hail pummeled Paula. Nobody in the bus shelter bubble moved to let her squeeze in. Monday-morning crush, yet few regulars. Forty minutes ago it was eighty degrees and sunny with a little haze from Sunday's wildfire smoke. This bizarre storm blasted out of nowhere. Who could prepare? Students, environmentalists, slackers, retirees, working stiffs like Paula, and folks down on their luck were afraid to squish close. An echo from the Pandemic, the virus doing a mutation uptick (Covid was still in the top ten causes of death!), or angst over a killer on the loose. *We're all victims, suspects, and accomplices!*

A second body was unnerving, so Paula didn't screech at folks letting her stand out in the cold. She refused to be unnerved. That led to despair. Stinging ice crashed into her eyes. She winced. The hail was pea-sized, fairy missiles of torment. She bruised easily, a terrible face for work. As if a druggie had tried to mug her and she fought them off rather than hand over bus fare and her indulgence fund.

Monday's indulgence was something to share with the St. Berdoodle. Treats tasted better when you shared. No lethal chocolate on dog day, a cheesy bun with soy bacon bits, the $1.59 (+ $0.32 tip) vegan special, a reasonable dinner that the dog loved. She'd be waiting for Paula in the shelter bubble even if the bus ran late this evening. Wagging her tail, doing a doggy tango, the St. B was a charmer. Just, a terrible witness.

Upstairs Karl was wrong. The police would laugh if Paula told vanishing-dog tales. They might lock her *and* the St. B up. No cops ever believed reports Paula made, except Oshun Jackson and Blue Rosenthal. For the first time in forever, the ace detectives sat across the street in the bay window of Haven Bagels, a way station at the crossroads of the multiverse. The Haven inhabited the first floor of an old robber baron mansion. The top floors were single-occupancy apartments. Wobbly round tables and chairs spilled into the street even in winter. Their gluten-free, soy-bacon bagel was heavenly.

Oshun and Blue were having a morning cup, defying gossip about an affair. Muscular gym folks, they PUMPED IT UP with Upstairs Karl. Blue was fifty, stocky, and a sharpshooter. He had a killer smile and curly red fringe around a bald spot. Oshun was two inches taller and three years older than Blue. A champion wrestler, she had wavy blond hair and a disarming smirk. Paula liked them both.

Unfortunately, Blue and Oshun didn't count anymore. Blue was under investigation for cover-ups and kickbacks. Oshun was his partner (lover?), so also suspect. Pointless telling them to question Oona; how far would they get? Paula had to do that interrogation herself. No good YouTube videos on interrogating dogs, let alone one with powers. The Iris Library (best in the region outside of the university) was 7.5 blocks from An'qwenique's, a lunch-break walk.

Belle Roberts was a stellar research librarian and loved a good mystery. Who didn't? Belle was almost a friend. She and Paula always gabbed on the 7:30 bus—Where was Belle? Good thing she was MIA. Paula might have blurted wizard- or alien-dog crap to her. Premature. Paula needed more intel. A detective had to be patient.

The wind was the edge of a blade. Paula shivered slush off the flimsy rain jacket she kept in her knapsack. Cleaning supplies and equipment were wrapped in recycled plastic, safe from the elements, yet weighty—enough to build serious upper body, ab, and quad strength, according to Upstairs Karl. He was *personal trainer to the stars*, not just *corrupt detectives*. Still, her shoulders would be aching soon. The hood on her jacket had a hole. Icy water leaked into her vest pocket. Her shoes were on their third life and soaked through. Wretched was not an exaggeration, yet dry people in the shelter looked away from her misery. Not just Belle AWOL, where were the other regulars?

"How long are we going to be standing out here?" A college woman in the corner muttered everyone's thoughts. The 7:30 bus was very, very late.

"Cheer up," Paula whispered at pinched faces, too softly to be heard in the hail. Maybe they would feel the vibe. "We drink oxygen that Hiawatha tasted with She Who Lives at the War-Road, Jigonhsasee." Dgi-gon-sa-SHAY—Paula stumbled over the pronunciation, a hard one. "Hiawatha and Jigonhsasee worked with the Peacemaker to bring warring Haudenosaunee into one longhouse." Hoe-dee-no-SHOW-nee came easier. "Jigonhsasee gets left out of the story a lot. That doesn't mean she wasn't there."

Warmth radiated through Paula at the image of Mohawk, Oneida, Seneca, Cayuga, and Onondaga warriors gathered around a fire, eating and joking as children played pranks and women rested their bones—ancient enemies had become fierce allies.

"People who remember the Peacemaker, Hiawatha, Jigonhsasee, and the rest, we can be peace on the War-Road too," Paula murmured.

An old hippie hovered half in / half out of the shelter. Another almost friend. "Speak up."

"What're you standing in the rain for?" a big-foot dude shouted. He stomped past Paula to the shelter bubble. "Plenty of room." He jostled the hippie into the street.

Her two faded copper braids were instantly coated in hail. Bare feet in sandals were already a raw red. Ouch. As she scrambled for balance, her journal flew from her hand toward the muck. Paula caught the leather-bound book. The hippie snatched it back and snarled. At Paula? At rude big-foot dude, the fairy missiles, or just everything?

A body stuffed in RC recycling Sunday, and Monday morning bus patrons ignored bully behavior. Big Foot shook hail from his hair and glowered. The shelter crowd shrank away from six and a half feet of muscle and attitude. He could give a damn if they thought he was the kidnapper or the murderer. It was reasonable to speculate (not assume) that the kidnapper and the murderer might be one and the same.

The old hippie lady hugged her journal. She was a blur of mad and slush, maybe tears too. Her chest heaved for sure. Big Foot didn't care about that either.

"Hey, you. Everybody's running late." Paula tugged the hippie's soggy sleeve and spoke just loud enough for her to hear. "It's me under this stupid hood."

"Me who?" The hippie had a monthly pass. She rode this bus all day and wrote beat portraits of the driver, other passengers, creatures on the street and in the trees, including beings nobody else saw. She drew careful pictures with nubby pencils. She sometimes smelled sour and her hair was a stringy riot, as if days had passed since a shower. Not today. She wiped her slushy face and tucked the journal under layers of paisley cotton. She glared at Big Foot like she wanted to wring his neck. Not good.

"Think of the viruses, bacteria, and fungus we share," Paula shouted. "Most are benign." The college woman at the edge of the shelter scrunched her face and the old hippie frowned. People hated bacteria and virus relations, and forget fungi. Bad choice. "Sorry." Paula tried a quiet, conspiratorial tone. "Feeling secret connections lets you resist unhelpful impulses and tap a well of power instead."

A barrage of hail bashed the hippie. She flinched. "Is that a fact?"

Paula blocked the storm wind. "Yeah." Her butt could take whatever the fairies dished out. "You strike me as someone who can handle the facts, ma'am."

The hippie sighed, grateful for the wind shadow. She squeezed Paula's hand. "The facts. You really think so?"

"I do." Paula had learned at ten, more than thirty years ago, never to share cosmic thoughts with just anybody. *Nobody wants to hear her nerd nonsense.* She usually hid behind blank brown eyes, a dull smile, and occasionally an Angry-Black-Woman snarl. Talking to a hippie beat poet, who rode the university route through the surrounding towns, was an allowable exception to general safety rules. "Your bullshit meter is in great shape. Am I right?"

A roguish smile creased the hippie's face. "Our ship!" She pointed across the street to a wooden bench carved in the shape of a Viking ship beached in front of the Haven. "I like you." The hippie licked her lips, tasting fond memories. "Why?"

"Why not?" Paula replied. Wednesdays after late cleaning jobs, she and the hippie ate cheesy popcorn on that bench with the dog. Wednesdays was Buy Two Get One Free at the Haven ($2.13, no tip). Paula managed $12.00 a week for snack-dinners with special buddies. Mostly at the Haven. Tuesdays was at Jojo's Ice Cream Parlor across from the Iris Library with head honcho Belle, after book club or a Change Gang confab. The Change Gang was hope junkies doing whatever they could to turn some mess around.

"A stray-hound follows us." The hippie's face crinkled with pleasure. "A big girl—silver hair and black eyes. A good listener."

The St. Berdoodle always wolfed her own bag of popcorn (plus some of theirs) in a blink. They never minded, too busy telling tales on the late-night crowd who were guzzling brews and stuffing their faces with bagels, lox, and cream cheese. The newly coupled took a break from hot sex. Insomniacs hoped warm milk or goat cheese was the trick to call down sweet dreams. Folks who lived on the streets rested their bones and, while warming up and drying out, also fueled their dreams. Students and other workaholics stocked up for all-nighters. Illicit lovers enjoyed a latte tryst far from jealous eyes. The hopeless got a midnight stay of execution, drinking the cosmic tea special, a secret blend of fermented twigs, oolong, and flower buds.

Desperados, fools for love, clowns, and dreamers. Paula, the hippie, and the St. Berdoodle fit right in.

"We have fun." The hippie choked up. "I think." The next day on the bus, she would burst into tears saying Paula looked like an old friend come back from the dead or her daughter-in-law who'd stopped talking to her or a famous writer buddy who was also dead, covid on top of cancer. After the weekend, Paula was a ghost in the woman's memory. Paula hated being forgotten, but didn't want to make the woman feel bad.

"I miss Melody. Not doing well with change these last few months," the hippie confided. "I started a new medication last week. Might help my memory. Wasn't that your idea?"

Paula tingled with hope. "I said you should check for conflicting effects." She always omitted *side*.

"That happened to my mom." The college lady nodded—shameless eavesdropping.

"You were right." The hippie stomped raw feet, splattering muck about. Paula stomped with her. The hippie grinned. "I thought you looked familiar. We used to sing together."

"At Crossroads, that African restaurant."

"You entertain wild ideas. I like you a lot. I do!"

Paula nodded. "I like you too."

"Your stray-hound brings people together. She knows more than she's telling."

"Indeed," Paula replied.

After catching the last of An'qwenique's dust bunnies, Paula would mention the St. B's vanishing acts and see what Ms. Podcaster, Investigative Journalist thought. An'qwenique also loved to entertain wild ideas. The thought of bringing her into these particular miracles and mysteries perked Paula right up.

YESTERDAY

AN'QWENIQUE—*Dizzy*

What the hell are we doing?

Sunday afternoon (before Oona found the body and a day before Paula waited for the bus in a hailstorm), the August sun blasted An'qwenique Robinson's early-twentieth-century mill-owner mansion. Hot, bright light blazed through flimsy curtains. The air conditioning rattled, blowing a cold draft in An'qwenique's face. It sounded like the angry voice in her dream.

I know you hear me. What the hell is it all about?

Was An'qwenique supposed to have an answer? To the big questions?

Yeah, 'cause how do you find where you are on a map if you don't know where you are?

A dog barked, a large creature. The bass boom blasted adrenaline through An'qwenique's bloodstream. Wide awake now, she was sprawled on the king bed in Saturday's scratchy tank top and shorts. Her right foot dangled over the edge, throbbing.

She'd been up half the night riding a new virtual rig, doing hummingbird adventures in the rainforest with her inner posse. Her review was due on Monday and her editor wanted something a chatbot couldn't write. It was already 12:45 PM. Sunday was half over and the air conditioning was giving her a migraine. An'qwenique scribbled dream notes/quotes in the journal by her bed, nearly illegible. The quick sketch of angry lips and teeth was clearer.

What the hell were we doing?

She stumbled to the bathroom and dropped everything. The shower felt wrong, slimy, like the back of her throat. Her hair itched her neck and forehead. "Allergic to myself!" She snarled at the mirror and pulled thick hair into an afro-puff on top of her head. Washed-out amber eyes were bleary and so much vampire gray in normally beige skin, too pale for August. "What are those West African genes doing up in there? Gotta kick it, y'all!" She needed to run 10K in midday sun, not at dawn or by the moon, if she wanted to turn nut brown. These days, it was always too hot.

Clean clothes caressed prickly skin: silk bra and panties, silk blouse and cropped pants, in a subtle camouflage pattern, no synthetics. Overpriced designer casual. She ignored her itchy back, a phantom itch, probably missing the hummingbird wings. They'd fluttered so fast, like helicopter blades. The rush of muggy jungle air was a comfort to irritable skin. The flower nectar was a serious high.

An'qwenique slumped at the kitchen table. Real life made her sneeze. She bit her lip eating stale bread and washed the blood down with suspect almond milk. Paula B. Queenie said corporate agribusiness enslaved bees for vegan almond affectations—so this was her last carton, and it was going off. Why should starting abstinence taste sweet?

"Don't go there," she yelled, then giggled at raw, unfiltered irritation echoing through the empty house—a museum more than a home. Hawaiian masks and West African statues glowered. Japanese wind chimes tinkled a reproach. The Monkey King chortled. What'd she expect from a tourist-shop trickster out of Mumbai?

Fortunately she lived alone. Nobody scolded her for bad moods or told her to chill. And, as an early-afternoon pick-me-up, she'd call Paula to make sure Monday was still a go. Paula would have already alerted her if there was a problem with tomorrow. Paula was a rock. Why couldn't An'qwenique fall in love with someone like that? Well, because Paula was straight, and An'qwenique's life wasn't an English costume drama where the lord or lady romanced the maid, stable boy, gamekeeper, whomever. Falling for your best friend was desperation.

"She's your best friend now?" Rather than answer her own question, An'qwenique decided to get the house ready for Paula. She was too muffle-brained to start writing the damn virtual reality review or the other ten things due by her Wednesday podcast.

She collected the recycling from the basement and the second-floor office and bedroom. The stairs made her dizzy. The rooms kept spinning, especially if she closed her eyes. The tang of fermenting apple juice and curdled protein drinks wafted from empty bottles and cartons. She almost heaved. Stupid to force down that bad almond milk, and after how many hours of VR? She warned everyone about hanging overtime in their rigs, then stayed too long herself. Next time, she should be a sloth, palm tree, or a swamp—anything instead of a hyper bird.

An'qwenique halted at the back screen door. Her next-door neighbor, internet sensation Tomás de la Cruz, stood under a gothic archway in his yard, sporting skin-tight motorcycle pants and a leather vest over a naked chest. A breeze played through wavy black hair. He pulled his juicy wife, Charlize Giddens, to his chest. Charlize wore a diaphanous white robe over nothing else it would seem. Her burnt-umber hair sparkled in the sun.

Tomás kissed Charlize like a camera was running. He backed her against a wall and buried his face in her ample cleavage. The robe slipped from her shoulders and puddled around his faint scruff of a beard. Charlize had her hands on his muscular butt as they writhed up and down the wall. Their eyes were closed and they moaned, getting off on doing it outside, in public view.

"Fuck you and your Instagrammable romance too," An'qwenique muttered, and stormed through a spotless kitchen. Forget going out there with the recycling. Charlize and Tomás always smirked at her Sunday get-ready-for-Paula ritual. They were careless, entitled slobs. Messes spilled out of every doorway. They assumed she was embarrassed by her mess, afraid to lose status in the eyes of the help. Way off the mark!

Paula's Monday clean was motivation, inspiration, an organizing principle for the week ahead. An'qwenique refused to waste Paula on tasks she herself could manage (given adequate prompting). An'qwenique saved Paula for the rash-and sneeze-inducing dust and pollen, for hunting down what she might miss, and for the bacterial, fungal, and viral miasma of the sinks, tubs, and toilets.

Paula claimed to like the little buggers and cleaned with nothing harsh to avoid *encouraging them to mutate from irksome acquaintances into lethal enemies.* Soap was better than hand sanitizer, which was horrible for the small intestines and colon. Vinegar or baking soda, and hot dry air were great on mold. Using benign products meant less damage to lungs and skin. Pipes appreciated a non-caustic regimen too. Paula's mind was full of great stuff most people could give a hoot about or barely noticed.

In the living room An'qwenique gathered magazines she never read (affectations? aspirations?) and emptied wastebaskets full of tissues and nasal spray bottles. The news blared from a giant flat-screen over the fireplace. The weather was blistering hot plus wildfires and pop-up showers. A hailstorm was in Monday's forecast, a climate crisis blip across New York and New England. The storm might miss her neck of those woods, but if enough trees came down tomorrow, power outages might reach them.

A motorist in Pennsylvania cursed the freakin' trees for keeling over and causing traffic jams, as if this superstorm was the trees' fault, and what about the skyrocketing price of peaches and apples? Not a word on how devasted the trees felt, cracking and splitting to their heartwood, roots wrenched from the soil as they knocked each other over, death all around. An'qwenique wanted to smash the wastebasket into the screen.

Nobody cared about other living, breathing beings who died because of us. Slave trees . . .

"Hyperbole. Stop." She set down the wastebasket. "What good is a rage fest?"

After the tree-massacre forecast came people-on-people violence. Given relentless coverage, you'd think everyone was doing it, and not much else. Machine guns blasted and viewers were warned (tantalized). She clicked off before more disturbing images rolled.

Instead of mass murder and apocalypse, what about people saving people or other species? What about Akan farmers in Ghana doing Sankofa, calling on traditional farming technique, Indigenous science, to save chocolate from extinction? Eddies of gray from the screen drifted across the room. She tripped, fell over the couch, and almost banged her head on the petrified wood coffee table.

"Get a grip, girl! Turn down the gain."

Paula would tell her be mad and hurt, then go save something, join the Change Gang—an activist group headed by a librarian, but no-joke do-gooders. An'qwenique struggled up. Being out of allergy medicine could explain the itching, still allergies rarely made her bitter and wobbly. Something else was up. She'd curse herself later for not paying attention to the signs, to the clues as Paula called them. Hummingbird hearts hit 1200 beats in a minute. Was that true? Well, her heart was still racing. Months working way too hard, and she'd promised herself a whole weekend off.

She was supposed to do a three-day getaway with Kitty Richards at her cabin on the lake. Beauty, quiet, and running trails every direction. Kitty forgot, wanted some better action, or decided An'qwenique was incapable of love. Perhaps all three. Hard to know. The bitch went off to NYC to suck face with some other babe. Too cowardly to break up live, Kitty texted Friday: *You and I are barely a thing anyhow.* Right.

Next door, Tomás traded his vest for a leather jacket and

rode off on his flashy motorcycle. Except for sex in the sun-kissed portico, Charlize stayed in air conditioning and protected creamy skin and fragile sweat glands while obsessively shopping deals and steals online. An'qwenique tried to squelch pissy thoughts. Charlize and Tomás wanted a family, lots of babies, three at least, and a couple big guard dogs. Charlize was feathering the nest; Tomás ventured out in the wilderness to bring home the bacon. A happy cliché, nothing wrong with that, a stupid waste of irritation.

The coast was clear. She stuffed the last of the recycling into a big blue RC recycling container and charged out the back door into her meadow lawn, a half acre gone wild. The dog did a plaintive whine that matched her mood, out of sight yet nearby.

Barely a thing.

Kitty never understood An'qwenique's desire to wander in the weeds or run through the woods and sing with the birds at sunrise or sundown. One evening during their last trip to the cabin, An'qwenique's half-hour run turned into three hours and pissed Kitty off. There was no Wi-Fi and cell service was spotty, nonexistent actually. What was Kitty supposed to do? A big nothing or imagine the worst—injury, bear attack, two-legged predators—as the dark crept in and An'qwenique hadn't returned. Hurt by callous disregard, Kitty had been out for blood ever since.

Stumbling over that thought, An'qwenique scarcely registered the weirdo lurking at the side porch four doors down.

T O D A Y

PAULA—*Warrior Women*

"Dave, the weatherman, warned you: *Monday, a tree apocalypse coming.*"

Big Foot sneered at people shivering in the bus shelter bubble. A superstorm wind had birds flying sideways through the hail. They looked miserable. The same wind tore through flimsy tee shirts. Everyone was miserable. Paula's shoulders throbbed. Laying down her burden in the slush was impossible. An unseen hole in the plastic wrapping and a fortune in cleaning equipment and supplies would be ruined.

Online, the bus company posted an apology for delays and pleas for patience. Drivers were out sick. Weather mishaps and accidents jacked up the buses still running. Paula texted An'qwenique an abject apology for being late. It didn't go through. *Try again later.* Upstairs Karl had texted and emailed with urgent updates on the murder case. Paula was at her morning cell phone limit, so she ignored him. No bandwidth for his theories on burly, Black, anti-fascist perverts. After work maybe.

The college woman stepped from the shelter and squinted down the road. A graduate student perhaps, she wore a shimmery bronze raincoat. Her little daughter, nine or ten, in bronze armor also, gazed into the storm with Mom. Cars full of out-of-state tourists slipped and slid about, no bus in sight. Paula danced around to stay warm. Hypothermia was no joke. The old hippie mimicked her steps, coppery braids whirling, a good dancer.

"I had an umbrella; God punched a hole in it. Not an umbrella day," she said. "We've had good times, right? My name is Elaine, Eleanor, Edith. What's yours again?"

"It doesn't matter." Paula had told her many, many times. The 7:30 AM driver said Elaine, Eleanor, Edith had been Babs, Beanie, Bug last year—before Paula's car croaked and she had to take the bus. (Her car repair budget was zip.) The driver claimed Triple-E's memory was the sketch/poetry journal. Paula might be in there. The driver sure was. Paula had glimpsed his Duke Ellington face over a big steering wheel on a charcoal-smudged page. The wings at the edge of his sexy mustache gave Paula a nice tingle. She hoped he was OK driving in foul weather.

"Of course your name matters," Triple-E declared, "although tomorrow I might not recall. Not age, never good at names." Right. A waste of irritation over the name game. "Triple-E" was better than "old hippie," even if those weren't her names.

"Paula B. Queenie," Paula whispered in Triple-E's ear so nobody else heard.

"Paranoid or . . ." Triple-E looked around. "Is someone after you?"

"Uh . . ." Paula was paranoid. Everyone should be. *We are being hunted!*

Exploiting birthdate, location, and name, anyone could break in and wreck your life. A fancy algorithm had declared Paula a fraud risk three times when she got food assistance. She kept providing the same documents. Proving them wrong never lasted. Big Tech didn't care who she *was*, just who she *might be*. How hard to fix the algorithm or cross-check allegations or put a note on Paula's file? Not the algorithm's fault, the people were too lazy, too cheap, too privileged and clueless to quit glitching her life. Hounding a nobody was misery for Paula, profit for them.

Profit is sacred, according to Upstairs Karl. *All anybody believes in is Money, Money, Money. Fuck people's lives.* He was right. Folks disappeared from a dodgy neighborhood then turned up naked and dead in a car wreck like Melody, from the Haven, or never turned up like wayward trans teen Gwen and little brother Lance. Real family, just not by blood. Their cases went cold in a blink—no social media hype. More proof AI wizzes worked against them. Maybe not the Cloud Heights Enterprises folks.

"Hey!" Triple-E shook Paula back to right now. "Thinking yourself into a hole. Who's after you? Answer me."

"I trust you," Paula admitted. "No one else here needs to know who I am."

"What's that fucker's name?" Triple-E pointed at Big Foot. "I want to report him."

Paula huffed. A warrior on the Peace Path, remember? "Report him to who? Why?"

Triple-E blinked. Like Paula, she had a long list and not enough words for every complaint. Reporting Rude Dude might mean trouble with unrestrained algorithms. They'd lock her up instead of him. That's how trouble worked, even for old white ladies, if they were poor and batty. Who coined that term? Same people who drew the neighborhood maps. Bats were grand beings, flying mammals, our cousins. Triple-E was a treasure.

"Who does he think he is?" she hissed. "What am I? Slush on his boots?"

The 7:30 AM driver said Triple-E had ancient ancestors from around New England. White but not quite . . . Nipmuc? Mahican? Pocumtuc? Too far east for Haudenosaunee. Some Vikings went astray on the way to Greenland? Mi'kmaq?

"He better watch out." Triple-E raised a fist. "I'll find somebody to listen."

"I'm listening to you." Paula got in Triple-E's face. "Hiawatha and Jigonhsasee shared peace stories and tended the spirits of future warriors like you and me."

Triple-E dropped her fist. "The Iroquois League wrote us into their constitution?"

"Haudenosaunee Confederacy."

"Right. Iroquois is French/Algonquin for sneaky snakes,

shadow warrior enemies." Triple-E gave her a Viking Queen, Mi'kmaq Elder glare. "So, summarize."

"Community starts in the mind. Peace is how we think," Paula declared.

Triple-E scoffed. "Change my mind and I change the world? Get out of town with that old news, 1960-what?" She raised an eyebrow, very *Star Trek*, Mr. Spock. "You're too young for 1960. Me too, practically. Were you at Occupy? That was also a bust."

"No," Paula sighed, "I wasn't there."

"You should have been. Occupy folks changed the world. Where were you? And what exactly have you been doing since?" She pointed at Big Foot and the crowd in the shelter. "Look at the mess we're in. Numb, pissed off, and armed to the teeth."

"Hey, bust or boom, we can . . ." Paula sputtered.

"We can what?" Triple-E pursed her lips. "Uh-huh. You got nothing."

"Not true." Paula regularly thought herself into being a warrior taking council from She Who Lives at the War-Road. "I . . ." Paula sat in a longhouse of the mind where strangers, ancient enemies even, transformed into allies and friends. This longhouse league stretched around the world, extended back in time way before 1960 and clear into tomorrow. "We all sweat like Harriet Tubman, Mahalia Jackson, and that Black woman scientist who plotted a trip to the moon in her head." Their pictures hung in Paula's closet, this week's inspiration gallery. Last week it was Hiawatha, Jigonhsasee, and the Peacemaker. Duke Ellington was the week before with Mos Def and Angela Bassett. "Boom or bust, you gotta have an Underground Railroad of the Spirit leading you to change."

Elaine, Eleanor, Edith wagged her head at what she might have once believed and was resisting now. She glanced at the oak and maple trees. Hail coated their leaves like her endless braids. So many limbs weighed down. She wiped her face again.

"What, you're a conductor on the Underground Railroad of the Spirit?"

Paula shrugged, patient.

"OK. OK." Triple-E swallowed her snarls. Hard to resist Harriet. "You're right."

Paula felt a swell of pride. Peace was contagious.

"I hope we're not looking at another tree apocalypse, like 2011." Triple-E waved at oak limbs bent almost to the ground. "This slop is pretty dry, and the air is warm. I wish I had a broom." She cackled like a witch, marched to the green life around the shelter—forsythia, flame bush, and yew—and jiggled the branches. Paula joined her.

They were gentle, especially with two baby tupelos, ten feet tall, spindly, and full of broad leaves. Shelter folks sneered, displaying their *why do anything, we're fucked* faces. Paula planted these tupelos last year with Belle and the Change Gang. They started at Iris Library and planted trees all over . . . Paula hoped Belle was OK or just sick.

"Paula, my dear, you're right. It's too late to give up." Triple-E wagged her butt. "I was at the first Earth Day in 1970, bright-eyed and bushy-tailed back then." Her faded copper hair turned into a wavy ginger cloud. Skinny hips were full and the sunken belly round. She had daffodils in her braids, seeds and bells on her ankles. Dancing barefoot, she smiled at Paula and beckoned her to dance too.

Paula grinned. "I can see you. Beautiful. On the Peace Path a long time."

"Oh yeah?" Triple-E crinkled pale brown eyes and leaned close. "You and me, on it together, like the ancestors who loved us." Then she added, "We're warrior women for peace." She gripped Paula's forearm. "I know what I saw. I could be next."

Did she mean next murder victim? Paula tried not to freak. "Really?"

"Warrior women?" The graduate student shook slush from her bronze raincoat and luxurious black braid. "Shaking the trees? What bullshit." She snorted as if certain the old lady was dead wrong, but she wanted Triple-E's words to be true, and felt betrayed. She pursed full lips. High cheekbones supported a mighty sneer. "Warriors for peace is a contradiction." Her daughter nodded solemnly at Mom's righteous truth.

"What do you know?" Triple-E strode toward the doubting faces. "Nothing about what I've been through. What I've done. Life is a goddamn contradiction."

"Shh." Paula pulled her back to the tupelos and murmured, "The next what?"

Triple-E patted the journal at her bosom and whispered, "I wrote it down, drew pictures. And look who's here." A double bendy bus pulled up to the stop and splashed muck into the shelter. "Oh là là, accordéon!" Triple-E exclaimed in French. Artists had painted an accordion keyboard and buttons on either side of the bus's bellows. Giant hands came out of the windows to play. "Ça alors!" She barged past passengers mobbing the front door. Even Big Foot yielded to her fierce excitement.

"Elaine, Eleanor, Edith," Paula shouted. "You're the next what?"

Triple-E charged through the half-open bus doors and flashed her bus pass. "Mover shaker, like you."

"That's you, not me." Paula banished thoughts of kidnapping and murder.

A dead woman found nearby didn't mean bodies would turn up everywhere, didn't mean Belle was lying dead in her library stacks, didn't mean Triple-E was the next target. Paula ground her teeth, insisting the odds of random lethal threats were unaffected by the recent recycling bin spectacle. Availability bias skewed her thoughts, made her think the worst. She had to reframe.

YESTERDAY

AN'QWENIQUE—*Subliminal*

An'qwenique squinted in the afternoon glare and staggered along the fieldstone path through her wildflower meadow. Bottles in the RC recycling container rattled and papers threatened to fly off. The creepy jump-scare wraith froze just beyond the hollyhock border. He? She? They? rocked a snakeskin raincoat and fanged hat in ninety-eight-degree sun. Pink mirror sunglasses and a high collar obscured the face. A neighbor? So tall and thin under the cosplay raincoat—not the tank girl who hayed people's yards as if she was going to war in her lawnmower (her thresher?). Tank Girl never came on a Sunday. Visitors and delivery folks went to the front door, not the side. So who the hell was this?

Barely a thing.

Kitty's text was a mosquito bite, stinging and itching the more An'qwenique scratched. Trouble crept up here and now, yet An'qwenique ignored it. She was lost in deep mind, slow thinking. Paula insisted that focus was An'qwenique's superpower. Of course, every superpower had a downside. The stranger pulled the reptilian hat brim low, although the sun blasted their back not their eyes. An'qwenique would kick herself later for feeling too sorry for herself to entertain reasonable suspicions.

Barely a thing.

Girlfriend Kitty was a stupid flail. Despite mutual lust and similar dating profiles, they had nothing in common. Take NYC, their favorite metropolis. Kitty loved the noise and chaos, the electric city, a screech and jolt in the night. She got bored trudging up the Custom House steps to the National Museum of the American Indian—Paula's suggestion. Forget exhibits at the Studio Museum in Harlem, the Met, or anywhere. Kitty refused food from places hard to pronounce. She avoided folks from far away or the next block over who weren't hip to the program. Which program?

NYC had infinite programs. An'qwenique loved the parade of startling people, carrying on, acting up, and inventing a new world together. She hated the sweaty clubs with shadowy bodies grinding away at 2:00 AM. Strutting around the dance floor, Kitty loved the legions of lusty ladies coming on to them. A post-Pandemic frenzy with the cameras rolling. Two minutes on the dance floor, and An'qwenique broke out in a rash.

She and Kitty might not like each other. They certainly worked each other's nerves. A slacker and a workaholic were an awful mix. Kitty texted An'qwenique every five minutes: wacky emojis, pictures of her high-heeled sneakers in odd poses, or the enemy engaged in lethal fuckups. Why waste precious time on jerks and trailer trash in camouflage driving off a cliff or fixing the toilet and almost drowning? Reading, writing, and thinking her way into the zone, An'qwenique ignored this drivel.

She neglected all her friends, not just Kitty. Terrible but true. Texting her was like screaming into a black hole. She regularly video-chatted with her inner posse and dutifully posted on social media, however there was no special person she wanted to spend live time with other than Paula, who, let's face it, came for the paycheck.

An'qwenique bumped her head against the gazebo door and lost this mean thought. She almost fell over again. Still dizzy. Promising herself a real break from the VR rig, she set the recycling container on the table inside the gazebo and turned on a solar-powered fan. She dropped into a comfy wicker chair and peered up at a pale moon rising in a cloudless sky swept clean by a recent thunderstorm. After a few deep breaths, the dizziness subsided. Should muffle-brain and dizzy hangover go in the review? Or perhaps she was blaming the VR rig when something else was wrong.

An old paperback sat on the table. It detailed how to survive in the jungle, on icy mountain cliffs, falling from a plane, or after the civilized world took itself down. Paula loaned this to An'qwenique two Mondays ago. They'd hung out in the gazebo till the final blast of light. They were quiet at first, watching the stars rise. Then came gumbo-yaya—talking on top of each other, throwing thoughts in the stew pot. A good time.

The book's cover had been chewed by Paula's dog, not really her dog, a special dog *friend* who walked her home from the bus at night and brought her books and other goodies. This gift was An'qwenique's current breakfast read, if she woke up before noon. The end times were now, only fools refused to hone their survival skills.

She tucked the paperback into her waistband and cursed. She had a 3:30 PM meetup with Azul Mendes, a nonbinary computer geek, CEO at Cloud Heights Enterprises. Azul returned her query call Friday, after Kitty blew her off. They agreed to a Sunday interview on Azul's Data for the Earth initiative (a fuck-just-surviving-how-to-prevent-the-apocalypse joint), only if it involved fun, like high tea at the reservoir. Azul offered to bring scones, vegan deviled eggs and shrimp (what?), fruit, gluten-free brownies, and a carafe of fancy tea for a picnic under the cedar trees that overlooked the waterworks.

It was already 2:12! An'qwenique considered canceling, although the interview might help her write the damn VR review. Canceling might hurt Azul's feelings—a sensitive being. Hurrying to the garage, she wondered when to tell Azul this wasn't a hookup. After the article was posted. She was upfront the first time they met: *I like girls.* To which Azul replied, *Me too.* Azul liked anybody.

She jammed the last of the recycling into a solar-powered EV from Germany, a tiny, lightweight miracle (designed by one of her mom's old lovers). Kitty said it was a glorified golf cart, a feel-good illusion solution: *unsustainable rare earth met-*

als brought to you by slave children in Africa. "Fuck Kitty." Newspapers blew out of An'qwenique's hands. She chased them around the yard. Junk mail floated behind the composter. She'd let that rot. Definitely an *if I can drop it I will* day, like her mom had. Mom claimed it was old age. An'qwenique was twenty-nine. What was her excuse?

The snake cosplay stranger stood next door by the showy Roman columns of the old mill baron's mansion that housed multitudes. An'qwenique wasn't sure who lived there. A Wild Bunch of artists and activists: Louise and Thelma, their grown children, babies, elder aunties, cousins, and long-term visitors from Ghana, Brooklyn, Vietnam, Copenhagen, and New Mexico—Abuelo or Tio Marco. They grew vegetables, had art exhibits, and performed rituals and sacred festivals agitating for the future they wanted.

"Charlize?" the stranger croaked, wrong, somehow. A broken special effect.

"Me? No, the next house over." An'qwenique immediately regretted blurting this.

Charlize and Tomás had called the cops several times on Louise and Thelma, their guests, and the wild turkeys from the Yucatán Peninsula they kept as part of a licensed experiment. However, there was no law against an intergenerational extended family or an international change-maker commune. The long-term guest from Ghana was a trial lawyer. Her husband was a farmer who specialized in chocolate and organizing. His side hustle was stage managing. In fact they both were stage managers. They met doing community theatre and could wrangle any mob into a movement. Louise and Thelma loved this. Lawyer Lady threatened to sue if Charlize and Tomás kept harassing them.

This made national news. Violent threats rained down, mostly on Charlize. Tomás's fans came to her defense and fired off counter death threats. That fiasco took six months to cool off. Occasional skirmishes still popped up on social media and Faux News. Last week, trolls attacked An'qwenique for not taking a side. Charlize and Tomás defended her. Unfortunately, they implied An'qwenique was on their team fighting to maintain high property values and keep the neighborhood unaffordable and safe. What the fuck?

Louise and Thelma had been giving An'qwenique the stink eye ever since.

"You need help?" The stranger (neighbor?) in snake cosplay lurked at the break in the hollyhock border between their lots. Ethnicity, region, and gender were unclear. Welcome to the twenty-first century. Kitty's alarm bells would have screeched. Podcast Journalist An'qwenique was fascinated. An iridescent blue turkey from the Yucatán waddled by, gobbling. The stranger leapt three feet in the air. The fanged hat almost flew off. Snake Child looked afraid of more than exotic turkeys. Trouble in the commune? A juicy story lurked under the reptile raincoat. They rasped, "Dressed in silk camouflage? What are you playing at?"

"Me?" An'qwenique chased last Sunday's *Times* as it danced with the hydrangea. Camo silk was her go-to summer fabric. She liked fading into the bushes. "What're you doing?"

Serpentine gestures and anxious glances over the shoulder accompanied a garbled reply about Guinevere and brother Lancelot. An'qwenique frowned. Guinevere and Lancelot were lovers, not siblings. "Camelot's never been our home. We'd prefer Avalon." Snake Child's jacked-up vocals and creepy-crawly moves were maybe more dark fantasy than the festival troop neighbors. "Know what I'm saying?"

"Actually no," An'qwenique said. "A magical island versus a magical city?"

"You should be careful," Snake Child admonished her. "You gotta watch out."

"On Mooseberry Lane? The Mexican turkeys usually mind their own business."

"They are creepy."

"*They* are creepy?" An'qwenique almost laughed. *What*

about you, dear? "Google can't find us, let alone trouble. Trouble gets lost on the one-way streets and that old bridge you can't cross on Water Street."

"I'm serious," Snake Child snarled. "You ain't living in Avalon either."

"I can't decode your metaphor, Gwen," An'qwenique said.

Snake Child jerked at the diminutive. "Shh!"

An'qwenique's skin prickled as she scanned beyond her yard to sculpture gardens and mansion monstrosities, a fake Avalon, inhabited by nouveau strivers. She respected the eccentrics next door—hard-working, big-talking, do-no-harm-for-real futurists. Their turkeys were jewel-toned like the hummingbirds she loved, always a beautiful sight. Exotic neighbors were set decorations to An'qwenique's life, but often indistinguishable. She mistook the danger radiating from Snake Child for their weird exuberance. Plus, she assumed her recent flickers of negativity were Kitty's fault. *You become the people you hang with.* Or perhaps VR afterimages were distorting her perceptions or . . . what? No time to think. Being late was against An'qwenique's religion.

"Sorry. I gotta boogie on down the road." She hurried off, soothed by ancient slang she'd picked up from Louise and Thelma, who insisted you never called them Thelma and Louise *'cause we fell in love way before that movie came out.*

YESTERDAY

ZSUZSU—*Stuck*

Before Oona found the body (but after sniffing out turtles and turkeys in the State Forest with Zsuzsu Marlene Hönig on their Sunday stroll to the Redemption Center), the St. Berdoodle caught an old-home scent. Blue sky over the forest was tinged with lilac as she dashed down the sunset boardwalk to search for the musician, magician, and clown. If she found her carnival family, they'd come back for Zsuzsu later.

Murder or danger was far from Oona's mind. Zsuzsu would be safe at the Redemption Center. Tourists were rare and had never posed a threat, although Zsuzsu felt everyone was suspect. Zsuzsu knew too many villains and creeps who masqueraded as normal. Still, she barely noticed the big St. Berdoodle dash off. Zsuzsu squinted at the lopsided turrets on the Redemption Center mansion. Did it look different? Her vision blurred. Memories of the Center were murky, even from *last* Sunday, forget Sundays before that.

Two large crows (ravens?) circled a crumbling chimney. Rickety walls leaned to one side, and wind wheezed through cracks in the upstairs windows. Two dragon weathervanes on opposing turrets couldn't decide where the wind was coming from. They pointed different directions. A light in the attic tower glowed—*to keep bats from flying down.* How did Zsuzsu know this yet forget so much?

Flimsy curtains fluttered out of a broken attic window and danced around shards of glass that called to mind dragon's teeth. The tumbledown old ruin could pass for a haunted house in an enchanted forest or a ghostly galleon tossed on stormy seas. Maybe a house haunted by an old ship. This place truly was spooky. Zsuzsu liked spooky. Why come if you didn't?

Not much breeze on the ground, yet fog from the nearby marsh slithered across the sundial courtyard. The diameter had to be thirty feet. The sundial's giant gnomon cut the fog river in half. Too many shadows wavered about the Roman numerals, as if the gnomon skittered from this dimension into other dimensions. Time was wonky here. Sensible characters should avoid this place, if they wanted to make it to the end of the movie. *Sensible characters are boring. Who's going to make a movie about them?* Zsuzsu barely let herself think any of this.

More people in the courtyard than ever—two was too many; three was a mob. Tourists were ruining the region. The brush fires and forever traffic jams were as bad as on the Cape. Zsuzsu used to run into Melody here occasionally, but Melody knew how to mind her own business. She loved Oona, the spooky vibe, and Faulenzen, German for *doing nothing*. Melody was a salty character, walking on the wrong side of people, as bad as Zsuzsu. They both came to the Center to escape the mob, to step into another world. Should Zsuzsu worry about the killer hunting her in these woods? They should all be worrying about him; he could be anywhere. Melody always helped Zsuzsu set out the spirit offerings. Maybe she told Zsuzsu about feeding the spirits in the first place. *My heartbeat place*, Melody said, but Zsuzsu didn't yet know what that meant.

"Where are we?" a woman in camouflage yelped. "I should be at the lily pad lake, not this funky swamp. What is this, bottle return? Religious conversion?"

"This is private property, not part of the State Forest," Zsuzsu snapped, defensive.

"Where's the no trespassing sign?" Camouflage Lady shouted. All the tourists chattered nonsense at once.

These tourists hadn't planned on coming *here*; they were lost. It was too hot, and they would never think to feed the spirits. So entitled! "Why no info or a warning?" Camouflage Lady muttered.

The Center was closed on Sundays—big sign hard to miss—yet ten pissy tourists hung around, asking stupid questions about GPS and dead batteries. Some fronted like they were resting before venturing back into the State Forest. A few expected directions from the freakishly tall park ranger person when she finished her rounds and checked by the Center. OK, Zsuzsu had to admit the front door was enormous, fit for a giant, but nothing suspicious about that, except in dark fairy tales.

Two medical technicians in fashion-forward purple scrubs and hike-worthy sneakers stumbled onto the sundial courtyard, almost falling down on Roman numeral III. They rocked identical hairdos: shaggy bleached-blond front, blue buzz cut in back. Siblings? Lovers? Whatever. No matter which path they ran down, they ended up back at the sundial and not in the lot where they'd parked their camper, supposedly twenty minutes away, ten if they jogged.

After this fifth attempt, the medical technicians insisted the boardwalk network in the State Forest was a poorly marked labyrinth. Dripping sweat, out of breath, they still had enough oxygen to blame someone else. Other tourists joined the whining, which quickly escalated to not just the Center, but America, the whole world was going to shit. Stuck in a maze with no cell service was proof of how far humanity had fallen! Except present company. They were innocent victims of somebody else's fuckup.

"Diese blöden Kühe, wir alle gehen schief." *Stupid cows, we're all lost.* Muttering German, a bad sign. Zsuzsu gripped the wheelchair's arms. "Grown-ass people need to take responsibility for getting lost or wrecking their own lives. Damn!" Zsuzsu allowed herself two curses and one heartbeat spike. In a former life, she'd helped several scumbags get away with horrible crap, then they did more horrible and that was on her. But she quit that gig, didn't she? Robust old-growth trees scrubbed the air, yet she gasped for breath to talk on. Actually, anger was messing with her cardio, not wildfire smoke. "It can't always be *someone else's* fault. And check the conspiracy theory, magical thinking. That's a black hole." Why was she scolding? Self-righteous scolding was counterproductive. She knew the research.

"You talk like we're guilty of something and that's why we're stuck here." Arguing this point, the medical techs and other tourists spewed nonsense: They hadn't broken the world. Not their fault that other people were stuck on stupid. And Zsuzsu should understand better than anyone. The simpleminded, neo-hippie blather directed at a BIPOC woman in a wheelchair made Zsuzsu want to shoot someone, and she loathed guns.

"The world is everybody's fault," she declared. Nobody listened or offered original thoughts. They mouthed the party line. Everyone mouthed the party line yet few admitted this. *We all think we're experts when in fact we know nothing or believe the opposite of the truth. Human nature.* Zsuzsu investigated public opinion for ecology and energy groups in the Cloud Heights policy division. She was lucky to have this job. Azul Mendes hired her despite the helping-scumbags rep. "I know what I'm fuckin' talking about."

The med techs stepped away from her expertise and passion, from slitted gray eyes with angry green flecks. Not who they expected. They went on about UFOs, secret (government) experiments on aliens, and congressional hearings about ET. Laughable. Zsuzsu whirled away from a barrage of drivel and almost rolled over—

A suit-and-tie white guy wandered out of the courtyard one direction and back in another, every ten minutes! He consulted an antique watch and chirped. *This can't be happening.* A white het couple looked embarrassed. They sipped spring water under one of several pink-froth umbrellas shading the picnic tables. They'd pinned their hopes on the super-tall park ranger, but doubt was creeping in.

Time to go home.

Zsuzsu wheeled around the suit guy and across the courtyard. She halted by the giant gnomon. It was carved from an ice-age boulder into the wing of a great bird. Bacteria, viruses, fungi, plants, and animals (including humans) were etched on the feathers. "Awe-inspiring," she admitted, then whistled for Oona. "Where are you?" Oona rarely disappeared beyond whistle range.

Boardwalks radiated from the sundial's Roman numerals like spokes on a wheel. These pathways crisscrossed, doubled back, and tangled up in the State Forest, a maze for sure. Zsuzsu had never tried to roll home from the Center without Oona, too many twists and turns. Except once, Melody sang them the whole way to Zsuzsu's backyard. Zsuzsu had also rolled in these woods with An'qwenique and Paula, but they never reached the sundial. A stupid May blizzard got in their way. An'qwenique and Paula might have hated the Center. Zsuzsu winced at their imagined disapproval.

"Amazing!" The gaggle of eco-tourists didn't sweat being lost. They applauded leaves dancing in the mist as they waited for their Girl Scout to return with a way out of no way. They'd planned to camp out, eat a vegan feast, and do mushrooms under the stars. Blocking the ramp to the sunset boardwalk (which led to Zsuzsu's house), they blathered about aid for refugees and the homeless.

Zsuzsu hated their pack-it-in, pack-it-out ethos, their designer water bottles and bamboo snot rags. High already, they stumbled over their feet showing off hand-me-down clothes, tents, and shoes—like they deserved the Medal of Honor or an Oscar for best costumes in the apocalypse.

"How are you going to save the world doing that?" Zsuzsu muttered.

A short middle-aged woman stomped onto the sundial behind her, tourist number thirteen, the Girl Scout. A familiar face, she was plump with pale olive skin and a topknot of kinky gray/blond hair, Afro-something like Zsuzsu. She plopped on a boulder at twelve o'clock. She'd been wandering in circles since before Zsuzsu and Oona arrived. "We're not trying to save the whole world," Girl Scout murmured.

"So how much of the world do you plan to save?" Zsuzsu snarked. *'Cause when the fire comes, your ass will burn too.*

The Girl Scout chortled. "We all need to save the world with everything we do."

Zsuzsu said something similar earlier. "Yeah, the world is everybody's fault. But doling out money to people too lazy to take a job. That worked so well."

The Girl Scout had the nerve to smile at Zsuzsu. "You assume people down on their luck are lazy, gaming the system, looking to get something for nothing. Are you like that?" She wore mismatched florals and paisley cinched at the ankle and elbow. Actually, a purple paisley hair tie matched the pants. "What if none of the bone-breaking, mind-numbing jobs you find pays a living wage, even doing double shifts every day?"

"Whose fault is that? Who made one bad decision after another? Who didn't work hard enough?" Zsuzsu hated these stupid arguments. No one ever changed their minds. Why did they bother fussing at each other? It was too hot for empty rituals. She wheeled away from the eco-freaks into the shade of the mulberry trees to wait for Oona.

The Girl Scout chased her. "The blame game is rigged. Luck is more important than talent or hard work for wealth and success. I'm Belle Roberts and who—"

"Luck is the most important factor," Zsuzsu said. "North African or Middle Eastern?"

Belle darted in front of her. "I recognize you. I'm the director of the Iris Library. You come in often. My sister has gray-green eyes like yours."

"You don't look familiar," Zsuzsu lied. Everyone knew everyone around here, an entangled mess, like the whole world. Belle gave a tear-jerking speech at Melody's celebration of life. An odd-couple friendship.

"Can you tell us how to get back to the parking lot?" Belle squinted silvery eyes at the sunset boardwalk then grimaced at the mob of trees lurking beyond.

"Which parking lot?" Zsuzsu scowled. "Do I look like a guide, a ranger on wheels?"

"You could be." Belle giggled, perhaps at Zsuzsu's petty hostility. "You seem to know what's happening and where you're going." She pointed at the other tourists. "The rest of us are confused." Understatement. Belle's crew was tripping!

"There's a map in the front hall of the Center. I saw it once . . ." Zsuzsu trailed off, straining for this memory. "But you're out of luck. The Center is closed on Sundays."

"I always have a map. I like paper." Belle held up a booklet of foldouts. "I just can't find our current location. I mean the Center is not on the park map, none of the boardwalk spokes either, and my phone's dead." She displayed a blank screen.

"Like I told them, the Center isn't in the park proper. Private property, yet open to the public." Zsuzsu shrugged. "No cell service, too far out in nowhere. I leave mine at home, so I can really be here and not caught in someone else's static."

Belle blinked and tightened full lips. "Yes, no, I understand, I do. And here we come bothering you. I am sorry. It's just . . . The phones are dead, batteries at zero percent, which doesn't make any sense, right?"

Zsuzsu shrugged again. "There must be a reasonable explanation."

"Or not. That woman talking to the nurses—"

"The gender-queer couple in purple scrubs are medical techs," Zsuzsu corrected.

"OK, so that lady in combat gear, talking to the nonbinary techs—"

"Jungle camouflage, I see her, yeah."

Belle whispered. "She thinks Pocomtuc warriors who died of European smallpox still haunt these woods. They are draining our cell phone batteries for spectral power."

"No! Does she really believe that? No way. Nipmuc ghosts more likely."

Belle allowed a chuckle and pointed at the suit-and-tie man wandering in again. "He thinks the Feds are jamming signals."

"Why? Do they have something against cat videos?"

Belle laughed full out. "Seriously, any path we take leads us back here."

Zsuzsu nodded. "That's how it is sometimes."

"I mean literally." Belle licked her lips. Fear? "Everyone says the same thing."

"Yes." Zsuzsu smirked. "So why are we listening to them?"

The med techs were arguing with Camouflage Lady about extraterrestrial life and government plots. The suit guy took the jacket off and mumbled *impossible* over and over. He had an important meeting. He'd walked miles and miles and got nowhere. His pale blue silk shirt was soaked. Slimy gray hair hung down his forehead; sweat streaked splotchy red cheeks; a heatstroke brewing, or worse.

"We must listen." Belle's voice was a caress, a woman practiced at deescalating conflict. Zsuzsu resisted liking her. Belle took a breath and coughed. The rain hadn't cleared all the wildfire smoke. "Nobody knows how to get back to where they started."

"So true," Zsuzsu said. They took breaths together and assessed the situation.

"We weren't trying to get here, wherever this is," Belle said. "Some people came from quite a distance." She glanced at the het couple waiting on park ranger rescue.

"Uh-huh." Not Zsuzsu's fault they were up shit's creek without a paddle.

Belle scanned the courtyard. "Most everyone else is a mess, one step from hysteria. You, however, don't seem agitated or even mildly concerned."

"I know where I am. My house is on the other side of those trees. I roll over any Sunday I'm able and hardly ever see a soul." Zsuzsu and Oona hadn't missed a Sunday since late February.

"Mostly me and the dog, Faulenzen, doing nothing together. Boss's idea."

Faulenzen was Zsuzsu's idea—sacred time, sacred space—which Azul Mendes turned into Cloud Heights policy then took credit for the whole thing. Gender-queer, yet Azul acted like the dudes and got treated like the man, even in Zsuzsu's mind. Big brown eyes, teddy-bear cute, yet a silver fox, Azul disarmed you, then slayed you. She was jealous.

"Can you show me on the map?" Belle set the booklet in Zsuzsu's lap.

"I'm terrible at maps." Zsuzsu handed it back. "I don't know how to get anywhere. The boardwalk system is a maze. I follow my dog." Or listen to the trees. Why say that?

Desperation darted across Belle's face. "You have a lot of faith in your dog."

"She is lay-down-your-life loyal. How many people do you know like that?"

"A couple, well one is dead. Melody, from the Haven." A catch in Belle's voice as she glanced at the eco-tourists. A willowy thing produced a mandolin and strummed a melancholy tune as Belle spoke. "This situation here is so disturbing, inexplicable."

"It's not that bad." Zsuzsu surprised herself by rolling close and touching Belle's arm with bare fingertips. Belle startled then clutched Zsuzsu's whole gloved hand (covered with boardwalk muck, yuck). Zsuzsu had to resist an urge to pull away. She was always pulling away, even from people her gut said trust. Stupid or what?

"What if something happened to your dog?" Belle asked. "What would you do?"

"Then I'd be shit out of luck." Zsuzsu should help these people. "You too, I guess."

"Oh? What are you saying?"

"My dog took off fifteen minutes ago. She won't leave me here long. Oona knows her way around these woods. She'll help you find your parking lot."

"I hope so." Belle's lips trembled. She wanted to believe Zsuzsu. "Melody was that good, loyal friend, since high school. Over forty years, even if we fought a lot." Her voice was thick with grief, as if they'd found Melody dead yesterday, instead of February. "Melody always came on our State Forest trips. She was our guide, and we never got lost in the maze. She knew the boardwalks, the tree songs. This is our first adventure without her." Melody and the neo-hippies, that must have been a trip! Belle sighed. "The last few weeks ripped me up. The world on fire and everything else, plus a killer still on the loose."

"They're always on the loose. Maybe even here with us, stalking the next victim." Zsuzsu winced. Why say that? Because talking about tree song felt risky?

Belle scoped the tourists. "The police should have found the creep by now." Unreasonable, the cops weren't wizards. "Or they just don't care."

"Or you could wake from a nap one afternoon, stand up, and your legs give out under you. And the doctors can't figure why." Zsuzsu spilled this quickly.

Belle squeezed Zsuzsu's filthy glove and quoted Shakespeare. "*There are more things in Heaven and Earth, Horatio, than are dreamt of in your philosophy.* We are not alone." She nodded at the eco-tourists. Her face crinkled with pleasure. "The Change Gang." An activist group she founded and led, hope junkies. "New recruits on this adventure today. You and your dog should join our nature jaunts."

"Interfaith optimists walking the moral high ground together," Zsuzsu sniped.

Belle slitted her eyes. "We welcome everyone to our self-righteous orgy."

"Sorry, bad habit," Zsuzsu muttered. "Oona will love you all."

Shrieking, Camouflage Lady cornered Suit Guy and ranted about Pocumtuc ghosts and the blood of other lost tribes besmirching our spirits.

"Is she with your Change Gang?" Zsuzsu asked.

"No," Belle replied quickly.

"Un-fucking-believable!" The suit guy shrieked back at Camouflage Lady. "We're stuck, going in circles, and you're making up revenge fantasies, bullshit excuses. There must be cameras in the bushes, drones for wide-angle shots, agents laughing their asses off in a van somewhere. They are playing with us." Camouflage Lady stepped away from him.

Oona needed to come back soon. Zsuzsu was about to lose it.

"Why are you idiots so chill?" Suit Guy scowled. The tourists were freaking out. He just didn't notice, too stuck on himself. "You little shits are in on it, actors doing a show, breaking into my mind for secrets, big secrets I don't realize I have. Like a uranium mine, radioactive secrets." CEO of his world, he tried for a fighting stance and almost keeled over.

The med techs and Camouflage Lady caught him before he fell on his pale face. "You need shade and water." Three muscular fems were saving his ass. Did he notice?

Despite irritation with Suit Guy for hiking in navy blue formal wear when it was over ninety degrees in the shade, Zsuzsu said, "The H_2O dispenser on the porch never runs out."

Suit Guy babbled on about chain reaction potentials and federal government overreach as they guided him up the Center steps. He mangled good truth. They set him on a chaise lounge, put a rag on his neck, and plied him with water. The mandolin player sang Melody's favorite (corny) song in a language Zsuzsu had never heard then shifted to English. She had an otherworldly yet beautiful voice:

Sing me a song that breaks the curse
Plant a garden to save the Earth

"Inexplicable, disturbing situation," a teary Belle repeated softly, pressing Zsuzsu's gloved hand to her heart then her forehead, as if they were in a secret league together.

"My name is Zsuzsu Marlene Hönig."

"Hönig is honey. Two Zoos, who told me about you? Oh . . . Ralph Carter is a fan."

"The trash dude: **DUMP IT ALL** and **START DOING BETTER!** He talked to you about me?" Zsuzsu shivered, desire she couldn't contain.

"Everyone talks to me. Ralph is cute. You say Marlene like Dietrich. Afrodeutsch?"

"Ja und I love libraries. I must have seen you at the research desk."

"You come almost every week. Ralph comes a lot too. He bragged about your work at Cloud Heights and took out old Dietrich movies: *Destry Rides Again* and *A Touch of Evil.* Yeah, Ralph's a big fan of yours." As Zsuzsu's cheeks got hot, Belle smiled—radiant and compelling this time, not covering irritation. She was resilient, a people-person like Azul Mendes. Belle was able to connect with anyone, magic Zsuzsu secretly longed for.

"My mother is Assyrian-American," Belle said. "She emigrated with her parents from Iraq. My dad hails from Indiana and the Great Migration." When Black folks ran from the South to the promised land and it turned out to be a fucking mirage.

"My parents are from Bavaria and Queens. World War Two brought them together." Zsuzsu rarely told anyone this. It made her feel overexposed. "Oona will be back soon."

"Who is that again?" Belle frowned.

"Oona, the rescue dog! A St. Bernard / poodle mix."

"Huh." Belle smiled. "I think I know Oona."

"She's very friendly, much friendlier than me."

Too many parking lots to locate, even for Oona. Zsuzsu would have to let these bizarro tourists call for help from her house. They'd track State Forest dirt into her kitchen, down the hallway, and into the bathroom. Maybe she could persuade Paula to come out and clean up after lost tourists. An'qwenique would drive Paula, and afterward they might stroll in the woods. Although, given the last time, An'qwenique and Paula might turn Zsuzsu down.

She should dump the tourists on the neighbors. Pete and Cal were farmers who didn't mind people tracking dirt and debris everywhere and they loved feeling helpful. Cal was a born-again Christian and drove a big truck. She'd transport these lost souls wherever they needed to go. Pete would ride shotgun.

T O D A Y

PAULA—*Good Thoughts*

Paula stumbled toward the big bendy bus. Traffic had picked up. Cars threw slushy muck on the unruly bus patrons. Her phone vibrated. She held it close, shielding the screen from fairy ice missiles. Upstairs Karl was pestering her about nothing or offering murder updates. He'd been warned: only urgent calls. She should never have given him her number. The ringer was on for An'qwenique. Temptation made her fingers itch. People shoved past her and stomped on board, waving monthly passes like magic wands. They grumbled about Melody stuffed in a tiny car at the auto junkyard with a dead raccoon, and DID ANYBODY CARE. Small-town cops—what could you expect?

Paula refrained from shouting: *Oshun Jackson and Blue Rosenthal got busted when they were working Melody's case, a case other detectives didn't want. Melody was a poor white nobody*. The ace detectives argued the clues for months, even around Paula. Oshun stood over Blue, shaking her storm-cloud hair and insisting the Melody crime scene was a horror science experiment. Blue proclaimed it a terror art exhibit and scratched his bald spot, till Oshun gripped his hand.

People thought they were an odd couple. Blue was a natty dresser and very sociable. Oshun was frumpy and ready to wrestle you to the ground. Paula thought they complemented each other perfectly. They never caught a break with Melody's case or with Gwen and Lance's. Foster kids, Gwen was Nipmuc and Black and her little brother Lance was Filipino. They allegedly got sick of straight white Christians, left a *Fuck Y'all* note, and took off. Why leave a note—then everybody's looking for you. Why not just run? Unless you wanted to be found. Or the note was left by someone else, misdirection. An'qwenique agreed with Paula on that.

Yesterday's recycling horror should put a fire under other detectives. Dead rich lady and turkeys might be the work of the perp who did Melody or a copycat crime. Instinct said it was one guy, flaring up after a pause. Couldn't rule out copycats, though.

Oshun and Blue had vanished from the Haven bay window. No point sharing her theories with them till they beat the corruption rap. What if they were guilty, and Paula had missed those clues? That would be weird. Liking someone might blunt her superpower. Maybe she had rationalized away inconvenient possibilities, like with Oona. Everyone did that. Or maybe Paula should trust herself. A hard call.

Her phone vibrated again, Karl leaving voicemail. Paula's hands shook and the screen blurred. A jangly feeling—needing to know right away—surged, because what if she was missing out on something, anything that everyone else already knew? Knowing right now, she wouldn't feel out of it, like she came from another dimension. What if this notification, update, instant message, was the jackpot? What if the secret to happiness/success was waiting for her to tap and tune in? Not just internet withdrawal, depression lurked in the wings, waiting for her to backslide.

"No!" Following An'qwenique's lead, Paula only checked for good news. Murder updates did not qualify. Instead of doomscrolling at lunch today, she'd walk to the Iris Library and do research for next week's inspiration gallery. The Iris was Paula's anchor in a digital storm. *Ask me anything!* Belle—Isabelle Shamiram Roberts—was head librarian yet helped Paula create inspiration exhibits for home uplift and then library installations for public benefit.

Belle's Change Gang gave Paula something to do besides worry, get mad, or go crazy. An action for every ache. Belle was close to Melody. Those two had signed a civil war ceasefire treaty to save friendship. Belle was a community treasure. Maybe Paula could share disappearing dog tales and other theories with her. Belle had not missed the 7:30 bus since Paula started riding, over a year. *Must be a good story.*

"My home exhibits work," Paula whispered what she wanted to tell Belle. Free-floating outrage had subsided. Digital cravings, post-covid blues, and civil-war angst faded too, though not completely. How the heck did the Haudenosaunee stand living with alien invaders? How did Black folks survive Jim Crow USA? They must have possessed secret juju that Paula could use right now. *America, my people, my people.*

She glared at the vibrating phone, Karl, a third time. Forget wasting her morning allotment on his BS or on the warnings, curated memories, and breaking news throbbing on the screen. Constant temptation! Warrior women for peace like Jigonhsasee stayed on track even if surrounded by bloodshed. Paula shoved the phone back in her knapsack.

The line to board the bus had stalled. Big Foot was cussing the driver out about expiration dates. *Fucker*, bus patrons hissed, happy at a target for overflow rage. A gloomy start to the week. Near the end of the line, what if Paula didn't make it on board this trip? "Crap!" She fumbled the fare from a soggy pocket.

She short-circuited irritation by realizing her bus jar had $67, almost enough for a monthly pass—able-bodied adult, $74. Only $10 for students, she was jealous. The last loan payment went in on Saturday, a week before the deadline. No more poverty loans at 400 percent APR. That payment plus rent and utilities wiped her out. Poverty was expensive. An'qwenique paid cash ($300 + $60 tip). Paula did her house Monday every week, a solid cash flow. "Think of something good," she told folks grumbling around her. "Don't waste your mind studyin' Big Foot." She mimicked Grandma Junebug's down-home chill and grinned, because, well, there never was much to clean at An'qwenique's.

Girlfriend had dreadful allergies and a dust/pollen phobia. A whole-house air purifier would have been cheaper than the weekly attic-to-cellar clean, but . . . *No way!* Paula had to do the full Monty. She caught micro-spills on counters and floors that An'qwenique missed. She removed the bug and bird debris caked on window screens, vacuumed skin cells and hair that fed dust mites, and prevented the accumulation of newspapers, bottles, cartons, magazines, dreaded plastic bags, and other detritus. Those were carted off to recycling before Monday because PAULA WAS COMING.

The graduate student mom bumped Paula as they neared the bus. "Sorry," Grad Mom whispered. Paula wanted a knee-length raincoat with a sparkly bronze hood like hers. Not in the budget though. "Sorry for earlier too." Grad Mom shrugged. "None of my business what you two warrior women are up to."

"We're not just planting trees," Paula replied. "Belle Roberts and her Change Gang do good work all over the region. Afterward, you feel wonderful." She smiled. The grad mom looked sad—about what she wasn't doing. Paula changed the subject. "Today is going to get better. An'qwenique loves chewing my ear with her silly habits, secret hopes or fears, and flights of fancy. Some clients do that." 1980s throwbacks (1950s? the Middle Ages?). "Blabbing while I'm trying to clean." The grad mom raised a disapproving eyebrow. Paula continued. "They never pay extra for emotional maid service. Sometimes they don't pay anything, for months."

"So retro." Grad Mom looked embarrassed for the stingy rich folks and relieved that she and Paula were on good terms. "That sucks."

"Yeah." Paula was sick of the private-client nonsense. Zsuzsu Hönig always paid cash like An'qwenique, yet lived out in nowhere. With a dead car, Paula had to take a cab. That cut into her wages. An'qwenique drove Paula once on a snowy Saturday last spring. Not sustainable. "I'ma fill up my business client list and dump private homes." No more loan payments made this possible. And a year ago she was worrying about being homeless. "I'ma give retro folks notice this week, after they pay me." Maybe.

"Good for you." Grad Mom bumped Paula's fist.

"Except An'qwenique," Paula declared. "Monday is hers, as long as she wants it."

"Sounds grand." Grad Mom scowled at Big Foot, who was still talking trash at the driver. "What the hell is the holdup? We're already late and it's still raining ice needles." She squeezed her daughter's hand. "Don't cry, Rosie. If your father won't wait, you can come to class with me."

Rosie blubbered, a sad angel in her shiny raincoat. "Can't I stay with you this week?"

Grad Mom wiped Rosie's face. "I don't know. I have a big test . . ."

Paula wished she could help out, take the kid with her on cleaning jobs, like in that old Whoopi movie Belle gave her, *Corinna, Corinna*. The library had a great media collection, no streaming fees (which were beyond Paula's budget), plus DVDs and Blu-rays. There were oldies and the latest releases.

"You know me!" Big Foot was yelling. "I'm a stand-up guy."

"Not any thirty-one days," the driver boomed, a deep, melodious voice, irritation thoroughly disguised, "thirty-one consecutive days."

"That's cheating," Big Foot replied. "I want my money back."

"Your pass expired last Thursday, and there are no refunds," the driver explained.

"Pay the damn two bucks, so we can move out," Grad Mom shouted.

Big Foot held up his pass. "Where does it say consecutive days?"

Entitled white dudes, man!

"Pay or get out of the fuckin' way." Grad Mom was on her last nerve.

The other bus patrons roared for Big Foot's blood. "Peace starts in the mind. Good thoughts make stupid time whiz by and sweet time linger." Paula murmured these words like a prayer. Grad Mom rolled her eyes. Whatever. Rosie stopped blubbering, tuned in to the Peace Path frequency, and whispered the prayer too, sadness forgotten. Grad Mom nodded, grateful. Prickly hail cooled Paula's angry cheeks.

Once she arrived at work, there'd be funny bus stories to tell on Big Foot, Triple-E, Rosie, and her mom. An'qwenique loved knowing what Paula thought of anything. So Paula spoke her mind, talked her nerd nonsense. An'qwenique always asked great questions. They agreed, disagreed, and talked wild, after work too, chilling in the gazebo. An'qwenique had hooked Paula up with Cloud Heights Enterprises, her first corporate gig: Fridays and a weekend clean-to-the-bones every four weeks.

"The latest body was in a Cloud Heights recycling bin," Paula blurted. "The geek squad has to know something."

"Yeah," Rosie agreed, and Grad Mom flinched.

Paula flinched too. "Oh, sorry." No way to keep the worst from the little girl. All manner of horror was just a click away. Still, Paula should watch her mouth.

At first the geeks had been cryptic around cleaning lady Paula, as if she was incapable of understanding their deepness or would be bored by tech talk, or they had corporate intel and government secrets to protect. She walked through scanners and detectors to get in and out of the building's upper floors. An exhaustive background check turned up pirate ancestors from Barbados and the Georgia Sea Islands (Grandma Junebug's great-uncles); her parents' jail stint for crimes they didn't commit (armed robbery and manslaughter); her sister helming an apocalyptic cult; plus Paula attacking random rich folks' car with a sledgehammer. Still the geeks hired her. What algorithm were they using?

After a couple months, they blathered like she wasn't there. This was instructive and entertaining. Unless there was a power outage, sabotage, or a glitch, whoever dumped the dead woman in the recycling had been caught on their video cameras. The geeks certainly gave camera data to the police. Paula would ask the silver fox with the big cow eyes (who had a crush on An'qwenique and chatted Paula up for helpful tips) to let her see the video too. Ozzie, or no, Azul Mendes, a trickster fronting sweetness and light.

"Pay or get off the bus," the driver said. "Right now, or else I will have to—"

"That's all I have." Big Foot brandished a fifty-dollar bill like a weapon and snarled at folks behind him. "I don't have anything smaller."

Triple-E snorted. "You're a nasty waste of benign bacteria here on the Peace Path."

"Huh?" Big Foot shook his head, confused by her bio-nerd slur.

"Harriet wouldn't sweat this nonsense, Jigonhsasee neither." Dgi-gon-sa-SHAY, Triple-E had no trouble spitting that name at him. She snatched the fifty from Big Foot, stuffed two ones in the fare box, then thrust two twenties, a five, and three ones in his hand. "Et voilà." She shoved him on down the aisle and the line was moving. Big applause and fingers snapping.

Paula murmured *bon*, *parfait*, *super* with a French accent and lugged her cleaning equipment up the steps. She paid her two bucks and resolved to invite An'qwenique to tonight's vegan bacon bun with the dog (hero dog!). Together, they'd gather clues from the St. Berdoodle and get a handle on those disappearing acts. They should go over Melody's case and find what was hiding in plain sight.

Paula's heart quivered. Was she playing detective? Also, a dinner invite might be inappropriate. What if Paula and An'qwenique were just friendly and not real friends? Paula had never managed real friends her whole life.

Today was the moment to go out on a limb, risk everything. Because, why not?

Y E S T E R D A Y

AN'QWENIQUE—*Detour*

"You are not changing your camouflage outfit to suit a stupid neighbor who was wearing a snake raincoat in crazy heat!" An'qwenique yelled at herself. She stormed out of her walk-in closet and down to the kitchen. She counted $360 in twenties and tucked them in an envelope for Paula. Writing the damn VR review, she'd be up all night and asleep when Paula arrived Monday morning. Paula had a key and always waited for signs of life to vacuum. An'qwenique wrote a silly note—more than a list of what to clean, an invite to high tea in the gazebo afterward. She decorated it with hearts, birds, and smiley faces. OK, she did like emojis. It was Kitty who aggravated her.

An'qwenique tucked the note in with the cash and quickly sealed the envelope before she changed her mind. Hopefully she and Paula would negotiate the job/money/power differential and be friends. She'd let Paula use the VR rig and read the review before she sent it off. Then next week, lounging in the gazebo at their second high tea, An'qwenique would broach the subject of a piece on Paula, a biographical praise poem for a humble philosopher queen/activist, followed by a podcast series together—"Gumbo-Yaya to Stream." This fantasy was possibly too transactional, but what the heck. A girl could dream.

Paula's survival handbook went in An'qwenique's backpack / mini go-bag. It smelled spicy, like Indian or West African food. Her pack would hold the curry scent forever, nevertheless she might snatch a moment to read more before the quiz on Monday. Paula was tough. Ms. SuperNerd didn't let you get a B. Ever.

An'qwenique always carried a mini go-bag now: weather-proof matches, several super blankets, poncho, her grandmother's lucky *Star Trek* watch (no battery needed), and a first aid kit, including emergency epinephrine autoinjectors, allergy pills, and nasal spray, which she could raid today and replenish tomorrow. She attached two lightweight, collapsible picnic chairs. Bare ass on the grass or random surfaces had little appeal. Ants, bees, spiders, and ticks were Paula's friends, not hers.

The Cloud Heights building was only a few blocks from the reservoir. Still, Azul Mendes would be late. The computer geek always dove deep into a problem and lost track of time and space. Instead of indulging irritation, she packed a fountain pen, a pack of colored markers, and an old-fashioned composition book with acid-free paper. The reservoir was a perfect place to think, draw, write, and simply be. And if Azul brought nothing edible (vegan shrimp, yeck), there was cashew butter, rice crackers, and gorp in her go-bag, plus a big bottle of lime-flavored filtered water. To hell with dying of thirst first.

Driving too fast out of the garage, An'qwenique almost ran over the stranger (neighbor?) striding across the driveway. She swerved, screeched to a halt, and gawked. The silhouette was definitely larger than before, a giant inside that reptilian raincoat—not the skinny wraith from before. Nobody in the Wild Bunch next door was so tall. A massive dragon hat had replaced the snake head.

The stranger tromped through the border of clover and dandelions like a heavyweight champ going into the ring. An'qwenique's uncle was a professional fighter. She knew those bluster bully moves—a contrast to the anxious creeping fifteen minutes ago. Much bigger hands and feet, and a nasty snarl and threatening stomp for the curious young turkey trotting nearby. There had to be two weirdos dressed alike.

This weirdo had skeleton tights, green mirror sunglasses, and a purple neck scarf. Religious fanatic afraid of the sun? Born-again pugilist? Doom and Gloom climate activist? More likely, internet troll gone live. The stranger approached, a definite big-dude swagger in neon-orange-and-pink sneakers. His green mirror sunglasses reflected an exhausted, anxious woman peering out of an EV window. Such a vulnerable bird woman, An'qwenique barely recognized herself. Surely the glasses distorted her face.

"No thank you," she shouted. "I'm about to be late. Sorry." She closed her window, turned on the AC, and accelerated. Whatever the pitch was, she was thankful to escape. Her heart fluttered as if something whizzed past her ear. *Dodging a bullet.* She glanced in the rearview mirror. Why did she apologize?

The stranger stomped across her wildflowers as if these living beings were nobody. He could have taken the flagstone walkway to Charlize and Tomás's monstrosity. The happy couple had torn down a perfectly good house to build a gothic nightmare with obscene turrets, stone stairs-to-nowhere, and precarious balconies. The front hall was outfitted as a torture chamber with a rack, thumbscrews, an iron maiden, and breaking wheels. An'qwenique resisted finding out what exactly a breaking wheel did. The stranger caressed a medieval side door and peeked into frosted windows.

Burping stomach acid, An'qwenique turned the sleek, solar-powered EV off of her tree-lined, dead-end lane and headed for the Mooseberry Mall. She resisted an adrenaline surge as she wound through the one-way streets. Her home security system was next generation, courtesy of Azul. If invaders tried to break in, the police would be there cracking heads before the shitbags figured out there was nothing much to steal.

The flat-screen over the fireplace was a monster. Getting it down from the wall would kill you. The upstairs screen in the master bedroom turned office/studio was cracked (from a recent rage fest). The VR rig was hiding in the closet, masquerading as tech to be recycled. Her laptop lived in the go-bag now. Where were these rat bastards going to fence Hawaiian masks and Dogon sculptures? Probably not connoisseurs of non-Euro art. Little comfort there.

It was 2:41 PM, almost late. McMansions to the left and right smirked at her anxiety until she reached the main drag. Coming up on the first red light, her neck itched, her stomach clenched, and her heart pounded. "OK." She should text Charlize, warn her, warn somebody, while there was time. Of what? The next-door futurist commune might have welcomed two new cosplay weirdos who had yet to become accustomed to wild Mexican turkeys. An'qwenique had errands to run and somewhere to be. Texting while driving was stupid. If there was trouble, Charlize had the police chief on speed dial.

The light turned green. It was three minutes to the mall. An'qwenique drove faster than the limit like everyone else. Behind the mall next to the autobody shop was a municipal recycling center that accepted plastic and metal containers, plastic bags, and paper. The mall liquor store paid cash for empty beverage bottles and cans. A twenty-two-minute job on Sunday, then fourteen minutes to the reservoir. She had a nine-minute margin of error for the unexpected and also to give her bottle refund to the homeless guy who sometimes hung around the parking lot with his donation jar.

A month's worth of bottled H_2O for one person was an obscene amount of plastic and giving the refund away was bullshit. Past time to ditch the fizzy water. Paula had scavenged a machine from a client to make your own fizzy. So why not use that?

An'qwenique slammed on the brakes as a logging truck burst out of a parking lot right in front of her. Traffic came to a standstill. Construction? Not on Sunday. Accident? Westbound traffic was funneled into her lane then back to their own. Her lane moved a few car lengths and halted again. The logging truck belched oily smoke. She wanted to scream. It was 2:45 PM and only a few blocks to go. She turned on the damn phone and texted Charlize: *Hey you! Urgent Alert! Political zealots or deranged trolls lurking about, don't waste time answering the door.* Was that who the dragon people were? Sometimes Kitty was right about creeps up to no good.

A text from her mom popped up: *Your brother is in BIG TROUBLE.* He was always in big trouble. Nothing to do about that, barely time for her own troubles. She switched the phone off and shuddered. She hated how the damn device could invade any moment and make it worse. Up ahead, a sign offered a detour onto an unfamiliar street. Nobody else took it. An'qwenique hated detours. She always got lost. Actually, she hated driving, even a solar-powered miracle. Species had gone extinct so each of us might zoom about in our personal chariot of the gods.

"Unintended consequences."

However, if folks realized and did nothing, like An'qwenique slurping water out of plastic bottles, that was consequences ignored.

"Stop it," she chastised herself. "Don't think. Who cares right now?"

When should you care?

The tree trunks stacked in the truck bed looked ready to tumble onto her hood. So many naked corpses stripped to their weighty bones. Suddenly she felt like vomiting.

What the hell are we doing?

"I'm doing the best I can!" Screeching hurt her throat and made her ears ring. Her best wasn't good enough. The cars inched forward. Up ahead, an Amazon van had crashed into a telephone pole. "Fuck!" She hoped nobody died, nobody was hurt.

Coming back to the mall after high tea with Azul was not an option. Recycling ended at 4:30 PM on Sundays. In a fit of high-voltage rage, An'qwenique turned onto the detour route and revved back up to speed. The mall was close, even if this road circled wide.

YESTERDAY

OONA—*Dodo (Fried Plantains) and Tracking Trouble*

Sunday afternoon before Oona found the body, there were several surprises.

She left Zsuzsu Marlene Hönig at the Redemption Center to track the scent of frying plantains. The Center was closed, still Zsuzsu was having a good time arguing with strangers, and Oona hadn't smelled dodo in forever. Her heart ached for the musician, magician, and clown. She was neither an optimist nor a pessimist, but a prisoner of hope, and hope was an action. Do what you had to do, what felt right, felt good for everybody, no matter the odds against you, and life was worth living. So, even if you didn't find that family you lost, searching for them mattered. Searching was a good life.

Oona bounded over the chokeberry bushes that bordered one of her favorite yards. The resident turtle thrashed on her back in white clover. Oona growled and barked at an intruder. A raccoon darted through the garage and out the back, away from her big-dog boom. Oona pissed on the garage door, a threat. Wild turkeys flew into the maple trees and cackled at her. They never wanted to play.

The turtle stretched her head to the side, slapped webbed feet in tall clover, and tried to flip onto her tummy. Oona yapped encouragement. The turtle teetertottered then fell back to flailing. This had occurred before, and Oona had been warned. *Be gentle.* She whined and tiptoed closer. The turtle waved stubby legs and hissed. Oona nosed the colorful shell and flipped her over. The turtle chirped irritation, in no mood for fun yet, and waddled to a tiny pond filled with lily pads and noisy frogs.

"My angel." Charlize snapped her fingers from the kitchen porch. She was alone. No whiff of the carnival crew. Oona whimpered, disappointed. Charlize laughed, a deep drum sound. Her voice was a caress, a singer's voice. Indeed, Charlize was a wonderful musician. Oona was determined not to lose track of this one. "That's twice this week you've saved Aretha. And from what, I don't know." Charlize stepped into the garden. "Not the wild turkeys, so I've been told. Skunk? Weasel? Racoon? Some son of a snake, internet troll?" Charlize growled. "Tomás doesn't want Aretha or any messy animals in the house. I need a big, brave dog to patrol the outside. You know anybody?"

Charlize's robe fluttered like clouds in the sky; frizzy hair waved like a field of scented grass. Oona savored the aroma of lavender soap, canola oil, lime, nutmeg, and plantains. Charlize regularly fried plantains, singing as the oil popped, almost as good as the circus crew. She held out her hand. Oona licked the greasy fingers. "You're better than nine-one-one to the rescue. Where's the rest of your team? Doing good deeds all over, I bet."

Oona's carnival family had traveled around to assisted living / nursing homes, schools, libraries, hospitals, or where people were feeling sad and low. They played music, juggled toys, and tumbled about with Oona till the audience laughed, cried, and clapped their hands. Sometimes the carnival crew disappeared, taking Oona with them. Disappearing then coming back was the most fun! The audience always went wild.

One day last September, the clown and the magician started fighting with each other, worse than usual. Oona hid under a table. Scuffling and screaming about lost transport and staying away too long, they broke a cello and a djembe drum. The musician ran out into a freak snowstorm. The clown and magician quit pounding each other and followed the musician into the early snow. *Come back, we'll find the shuttle*, they yelled, *we're sorry. Nobody's to blame.* Oona's heart was thudding, her paws shaking. She stayed under the table a long time and waited for them to return. She ended up at the Wild Animal and Pet Rescue, and hadn't seen her carnival family since. She had visited their old haunts, but they weren't there, and sometimes angry people chased her away.

Charlize hugged Oona. "You do realize, I'd steal you in a hot second."

Oona flopped in the clover. Charlize rubbed her tummy. Inside the house someone banged into furniture and grunted. Oona's ears perked up and her nose quivered.

"Tomás, back already? That was quick. Did you forget something?" Charlize kissed Oona's nose. "You want to meet Tomás? He thinks I made you up." Oona had smelled Tomás many times before; they just had never been formally introduced. "Wait here." As Charlize dashed onto the porch and into the kitchen, her cell phone dinged—a warning from An'qwenique she never got.

An old gym-mat odor wafted from the door before it slammed shut. Paula had a friend who smelled like that. Tomás carried this scent too, yet the person in the kitchen was someone else, vaguely familiar. A big-man smell. He was agitated and uncertain, irritated and thrilled too. Oona was confused. Aretha, ready for slow-motion fun, waddled under Oona's belly and nibbled her toes. After running around the slowpoke turtle a few times, Oona jumped onto the side porch and dropped down in the shade.

The temperature would top one hundred degrees before she found the body in the recycling bin. That fateful moment was drawing near, yet fate was often a total shock, a lightning strike from a cloudless sky. Oona expected good times with friends to last forever. So when trouble came (and trouble always came), she wasn't already exhausted, despairing. Her heart spirit stayed charged up. Oona was always ready to tackle trouble full force.

The aroma of fried plantains and nutmeg from Charlize's

kitchen carried delicious memories: living on a riverboat with her carnival crew and swimming in cool water whenever you were climate-crisis hot. The musician, magician, and clown were undoubtedly searching for Oona as doggedly as she searched for them. Fried plantains were a trail they left for her to follow back to them. It was just a very long journey.

She licked her chops, excited for Charlize to come back outside and chase her and Aretha around the pond. Aretha ate any bugs the speedy mammals threshed up when racing past her. No jumping in the pond for Oona though, Charlize's rules.

"What are you doing here? How'd you get in?" Charlize talked from beyond the kitchen to the big man who smelled like a gym mat and Haven Bagels. "What are you wearing? What's with your voice?" The big man mumbled a long speech. Charlize laughed over him, loud hoots and guffaws that had Oona wagging her tail. "Whoa! You and me? Ha! I don't even remember your name! We were never anything. All in your mind. I love Tomás. He loves me. And guess what, I don't care who else he loves or what anybody thinks." Despite laughter, she sounded upset.

Oona pressed her nose on the screen. The big man grumbled at Charlize from the shadowy hallway to the dining room. He made snake and angry-bird noises.

"I'm sorry we disappoint you so much." Charlize replied in an angry voice too.

The big man grunted. Fury rode the words he spat out. Oona's hackles went up. She was never allowed in the house, Tomás's rules. However, Tomás wasn't here. Charlize needed help. Oona pounced on the door handle. It was jammed.

"It's time for you to leave. Tomás will be back any moment," Charlize declared.

"Liar," the big man replied, full voice. "Who cares anyhow?"

Oona pawed the door handle again. Still jammed. The stranger grabbed Charlize and whispered. He smelled excited and happy, yet he was an intruder, a threat, ready to eat somebody alive. No time to map another route. Oona lunged at the screen.

"There is no fuckin' planet where that would be remotely possible!" Charlize yelled.

"Shut up." He put a cloth over her mouth. She gestured at the ceiling, staggered, and almost fell. He caught her then shook till her head flopped back and forth. Oona sprang at the door again, warping the screen, without breaking through. Blood spurted from a toe, and she swallowed a yelp as Charlize and the intruder staggered into the dark recesses of the house.

For the first time in a long time, Oona wanted to bite someone, a bad man. He dragged Charlize deeper still. A door slammed. Oona jumped from the side porch, raced around the stairs-to-nowhere and across the front yard. Turning the corner, she bounded over the hydrangea bush, into the gothic archway.

The bad man shoved a wobbly Charlize into the back seat of a car idling just beyond the garage. He slid in beside her. Oona hesitated. Cars often tried to run her over. She crept closer, hidden by wildflowers. Gwen, a friend from the high school, was driving. Gwen and Oona played Frisbee with little brother Lance, not recently though. Backing the car into the street, Gwen smelled scared, like Charlize. Oona snarled.

Charlize vomited out of a window and flopped against the bad man. They drove off with the window open. Oona trailed them through the maze of one-way streets and dead ends. Gwen obeyed four-way stops and stuck to the twenty-mile-per-hour limit over the speed bumps. Oona never lost sight of the car. They paused at the big road where traffic roared over hot blacktop: right turn for the Mooseberry Mall or left for Crossroads African Restaurant. They headed for Crossroads, thirty-five miles per hour in steady traffic.

Trouble had blasted out of the clear blue and now disappeared into a hazy afternoon. Oona licked a tender paw and panted under a maple tree. She decided to cool her feet in the clover a bit longer, then take an easier route to Crossroads. A musician from Mali played there and always set a water dish out for her. There might be a snack too. If not, Melody or somebody would have a bowl behind the Haven. Fortified, Oona could comb the streets and catch the scent trail wherever Charlize, the bad man, or Gwen got out of the car.

Oona's carnival crew always said, *Search and rescue, tracking trouble and navigating the multiverse, that's in the dog's blood.* They spent months training her, in the woods and strange cities, across mountains and rivers, when it rained and snowed. Nobody was better at hiding than the magician, who knew more secret, dangerous places than anyone. The clown set booby traps and tried to fool or scare Oona. The musician distracted her with toys, music, and treats. Oona sidestepped danger, gobbled the food (only if it smelled right), and found every tricky hiding place. Except last fall.

It never occurred to Oona that maybe her family wasn't playing hide-and-seek or lost on an aggravating map. Maybe they'd gone somewhere she couldn't follow, not without technical assistance. It did occur that Charlize was in mortal danger. The bad man had a predator smell. On a hunter's high, he might do anything. Tracking trouble, Oona trotted off, determined not to lose another musician.

T O D A Y

PAULA—*Understanding*

Hooray for the big bendy accordion bus! On board at last! Air conditioning blasted a polar wind on soggy people. Fairy ice-missiles battered the roof and sounded like the popcorn machine at the old movie theatre. Triple-E shimmy-shook to the beat. She sat behind the Duke Ellington driver in a seat reserved for the elderly and disabled. The batty old hippie was magic like the St. Berdoodle, no matter what anybody said.

Paula stood on the yellow line and soaked up her good vibes. Cranky bus patrons showed passes or paid two bucks and squeezed by. The driver winked at Paula, as if she was cute or something. She winked back. "Mind if I call you Duke?"

"You and everybody been calling me that behind my back." He beamed at her. "I like the sound."

"Me too," Triple-E declared, and opened her journal. Words and sketches flowed onto the page. Duke never let other passengers sit in her window seat on the world. He watched out for the regulars. Duke had loaned Paula round-trip fare when half her clients forgot to pay, and the rent and utilities were due. She paid him back with interest.

"My nom de guerre!" Duke winked again.

"Don't set yourself on fire now," Paula warned.

"What you mean by that?" Duke handed out transfers to a few college bros.

"It's good advice, isn't it?" Paula had to watch saying just anything. He might be a suspect or married or into handsome young men.

"You can't stand there daydreaming and grinning at me,"

Duke said. Everyone was on board. The doors whooshed shut. "Step behind that yellow line. We're late."

"Sorry." Paula stepped back, and they were underway. So many wet bodies, shivering and muttering, and nobody wanted to make room up front. They glowered at the HEPA vacuum cleaner banging her shoulder. Triple-E shouted *Queen Bee* as Paula slogged past the two empty seats in the accordion section—mostly kids sat there.

The bendy bus was too full before the Haven stop. Hardly anyone got off. Drivers missing their shifts or worse. Duke was very late. He sped up and Paula almost fell. She clutched a grip by the back exit and ignored grumpy faces. Why was everything too hard and taking forever today? Time was in a bad mood too. Since covid.

Outside, the street was a moving-picture fantasy. The sun broke through departing clouds. Fog ghosted above the blacktop. Slush slid off leaves and tree limbs sprang up. Drab buildings glittered like an enchanted village. The fairies must be happy. Paula's new neighbor streaked by on Air Jordans. Purple-and-green dreads were a bold contrast to the mist. A silkscreened cosmos on his back gleamed. A burly Black man suspect.

Paula scanned the aisle. More suspects peered back at her, picking their noses, poking their phones. Ominous. In the welter of clues, how did you sort the signal from the noise? The bus halted at the Cloud Heights building. The Pet and Wild Animal Rescue occupied the ground floor. Paula deep-cleaned the Rescue on Thursdays. Azul Mendes and the geeks had recommended her when some joker abandoned a wounded skunk at the door and their cleaning service up and quit.

"Just Tuesdays and Wednesdays to go!" Paula exclaimed to Big Foot, who rolled his eyes. He and everyone else decided she was batty like Triple-E. Whatever.

A fem performer in top hat and tails with a golden retriever service dog squeezed down the aisle. The performer had a sexy mustache like Duke's and stippled cheeks mimicking a five-o'clock shadow—a drag-king act or trouser role in an opera. Probably not a suspect. The dog danced across the pivot disk and shook rain on folks nearby.

"Watch your mutt." A muscular man in T-shirt and shorts offered the drag king a rosy-cheeked smirk. He had sweet dimples and large hazel eyes. Soulful. A mop of spiky curls looked improbable. Wig? He sat shoulder to shoulder with Big Foot, as if they were great pals. They both had gym bags: PUMP IT UP! BE THE BEST YOU! Upstairs Karl's gym, the only serious workout spot, open 24/7. Too expensive for Paula.

"People pretend pets are service dogs. One like yours peed on my shoes yesterday." Dimples laughed, at what, Paula couldn't say. She got little sense of who he was, what he was up to. Unusual to find someone so hard to read. A performer? Or caught in middle-aged muddle, same as Paula, yet fronting like he was in control of himself, of the world. Control was a mirage. Dimples nudged Big Foot. "Can you beat that?"

The drag king stood between Dimples and the golden retriever who looked ready to jump off the bus. Duke honked at a van blocking the road, and the dog quivered. "Damn, man." Big Foot shoved Dimples, picking on someone his own size. "The mutt is way the hell over there. What the fuck?"

"Yeah, OK," Dimples replied.

Paula sniggered, and the retriever plopped on her cold feet with a contented sigh.

"Get up from there, Benjie." The drag king tugged the dog in vain and looked terrified at Paula. "Sorry. Benjie never acts like this." *As far as you know.*

"It's all good," Paula said. Benjie gazed at the tangle of soggy shins around him then up at Paula. "With this polar AC, a warm butt is appreciated."

"Benjie hates the bus," the drag king said.

"A dense forest of strange legs," Paula ventured.

"I know." The drag king felt awful torturing such a sweet

dog. "We had to take the bus. Almost late for my rehearsal. My car died." A lie. Something else was up.

"I'm glad my heap croaked," Paula said. "Forced me to do the right thing. Cars are a death wish. Everyone should take the bus—electric, from a solar plant, carbon neutral." Big Foot and nearby passengers eyed Paula like she might foam at the mouth. "Every bit helps. Ants aerate the whole world's soil one tiny pile at a time."

"So get a fucking grip, people." Dimples smirked. "Stop acting like you don't matter. Do something, goddamnit, and make a difference."

Paula cringed. Her thoughts coming from his mouth sounded too derisive, too self-righteous or condescending to do any good. She wanted to take back her little-ant speech, yet folks nodded at Dimples. A few laughed. *Speak truth to power, man.*

"That was easy." Dimples sneered at Paula. Everyone was charmed—by him, not by the point she was hoping to make. He knew it too. She pretended not to care and shrugged.

"I can't get myself anywhere without Benjie." The drag king confided to Paula. "I've been scattered, lost, but sometimes, the road finds you."

"Yeah, but we gotta make sure who we happen to be is who we mean to be."

"Word." The drag king wiggled bushy eyebrows, like upstairs Karl. "Understanding is what it takes." Benjie nosed Paula's calf.

"I love animals. Easier than people," she murmured to the dog. "I have a dilemma." Benjie thumped his tail and tilted his head. "Is this the day to betray a friend?" Benjie licked his chops, attentive to her serious tone. "Sorry." A working dog, Paula should leave Benjie be and untangle dog / murder mystery crap herself.

Despite what Upstairs Karl thought, she had no useful info to offer police on the St. Berdoodle. What to say that anybody would believe? Detectives would most likely check animal shelters. The Pet and Wild Animal Rescue might not know who ended up adopting the St. Berdoodle. The Rescue's computers had crashed in March. Cloud Heights geeks helped them retrieve a lot of the data, except for recent records. And let's be real. If the cops tracked the St. B down and acted imperious or mean or locked her in a government escape-proof prison, she'd never tell them anything.

The dead woman in the recycling was probably family, a friend. The dog was sad, grieving. If no one had found her yet, maybe she never went home to the folks who thought they owned her. Maybe she went off to some safe place to howl and find love. That could be anywhere—she had a wide range. For sure wider than Paula imagined.

"I made it. My stop is next," the drag king said. "Today might be our first show—"

"Since covid?" Paula ventured.

The king stuck a flyer in her hand and pranced down the steps with Benjie. "Tonight's appearance at Crossroads is up in the air. But come to our farewell concert at Iris Library. That will be out of this world."

"I'd love to." Paula waved the brightly colored flyer.

On the sidewalk two drag queens screeched a welcome. They were big girls, rocking high hair, platform boots, sequined bell bottoms, and glitter glam robes, carnival all day every day. A giant book (prop?) was jammed in a shopping cart. READ THE WORLD was on the cover. "That's what I'm talking about! Getting River here in one piece" They had resonant voices and much heart. "Keeping the act together! Go Benjie!"

Paula nodded. "Yeah, go Benjie and River!"

Benjie barked at Paula, and River bowed to Paula. "I was ready to turn back. You got me to the right stop. The cameo at Crossroads tonight is looking possible, but no promises." The drag queens sashayed onto the bus, squeezed Paula's hand, and jumped out before Duke could fuss. The doors closed as they did a group hug over Benjie.

The flyer smelled like good food and good times. Paula tucked it in with the HEPA. Positive energy was fuel for Harriet Tubman and for Jigonhsasee. Paula whispered Dgi-gon-sa-SHAY over and over to nail the pronunciation and let the spirit flow. Suddenly she was impatient to work the recycling-bin case with An'qwenique. The killer was out there, plotting the next deadly attack. He had a day on them, maybe a lifetime of getting away with nefarious crap and letting someone else take the rap. The next victim might be anyone, a passenger on this bus. Solving this crime was better than doomscrolling through grisly details and feeling pointless and mad as hell. An antidote to despair!

An'qwenique had laser focus. Together they'd hone in on hidden patterns and figure the how and why of random clues. They'd persuade the St. Berdoodle to sniff out the killer and take them wherever she took that burly Black man, her safe place, off the grid no doubt. Way off the grid. This was not a simple who-done-it. Paula found that exciting. Maybe later, she'd be scared. Right now, she wanted Duke to drive the bendy bus over the speed limit and make up for lost time. Every second counted.

YESTERDAY

RALPH—*Found*

RC's Disposal—**DUMP IT ALL AND START DOING BETTER!**

On Sundays Ralph Carter indulged himself. He slept late, read a good book, and ran with the dog. The rest of the week, he worked like a demon, twenty-hour days to build the **DUMP IT ALL** business up. He trained his team, solved routine and exceptional challenges, and crafted that serious, shiny reputation which resulted in success. According to his accountant, the (almost) 24/7 grind was working.

At thirty-nine Ralph ignored the toll success was exacting on his body. Some folks called him brawny, a bruiser—most of that was muscle. He biked to work and had free weights in his office. He broke his nose, showing off at the **Pump It Up!** gym. Yet, blood pressure was creeping up and resting heart rate stayed a little too high—stress. *The world, man!* Like Paula said. At least his cholesterol was OK. A coffee mocha with caramel ice cream at Haven Bagels once a month was his worst sin. Darlene was his biggest regret. He almost broke her jaw. She deserved every penny he paid her.

Ralph was a glorified garbageman—a job his grandfather warned him against, but it wasn't like the old days when Black men couldn't get much else. RC's Disposal helped you reuse, recycle, or dispose of just about everything, and still feel good about yourself. Ralph offered people a chance to clean up and do right, what somebody offered him once, after Darlene. Satisfied customers considered themselves responsible citizens of the world, of a sustainable future. The trash they dumped told another story, however it wasn't in Ralph's contracts to shatter illusions. **DOING BETTER** was on the clients.

Every Sunday, an hour before sunset, Ralph chained his fancy commuter bike behind Cloud Heights Enterprises. The upstart tech company hired RC Disposal ten months ago to refurbish or recycle e-waste and deal with shredded paper that gummed up municipal sorting machines. Who knew people in the digital age would deal with that much top-secret, sensitive paper? Ralph persuaded them to use vegetable ink and cut back on the shredding. Cloud Heights had a Data for the Earth mission.

Their current big project was tracking the waterways and oceans for nurdles—tiny plastic pellets made from fossil fuels and used as the building bits for most plastic products worldwide. This carcinogenic pollutant was turning up everywhere, devasting coastal ecosystems, and generating massive denial. Everybody used nurdles, yet no one took responsibility for the poison mess they made. The Cloud Heights geeks were masters at puncturing denial. Chief Nerd Azul Mendes was almost a friend. Ralph offered Cloud Heights a discount. They gave it back to him as a bonus with interest.

Dropping off and picking up their recycling kits and bins, Ralph had discovered the perfect run/walk just beyond the parking lot. Actually, the dog helped him find it last February, during a freak warm spell. All the weather was freak now. The dog stole a glove and he ran after her. The sandy trail meandered through scrub brush, a tunnel, and over the roots of scrappy trees along the river. Native flower blooms were an unexpected delight as well as wildlife caught in the act.

Ralph treasured the Sunday quiet, the water, and the dog—a big fluffy ball of energy who, in addition to gloves, loved to steal his hat, fanny pack, or sunglasses. He had to chase after her to get his stuff back. Like the women he was always falling for. Ralph had too little time for love or even friends these days, although after communing with nature and chasing the dog, he liked to splurge on a feast at Crossroads. The Pan-African restaurant served up good food and live music. He often picked up the tab for a table of strangers, because why the fuck not.

This Sunday, Ralph arrived in the parking lot, and the dog was nowhere to be seen. She'd never been late before, never missed a Sunday since that first meetup. Neither had Ralph, despite blizzards, blackouts, and floods. He stared at shadows for twenty minutes, hoping she'd magically appear. He glanced at his watch and reluctantly decided the dog had stood him up. After a week with the clients from hell, he'd been counting on her to cheer him up. He was devastated.

There were no witnesses, yet Ralph resisted the urge to curse, howl, or weep. He tied on his trail runners and pretended not to be disappointed or jealous of whoever the poodle mix was spending time with. A St. Berdoodle most likely—he'd done a background check—so a designer dog bred to be friendly, smart, and loyal. Breeding wasn't everything. Breed statistics were no good at predicting the individual. For the first time Ralph wondered how the dog figured the day and the before-sunset time to meet. She was a big unknown. Whoever owned her would most likely disapprove of their regular Sunday rendezvous. Too bad. Ralph shook out his muscles, did warm-up exercises, and pretended the ache in his gut was hunger. Chewing a few figs and nuts had zero effect; neither did the swigs of lemon water. The dog wasn't coming. His breath came with a hitch. "Are you shitting me?"

Ralph never allowed himself to be sentimental, even in private, except with the dog. A real macho cliché. He jogged down to the river and found two otters hunting. One dove into a murky patch and surfaced with a flailing fish in its mouth. The dog charged at Ralph, howling and growling, and scared the otters off. Ralph couldn't believe how glad he was. She jumped against his chest full force and almost knocked him down.

"What's wrong?" He hugged her close and let her lick his

face. "That bad? I wish you could talk. Well, not like in those stupid movies with wiseass celebrity dogs."

She whimpered and slobbered, more upset than he'd ever seen her. The agitated mood was contagious—Ralph's heart fluttered. She dropped to the ground and dashed off without stealing anything from him. Ralph raced after her toward the Cloud Heights parking lot. She usually dallied here and there, let him get close, then dashed off again. Not this evening. He ran full out just to keep her in sight and then boom!

Ralph almost fell in the gravel. For a moment he lost faith in gravity and light. He refused to believe what he was seeing. Blinking didn't clear the vision away. He wondered if (hoped?) he was dreaming, stuck in a nightmare. A naked woman, dead it would seem, murdered most likely, was jammed feet first into one of his shredded-paper recycling bins. WTF, right? As far as he could tell, the dead woman was nobody he knew. She was in fact unrecognizable. His gorge rose. A murder victim in real life was exponentially worse than the TV series and internet videos he'd seen.

He shrieked like in a scream movie then broke into a cold sweat. The murdered lady had an arm around a burnt wild turkey. Colorful feathers had been singed, the feet seared, and a red wattle hung over a broken beak. The dog licked Ralph's shaky knees and paced between him and the dead woman.

"Did you know her?" he asked the dog. She whined. He took that as a yes. The smell of dried blood, of pain and suffering made him almost throw up again. The dog butted the back of his knees and tugged his running shorts. Ralph refused to budge.

Two wild turkey corpses were in another bin—iridescent feathers, purple and orange, more like peacocks than the wild gobblers he usually saw strutting around. The birds were stuffed in shredded paper. Rainbow confetti, sparkly. Ralph emptied these two bins himself on Saturday and ferried a load to Mulch Works. No way should they have been even half full.

The Cloud Heights crew always took Sunday off, to have fun, to do nothing. Zsuzsu Hönig called it Faulenzen. She and everybody at Cloud Heights got Ralph started on the day-of-rest kick. A sacred day. Plus they never used colored stock. The killer must have filled the bins himself and then stuffed his victims in.

"Shit," Ralph muttered. "Who cares?"

He was avoiding the murdered-woman spectacle—like if he didn't look, she'd vanish, she'd go torture some other poor slob out for an evening constitutional.

The dog sat on his feet, leaned into his legs, and whimpered.

"Yeah, right. I don't know torture." Ralph forced himself to look at the dead woman, at the evidence of what she'd gone through. Everybody deserved that, right?

He'd seen everything all at once. Cuts and bruises everywhere. Her long, frizzy hair had been shaved off in patches. There were needle marks in her butt. Tubes in her ears, up her anus; electrodes on her breasts, feet, and skull; clamps on her lips, and . . . It wasn't like at the hospital with life support. This was some kind of science/torture experiment—put on display here. Definitely not what his heart or blood pressure needed. The killer wanted Ralph and everyone to find this dead woman and feel terrible and terrified, feel humiliated and violated. The killer got off on staging a nightmare exhibition that no one could unsee.

Ralph closed his eyes and sank down by the dog. She crawled into his lap and put her head against his cheek. He hugged her and swallowed the acid taste in his mouth. After a moment their hearts slowed down.

People around this way generally didn't kill other people and trash them in Ralph's or anybody's bins. Shit like this made him leave the city and move up here, way out in the middle of nothing. Murders in these sleepy New England towns were rare, and mostly crimes of passion, not serial wankers or mad scientists putting on a terror show. Some poor slob came after you because *you screwed me over or screwed my whoever and I lost my mind and picked up this baseball bat, knife, or gun.* Who remembered the last one of those? The shootout in front of Fitzroy's bar was six years ago. No automatic-weapon massacre to date, thank you Jesus.

Death headlines were mostly stupid car accidents. That poor kid who backed out of the garage and ran over his best friend, or the hit-and-run by the meadows. There was Melody from the Haven, stuffed into a Toyota BEV at the auto body shop behind the mall. Guys at the gym claimed Melody was a real bitch. She threw your order at you, never smiled, and let funky homeless people nurse a cup of coffee for hours. Ralph never noticed any of this. The murderer shaved Melody's head too and stuck tubes and whatnot in her. She clutched a dead raccoon, not an alien turkey, but a similar deal.

The dog scrambled from Ralph's lap. She gripped the hem of his shirt and tugged.

"What do you think I can do?" The dog flinched at his tone. "Sorry."

Ralph stood up slowly and called the police. He almost threw up on the first officer on the scene. A tall, muscular Asian-American with a broken nose similar to Ralph's arrived too quickly. Time was like in a nightmare or horror movie. Jump scares whenever you turned around.

The officer cut dark eyes at him. Ralph knew that look. This lady cop thought he was the perp. Nothing personal, Ralph told himself. Suspicion was her main mode, how she approached anything, anybody. "I said I'm Officer Wang. So you *found* the body?"

"The dog found her." Ralph pointed at the St. Berdoodle. "I called you guys, you people I mean, and . . ." He waited twenty minutes according to his phone, even though he worried they might arrest him. Ralph was paranoid for good reason. He'd been arrested several times for shit he had nothing to do with. An AI glitched, facial recognition fiasco. Unfortunately, his DNA was all over those bins and also in the FBI database. "I was jogging down by the water. The dog came and got me."

Officer Wang scowled at the river. "There's no path down by the water."

"Yeah, there is. After the tunnel," Ralph replied. "Rugged, you know? I like the effort, bushwhacking through virgin territory." Wow! What a stupid turn of phrase.

"Tunnel?" Officer Wang wrote furious notes. "You say *the dog*. I take it, not your dog."

Ralph had explained that already, when he called it in and when this officer arrived. Trying to trip him up maybe. "Me and the dog, we're just, she . . ." He shouldn't say friends or running buddies. "We see each other down here sometimes."

"There's a leash law. We'll have to take her in."

The dog sat down on her haunches a few yards away. She tilted her head to the side and watched them. She seemed so far away, Ralph felt abandoned. He never liked talking to the cops. They never liked talking to him. He wanted to run away. The dead woman was pale with frizzy hair, a white girl or light-skinned BIPOC. Ralph was blue black, like he just stepped off the boat from Mali, West Africa, with goat hair in his afro and a donsó ngoni, hunter's harp, slung over his shoulder. Terrible optics.

"Where'd you buy those shoes?" Officer Wang squinted at Ralph's large feet.

"Sidewalk sales. The orange with pink highlights in big sizes didn't sell well." He got these for $29.99, down from $129.99. Ralph liked orange. The pink reminded him of the watermelon sherbet he loved as a kid. "Every big-foot dude at the gym did. Why?"

"A gym rat, huh?" She eyed his muscles. Hers were big too.

More cruisers showed up, lights whirling, sirens blaring. A horde of uniforms blocked the parking lot from bystanders beyond. When did they arrive? Ralph was in shock, short-term memory fritzing. The dog plunged into a blackberry bush. Two cops chased her, but stopped at thorns and lopsided trees getting strangled by bittersweet.

"You didn't tell me your name, sir," Officer Wang said. "Do you have some ID?"

"I didn't tell you already?" Ralph had committed no crime, still he was about to freak out. How guilty would that look?

"Call your dog out of there!" the tall, white boss man yelled. "Now."

She wasn't *his* dog. Ralph never looked inside her collar. He didn't want to know who laid claim to her. Someone at Cloud Heights? "I don't know her name."

"Go get your goddamned dog!" the second-in-command yelled, a shorter white dude. Most of these cops were white guys, in fact all except the interrogating officer.

"No need to curse," Officer Wang chastised the number-two cop. Understanding flickered in her eyes. "The dog might be scared to come out. She doesn't know us."

Ralph stepped close to the bittersweet/blackberry mess. There was plenty of room to maneuver even with their cop gear. They were afraid the mutt might bite. Ralph honestly didn't know how she'd react to their twitchy energy. He slipped past a snarl of spikes, bristles, and barbs. For a moment he felt like he was in two places at once, ripe blackberries and sharp thorns in both places, yet different air, different magnetic energy. Ahead on a gravel path, the dog wagged her tail. She barked: *Chase me.*

"Hey, everybody, come on. It's OK. She's trying to lead us somewhere. She does that." Ralph jogged toward her, then looked back to . . . a mass of dense vegetation going dark as the sun went below the mountains. He froze. No whirling lights, chatter, crunch of gravel, or radios crackling. The cops and bystanders had disappeared. How did they do that? Thoughts tangled up in Ralph's mind. Time was wrong, east and west too. Maybe he'd come farther than he thought. He checked his phone. Dead. The battery had been at 44 percent when he called the cops, and now suddenly it was out of juice.

The dog did an urgent command bark: *Chase me now, fool!*

Ralph turned back to her and wobbled. Maybe she had found another body. “Fuckin’ A!” He wasn’t up for another body. The bushes rustled and he froze. What the hell was he doing? The killer might still be nearby, enjoying their freakouts. Or some yahoo with a badge and a gun might think Ralph was running away, even though he called it in and they told him to *go get your goddamned dog.*

Ralph whirled around with his hands up and his heart in his mouth. Nobody was following him—just wind in the branches. Paths went every direction from where he stood. He was unsure which led back to the parking lot. Usually he was a wiz at mapping novel routes and retracing his steps. Since he was eight or nine, his inner compass had never glitched like this, other than navigating around Darlene, and that was emotional geography. Not the same, right?

What other kind of geography is there? Darlene in his head, calling bullshit. Would he ever trust himself again, with Zsuzsu or anybody?

His head throbbed and his stomach was ready to riot. He felt as if he stood not just in two places, but in many places at once. How was that possible? He turned back to the dog. She paced on a wooden bridge he didn’t remember. She wagged her tail and grinned at him, like *isn’t this better*, like she’d forgotten the dead woman, the dead turkeys, and whatever else was in the bins. She trotted onto a boardwalk that snaked into a grove of hemlock trees.

Ralph didn’t have a clue where they were—a novel experience! The dog knew though. As he jogged after her, his feet were lumps of lead. His heart was also heavy—he kept flashing on the dead woman. The dog waited for him. When he stepped close, she raced ahead, their usual game.

"No. Where are you taking me? We should go back and deal with the cops."

Ralph wasn't sure how to go back and he didn't want to lose the dog, so he ran on. Maybe this direction would help him figure out what the hell happened. Or not.

T O D A Y

PAULA—*Hawaiian Romance*

A mob barged past Paula and out the back door, exiting the bus before Duke drove from the borderlands into some good neighborhoods. Another soggy mob boarded. Thirty more minutes to the end of the line near An'qwenique's street, if the red-light goddess smiled on them. A thirty-five minute trip from the Haven as the crow flies, but the bus went the long way via the university. Normally a ninety-minute ride, endless today, especially with the accidents, construction, and hail. Squelching impatience, Paula meditated on the clues.

"You're kidding, right?" a college guy hooted, loud so everyone might hear. "Naw, man. No way." He interrupted Paula's deep dive into the recycling bin murder. A graduate student or, no, an adjunct who still played sports. College sweatpants hugged muscled buttocks. A number 42 shirt clung to his sweaty back, Jackie Robinson's number. A baseball cap was off to the side, jaunty. A pretty thing. He had pouty lips, long eyelashes, and a luxurious curly mop, similar to Dimples, not a wig though. "Get out of town!" he shouted, theatrical outrage for the back row.

For a second, Paula thought he was talking to himself, brash and carefree. Then she spied an earbud and a sleek device clutched in his hand. He was FaceTiming a college buddy on a moonlit beach in Hawaii. Like Big Foot and Dimples, College Bro #42 was the head of a pack, and somehow, he was above it all, floating over the grime, the crime, and the whine. Paula marveled. He was so aloof he could touch the stars—except for the size-thirteen feet dragging in the dirt. Fancy orange-and-black sneakers with a flash of fluorescent pink—where did the guys with ginormous feet find these shoes?

Duke cussed at tourist drivers and August ice storms. The bus skidded to a halt. The college bro banged into Paula's HEPA vacuum and almost knocked her into people's laps. The cell phone flew from his hand and slid into the dark. As he scrambled after it, bus patrons ogled him like cheesy popcorn they wanted to snarf. He pounded the dirty floor and cursed. His phone didn't seem to be anywhere, as if it had vanished to another dimension. His pretty face twisted as he pulled out the earbud and cursed at Paula.

"Sorry," she said, although the accident was no way her fault.

Earbuds off, the college buddy in Hawai'i could now be heard, yelling about full moon, skyscraper tides. "You went dark, man!" Sound from the phone speaker was warped, creepy.

Bus patrons joined the search. The two friends shouted back and forth about idiots lugging heavy equipment on a crowded bus and crashing into innocent bystanders. Paula brought her cordless HEPA to every job apart from Cloud Heights. People's random machines full of unknown filth were unacceptable and unprofessional. Cloud Heights had purchased equipment using her specs.

"Sorry," Paula said again. "Actually you banged into me." No one remembered that.

"It's gotta be somewhere." College Bro #42 was ready to cry. The phone was worth a small fortune. He was recovering from a ransomware attack, avoiding cloud storage, and deploying super encryption. The device contained all his sites, his whole life, photos and shit no one else should see. Porn? Sexting?

Big Foot and everyone glared at Paula. Dimples broke into a smile. "Nobody's fault," he said. "You stumbled into her." He'd noticed. Paula resisted gratitude.

"Look!" Ten-year-old Rosie scuttled off the accordion seat and dove between wet pant cuffs and muddy shoes to grab the phone. It was wedged behind a metal bar under a seat in the way back. "Not cracked or anything," the little girl declared.

Scowls turned to smiles at the college bro getting his life back, at the mud on Rosie's nose. A cute nose, like her proud mother, tapping a computer, consulting hefty tomes—definitely an innocent, victim type, making something of her young mother self on a long bus ride. Paula bet Grad Mom was taking a summer course to help write a thesis and had low-interest overdraft protection at her bank. She was a good risk, not like work-yourself-to-death Paula, out here degrading the public sphere.

Grad Mom joined the FaceTime celebration, flirted with the college bros, and scored an invite to Hawai'i from them both. Paula's mouth dropped open. Did they really mean that? Grad Mom's face glowed. Would she go and take Rosie too? Mom was tall and pretty: luxurious bangs and thick braid, high cheekbones, big eyes, and full lips. Very symmetrical, like that singer Radmilla Cody. Easy to believe she could do anything. Rosie had yet to grow into herself and was headed a different direction than Mom. She had haphazard features: cute button nose, beady eyes, and sparse hair. Mom would nevertheless drag her to Hawai'i for the adventure of their lives.

"O'ahu. Damn, I'm jealous." Dimples leered at mom and daughter, pretending to joke. "I mean, not really." Liar. He and Paula were both jealous.

"You should be." Grad Mom smirked, enjoying her cutest-girl-for-miles status.

"You'll love the volcanos and skyscraper waves." College Bro #42 hugged his phone, ecstatic. "The food, culture, and hospitality, are the best in the world. My mom dances everyone into the dirt. She does hula kahiko and hula 'auana." He did some fly moves with those black-and-orange kicks. Maybe he was Native Hawaiian.

"I'm a dancing fiend," Grad Mom declared and joined the dance, to everyone's delight. She looked Latinx or Native. What people, Paula couldn't say, possibly Greek or Turkish too. "I'm going to take you guys up on that invite." Way too trusting.

"Fuck yeah!" College Bro #42 chortled. Unfettered, impulsive youth. They made a date for coffee at Haven Bagels and exchanged cell numbers. Passengers chuckled, eating pineapple and dancing hula across the Pacific with the happy Brown couple. They scowled at Paula: ruined shoes, battered rain jacket, and cheap pants bunched up at the ankles. Paula had zero fantasy quotient.

Of course, she also wanted romance and adventure. "I said sorry twice and I didn't even do anything," she said. "What the heck?" Almost the angry Black woman!

Big Foot shook his head. Clearly, Paula was too dumb, too inept to make anything of her life. A loser without a bag of books to learn or a cute nose. Paula had wide nostrils, big eyes dim as dirt, and a humble afro—the opposite of Angela Davis's, Wole Soyinka's, or Erykah Badu's wild bushes. Twenty-five more pounds hung around her hips than folks thought women should carry, although her booty was perky. A warrior woman on the Peace Path needed heft. One lady sucked her middle-class teeth. She probably got a tax break for those pearly whites and paid a fortune for her weave.

"What? You want me to disappear? Farts and Fleas!" Paula kissed her teeth with Grandma Junebug's Bajan and Gullah disdain. The lady recoiled. Paula sneered. "I know what you're thinking." If she asked these folks or anyone about mean thoughts that dismissed her, they might lie. No, they always lied. Along with listening, her other superpower was reading liars (or anybody) before they opened their mouths. She was right nine times out of ten. *Better than a gold mind* or *a gold mine*, a social worker told her at thirteen—Paula's wordplay though. Reading folks never meant she understood them. Knowing *what* never gave her the whole *why*. Whoever figured that, though?

"The storm has passed. Everything's melting, rainbows in

the air." She pointed out the window. "Fewer potholes too." The middle-class woman turned away. All eyes shifted to an enchanted landscape. Paula sighed away anger. She hated the spotlight.

College Bro #42 loved it. He talked on to the grad mom (and everyone) about how messed up the world was, from Paula to infinity. An unapologetic rant. No, he hadn't heard about the rich woman found naked and dead in a recycling bin. He was skeptical of the electrodes and tubes. They shouldn't believe social media spew. Disinformation bots from Russia, China, or Hungary tried to make us in the land of milk and honey feel bad for thriving when many people in unfortunate places were suffering hard times. Disinfo-teers were everywhere. Paula agreed. This college bro was among them.

"One person has very little impact on the flow of history," he trumpeted at Paula. "It doesn't make sense for individuals to risk themselves." He was smacking her for blabbing truth about ants aerating Earth, one tiny pile at a time. Dimples scowled and sucked his teeth for Paula's and Rosie's benefit. College Bro continued. "Altruism isn't rational."

"Who said people were rational?" Paula muttered. Why wasn't the bus moving? Was that smoke up ahead?

"Most serial killers are average IQ, not evil geniuses," College Bro lectured. "Ain't only white either. They will catch this perp. Can't get away with shit these days. He left DNA behind. He follows unconscious patterns. Don't forget cameras track our every move. Cell towers ping our phones, even if off. You know what else?" He sniffed, proud of his above-average IQ. "Men kill more men than women, despite what streams into people's minds." This speech was what a perp might say to divert suspicion.

Grad Mom raised an eyebrow. "We shouldn't care about dead women?"

"Men kill more everybody," Paula murmured. "Telefascists and their infodemic of misinformation are the worst. Less truth equals more death. Disinfo-teers know how to toggle our switches." Passengers stared, anxious. Back in the spotlight, she squirmed.

"You're right." Grad Mom patted Paula. "And full of surprises."

"Yeah," College Bro #42 said. "Are we there yet?"

"No. Not even moving." Grad Mom looked at her phone. "Shit. I am so screwed."

"Hey, who's your professor? I'll write you a note—caught in construction traffic jam." College Bro #42 grinned. "Get you back on the good foot with this guy."

"*She*'s a witch, but I'll let you try to work your magic," Grad Mom replied.

They did a dance move together, and snap! Murder forgotten, just like that. Next stop, Waikiki. Paula was so jealous she wanted to scream. Big Foot and Dimples shook their heads at the lusty couple. Jealous too. Dimples mouthed *disinfo-teers know how to toggle our switches* and winked at Paula, devilish like Duke. Two guys flirting with her in one day. Suspicious. Dimples's lips trembled and hazel eyes smoldered. Really, dude?

"Don't set yourself on fire," Paula warned. Dimples chuckled, and Paula made herself look away from his handsome delight in her witty rebuff. She wasn't taking any chances. Not with killers on the loose and nobody knowing what the hell happened.

YESTERDAY

ON CAMERA—*What the Hell Happened*

Mooseberry Lane, outdoor cameras, motion sensitive, Sunday starting at 2:33 PM

A hefty figure over six feet tall, male most likely, wearing a reptilian raincoat and bug-eyed mirror sunglasses, strides down the flagstone path to Tomás and Charlize's medieval side door. Specific facial features and bodily form are obscured. Muscular legs are enhanced by skeleton tights. Black, orange, and pink athletic shoes are fluorescent. A dragon's head serves as a rain hat. Fake fire from the mouth is the brim—an outfit reminiscent of cosplay, Day of the Dead, or Halloween—excluding the pink shoes.

His gloved hand caresses the stained-glass window in the door. Skeleton gloves. Off-screen, a car races down the street, tires screeching, engine rumbling. His head follows the car, which is reflected twice in the green mirror sunglasses—a solar EV, German made.

Dragon Man scans the surroundings and turns to the door. He attaches a gadget to the window. Sculpted into the glass is a Day of the Dead image—a woman with a skeletal face wearing a long dress and veil, the wailing woman, La Llorona. The pane falls into his gloved hands. He traces La Llorona's form and skull face then sets the glass gently behind a hydrangea bush. He reaches inside and the door clicks open.

A dog barks, and Dragon Man is startled still. He backs away from the open door. He scopes the yard behind him, and broad shoulders relax. Stepping over the threshold into the house, he disappears from the frame and the door swings shut. After thirty seconds the camera freezes.

Seven minutes later, Dragon Man hurries out of the terrace door at the back of the house. He heads through the gothic archway toward the garage. Wings are curled on the back of his raincoat. A jagged tail with a sharp tip looks lethal hanging between the back panels of his raincoat. In each hand he clutches two dead birds by their feet. Ocellated wild turkeys from the Yucatán. Colorful heads flop about on broken necks.

Dragon Man is agile, athletic, in a hurry, yet not frantic. His movements are precise, almost choreographed, the apex predator brandishing a big haul. He slips out of the frame then returns empty-handed. Green mirror glasses reflect the sun, overexposing the image as he trots into the house through the terrace door.

In ten minutes he returns leading Charlize, skeleton hand around her waist. Her head lolls back and forth as if she is drugged and semiconscious. She is barefoot and wears a silky white bathrobe. The robe almost slips off. She stumbles, struggling to keep herself covered. Dragon Man grips her more tightly, pulls the robe over her shoulders, and leans her against the archway. He rushes to the medieval door, grabs the La Llorona panel, and runs back to comatose Charlize. They stumble out of the frame.

Fifty-nine seconds later, the St. Berdoodle bounds by the stairs-to-nowhere. She lunges over the hydrangea bush into the gothic archway. She pauses where Charlize stumbled and licks the odors across her nose. Off-screen, a car engine roars. The St. Berdoodle bares her fangs as the car drives away. She races off.

Nobody except a turtle and a lone Mexican turkey until 2:59 PM. Tomás de la Cruz rides his motorcycle to the terrace door at the back of the house. He jumps from the bike, hangs his helmet on the handlebars, and grabs a bag from a compartment behind the seat. He sings Selena's "Amor Prohibido" (*Forbid-*

den Love) loudly as he dances into the house and out of the frame:

> *Y cuando al fin*
> *Estemos juntos los dos*
> *Que importa que diran*

The singing fades after a few minutes. Tomás comes back outside from the terrace door. "Where are you, mi amor? I need some harmony for our wild love." He wanders out of the frame and yells, "I bought the chocolate croissants you love, from Haven Bagels. Still warm, ready to melt in your mouth. Peaches and cream too."

Cameras catch Tomás as he charges twice along the field-stone path around the house. He yells Charlize's name several times. After the third pass, he halts in the gothic archway. He taps his cell phone and paces with it pressed against an ear.

"Where the fuck are you? Pick up!"

He leans against the wall and gulps breath. A gargoyle looks down on him, as if about to attack.

"Hey, babe, it's me. You doing a surprise? I hate surprises. You know that. Call me."

His eyes dart about. He taps his phone again.

"An'qwenique, this is Tomás. I'm sorry to bother you. Three minutes to talk, great. Have you seen Charlize? Your car is gone. Did she go with you somewhere? My lady hasn't gone out, not alone, since the uhm, you know, death threats and things. She doesn't want me to leave the house. The eat-the-rich trolls are serious.

"Monsters and aliens mobbed us at Crossroads last week between the appetizers and the main course. Trolls bombed Charlize's new account today. They posted what nasty they were gonna do to her and you too. Charlize takes these threats straight in the heart. What do you call it, digital hyperbole? That toxic bullshit is busting out in real life. It's killing her."

His mouth refuses words. He closes his eyes on a few tears and clears his throat.

"Sorry, sorry. You're her best friend. You know how she is. Gabriella was supposed to come in today. She was a no-show, so . . . Charlize thinks we need bodyguards and a monster dog. I said you were next door on the lookout. She had to stop worrying. I told her, she'd be fine. To the Haven and back is no time, unless traffic. I wasn't gone long. But my lady's not here. No text, no note, and that's not Charlize. Do you know anything? Call me when you get this, OK? 'Cause—" His voice cracks. "I'm worried."

Tomás wanders out of view till he slogs by the medieval side door. He slumps down on the front porch next to the stone staircase to nowhere. For fifteen minutes, he stares back and forth between his phone and the street in front of the house. A Mexican turkey trots across the wildflowers toward his feet. Wings are spread as if the bird is about to take off—a flurry of iridescent blue violet accompanied by distress gobbling. Tomás throws rocks at the turkey. It flies up the stairs-to-nowhere and out of view.

"The video feeds." Tomás jumps up, taps the phone, and slams through the front door. After thirty seconds the camera freezes.

Cloud Heights Enterprises parking lot, river side, tracking camera #3, 6:55 PM.

Low-angle sun blasts a deserted concrete square except for two e-vehicles in the Pet and Wild Animal Rescue spaces near the bike rack—company cars. A hawk drops from the sky and tries to catch dinner in the brush. A furry critter skitters away from sharp talons. The hawk soars into nearby sumac and Norway maple trees as—

Ralph Carter wheels in on a custom-made hybrid bike. He is large, over six feet, athletic, and agile. He double-locks the bike to the rack and removes the headlight and computer from the handlebars. He does a 360 scan of the parking lot, bushes, buildings, and alleyways. Fighter jets blast overhead and he jumps at the booming sound. He is agitated. Something is off. For twenty minutes, he paces, frowns, and mumbles to himself. Finally, he puts on black, orange, and pink athletic shoes—same style as Dragon Man. He stretches, eats dried fruit, and takes a swig from a water bottle. He smacks the trunk of the nearest e-vehicle, stomps, and curses.

"Are you shitting me?"

He checks his watch and runs off toward the river.

Cloud Heights Enterprises parking lot, center tracking camera #1 at the back of the buildings. Camera #1 went offline at 7:04 PM and rebooted at 7:27 PM, reason unknown.

A slight figure, five feet eight or nine, female perhaps, wearing a snake raincoat, pink mirror sunglasses, and a hat with fangs, stuffs confetti in an RC recycling bin. Small feet in black sneakers. The snake person touches the DUMP IT ALL AND START DOING BETTER! logo with gloved hands then startles at the off-screen noise of a shopping cart. Staring at what approaches, Snake Person tries to smother a full-body tremor. Unsuccessful. The creak of the cart's wheels grows louder. Snake Person runs from the recycling bins into blackberry and bittersweet bushes. They squat down and dissolve out of the image. An FX special effect in real life. Inexplicable.

Dragon Man wheels an oversized shopping cart into the frame. His wings are unfurled, tail erect, a strutting demon. Fluorescent-orange-and-pink athletic shoes are spattered with muck (mud or blood?). He comes from the shadowy alley between Cloud Heights and the boarded-up Chinese restaurant. A blind spot. Snake Person flickers back into the picture, crouching in blackberry bushes, a second inexplicable FX.

Dragon man pauses, does a 360 scan like Ralph. Under the

streetlights, the cart's contents are visible: three dead Mexican turkeys and Charlize Giddens, who is comatose or more likely dead. She is naked with a gag around her mouth. Tubes have been jabbed into orifices or wounds, and electrodes clamped on her breasts and ears. Dragon Man reaches the blackberry bushes.

"Hey, you! No time for bullshit." Dragon Man deploys a device to distort his voice at the source, a thunderous rumble.

"Pee-pee," is Snake Person's response, voice also distorted at the source—annoying, that kid you want to smack.

Dragon Man looks right into the camera. "Do your business and get out of there. We're on the clock." So matter-of-fact. He glances toward a setting sun. A corona of haze from wildfire smoke glows.

Dragon Man wheels the shopping cart to the recycling bins and lifts Charlize's five-foot-nine, 140-pound dead weight from the cart without strain. He thrusts sandbagged legs into the bin then adds more confetti. He takes the gag from her mouth and clamps the lips closed. He tucks the gag under a turkey wing and places the bird in with Charlize, carefully draping her arms around the bird's burnt body. He stuffs the other turkeys into the second shredded-paper recycling bin. Snake Person whimpers.

Dragon Man pulls off a glove and takes pictures on his phone. Examining the images, he shakes his head, as if dissatisfied. Replacing the glove, he rearranges Charlize and the turkeys, sprinkling confetti over their heads. He takes other photos, then selfies with an arm around Charlize. Special-effect fire spews from the hat brim. He bows to her before striding to the blackberry bushes. He peers into the tangle of barbs and creeping vines. Snake Person scrambles away from him, flickers in and out of view twice, and then completely dissolves. Third inexplicable FX.

Dragon Man squelches a yelp and almost falls. "Quit playing around." Rattled, he reaches into the bushes where Snake

Person should be. Nothing. "No fuckin' way! Shit!" Voice distortion extends the curse. He steps where the anomaly occurred and does not disappear. Something falls from under his raincoat and vanishes. The fourth FX. Unclear if he notices. He flails. "Where are you hiding?" His tail snags on a barb. "Fuck!" He leaps out of the brush. "Think about your brother."

Off-screen, distant, a dog growls. Dragon Man glances at his watch and roars—an eerie sound. His hands shake. After a few breaths and foot stomps, he salutes camera #1 then sprints to the empty cart. He wheels it off-screen—down the alley between the old Chinese restaurant and the Cloud Heights building.

The hawk descends into the blackberry bushes near the anomaly. Clutching a small rabbit, the bird soars into the sky and disappears midair. A fifth FX in real life.

The St. Berdoodle bounds into view from the street entrance to the parking lot. She runs to Charlize in the recycling bin. Whining, she jumps up to lick Charlize's hand. She sniffs the dead turkey in her arms and sneezes. She scrambles as if trying to climb into the bin, then tumbles down. She jumps up again, rests her paws on the lip of the bin, and licks Charlize's face. Something catches her attention. She tests the air and dashes up the dark alleyway. A few minutes later, she returns with bug-eyed mirror sunglasses in her mouth. Dragon Man's glasses.

The blackberry bushes rustle near the anomaly. A momentary flicker of a human form, accompanied by sobs. The St. Berdoodle whimpers at Charlize then runs straight into the bushes and vanishes. The sixth inexplicable FX.

Camera #1 freezes at 7:57 PM. Camera #3 picks up Ralph and the St. Berdoodle coming into the parking lot from the scrub-brush trail along the river at 8:18 PM. No cameras in the vicinity of Cloud Heights pick up Ralph, Dragon Man, Snake Person, or the St. Berdoodle right before or after their appearances in the lot.

Behind Cloud Heights is a warren of alleys, decommissioned factory buildings, and river loading docks. Surveillance devices aren't deployed there or on the river trails.

No spatial anomaly found near the blackberry bushes and no sign of human urine or feces or whatever fell from Dragon Man's belt. A bug in camera #1's software or hardware is insufficient to explain the dragon man's *behavior* around the anomaly. Perhaps he was acting/overacting for the camera.

YESTERDAY

ZSUZSU—*Tripping*

Sunday evening (after Oona found Charlize's body and led Ralph to the parking lot to bring her back to life) Zsuzsu sipped her lime water and eyed the Redemption Center's weather-vanes. Why *did* they point different directions? She acted chill, fronting, as bad as the tourists. Oona had never stayed away so long. What if something bad had happened? A mandolin interrupted Zsuzsu's dire thoughts. Head librarian Belle sat on a rock bench in the sundial, bobbed poufy gray hair, and sang Melody's corny anthem. The lyrics were carved on a boulder by the stone steps to the haunted mansion. Everyone except Zsuzsu knew the words. Well, the Change Gangers did.

Write a formula for good sense
Build us a bridge over that fence

Belle had a decent voice. Her pupils were large, her smile dreamy. Maybe she'd been tripping on magic mushrooms all along and was excellent at fronting, or maybe the shrooms were just now kicking in. Belle and the mandolin player harmonized. The music improved Zsuzsu's mood, although she'd never admit that.

Belle gripped Zsuzsu's hand and babbled like they were besties. Library gossip: action/adventure in the stacks, political intrigue in the potty, love affairs on an elevator stuck between floors during the blackout last spring. "Seven hours in the dark." Belle grinned. "With a bus driver, a younger man, fifty-three. Hollywood hunky and a good person. They call him Duke."

Zsuzsu thought of Ralph Carter and smirked. "Younger men are trending." Ralph was thirty-nine to her fifty.

"I sent bus driver Duke a special-delivery invite to the benefit tomorrow for the Literacy Project and Tech Up Your Skills. Tomorrow's Monday, right?"

"Comes after Sunday, usually," Zsuzsu said. Should she invite Ralph?

"The dark has been moving in earlier, as summer wanes," Belle murmured. "Not tonight though."

Head toward sunset, directions from whoever said. *Light discourages bats from swooping down the stairs*. Elusive memories ghosted through Zsuzsu's mind. "We should gather the tourists and hit the road." Her house was at the park's western edge.

Belle or someone sober could help Zsuzsu navigate the sunset boardwalk to her house before dark. No. Without Oona, Zsuzsu or any of the bizarro tourists might roll off the boardwalk into poison mess, stinging insects, or a den of sharp-toothed mammals. Where was Oona?

Zsuzsu had warned her this morning, but she loved to stick her nose in trouble. Oona regularly chased coyotes away from the groundhog who lived under the back porch. Last week, she scared off a bobcat going after baby crows in the barn, and the damn crows were eating her dinner! The firebug who torched Cal and Pete's garage (and then stuck around to watch) had to scramble up the red mulberry, or Oona and the next-door mutt might have eaten him. Zsuzsu's favorite tree would have burned if not for Oona barking an alarm. A hero dog, an outlaw dog, an ornery alpha dog.

Oona had buddies everywhere: musicians at Crossroads, homeless people living under the East Street bridge, students from the high school, and the wizened rent-a-bum who worked the mall parking lot for spare change. Something bad must have happened to a friend or a stranger, and Oona to the rescue! Her love of strangers was admirable. Xenophilia—Paula's word. Hopefully, wherever Oona roamed, she was keeping a low profile. Animal Control could give a crap about a dog's high moral character. Even if Oona bit an evil murderer, they'd lock her up and put her to death. Doing good never added up to much.

Zsuzsu scowled at the CEO cursing a dead phone and the med techs rehearsing a dance greeting for the aliens. She hated their stringy blond bangs and pool-blue buzz cuts. She'd love to sneak off and abandon these idiots to their own devices. Yet no way was she abandoning Belle. That meant saving everyone because Belle, like Oona, *would hate to leave a soul behind.* Who told Zsuzsu this? Someone from the Redemption Center, a giant of a woman with dagger fingernails. Birds roosted in her colossal afro, and she dressed more like a pirate than park ranger. One of Oona's buddies. The pirate woman warned Zsuzsu about offerings to appease the spirits, not Melody.

"Look." Belle shook her topknot and gestured at shadows. "A vision."

A gaunt young woman(?) in a reptilian raincoat crept from the birch trees to the sundial. She was silent, murky, like the fog. Cartoonish fangs adorned her hat. Pink mirror sunglasses covered half her face. Why wear shades in twilight dim? The scrawny wraith broadcast a running-for-your-life vibe. Indeed, all the tourists gave off that vibe.

Splotches on the kid's white surgeon-gloves looked like ketchup, dye, or blood. Blood on the coat too. Sinking onto a stone bench, the kid hugged long legs. She had to be sweltering in that plastic raincoat, yet she shivered.

"We haven't seen you in a dog's age!" Belle screeched. The young woman winced. Belle turned to Zsuzsu. "Popping up out of nowhere. Isn't it wonderful?"

"No." The CEO put his jacket on. He'd recovered sufficiently from heatstroke to threaten the med techs and Camouflage Lady with jail time. They should have let his brain boil. He accused them and Belle's Change Gang of kidnapping him then trying to break into his mind. "My wife ratted me out. Had our son hack my private files. She turned him against me. And I'm not telling you anything. Talk to my lawyer."

Camouflage Lady snorted and tapped her phone, a desperate beat. She pleaded with whoever was in charge to reconnect her to the outside world. They absolutely had to leave before nightfall. After dark, instead of just draining cell phones, Pocumtuc ghosts drained the spirit out of the people themselves.

Zsuzsu chuckled. "It's Nipmuc ghosts haunting these woods, I believe. Or both."

The snake kid grunted agreement and inched away from Belle.

The med techs swore aliens not First Nations ghosts stalked these woods. They detailed recent UFO sightings, talking on top of one another, finishing each other's thoughts. The Change Gang scoffed as the techs insisted, "Zooming a billion light-years across the universe, ET won't be a slime monster coming to chomp you. Odds are, we're poisonous as shit. The aliens have the big picture so they might help us out."

Zsuzsu sniggered. These people had to be joking. They were tripping for sure. *Why come a billion light-years to save people too stupid to save themselves?*

"Why stand around, telling bad jokes, and doing nothing?" The CEO asked a reasonable question.

"The last ten times we tried to go anywhere, we ended up back here." Belle was calm and clear, not a stumble or a mumble. "Spiraling around the sundial courtyard, getting nowhere. Freaky." She patted Zsuzsu. "But we're no longer lost in the maze. Zsuzsu Marlene Hönig, Ralph calls her "Two Zoos, Marmalade, and Honey," she knows a way out. Her farmhouse is that direction." She gestured at the sunset. "Frau Hönig is waiting on Oona the rescue dog, who should be here any second. I know Oona. She'd never let us down." Belle turned to the newcomer in the snake raincoat. "What's your name again? Gwen, a big senior at the high school this fall, right? That baby dragon disguise doesn't fool me." She plucked the pink mirror sunglasses off her face.

Gwen snatched her glasses. "I'm a snake." She looked ready to bolt.

"You and Paula Queenie did the Iroquois, I mean Haudenosaunee display for the library with that bitchy professor." Belle lurched toward Gwen. "So why are you dressed like a baby dragon? Wait. What are you doing here? I thought you and your brother were lost, kidnapped, or possibly dead according to Paula."

"Start at the beginning," Zsuzsu commanded.

"Right." Belle exhaled. "Lance was/is ten. He wants to be an astronaut or a wizard, so sad. Hey no, you're alive. Is Lance?" Gwen nodded then shuddered as Belle babbled on. "We all are. Isn't that wonderful?" Belle giggled at the tourists. "OK, nobody knows where we are or what time it is . . . Melody never needed a device to tell time. She felt time." Belle's smile broke into pieces. Tears and snot dribbled down her face.

Zsuzsu wheeled close. "Melody was a beacon. Everyone liked her." Not totally true.

"Who?" Camouflage Lady and CEO said in unison. They looked mystified.

"Melody Davis," Belle snarled, rage bursting out for an instant. "Melody worked the graveyard shift at Haven Bagels, so full of life." The med techs shook their pool-blue heads, clueless too. "Where have you people been? Melody disappeared the same time Gwen did, only Melody ended up tortured. Murdered!" Belle winced. "Paula was afraid you and Lance would end up dead in a junkyard too." Gwen flinched.

Camouflage Lady grimaced. "Why should we remember these gruesome tales?"

"Big news around here last winter," Zsuzsu said. "Where are you guys from?"

"Don't you already know?" The CEO scowled. "If not, why should I tell you?"

"What do you have to say for yourself?" Belle stood on a boulder in the kid's face, tiny but fierce.

"I don't know what to do," Gwen replied. "It's fucked up . . ."

"You can be whatever you want." Belle hugged Gwen and blubbered about Melody bushwhacking through stupid expectations. Zsuzsu had heard these stories ten times at the celebration of life, except—"An ignorant library patron told Melody, *You don't think you can be a real musician, do you?*" Belle clapped a polyrhythm. "Melody and that fellow from Mali played for the kids, Saturday morning, story time."

"They played for the drag shows too," Zsuzsu added. "And at Halloween."

Belle teared up again. "I know Melody was aggravating. Still, why stuff her body in a car wreck with a dead raccoon?"

"Otter," Gwen said. The tourists twitched, uncomfortable, baffled. Peering at naked human nature, not a pretty sight. Gwen retreated to the edge of the woods.

Belle pounced on Zsuzsu. "He tortured her to death. Why? Tell me that."

"Evil," Zsuzsu said.

"Tautology." Belle wiped her eyes. "Calling it *evil* doesn't explain anything."

Zsuzsu bristled. "Sorry, Ms. Librarian. *Why evil?* is an impossible question."

"Evildoers have logic, rules." Belle forced a smile. "The rules they keep, the rules they break, the story they're telling themselves."

Zsuzsu shook her head. "Everybody has that."

Belle leaned on the wheelchair arms and glowered in Zsuzsu's face. "Exactly."

Zsuzsu glowered back. "OK, a story, that's what you want?"

"No. We want to know the way out of here," the CEO yelled, his voice raggedy. "Which you claim to possess. Why keep that secret?"

Zsuzsu ignored him. "I bet the killer took Melody out because who she dared to be challenged him to his core. He had to snuff her out."

Belle gasped. "So not just random prey."

Zsuzsu thought of the firebug sticking around for the show at Cal and Pete's garage. "And he's been enjoying our freakouts ever since. A terrorist."

"You talk like you know him," Gwen said.

"I roll by him in the stacks at Iris or drinking coffee at the Haven." Zsuzsu appraised each tourist. "We're all suspects." Although unlikely that the killer was a woman.

The Center groaned and creaked. Wavering in the mist, it looked and sounded like a steampunk rocket ship readying for takeoff, as if it had just masqueraded as an old haunted house. Change Gangers jumped. The CEO shrieked. The quiet het couple clutched their picnic table. The pink umbrellas flipped inside out as if hit by a storm wind and now resembled an array of satellite dishes.

Zsuzsu laughed off this vision and the sound effects faded. "No more scary stories."

"Let's head west, before the sun is gone," Belle said.

"No. Why trust you two?" the CEO declared. "We break into the Redemption Center, find a landline, and call for help, helicopters, a real rescue." He marched up the stone steps, grabbed a metal chair, and slammed it against a window. The chair bounced back against his chest and he almost fell. The window was undamaged.

Belle raced up and wrenched the chair from him. "Who says there's a landline?" The med techs clutched the wobbly CEO. Belle hummed Melody's anthem and hugged the battered chair. "Oona's coming. I feel it," she murmured.

"Heller Wahnsinn," Zsuzsu said in German, literally *bright madness*. Everyone except Belle gawked at her like she was the architect of their misery. She translated loosely, "Contact high. I feel like I'm tripping too."

T O D A Y

PAULA—*No Answer*

"Does this ride always take forever?" College Bro #42 yelled at Paula, like the holdup was her fault. College Bro slipped off prickly topics (murder and such) to rail about god-awful mass transportation, as if riding with the public was a health risk. A death-wish car wouldn't get you there sooner, not today. The red-light and storm goddesses thwarted us all, plus an Amazon van was on fire up ahead.

"Public transportation is a treasure," Paula yelled over him. She was grateful the university subsidized the route through surrounding towns even if it was an endless ride. "Did they find the St. Berdoodle? That's what I want to know."

"No," Grad Mom replied. "Why?"

Paula shrugged. "The dog is key to solving the case." Oops! TMI.

Big Foot smacked a pole. "The dog's a dead end. The police should focus on something worthwhile, instead of wasting time and money chasing a goddamned dog who can't tell us shit, even if he witnessed the crime."

True, but Paula barely resisted screaming *the dog is* she *not he*.

"Amen, brother," Dimples said. "Tell us what you really think."

Big Foot went on and on about TikTok wildlife videos and sentimental animal-loving fools (like Paula) who acted as if dogs, crows, cats, trees, and even fungi were practically people. He balled his fists, in a bomb-throwing rage. You'd think this assault on our (Homo sapiens sapiens) status as the supreme beings of Earth (the universe?) was worse than shitbag(s) snatching women and doing whatever to them. Hubris, man!

Paula shouted over Big Foot. "You know why they're making a fuss now."

"Yeah," Grad Mom said. "Celebrity melodrama."

"Celebrity victim plus burly Black man suspect," Paula added. "Nothing this big about Melody."

Elaine, Eleanor, Edith cackled from the front of the bus. "Melody was a surly wench. She never smiled, rarely offered a good word to anyone. I know some of you worried she spit in your coffee or worse. Don't act like you all loved her." Passengers squirmed. "No one wanted her dead though. Oh. I guess someone did."

"Melody preferred talking with her hands." Paula spoke and signed. "Where's the uproar for women, men, and gender-free folks disappearing from the dodgy sections."

"Yeah." Grad Mom shot a worried glance at Rosie. The girl bounced in her seat, still enjoying the ride in the bellows of the accordion bus. Sparing Rosie was a convenient excuse. Nobody (other than An'qwenique) ever let Paula go on about injustice.

Gwen and little brother Lance were classified as runaways despite evidence of foul play. Their room in the group home was trashed and splattered with blood. Foster parents claimed the kids fought then ran away. Oshun Jackson and Blue Rosenthal had promised Paula they'd pursue wayward youth kidnapping with Melody's case, but corruption exploded in their faces. Nobody followed up, as far as Paula knew—which admittedly wasn't far. Still, violent crime was expected in dodgy neighborhoods, like the higher rent per square foot to live in a subdivided dump.

"I can't afford to be late or to live in the same town as class," Grad Mom said. "My professor doesn't care if the weather is on the warpath or if the buses blow up."

"Despite wishful thinking, bus service always sucks." College Bro #42 repeated himself and directed a snarl at Paula.

Why? "I loaned my car to a friend over the weekend. He got stuck in Pennsylvania slush. Normally, I wouldn't be caught *dead* on the bus." Awful choice of words.

Rosie furrowed her brow. "A driver might find you dead in the aisle one morning, when they opened the door to get ready for the first ride. Bodies don't only get stuffed in recycling." Her mom and College Bro #42 froze. Triple-E repeated Rosie's words and chuckled. Paula and Duke nodded. The killer wasn't just coming for folks living on the wrong side of everything. "Right?" Rosie asked, so earnest it could break your heart.

Yeah. Shit happens, and not only in the dodgy sections to Melody, Gwen, and Lance.

Grad Mom hugged Rosie. "Let's hope we don't see anything like that."

"Celebrity victim?" Big Foot said. "Who are we talking about?"

"Breaking News in the *Times*: Charlize Giddens," Grad Mom said. "Her husband's a famous music producer. Tomás something. They moved up to the country during covid to get away from city mess and start a family. He must be devastated."

Terror ripped through the bus. Phones came out for live updates. Paula quivered. Charlize Giddens and Tomás de la Cruz were An'qwenique's next-door neighbors.

"Tomás came home yesterday afternoon with fresh croissants, peaches and cream, and Charlize was gone." Grad Mom's voice was shaky. "Nobody saw a thing. Then she turns up in the recycling last night. At least she didn't suffer long."

"Yeah? How long is long?" Triple-E shouted. "Ten seconds can be eternity."

Paula covered her mouth and caught a scream. Last Monday, Tomás rode his motorcycle over An'qwenique's backyard heather. She broke out in hives cursing him from the kitchen. Paula suggested a direct, calm confrontation. *Next time*, An'qwenique promised. *I'll be straight with him.*

"My client lives next door to kidnapping and murder," Paula mumbled. "Someone has to, right?" Only Dimples and Rosie heard her. They nodded, a wave of sympathy.

"We know Tomás and Charlize." Big Foot sounded excited not unnerved. He nudged Dimples. "Monday, Wednesday, Friday Tomás from the gym."

Upstairs Karl coached Tomás. He really was personal trainer to the stars.

"Tomás sings in the shower," Big Foot continued. "His wife's a babe. I mean was—"

"No. Him? He's not that famous," Dimples said. "Is he?"

"Charlize was a one-hit wonder," Big Foot said. "Tomás is a composer/producer."

Dimples scowled. "I heard—" Everyone leaned in. He sucked up their morbid fascination. "I heard Tomás was cheating on his wife with some slut who was supposed to be her BFF. A neighbor?" He eyed Paula.

Big Foot sniggered. "Tomás was gay till Charlize bewitched him. He was cheating on her with some guy."

"Whoa!" Dimples bounced in his seat. "The burly, Black person of interest sounds like Ralph Carter. We know him too."

So did Paula. "The **DUMP IT ALL** trash guy." Ralph met Paula at the Haven after she deep-cleaned Cloud Heights and he emptied their recycling bins. Ralph ordered coffee mocha with caramel ice cream. She had hot chocolate. He paid for both. Not a date, almost a friend, like An'qwenique. Paula's nerd whimsy tickled him. They ran into each other yesterday. Paula stuttered, "Ralph is not the killer. He'd never mix trash like that—"

"Some guys use charm as a shield," College Bro #42 lectured her.

"Charm is more of a stealth weapon," Paula countered.

"Ralph and Tomás are always showing off together at **Pump It Up!**" Big Foot said. "One-armed push-ups. Ralph fell on his face and broke his nose on Halloween."

Dimples shook his head. "Tomás, cheating with a guy, huh?"

Big Foot chuckled. "Maybe cheating with the neighbor slut and a guy."

Dimples shook his wig of spiky curls, eyes wide and shining. "Tomás is less of a cliché than I thought. A man with secrets, I mean, what else? A dark side?"

"You think hubby is a person of interest too?" College Bro #42 stepped close.

"We don't *really* know Tomás," Big Foot said. "Not friends or anything."

College Bro pressed him. "Women are usually involved with their killers. It's the boyfriend, husband, or—"

"Charlize was a world-champion flirt. There must be a shitload of suspects. Half the gym." Half the bus! Big Foot's eyes flitted over his phone. "Cops are on the lookout for more bodies. Tomás's neighbors lost five exotic turkeys. Only three dead in the bins."

Paula had pictured plastic wrapped turkeys not purple ones from Yucatán. Panicked, she tried An'qwenique's landline again. It went straight to voicemail: *Sorry to miss you! Anything's possible, right? So what's your story? You got three minutes. Let go, let flow.* "It's me." Paula gibbered nonsense about small towns, entangled fate, and then ended the pointless call. An'qwenique answered any phone she heard ringing.

Dimples shivered. "More bodies. That *is* ominous."

"Yeah." Paula agreed. Why wasn't everyone freaked out? Guys played games on their phones, stared out the windows at nothing, or nodded off. Oblivious.

Big Foot punched Dimples's shoulder. "Don't worry. You're not the killer's type."

Dimples punched him back. "Oh, no?"

College Bro #42 snickered. "How do you know for sure until it's too late?" He and Big Foot cracked up. Other guys laughed too, finally even Dimples. Women passengers rolled their eyes. Big Foot had his phone out, snapping pictures, writing smack on social media. College Bro looked at the screen. "Wow!" He was flattered. "Hey man, wait, don't post that!"

"What are you posting?" Dimples tried to grab the phone. Big Foot fended him off.

"Too late." Big Foot grinned. "Ten hits already. Thirteen, seventeen, it's going viral!" He pocketed the phone and smirked as Dimples shook his head.

Charlize dead was no joke. Paula imagined sticking the HEPA nozzle up their noses and vacuuming the arrogant snark out. She looked away. Violent fantasies were forbidden on the Peace Path and the Underground Railroad of the Spirit, violent actions for sure. Jigonhsasee and Harriet faced greater challenges than Paula did. Fury jumped on the bus with her today. Nuclear fury, a chain reaction that could take out—

Elaine, Eleanor, Edith bellowed a jazzy song:

The bee's knees
Not a drink where you sink
More dapper than a flapper.
And look, she rides a skyhook
Flying high, flying free, our Miss B.

She held up her journal: Paula rode a vacuum cleaner rocket surrounded by a swarm of bees sparkling like stars, a beautiful image. The bus chortled. Hard to tell if they were laughing at Triple-E, with her, or just relieved to focus on something other than the local murder spree. Paula sighed, still unnerved, yet back in control. *We are all too mad.*

Triple-E sketched a cloud of torpedo bugs or fairies around a screen. "Internet trolls bombed Charlize's social media accounts. They sent automated death threats."

Paula blurted. "Cell phones plus social media plus internet hyperbole equals a forty to fifty percent drop in empathy among young people. Among the rest of us too. We're turning into trolls in real life."

"All of us? Naw, come on," College Bro #42 said.

"Some of us, too many," Paula snarled at him. "What we need are unlimited free passes on the Underground Railroad of the Spirit and a Peace Path to our best selves." Over the top. Only Triple-E, Rosie, and Dimples met her eyes. Everyone else jerked away, as if she had a nasty contagious disease. The same people had listened eagerly to Big Foot and College Bro ranting.

"So you think a troll broke out in real life and . . ." Rosie trailed off.

"Charlize was beautiful and rich and that's no shield against trolls," Triple-E replied for Paula, who refused to utter another word. "C'est la vie, ma petite. *Life, little one.*"

Grad Mom looked stricken. Sirens wailed, and a fire truck whizzed by. Adrenaline coursed through the bus. Veteran driver Duke got boxed in between a stalled pickup truck and a double-parked Amazon van. It took five minutes to extricate the bendy bus from that tight spot then—DETOUR. The passengers hissed. They wanted to shriek.

"Good thing none of you unempathetic trolls has an automatic weapon." College Bro #42 made a joke of Paula's peace-path, Underground Railroad outburst.

Passengers tried to laugh away tension and dove into their phones. Paula swallowed anger and called An'qwenique's cell. A pointless flail. A robot declared the phone OUT OF SERVICE and refused messages. An'qwenique always muted her cell and stashed it in another room when writing or hanging with friends. *Why carry a slot machine in your pocket?* OUT OF SERVICE was something else, like the phone didn't exist anymore.

"Daddy won't wait. He'll say we're late on purpose," Rosie muttered, glum. "We should have started earlier."

"I texted him earlier, no reply. The seven- and the seven-fifteen-AM buses were no-shows," Grad Mom said. "The seven-thirty was more than half an hour late. Earlier wouldn't have helped."

Rosie pouted. "Your class is boring. Can't I just read in the grad office?"

Mom formed a C with her right hand and used the right thumb to make circles on the back of her left hand, like stirring a pot—*chocolate* in sign language. She offered Rosie a fudge bar. The little girl knocked the candy away and tapped her first two fingers against her thumb—*no*.

Paula's heart thundered and her muscles seized. Melody taught beloved customers to sign. Haven Bagels was the favorite haunt of just about everybody, an ideal spot to stalk victims. Customers exchanged phone numbers and blabbed intimate secrets in range of each other. An'qwenique went occasionally with Charlize and Tomás for blueberry green tea and chocolate croissants. She was in the killer's crosshairs.

"We're all . . ." in the killer's sights. Paula gulped. Why let him know she was onto him if he was riding the bendy bus. She glowered at everyone.

An'qwenique usually called on Sunday with a cheery see-you-tomorrow message. Not yesterday. And no text today to see why Paula was late. So what other explanation besides disaster? Paula forced herself to go through best-case scenarios. Availability bias was making her jump to the worst conclusions.

1. Perhaps An'qwenique stayed up all night on the VR rig doing a hummingbird. She turned the ringers off then forgot to turn them back on. She might still be on the rig, hanging in the Amazon jungle with her inner posse, or maybe she was writing.
2. She could be in a mood over the cheating girlfriend she wanted to love, the bad-boy brother drifting in and out of rehab, and parents who demanded she make a man of her brother, give them a couple grandkids, and do something

with that $500,000 education. In a *mood* An'qwenique had to stay away from phones.

3. Several months ago, she broke out in hives and her throat closed over bad news from around the world spewing from her fancy tablet computer. She smashed the $2000 device against an ancient food processor. The tablet shattered; the food processor had a few scratches. Paula gave her an epinephrine shot in the thigh. An'qwenique refused to let her clean up device innards. OUT OF SERVICE might mean she'd stomped the phone.

The local, national, and world news was terrible. Paula had glimpsed the headlines—fascists on the rise, shoot-outs, invasions, war, wildfires—rape and death live streamed. An'qwenique might have checked this morning, even though they'd made a pact to resist temptation and take actions instead with Belle's Change Gang. Charlize-news would smash An'qwenique, even if they weren't *great* friends.

Paula tried the landline again without thinking through worst-case scenarios. What good would that do? She decided against leaving an I'm-worried-about-you message. If kidnappers were listening, she didn't want to give herself away or make them hurry on to the murder part. If An'qwenique was in a fury mood, she didn't also need to worry about Paula worrying. If a stranger was listening, what were they doing in An'qwenique's house, snooping phone messages?

At the beep, Paula turned away from nosy passengers and mumbled the truth about storms, tourist traffic, an Amazon van on fire, messed-up detours, and dudes so bored they flirted with Paula. Was that it really? Maybe Duke thought she was a stand-up lady. Maybe Dimples appreciated her wit and wisdom. Maybe they both were into short afros and ample-bodied ladies like Charlize . . . Ouch!

"Anyhow, don't worry, An'qwenique. I'ma get there when I get there. You don't mind how late, do you? Maybe after work, we could have vegan cheese buns with soy bacon bits at the Haven? My treat. You could help me with that dog friend I told you about." What if the dog was a dead end, like Big Foot said? Paula shook off doubts and risked even more. "We're friends, right? You can call and tell me anything."

Paula cringed. Saying too much all morning. She hung up as traffic cleared and Duke put the pedal to the metal. He pressed the bendy bus faster than the speed limit. Everyone cheered.

YESTERDAY

AN'QWENIQUE—*Lost*

Following endless detour signs, An'qwenique careened onto a dirt road doing almost fifty miles per hour. The washboard surface rattled her bones and she slowed down. Distant mountain ridges that might have oriented her were hidden behind oak, maple, and birch trees on gentle slopes. Definitely far from her usual routes. Did Zsuzsu Hönig live out this way? No, she lived the other direction, toward the State Forest.

The last time An'qwenique visited Zsuzsu was after Melody's celebration of life in June. An'qwenique should walk with Zsuzsu to the marsh or do a West African dinner and concert at Crossroads. Zsuzsu was decent company, if she wasn't in the conservative bitch-lane, and if An'qwenique wasn't in an apocalyptic *mood*. They should order jollof rice, red beans, and fried plantains, then cry over the donsó ngoni—hunter's harp—music together. The big calabash sound box on the ngoni was like a smooth booty. Six strings up a graceful neck ended in a metal rattle at the top—a segesege or nyenmyemo.

Melody said the ngoni *twanged her breastbone and made her heart sing*. An'qwenique took her hands from the steering wheel and signed *heart* and *sing*.

The whole community turned out to celebrate Melody's life with drums, rattles, and shakers, and also berimbaus, koras, and a cello. An'qwenique was surprised. Before Melody died, no, before some scumwad *murdered* her, Haven regulars were always complaining, demanding a smile. Actually, only a few guys ranted, why tip or order another cup with evil witch glowering at them? Melody's response: *You need a smile, grin in the mirror. There's one in the john*. Favorite customers knew if you wanted to catch Melody smiling, you went to Crossroads and watched her drum with the donsó ngoni player. The memory twanged An'qwenique's breastbone. She wiped away tears.

The sun retreated behind cloud mountains. All she needed was a storm turning this carriage trail through the woods into a mudslide, a raging river. A Mi'kmaq birchbark canoe glided through her mind, a gift from her godfather. Paula said that was the way to travel the world. Paula paddled in the back, An'qwenique up front. Her favorite mountain lake was a dark mirror under them. Their strokes were effortless, in sync, a smile in each stroke.

An'qwenique bumped her head against the steering wheel, and the stupid fantasy dissolved. Canyon potholes loomed ahead. She should pay better attention. A detour around construction on the main drag to an unpaved mess made zero sense. No wonder she was the only car who came this way.

The road wound through a grove of mulberry trees. The purple and red berries looked delicious. She'd hardly eaten today. Following another detour sign, she turned into a sandpit and zigzagged through endless mounds of slag—a maze. Where the hell was this place? She felt sick to her stomach. Even skipping the mall and driving straight to the reservoir she was destined to be late. Cutting things too close, worse than usual. She had no idea what time it was. The dashboard clock pulsed from 2:59 PM to 6:57 PM to 9:51 AM. Outside it was storm dark, so no help from the sky.

A red-tailed hawk clutching a rabbit in its talons swooped low and grazed the windshield. She startled and veered off the road. The solar EV's engine shuddered, clanged, and died. The car rolled to a halt by a splotch of purple clover in who the fuck knew where. "No!" An'qwenique smacked the dashboard in disbelief.

All systems were unresponsive. The smart battery was 98 percent when she left home. What happened to all that juice? The EV failed to alert her that it was running low. Such a scenario was supposedly impossible given the solar backup, even on a cloudy day—which this wasn't till a minute ago. She pressed the reboot button several times. The solar charging system remained unresponsive. The vehicle was truly dead in the dirt.

"I don't believe this." She turned on her cell, reluctantly, because a live phone was invasive, colonizing precious moments. "True . . . Stop! Better thoughts. Now."

Cloud Heights CEO Azul Mendes was bringing a vegan feast for her. The biscuits would be warm, the fruit pleasantly cool. There'd be portable solar fans, an umbrella for rain or sun, and candles to discourage bloodsucking bugs. The temperature was cooler under the cedars anyhow. Azul had inside intel on Data for the Earth and great perspectives on AI and VR, a perfect interview prospect. An'qwenique was never late. Azul might take this personally and clam up. She needed a better story than the car died. Shit! Deception wasn't really in her wheelhouse.

The phone was taking its time. Upgrading. She had a moment to spin the truth: *Big brother was in BIG TROUBLE again* or better, *Weirdo neighbors doing Dragons and Covens (or whatever) had threatened Charlize. An'qwenique intervened.* Almost true, and plausible. In April An'qwenique removed a mice family from Charlize's compost bin and chased thug raccoons out of her garage. The bat dive-bombing Charlize's birthday party was epic. An'qwenique climbed onto the kitchen counter, caught the bat in a butterfly net, and released the poor thing behind the house. Tomás captured this on video. An internet sensation. Azul would definitely believe a Charlize-emergency made her late.

An'qwenique's cell registered OUT OF SERVICE then powered off. The battery was empty. The stupid thing had been 83 percent when she texted Charlize. An'qwenique swallowed a scream. GPS was unavailable without a charged-up car or phone and might lead her into quicksand anyhow or over a bridge to nowhere. She pulled a crumpled map from the glove compartment.

How do you find where you are on a map if you don't know where you are?

The ancients were geniuses, figuring shit out from nothing. We're stupid, domesticated cows. Fuck! Vision blurred. She itched all over. It felt like she hovered in two places at once or in many places, a maze of mazes. Was she experiencing quantum mechanics phenomena at the macro scale, God playing dice with the universe, the multiverse, or what? A horror-movie scenario. Kitty loved horror and dystopia mess, training for the apocalypse. An'qwenique hated it. No need for any more horror training—she and Kitty had *barely been a thing,* and now they were over.

An'qwenique gripped the steering wheel and pretended to be calm. Calm helped you survive any disaster. Break-up by text was not a disaster, not a sign we were all turning into cowardly trolls, ghosts of our fleshy, empathetic selves. Yet, An'qwenique hadn't confronted Kitty at her real estate office or camped in front of her condominium with wildflowers and champagne, like epic lovers back in the day. No. An'qwenique deleted all of Kitty's stupid texts and blocked her number, her social media too. Both of them afraid to look hurt in the face, afraid to feel each other's pain. Cowards.

An'qwenique closed her eyes and indulged several minutes of alternate nostril breathing. Hooray for yoga. Her runner's heart slowed to fifty-five beats per minute. Gravity connected her to the center of the Earth, to the solar system, and beyond to the entire universe, the multiverse. There was always comfort in the vastness of that connection. A cliché, still she felt held, known, and right where she needed to be.

She opened her eyes. The view was bright, sharp, in focus. Adrenaline clarity. Advice from early chapters of Paula's survival book came to her: *First, assess your condition, situation, and resources.* An explanation for the sudden death of the car and phone batteries eluded her—so work that problem later. She was lost yet uninjured. Thanks to deep breathing, the itching and dizziness had faded along with her headache. Her skin was cool, tingling with anticipation. This was the best she'd felt all day, the best she'd felt in weeks.

Paula would say, *Gravity, man, what a tonic. Yo, I believe in gravity.* Gravity was better than an allergy pill sometimes. An'qwenique would have quite a story to tell Paula tomorrow. Something marvelous to look forward to, so survive till Monday!

Driving ten minutes at forty-five miles per hour meant 7.5 miles from somewhere, less if she'd driven in circles, more if her time sense was busted. *Let's hope it isn't badly busted.* No buildings nearby and nothing recognizable. Many small New England towns perched at the edge of farms and woodlands. Smoothing out the map, she checked a five-to-ten-mile radius from her last known position. The State Forest was nowhere near the mall. She should be looking at cozy neighborhoods or McMansion suburbia.

"Huh," she muttered, wanting to believe the map instead of her own eyes. The horizon rocked and rolled, phasing between static snow, beige mounds of slag, and technicolor rain forests, as if someone flipped through the channels on reality. Vertigo and nausea gripped her again, because, like everyone, even Dragon Man later, An'qwenique wanted to deny the evidence of her senses. She resisted inhabiting more than one world at once. Who could blame her? But she also refused panic.

"*Anything's possible, right? So what's your story?*" She whispered her phone message. "*Let go, let flow.*" A line from a cheesy romance. An'qwenique was a cheesy romantic. Suddenly, she felt like a hummingbird flying backward, wings a blur as she contemplated one marvel after another. Life truly was short and here was her chance at multidimensional adventure. Right?

She stared at the sandpit maze that shouldn't be there. It

was on somebody's map. No sign of trucks or digging machinery. The pit was in a valley, close to river level. Even with the sun below the tree line and behind clouds, the temperature was ninety-nine degrees—if the thermometer was still working. Up ahead were the mulberry trees with the plump berries she'd wanted to eat before getting lost in the maze. She'd ended up near where she started.

Nobody was coming to rescue her. Nobody knew where she was. Walking ten miles back would be a challenge in hot, thick air; however, she had plenty of H_2O and forget waiting for the cooler dark. She threw open the door. A muggy breeze was intoxicating. Her silk camo ensemble was perfect for the weather.

It was Sunday and the gravel pit was silent. No machines clanging, air conditioners chugging, no distant highway roar. The quiet was eerie, otherworldly. Even at her lakeside cabin, the industrial din of civilization always hummed in the background. This place felt like nowhere in particular, a setting constructed for an experience or a test. It was as if she was still on the VR rig, trapped in someone else's imagination, someone else's idea of adventure.

Not silent. Birds chattered at one another, very reassuring. Water rushed over rocks beyond the mulberry trees. Frogs and insects chittered. Squirrels chased each other through the high branches. Nothing eerie. The hawk was in the tallest tree, dining on the rabbit, maybe sharing the scrawny meal with a spouse and the kids. She was jealous. The go-bag food was dry and unappealing, apocalypse rations.

Her new trail runners perched in the passenger seat, waiting for their next adventure. She'd forgotten to put them away in the house. Talk about luck! So much of life was luck, good or bad, yet so random. Her stomach clenched. Perhaps she'd dodged a bullet earlier only to end up lost in a strange world or an alien dimension. The Fates were insisting on tough luck for An'qwenique Robinson this hot summer day.

"Resist bullshit theories."

She was resorting to magical, conspiracy-theory thinking because blaming the gods was better than nobody to blame. Paula would chastise her. An'qwenique shoved her feet into socks and shoes and stepped out of the car. She pulled her grandmother's mechanical *Star Trek* watch from the go-bag. It had run down at 2:45. She wound it up and grinned at the *Enterprise* ticking off the seconds.

"And I'm a *Star Wars* girl!"

She stuck the map and hiking sandals in a side pocket. The bag was almost too heavy with the fancy chairs on top. No leaving them behind. Thieves were welcome to break into the EV for the recycling, a small fortune in empty bottles. Gulping several swigs of water, she locked the car with her metal key—the electronic one was dead—and started walking. Perhaps magnetic rocks got dug up with the gravel and drained the batteries. She snorted at another bullshit theory.

The path beyond the mulberries into the woods went the direction the mall should be. The shade looked cool. Two gingko trees leaned into one another, their canopies creating an archway. A stringed instrument resonated through the branches. She halted, heart thudding against her breastbone. Not donsó ngoni music. Cello? Mandolin? Both.

A flock of wild New England turkeys strutted across the path, butting in front of her, unafraid. Two glanced in her direction, placid curiosity, cursory. Blue heads, bumpy red wattles, and red snoods dangling over their beaks gave them an alien look, or antediluvian. Yes, dinosaurs had come through a portal to visit our time and see what had become of their world. She groaned at what the birds would discover.

After five brisk minutes, she came to a boardwalk that traversed marshland before disappearing into more trees, like near Zsuzsu's house. Voices rode the breeze—animated conversation and a delightful tenor/alto singing with the mandolin and cello. Melody often did this song with the donsó ngoni player at Crossroads Restaurant:

Draw me a map that sets us free
Tell me a story I could be

An'qwenique hummed along and hurried across the springy wood toward the sounds. A dog barked. He had a commanding tone, like the neighbor dog yapping in her dream and waking her this morning. She disliked dogs, their fangs and slobber, their hair shedding over anything. Not allergy bombs like cats, still they were annoying, or maybe dog owners were annoying, thinking the world should love their mongrels as much as they did. Hopefully this dog wouldn't want to eat her.

T O D A Y

PAULA—*A Person Is a Person*

Finally, on the other side of accidents and detours, the bendy bus cruised through the *best* neighborhood. Only a few more stops to Shady Grove, An'qwenique's celeb enclave and the end of the line.

Paula breathed in for five counts, then out for five with a shaky pause in between. A trick from An'qwenique, who always insisted: Don't think the worst till confronted with actual disaster. Hard for Paula to manage that. Big Foot and Dimples stood at the back exit as it whooshed open at the Iris Library, Belle's stop. Hopefully she wasn't dead somewhere in a trash bin. "Don't give terror your mind," Paula whispered.

"This is wrong." Big Foot blocked Dimples. "The library's a couple miles from **Pump It Up!**" The doors closed on Big Foot's nose. He was a car man, however both his vehicles were in the shop. "We should have done an Uber or a cab."

Dimples shook his head. "Nothing kicking this morning. Tourists, dude."

"Riding the damn bus, shit looks different." The two men slumped into the bendy seats, clutching their gym bags and pouting like lost kids. "**Be The Best You!** should be two stops after the university," Big Foot whined. All the real jocks were members, according to Upstairs Karl: Duke; Ralph; An'qwenique's celeb neighbors, Tomás and Charlize; plus detectives Oshun and Blue. A jock paradise! Big Foot slapped his phone. "Fuck!"

"It's two stops before University Drive," Paula declared. "Same as the museum."

Dimples shook his head and groaned, perhaps for Paula's

benefit. "There aren't any earlier buses coming around. We have to go to the end station, then back."

"Our before-work session is a total bust. Not my fault." Probably nothing was ever Big Foot's fault. "GPS was sending us to the Water Sewer Works or some shit."

"Wrong pump." Paula snickered. "The public works plant is out beyond Shady Grove. A long walk."

"I'm supposed to know that how?" Big Foot smacked an empty seat.

People never knew where they were anymore.

"We're lost most of the time," Paula murmured.

"Yeah." Dimples lifted his eyebrows, pursed his lips, and smirked, definitely for Paula. He had perfect teeth; green, brown, and gold flecks in his irises; and a warm tan on his face, neck, and bare arms. Quite a specimen. "Hurtling over five hundred miles per second with the Milky Way through space, that's one million, eight hundred thousand miles per hour. A miracle, right? And what are we doing with all that momentum?" He spoke softly, yet under the quiet, he sounded disappointed, pissed off. Reading him was getting easier.

"I keep asking that question." Paula met his intense gaze. They engaged in an intimate, wordless exchange, as if they were on the same genius team, surrounded by know-nothing dolts who invested all their (all our) resources in the planet's demise. "Spiraling through infinity, tracing a unique path, for what?" She glanced at Big Foot.

He cussed out the gods, nature, and society for thwarting the good men who had somewhere important to be, something significant to accomplish. He shook Dimples, who wasn't listening, and yelled, "The shitbags think they can put me on hold or dump a bot on me. They fuckin' waste my time then pick my pockets. Like, my new car is on the fritz every second. Both cars." Half the people on this bus had car trouble. That's why they took the bus, Paula included. "I hardly used that fuckin' bus pass. How could it be expired?" He was still stuck on that.

Paula wanted to stuff the HEPA nozzle up his nose and vacuum the stupid out. Variations on this recurring image were hard to repress.

Big Foot balled his fists. "Like I'm a sucker and—"

"Whoa there, Hoss! We'll do double sets at the gym tonight." Dimples punched Big Foot's meaty upper arm. "Don't sweat this. You and I are gladiators, facing down the big cats every day. GPS glitch can't foil us." Dimples glanced at Paula. "We're too upset over nothing, aren't we?" He spoke her thoughts. She couldn't help smiling. Other passengers nodded. "See." Dimples shoved his friend. "Chill out."

Big Foot rolled his eyes.

"You're courting a heart attack and a stroke." Dimples made a sour face. "Why do I put up with your faucet of fury?"

"Because," Big Foot banged his chest, more gorilla than gladiator, "I bench-press just as much as you do."

"You smell like rancid cheese curds," Dimples said, and they laughed.

"Thanks, man. I . . ." Anger defused, Big Foot bearhugged Dimples, so grateful for grace that he was speechless, a rare moment, no doubt. Earlier, he had called Dimples on harassing the drag king over a service dog riding the bus. These guys were running buddies, comrades-in-arms, on the lookout for each other. Paula was impressed. Big Foot sniffed. "What do you smell like? Hand sanitizer? Bleach? Disinfectant?"

"Mr. Clean," Dimples said, and they laughed again.

Paula had the unkind fantasies, not Dimples. Ouch! She'd felt mean-spirited and jealous all morning. Everybody needed someone to see who they were and who they could be. Even bratty hunks like Dimples were useful, because on a whim, they tantalized and aggravated you into doing better. "My stop's coming. Catch you guys tomorrow." She didn't mean to say that. Careless.

"I hope so." Dimples stood up. If he flexed, he might have ripped his flimsy white T-shirt. "I hope to see a lot more of you." He batted those sexy hazel eyes at her. Definitely flirting. "Umuntu ngumuntu ngabantu," he murmured.

"What?" Big Foot asked.

"Zulu—*a person is a person through other people*," Paula translated, and hid her shock. Captain America dropping African philosophy on her, a serious come-on. Weird. Handsome white dudes usually looked right through her, as if she wasn't even worth disgust, forget lust or whatever this was, genuine interest? Her bullshit meter pinged a soft alert. Usually, Paula was invisible to hunky white dudes, hinkty Black guys, and Brown and Asian ones too. Only desperate derelicts and perverts ever came on to her.

Big Foot was more surprised than she was. He pulled a grinning, triumphant Dimples back down on the seat. "My car should be fixed by this evening, man. Forget the bus." Big Foot planned to forget Paula as soon as possible.

"Too bad." Dimples eyed her booty for sure. "Scrubbing your life away in the high-rent district. That's a colossal waste of resources." He shook spiky curls, leaned that muscular torso forward, and waited for Paula to make the next move. Desperate for romance and cosmic connections did not equal reckless. The world was too cruel. Even before the murder spree, Paula never dared to hook up with random dudes (random whoever), hunky or not. She could however talk to almost anybody.

Smirking at Dimples, she tapped Big Foot's shoulder. "I bet you bench-press thirty pounds more than he does."

"Forty pounds more," Big Foot corrected her. He babbled on about his weight lifter prowess. Paula mm-hmmed and uh-huhed, egging him on with technical questions till he shared diet and workout secrets that he had never revealed to anyone.

Dimples leered at her. He thought her superpower was sexy. "Yes, however I like the gym and the museum."

Big Foot snorted and the bus careened around a curve. Paula lurched into a pole and banged her head. Why was she performing for these muscle boys, letting them distract her from the mission? Their approval was insignificant compared to what else was on her mind. Too easy to lose yourself in other people's static. Big Foot was clueless. *The dog's a dead end.* What'd he know? Paula and the St. Berdoodle could read each other, person to person, wordless intimacy. They had already navigated several tricky situations. Figuring out the murder mystery together was totally possible.

Paula raced away from hunky distraction to the door up front, easy going with so few passengers now. She hollered over her shoulder, interrupting Big Foot's soluble fiber monologue. "See you when I see you."

Dimples frowned, disappointed.

"What the fuck, man?" Big Foot shouted disapproval for women who never hit the gym and just let themselves go when they careened into thirty.

Paula laughed, "I'm forty-one. Letting ourselves go then or anytime is fine."

YESTERDAY

OONA—*Smelling Time*

Sometimes, rather than meet trouble head-on, you ran where trouble couldn't follow. This wasn't failure or defeat. This was Oona and Ralph surviving danger to live and love another day. Still, Oona felt terrible leaving Charlize behind with the flashing lights and angry, anxious people. Charlize smelled wrong. She couldn't move, couldn't get out of the bin to run away with Oona and Ralph. Would probably never get up out of that bin. Neither would the Mexican turkeys.

Oona had smelled death many times—at hospitals and nursing homes, on the streets, and in the barn and the woods. She always poked a hand or a paw, licked a face, hopeful somebody was just very sick, hopeful they'd get up and fly. Who wanted to believe death had snatched away an old friend or a new one? However, Oona knew the difference between the barely-holding-on-to-life odors and what had filled her nose in the parking lot. Death was definite, final. No one ever got up again, sang a song, and chased you through the grass around Aretha the turtle when they smelled like that.

Oona howled sorrow, then paused three-quarters of a mile from the Center, a safe place for Ralph. She panted under hemlock and oak trees, old-growth survivors hidden in the State Forest. Their air tasted good. Oona usually loved roaming this ancient forest that sprang up before Europeans invaded and was still standing tall in the twenty-first century. What the magician called *wise woods.* A favorite place, yet sadness dripped down her tongue and wafted from her pores. Her feet throbbed from chasing around on raggedy pavement after Charlize and the bad man. Battered paws were grateful for the cool, smooth boardwalk, but her whole body ached. She trembled and howled again. Losing Charlize was like losing her carnival family.

Oona had come to love her new pack as much as her first family.

Ralph trudged close. He gave her the last of his bottled water. Sadness drifted from his pores too. Each breath was a labored wheeze. He had no trouble staying on Oona's maps, although he was as slow as Aretha the turtle this evening. Oona took off again. Ralph followed, grumbling. They'd both feel better at the Redemption Center. There'd be plenty of water and delicious-smelling food in a bowl on the porch for Oona, plus something yummy for Ralph in the foyer. He and Zsuzsu would eat and laugh together then slip Oona greasy leftovers. Aroma-memories energized her. She picked up speed.

A patch of white baneberry or doll's eye shrubs had blown over onto the boardwalk in this morning's storm—right before the bridgeway through the marsh. Oona halted and huffed at knife-sharp leaves that burned and left blisters. White berries with dark purple "pupils" were clumped on bloodred stalks. Creepy, as if someone had massacred old china dolls and mounted their eyes here to warn intruders or threaten them. Songbirds interrupted their eyeball feasting and soared into oak, maple, and birch branches. The berries smelled like a heart attack, a disturbing odor.

Beyond the creepy, well-armed shrubs, a drum perched in what the magician referred to as a *between place,* a borderland where many, many maps overlapped. It was Melody's drum, lost for a while now. Dogs smelled time. They charted how fresh aromas faded, decayed. Melody's odors on the drum were from last winter. In fact years of her scent clung to the drum. The musician, magician, and clown gave it to her when Oona was a puppy. Melody performed with Oona's carnival crew at Crossroads Restaurant. Their scents lingered on the drum too. Tantalizing.

"How far are you taking me?" Ralph almost stumbled into

Oona's butt. "I ain't got much more tonight." He hung his head between his legs. Oona licked a salty cheek. "The heat doesn't usually bother me. I mean, when the sun is down, that's my time." He stood up straight and hugged himself. "The air is better here, not so burnt."

Oona wagged her tail, turned toward the drum, and barked. Ralph should carry it to the Center. They could take it back to Melody later. Ralph grabbed Oona's collar just as she was about to lunge over the shrubs.

"No. These flowers are poisonous. The whole damn plant. We go around."

Oona tried to break free. She was powerful, a handful even for someone as strong as Ralph. They tumbled onto the ground. A doll's eye leaf cut his naked thigh.

"Ouch! Stop it!" he yelled. Ralph had never yelled at her before.

Oona whined. Melody loved her drums. Oona scented that still. Leaving this one standing where nobody could play it was a terrible idea. The musician (the clown and magician too) never abandoned instruments. Oona had practiced finding precious drums and cellos, also rattles and whistles.

"Wait," Ralph sputtered. "Is that Melody's conga drum?"

Oona barked.

"Shit. How the hell did Melody's drum end up way the fuck out here? Her bell too." Ralph shuddered. "At least it's not another dead body. That's what I was afraid of." He cleared his throat. "Kinda like a body, though, isn't it?"

Oona whimpered, echoing his tone.

"So, that's why you dragged me out here. Look, we'll come back, I promise, with the right gear, and I'll plunge in there." Ralph hugged Oona. "You and Melody were friends, huh? I miss her too. Not conga drum, what do you call that? She told me, from Israel, or was it Egyptian, or both. Middle Eastern."

Oona hadn't run into Melody since right after the monster storm in February. She burst out of the Haven's screechy back door with the Middle Eastern drum over her shoulder and a bigger drum across her back. Oona ignored treats stuffed in her pockets and tracked a bad mood. Melody was angry every day because of whiny Haven customers. She fussed to Oona about them, her hands cutting the air. Sometimes she drummed the rage away.

This last time was worse than usual. Melody wanted to rip something or someone to shreds. She tramped across the cobblestone alley to the dumpsters and played furious riffs to the shadows. Oona whimpered, concerned.

People usually felt better in the ancient woods and at the Redemption Center for sure. Oona butted Melody onto that map. They stumbled into a snow field near the boardwalk. Doll's eye shrubs lurked below Melody's feet, waiting for spring. The marsh was frozen under the bridgeway, an ice sculpture that reflected the sickle moon—a white slice in the dark. Melody, feeling better already, signed, *Magic*, her fists exploding in the air. She loved roaming any map. Oona barked encouragement.

"You can't hear how loud you and that mutt are, bitch!" Someone yanked Melody back to the alley behind the Haven. Off balance, she dropped the Middle Eastern drum and a gankogui, West African double bell, in the snow over the doll's eyes.

"What's wrong with you?" Melody spoke these words from the Haven side.

"What's wrong with me?" An angry reply.

Oona snarled at a powerful scent and voice memory. The bad man.

"I got patents and blueprints for the future," he said. "You're a dead end."

"And you're the fuckin' apocalypse now!" Melody stormed into the Haven kitchen, disappearing into steam from a mushroom soup pot.

Oona didn't get to eat the tempeh bacon in Melody's pockets, although she waited at the kitchen door a long time. Melody never came back out. What Oona didn't know: Nobody saw Melody alive after her graveyard shift, and all her instruments disappeared.

"Dumbek," Ralph whispered, here and now. He scratched Oona's itchy ear. "Melody's favorite drum."

A piercing whistle made Ralph jump. Zsuzsu was calling. Oona scented tension at the Redemption Center, a quarter of a mile away. She'd have to come back for the drum later. Slipping Ralph's grip, she ambled across the bridgeway, glancing over her shoulder to make sure he followed. He lumbered and wheezed behind her, in a foul mood—no help for that. Certain he'd feel better soon, Oona raced through the silvery trunks of centenarian birch trees.

The Redemption Center was so close. She could almost taste her fishy treat.

T O D A Y

PAULA—*Hot Dates*

It was stupid for Paula to yell her age at Big Foot. What was he, forty-one or-two? Why let him provoke her? Plus, he could be the perp. A weird bus ride this Monday morning, big mouths running on and everyone snooping. She stumbled into Triple-E's knees. The old hippie offered a toothy smile, like they were best friends forever. *Give it a week and I'll be nobody again.* Paula hated being forgotten, but foolish avoiding her the whole ride.

"I wake up, yesterday is mist, and I don't know who I'll be today." Triple-E confirmed Paula's fears. "I stutter between sunset and sunrise, an image that won't resolve. Since covid, the days are endless gray, yet over too fast. Night goes on forever. I choke on toxic lies, forever wars. Helpless. Finally asleep, I don't want to wake up."

"You talk like a poet," Paula said.

"Why not? Poetry is our default setting." Triple-E's eyes glistened as she whispered, "I started a new medication Friday, your idea, and this morning, l'amour rides the bus."

Paula's stomach clenched. "But . . ."

"What's worrying you, honey? Not those rude dudes. You got better beans to stew."

"Better beans? Yes." Paula also spoke softly. "My Monday client, her cell is OUT OF SERVICE. She always pays her bills. Have you heard that hail or some disaster knocked out cell towers? There would have been mayhem on the bus, in the streets." Upstairs Karl left three voicemails and five texts. "Towers are operational. It's something else."

Triple-E patted her. "Worry is a waste of good energy."

"Right." Paula forced herself to assume the best for An'qwenique: a technical glitch at the source. "I've been thinking through recent events."

"Of course. You're a bright bulb." Triple-E looked excited. "What's up?"

The perp came close, took out Melody, then went next door for Charlize. He left An'qwenique alive. She wasn't a Haven regular, and he probably worked one human target at a time. Exponentially fewer opportunities for things to go sideways. Doing just one, he could enjoy the deed with a dash of I might-get-caught spice, but not too much. "Trying to read someone I haven't met or don't know I've met."

"Tricky." Triple-E narrowed her eyes. "For every clue, many possible stories. That calls for slow thinking, not zip zap, this bias, that assumption."

"Exactly." Paula nodded. Triple-E was regularly impressive. "Time, however, is not on our side." Prospective quarries were probably in the loop already. Melody's and Charlize's murderer (Paula hated thinking those words) would do prep while waiting for the hypervigilance to fade. That's what she'd do.

"Where are you shining your light?" Triple-E said.

"He—" Paula coughed rather than spill her theories. A Haven regular, he hung out in public, collecting secrets careless people (like Paula) tossed his way. He lurked in the background of their lives, not a shadow, just unremarkable. So, not Big Foot doing chin-ups on a support bar while Duke hollered at him and Dimples laughed. Big Foot loved the guys videoing his antics. Maybe one of them was gathering intel.

The man with a hat pulled low was her new neighbor! She recognized his purple-and-green dreads, galaxy T-shirt, and Air Jordans. When did he get on? Why not say hi? How'd she miss him? Shadow men, everywhere . . .

"Talk to me." Triple-E pulled Paula close.

"Yeah. What you know good?" Duke wiggled his mustache and winked soulful eyes into the rearview mirror. Paula flinched. His wavy hair, full lips, and bright smile were uncanny. He spun the steering wheel like he was conducting a jazz orchestra. "I see what you do," he said. "I know how you are."

He flirted with Belle last week as she got off at the library stop. Cute guys like Dimples and Duke were never up for a low-class, frumpy nerd like Paula. Her bullshit meter pinged louder. Flirting was Duke's default mode or . . . A bus driver had extensive intel on his regulars. Was Duke a suspect or a prospect for Paula's detective team?

"A hard-working lady like you should let someone wine and dine her," Duke rumbled, charm at full, "at Crossroads after his double shift today."

"Sounds good to me." Triple-E clapped.

"Let me spoil you," Duke insisted. "For a good cause. You gave me the Change Gang flyer: a benefit dinner for Tech Up Your Skills and the Iris Literacy Project. I bought two tickets. Give us something to look forward to after working too hard."

"I like hard work." Paula stalled. Was her new vegan deodorant ($17.99!) driving the fellows wild? Or did he want an in with Belle, like Azul with An'qwenique, and Ralph with Zsuzsu? Men were always using Paula to get next to some other woman!

"My treat. There will be music." He held forth in a beautiful singing voice:

Holler the truth before we break
Dream the next move we need to take

Melody's community anthem was just what Paula needed. Smooth operator.

Paula reminded him, "My friend *Belle*," an acquaintance really, "Iris Library and Change Gang head honcho, she's usually on the seven-thirty-AM bus." Duke nodded, all sweet and innocent—yeah, trying to get next to Belle. "Belle gave me a dinner ticket last week." Paula had to resist other people's static, even good static. "But I have plans tonight." The date with the dog and An'qwenique was essential.

"Last week, you acted like you wanted to go with me." Duke sounded hurt. What could Paula be doing that was better than him? He looked as bewildered as Dimples. Who did she think she was? *Don't set yourself on fire.* Paula had warned them both.

"I have to deep-clean a big mansion, like in a Jane Austen costume drama, from basement to attic, suck up mega dust mite doodoo. I won't be fun after that, and I—"

"OK," Duke interrupted her, almost irritated. "I don't want to harass you."

Triple-E yanked Paula's sleeve. "You're always fun."

"Belle likes you, and I already have two hot dates." Paula stretched the truth only a bit. The dog was a sure thing, and An'qwenique had yet to call and turn her down.

Duke and Triple-E were shocked. Why? An'qwenique *got* Paula, *understood* her nerd nonsense and save-the-world angst. Definitely a better risk than the dudes. No matter what wild mess Paula blurted or freaky past she revealed, An'qwenique came roaring back for more. She flirted too. Watching the boys work this morning made that clear.

Two weeks ago, barefoot on the clean kitchen floor, Paula and An'qwenique danced to Brittany Howard and the Alabama Shakes: *I don't wanna fight no more.* An'qwenique showed Paula the latest moves then spun her around, old school. They ended up cheek to cheek, bosom to bosom, giggling. Paula had been uncertain what to make of her breath fluttering, her skin tingling. And what about Kitty Richards? An'qwenique wanted to love Kitty even though she didn't like her very much, even though they worked each other's nerves. No matter. If not friendship or romance, An'qwenique would be up for solving the murder mysteries with Paula. Wouldn't she?

"We're happy for you," Triple-E said.

"Yeah, sure." Duke raced down one-way streets over speed bumps.

Paula bounced up and down. "Really?"

Duke chewed over a response then pointed up. "I gotta watch the road."

The sign above his head said NO TALKING TO THE DRIVER. Paula squirmed.

"I told him to ask you although it's against the rules," Triple-E confessed. "Sorry."

Paula sighed. "It's fine."

"Hot dates? Ha! You have a mission stewing tonight, about recent events." Triple-E spoke softly, almost inaudibly, so not even Duke could hear. Eleven people left on the bus, no point in taking unnecessary risks. "Come on, tell me the truth."

"Ahh . . ." Paula had a fantasy: watching the Cloud Heights parking lot videos with An'qwenique. Geek lord Azul Mendes had it bad for An'qwenique, so, not impossible. Despite a silvery mane, Azul was only thirty and so successful. Paula felt jealous, even though Azul would be much better for An'qwenique than Kitty. More importantly, Ms. Investigative Podcaster would figure what Charlize and Melody had in common.

Staking out the Haven with An'qwenique and the St. B was perfect. The dog could smell the killer a mile away. If Charlize was a friend (even if not), the St. B wanted to take the perp down, not guide him to a secret sanctuary. Proof that Ralph Carter (or whatever burly Black suspect they were chasing) was innocent. Since the dog liked most people, it'd be easy to hang in the shadows and ID the perp when he turned up at the Haven or anywhere. Paula gasped as fears flooded her.

Triple-E searched her face. "Take your time. We worship speed, a false god."

"No, it's that—" Oshun and Blue had been sidelined. No other detectives would listen to Paula or take a dog witness seriously. Big Foot was right. (So why *were* the cops after the St. B? Or was that disinfo-teer mess?) An'qwenique did podcasts on the cops' bike brigade, community outreach programs, and Oshun and Blue's stellar record defusing violent situations. Not kiss-ass, just fair critique. Any detective would take a tip from her without pressing hard for the source. No reason to mention the dog.

Triple-E poked her. "People underestimate us both at their peril. I'm one of your best assets, 'cause whatever wicked tricky is going down, I've seen it ten times at least."

Not this. Paula toed the yellow line behind the driver's seat. She had no idea how the St. Berdoodle did whatever she did, but the disappearing act was not a camera glitch. The dog behaved like a great stage magician or an alien from another world/dimension with advanced tech. The police (the Feds?) must want her for a controlled, reproducible experiment. Scientists needed rigorous proof to believe, Paula also. After testing theories and gathering data, what nasty would they do to such a special being? She cringed and muttered Grandma Junebug's cleaned-up curse, "Kiss my grits!"

Triple-E groaned. "That bad?"

Paula would be unable to protect the St. B. The dog would become government property. National security trumped everything, eminent domain or some similar law. Dizzy with this thought, Paula almost fell over.

YESTERDAY

OONA—*Barely Holding On*

Conjure a spell to feel the sky
Weave me a way that leads to why

Musicians played on the sundial courtyard as Oona darted in from the woods. Cello accompaniment drifted from the Center's attic window. There was no fresh aroma of her carnival crew. They hadn't been on the sundial since last fall (when the air smelled of ripe apples, corn, and wild asters), yet this song was their favorite. Oona was ecstatic. She barked greetings and wagged her butt. Unapologetically sentimental, she raced over to Zsuzsu.

"Where have you been? I told the tourists you were coming to save us." Zsuzsu scooped Oona onto her lap and cried a few tears in the thick ringlets. Good to beat hearts together again. "You need a trim. Your fur, sorry, your hair is heading to dreads."

"This goofball mutt is going to rescue us?" A bitter-breathed man with blotchy skin and stringy hair shook his head as others screeched and cried.

"The tourists stopped believing in you," Zsuzsu whispered. "Me too almost." She fussed over Oona and soothed the ache in her spirit. "Just for a second." Oona whined with Zsuzsu and everyone. A long, hard, sad afternoon, trouble every direction.

Belle bent down and patted Oona. "Your dog visits the library." Her hand smelled of old books and the mushrooms she grew in a glass house. "Her troupe did a benefit show once. Clowns, musicians, jugglers, and a magician." Belle's tongue was thicker than usual, her sweat spicy. "They walked into a closet or something and disappeared. I don't know how they did it. Reappeared in the hallway. A class act."

"Not surprising. Oona knows her way around," Zsuzsu replied quickly.

A woman in camouflage garb squealed. "OK, so let's get outta here NOW!"

"Sure. Oona just needs to tank up first." Zsuzsu kissed her nose.

"This dog could walk us into a worse trap," the bitter breathed man snarled.

Everyone yelled at once. Zsuzsu set Oona's paws on the ground. "Stop!" she commanded, and wheeled in between two tall men before they bit each other. Oona squeezed in too, a game she did with the carnival crew: *keeping the peace*. "We head out ASAP to beat the dark, escape government agents, aliens, Native ghosts, whoever."

"Or Bagwajiwinini," Gwen added. The jittery crowd all turned to her. Gwen was shaky although not as bad as in the parking lot. Dried blood streaked her raincoat. Charlize's blood. Oona growled softly. "They're called Pukwudgies around here."

"The gnomes in *Harry Potter*?" Two tourists smirked together.

"No. Pukwudgies are Native tricksters." The camouflage woman patted Gwen.

"Yeah. Grandpa told me," Gwen said. "He's Black and Nipmuc. Pukwudgies are Wampanoag. Haudenosaunee know them too, and so do folks all over. Little wild people of the forest. They tease or torment you, maybe steal your children, then they vanish, like you're hallucinating, tripping, or whatever."

Zsuzsu nodded. The tourists glowered at Gwen and panted, anxious and distressed, unusual at the Redemption Center. Not Belle, she bounced on her toes and twirled. Oona joined this happy dance. "Pukwudgies! That's it." Belle grinned. "You and

Paula planned a library exhibit on Indigenous tricksters, then you and your brother vanished."

Gwen dropped onto a stone bench. She took off her sunglasses and rubbed her eyes. "Some Pukwudgies don't like people 'cause we're so f'd up," she murmured. "They torment you till you show respect for the spirits of the forest. We should leave food/gift baskets, to guarantee a safe journey." Tourists sniggered.

"I always do that! Courting disaster otherwise." Zsuzsu turned to Oona. "We want to move out before the sun deserts us. Go see what your buddy left you on the porch."

Oona headed for the stone stairs. She paused to bark reassurance at Gwen. The bad man had yet to navigate Oona's maps. Everyone was safe at the Center. Oona snatched Gwen's pink mirror sunglasses and dashed onto the sundial.

"Give those back." Gwen held out a trembling hand. She didn't want to play. Everyone was in a bad mood. Oona deposited the glasses at Gwen's feet. Tears dribbled from her eyes as she put them back on. "Sorry." She hugged Oona and whispered, "You've seen what he does. I can't do that anymore. I can't." Oona growled, ready to take on danger. "Right. I can't just ditch Lance. We have to help him." Gwen let Oona go. "But how?" The Cloud Heights parking lot was a danger zone. No going back there. Oona gave Gwen a comforting lick. She'd take her to the high school after Zsuzsu went to bed. Gwen would be safe here till then.

"So come on! How long before we leave?" Belle's Change Gang yelled. Impatience and irritation mixed with the oily mist rising from the marsh.

"OK, Oona, enough horsing around. You hear them? We're in a hurry," Zsuzsu said. "Go eat your treat, then we leave."

On the porch Oona nosed a tiny door in the wall under the table. A double dish with food and water slid out. She gulped the fluid then wolfed a mix of cooked trout, duck eggs, pumpkin, and green beans. As she licked the bowl clean, Ralph stumbled in from the birch trees. He clutched the sundial's giant gnomon and steadied himself. Tourists jerked away as he staggered to the stone steps and sank down at the top.

Oona raced to him and licked the wound on his swollen thigh. It tasted like the heart-attack plant. She sneezed this out. The tourists crept toward the porch.

"You look worse than we do," the bitter man grumped. Others grumbled too.

Ralph smelled wrong. Oona barked at Zsuzsu: *Do something, anything.*

"Hey there." Zsuzsu rolled up the ramp to Ralph. "**DUMP IT ALL** and **START DOING BETTER!**" Ralph stared at her, confused. "I'm Zsuzsu Hönig from Cloud Heights. You know me, right?" Pain in her voice made Oona whine.

Of course I know you," he said, bleary. "Two Zoos, Marmalade, and Honey. *Airy fairy*, Paula says. Full of mischief and spirit. Telling us to do nothing once a week at least. Faulenzen . . ."

"Ralph Carter! We were just talking about you." Belle stepped close. "We conjured you."

Ralph leaned his full weight against Oona. "Your dog?"

"Sort of," Zsuzsu said. She put a hand on his forehead.

"You ran in this bad air?" Belle shook her head. "Here. Sip it."

Ralph took swallows from Belle's cup then smiled. "The Belle of the Iris Library." He dribbled water on Oona's tongue. "The gang's all here."

"What misadventures were you and Oona up to?" Zsuzsu asked, calm voice, anxious breath.

"Her name's Oona? Hey, Oona." His smile fell apart. "We were in the parking lot. There was a . . . In my shredded-paper bin, a body, a murdered woman, Oona's friend. Naked, with . . . dead turkeys. It was horrible."

The tourists mumbled *murdered* and backed up almost to the marsh, except Gwen. She raced over to Ralph. Her hat fell off and skinny braids tumbled down her back. She stammered. "In the parking lot, did you see him? A big dragon? Fierce. Deadly."

"For fuck's sake! Him? No way!" Belle said. "This morning, stealing mushrooms, threatening me with green mirror eyes. A papa dragon to your baby dragon?"

Zsuzsu wrinkled her face. "Who are you talking about?"

"No dragons," Ralph declared. "I called nine-one-one and the cops blew in so fast, too fast, acting like *I* was the perp, the bullshit story of my life." He blinked and gestured. "Then I was on a boardwalk, chasing after Oona, lost in the woods."

"Everyone tells the same tale," Belle murmured. "Gives me a pain in my brain."

"No, that's from doing too many mushrooms," Zsuzsu replied. "You're tripping."

"Oona led me to Melody's dumbek and her bell. I had to leave them in the poison berries, doll's eyes," Ralph said. "Melody from the Haven, who was stuffed in a, a . . ."

"In a car wreck." Gwen whimpered. "With a dead otter."

"No, a dead racoon," Belle shouted, mad all of a sudden.

Zsuzsu was mad too. "Otter, raccoon, who cares?"

"Melody's drum?" Gwen bit her lip. "Where'd you find it?"

"I don't know. I couldn't feel the direction we were going. That's not me." Ralph winced. "Where the hell are we?"

"Somewhere safe." Zsuzsu patted his shoulder. "Oona to the rescue."

Ralph gripped Zsuzsu's wrist. "I'm never lost, you understand? Never in my whole life. I have a compass, right here." He pressed her knuckles against his chest. "I *feel* north, south, east, and west. I don't know how to be lost. Except once, with Darlene." This speech exhausted him. He gulped air as sweat streamed down his forehead.

"I got you." Zsuzsu leaned out of her chair and wiped his face with a sleeve. "I know where we are."

"You do?" Ralph replied. Oona snarled at the barely-holding-on-to-life odors on his breath. "Don't worry, Oona." He tickled her chin. "Two Zoos says Sunday, Faulenzen, and not lost." He slumped. The tourists gasped.

"Ralph?" Panic wafted from Zsuzsu as she gently shook his shoulders.

"I am so glad to find you all!" Everyone jumped at a voice booming from the trees.

An'qwenique, Charlize's next-door neighbor, strode onto the sundial, carrying the scent of today *and* tomorrow, of someone Oona was about to meet up ahead, on the other side of the sunrise. Oona scarcely registered this contradiction. Dogs smelled time, yesterday, last year, ten minutes ago. Why not tomorrow? An'qwenique paused by Gwen, who bolted for the bushes like a rabbit, afraid for no reason Oona could sniff. Gwen's raincoat got snagged on a branch. She almost fell and the mirror sunglasses flew off. She wriggled free and raced on.

An'qwenique set a backpack by the giant gnomon. The pack exuded a bouquet of jollof rice, dodo, and healing aromas. Oona wagged her butt, hopeful. "Guinevere? What are you doing here?" Gwen disappeared in the mist. "Wait!" An'qwenique yelled.

"Nowhere to run. I'll get her and her story." Belle ran off too.

"What's up?" An'qwenique asked the tourists gaping at her. She kicked off her shoes. "Blisters."

Oona poked her crotch. She smelled hungry, confused, and tired, although happy to be at the Redemption Center. Oona gripped a pants leg and pulled her toward Ralph.

An'qwenique gasped, nervous as she stumbled along. "That kid did a snake dance in my yard and talked nonsense about Camelot, Avalon, and brother Lancelot. Right before I took the worst detour ever and drove off the damn map. This sounds strange, but I think leaving my home dimension, my particular wrinkle in space-time, drained the batteries and killed my EV. Luckily, the sun refused to go down, so I didn't have to wander in the dark. I heard cello and mandolin." An'qwenique and Oona reached the stone steps. "Zsuzsu! What are you doing here?"

"What are *you* doing here?"

An'qwenique startled. "I know I sound loopy. Sorry."

"You'll fit right in!" Zsuzsu snorted. "Pukwudgies, aliens, ghosts . . . We conjured Ralph, then he collapsed." Oona huffed and licked Ralph's swollen thigh.

An'qwenique looked down at him. "Collapsed?"

"Heatstroke or I don't know. Chasing Oona," Zsuzsu said, then whispered, "He found another murdered woman in a DUMP IT ALL bin. Talk about horror . . ."

The barely-holding-on-to-life odors were overwhelming. Oona barked. They needed to quit talking and do something to help Ralph RIGHT NOW!

T O D A Y

PAULA—*Who Do You Think You Are?*

"Hey, you keep falling into deep holes." Triple-E stood up and steadied Paula as the bendy bus traversed a cobblestone crosswalk in the heart of the high-rent district. She pressed her lips to Paula's ear. "You're thinking about these awful, these women tortured to death, aren't you? You have a lead. Clues."

Paula put a finger over Triple-E's lips. "I was considering taking action." Who the hell was Paula B. Queenie to figure out an alien Houdini dog or chase after a serial killer who had everybody in his sights? (Long shot, her sights) She could get someone or herself killed. Arrogance, man! "It's hare-brained."

"Do something smart instead. I'll help." Triple-E shook her. "We're channeling warrior women for peace. They knew how to act. So do we."

"Yeah . . ." Paula should take Upstairs Karl's advice and send anonymous tips to Oshun and Blue. Let them pass the info to detectives not under suspicion who could work the case. *Leave dangerous mysteries to the professionals.* "It's all risky."

Triple-E smirked. "I see everything. I forget a lot, so I do sketches, memory visions, all day, along the route." She brandished her journal. "One each month. Plus *Storm Musings*. We go over these, and you'll remember with me, see what I know. I saw Melody's last concert at Crossroads before her graveyard shift at the Haven. I drew the audience and the musicians. She and I fussed about jasmine tea. She hated nutty, fruity, flower flavors. She wasn't drinking it, was she? That's in February's journal, under my pillow. Each morning I read the Melody entry so I remember to do something with the time I have, instead of whine and complain about the time I wasted and can't get back." Triple-E shuddered. "I don't want to know or be the next naked lady dead in a bin." She gripped Paula's arm. "Promise me. We find the nasty fucker before shit happens to me, you, or anyone else. We put him away where he can't hurt people, not even himself. We make him feel what he's done."

"I can't promise all that." Paula freaked. "Who do you think I am?"

"They can't steal my hope. Nobody steals my hope." Triple-E gnashed her teeth. "Jigonhsasee and Harriet sweated blood for the times we're living now. Our lives are a gift." She gave Paula the Viking Queen, Mi'kmaq Elder glare. "You're a conductor on the Underground Railroad of the Spirit. You can promise to try, can't you?"

"I guess," Paula muttered. "We'll hand over what we find to the pros."

"Shit yeah! What else would we do?"

"Uhm . . ." An action-adventure chase scene: Paula, Triple-E, and the St. Berdoodle ran through a swamp away from men with shotguns and slobbering hounds. Harriet was up a cypress tree in the middle of murky water pointing to Jigonhsasee who waved a pine torch in the distance. *This way to peace and freedom.*

"Promise like you mean it." Triple-E dug sharp nails into Paula's flesh. "This latest Brown girl, rich celeb or not, could turn into another cold case before you blink." The bus was suddenly full of elder ancestors. Silver-haired women gnashed sharp teeth like Triple-E and glowered fire at Paula. High expectations were etched in their gnarly faces.

"I promise." Paula wanted to mean it.

"I'm writing that down." Triple-E did a sketch of Paula zooming through the galaxy on her HEPA. She wrote a caption in an unusual script. "Klingon," Triple-E explained. "I'm fluent, in Vulcan too. I watched the original series, when it was first broadcast."

Paula flinched, skeptical again of the whole enterprise—no pun intended. Her spirit was too fickle today. She groaned as Duke turned the bendy bus into a circular driveway. He glided by the Shady Grove Cemetery where enslaved Black people, Nipmuc, Mohican, and maybe Pocumtuc had been buried, forgotten, rediscovered.

The bus shelter resembled a glass spaceship, hovering in hydrangea bushes. It was about to land and bring ET visitors to Earth or take off and carry passengers to alien worlds. Who could say? The bus doors whooshed open. After a break at Shady Grove, Duke would return the way he came for another long loop past the university.

"Madame," he said with a bright French accent. He no longer seemed upset, a quick-change artist. How did the man stand being nice to whoever got on board?

Paula stumbled down the first two steps then hesitated at the last one. Hydrangea blooms bobbed in the breeze, their late-summer exuberance unaffected by a hailstorm. Usually she was tickled by neon-purple blossoms (the size of basketballs) bouncing around the shelter spaceship. Not today.

The other passengers disembarked out the back, except Dimples and Big Foot. Her new neighbor had slipped off without her noticing, definitely a burly Black man in stealth mode. Dimples waved at Paula, too cute for his own good.

"Coming or going?" Duke asked her.

"I don't know." Paula's heart pounded.

The perp took the St. Berdoodle seriously as a witness. He hoped to hunt her down before the Feds. The dog was his next victim! What the heck was Paula going to do about that? About anything? What mess would she find at An'qwenique's? Perhaps girlfriend trashed her phone and other gadgets over bad boy brother or over poisoned rivers, toxic lies, and so many dead children. And now she was stranded in a bad situation, danger on her heels and no way to call for help.

"Feeling overwhelmed?" Triple-E shoved Paula onto the

street and stepped off the bus. "Waste of time. We'll be fine. I'll scope my journals for clues."

"I'm worried about the stray-hound." Despite sitting in the longhouse of the mind doing big talk about ants and people making history and changing the whole world one tiny pile at a time, Paula was a coward. "I don't know if I can handle what's ahead."

"Who does?" Triple-E hugged her and sang Melody's anthem.

Ask me to lose bomb, match, and fuse
Ask me to find what'll change my mind

"We're both recovering overachievers," the old hippie declared. "We always take the stairs and never coast. We even pedal downhill, so we're in excellent shape."

"Elaine, Eleanor, Edith, you have to get back on board," Duke shouted. He winked at Paula, flirt default-mode. "No real break this morning, we're running too late."

"Coming." Triple-E held Paula at arm's length. Faded copper braids unraveled into a frizzy wild-woman cloud, like the elders haunting the bus. "Don't mind Duke. We do have time, to breathe and smile together, then do the hard shit." She put a palm over Paula's heart. "No arguing." She jumped on board. "My money's on the dog." The doors whooshed shut and Duke drove away.

Trying not to worry too much, Paula marched off. Steam rose from the dark pavement. Her clothes were dampish and cold from the air-conditioned bus. Hopefully she'd dry out in the heat. Speeding up, she stumbled over nothing. She kicked off her soggy, ancient shoes, stuffed them in a trash bin, and slogged along in ratty socks. The big toe on the right foot ripped. She halted and gasped. "Who do you think you are?"

The street was empty. No witnesses, except high above the red oak and black gum trees, two red-tailed hawks swooped close, clutched each other's talons, and spiraled toward the ground. Just shy of the treetops, the raptor lovers caught a warm updraft and soared high. They disappeared in a low-riding cloud. Gravity, man, a death-defying thrill. "OK. I hear you. Keep it moving."

By the time she reached An'qwenique's street, the HEPA had rubbed her shoulder raw. She barely noticed. Cop cars at Charlize and Tomás's also did not register. Nor did the Wild Bunch: Louise, Thelma, their grown children, siblings, Abuelo Marco, elder aunties, grandbabies, and guests from Accra, Brooklyn, Copenhagen, and Saigon. The Wild Bunch huddled with the Mexican turkeys on the old mill baron's porch. The turkeys yelped at whoever would listen. Later, Paula realized the turkeys had witnessed Dragon Man snatch loved ones, break their necks, and drive off with the corpses and a comatose Charlize. The grieving birds stayed close to their people.

Paula was focused on the German EV hovering half in, half out of the garage. Brand-new trail runners perched on the hood. An'qwenique had to be home. The sun blasted the hand-carved Dogon door—West African space lore: alien travelers arrived in ships from the sky. As Paula raced up the flagstones past undulating Queen Anne's lace, the air shimmered like a portal to another dimension.

BOOK II

BETWEEN TIME

JOURNAL ENTRY:

*Paula told me: Yo, I believe in gravity. I feel the stars calling.**

STORM MUSINGS:

*It ain't just about fate or trolls. We're waging a story war!**

* Captions from the Iris Library's International Trickster Exhibition

AN'QWENIQUE—*Trouble*

Two red-tailed hawks soared out of a solitary cloud hanging over the Redemption Center. They screeched a high *kee eeeee* to a low raspy *arr* and disappeared into the marsh reeds. In the middle of the courtyard, an enormous sundial's gnomon looked like a knife jammed in a giant's heart, or maybe a lightning bolt. An'qwenique's hand tingled with static from twenty feet away. Momentarily paralyzed, she blinked at Ralph Carter sprawled on the Center's ramshackle porch. One thigh was twice the size of the other. His breath was so shallow that his chest barely moved, an ebony statue.

What are you doing, girl? What the hell is it all about?

A lanky CEO in a pathetic red tie and ruined designer suit spouted pseudoscience and conspiracy theories at An'qwenique and the anxious crowd scattered behind her on the giant sundial. He was a total cliché.

Is anybody a total cliché?

She tore at a plastic packet that refused to open and wasted energy ignoring the dream voice and the CEO's blather. The poodle wolf snarled a death threat. The CEO stuttered quiet. An'qwenique nodded thanks to the dog and pressed an epinephrine autoinjector into Ralph's thigh to counter a massive allergic reaction.

She itched all over, the third time today. Empathetic hives. The dog woofed support, a familiar deep voice. This was the hound she heard on the boardwalk and who barked her awake this morning (well, at 12:45 PM). That made as much sense as anything else.

Zsuzsu Hönig unfurled one of three super blankets that lived in An'qwenique's go-bag and laid it over Ralph. "Weightless cool or warmth. Why do you have these?"

An'qwenique shrugged. "I can't quite remember."

"I think this blue/green one is mine."

"Oh? Well, you can take it."

"I will." Zsuzsu was steely and sharp, and also fragile and flimsy in green rayon gauze. *So airy fairy thin* like Paula said. She leaned too far out of the wheelchair to pick a twig from Ralph's hair and whispered, "Come back to us." Had the **DUMP IT ALL AND START DOING BETTER!** guy pierced her frosty armor?

Ralph wasn't out of the bog yet, but An'qwenique's go-bag had two packets of epinephrine autoinjectors, four doses. What were the odds? "Luck, man!" She sounded Paula-esque. The CEO sniggered at her alternate nostril breathing. She turned away and peered at the Redemption Center, a gothic mansion with too many fussy balconies and lopsided turrets. Lizard railings framed stone stairs to the sketchy porch. Sickly light seeped from a round attic window—reminiscent of a lizard's eye. Dragon weathervanes breathed fire at each other and didn't agree about the wind.

Greenish swirl from the marsh skirted the foundation and gave off a ghoulish odor, or wildfire smoke stunk up the air. Both maybe. A dwelling for Charlize and Tomás, except, the paint was peeling and windows were busted or boarded up. The glam couple preferred high-end horror. This aging wreck was down-and-dirty weird, Kitty's postapocalyptic horror. Even though Kitty was alive and doing sex in the city, that wicked witch was haunting An'qwenique, here and now.

Plucking a mandolin furiously, a woman on the porch swing interrupted An'qwenique's self-pity. Long-haired and winsome, the player looked like that hippie ancestor who came back from a stroke and had a moment in the meme-verse—Joni Mitchell? Saucer eyes gleamed—high as a spaceshot like half this crew. (Hallucinogen brewed up in the marsh?) No cello in sight, perhaps An'qwenique had imagined that?

Eco-tourists in mismatched elegance chanted over a candle. A redundant flame; it wasn't getting darker. The sun had been motionless since An'qwenique stepped into the woods. Her grandmother's *Star Trek* watch did a heartbeat ticktock, keeping relative time. All time was relative, but . . . The sun looked to be caught in hemlock branches, a fiery ball stuttering in place. The shadow on the sundial courtyard was in the same spot as when she arrived. Wasn't it?

An'qwenique was afraid to ask the tourists wandering the sundial if they'd noticed. She feared a yes or a no. Roguish sprites flitted past zombies gazing at dead phones. The two factions snarled smack back and forth. Everyone was lost and blaming each other instead of working together to find a way out. Not the refuge/rescue she imagined.

The mandolin player riffed on the tune that led An'qwenique here, a song the donsó ngoni player at Crossroads loved to do with Melody. An'qwenique tapped her middle finger twice against her chest to sign *heart* and sang along.

Draw me a map that sets us free
Tell me a story I could be

"That's from Melody's last concert." Zsuzsu signed *sing*. "The donsó ngoni player taught the crowd harmonies. He said they made up the lines." She snorted. "Quiet as it's kept, Melody thought a community ditty was cheesy. Neo-folk music?"

An'qwenique flinched. "No good term for music like that anymore."

Zsuzsu sighed. "I don't mean to be harsh. Just chattering. Nerves. Melody played along, happily. The audience creating the verses was her idea even."

"I didn't know that." An'qwenique checked Ralph's vitals. He was still unconscious. Each breath was a burbly wheeze, yet his pulse was steadier. "In twenty minutes, I'll jab him again if he doesn't come around."

"Fuck you and the horse you rode in on!"

The CEO and another tall white man, a Change Ganger in tie-dye spandex, were ready to rumble on the sundial at 6:00 PM. Feeling out of control a few hours was the end of the world for these guys. *How about a lifetime!* The poodle wolf launched from the porch steps to the gnomon, almost flying. She curled her lips, fangs ready to rip flesh and crunch bones. Who wanted to tangle with that? The fight energy dissipated. The dog flicked her tail and trotted back up to Ralph.

"Diese blöden Kühe, sie spielen Kopfkino." Zsuzsu muttered something about *dumb cows playing head games* or *mind cinema*. The dog barked agreement. "Ich hasse Touristen." *I hate tourists*. Zsuzsu thought An'qwenique was fluent in German.

Not really. Her family lived in Bavaria when Mom scored a solar engineering job there. Dad could write anywhere. Big Brother hated Munich. He stole a moped, crashed it, and broke an ankle to piss the parents off. An'qwenique learned German to piss him off. She'd forgotten most of it. Staring at Ralph's swollen thigh, she imagined brother's *BIG TROUBLE:* sex, drugs, and mayhem with his cutthroat crew.

She should have texted Mom, gotten the skinny, offered comfort. Impossible to reach anybody now, she was in *BIG TROUBLE*. Geek wizard Azul Mendes might never forgive her for ditching the picnic, and her VR review was going to be late! What would Mom, Dad, and Big Bro think of that? She cringed. *That's what you're worried about?*

But she was never late, not once in twenty-nine years. Born on time, according to Dad. Azul regularly moseyed in late. Busy solving mighty problems, cruising from genius insights to miracle breakthroughs, who could be upset? An'qwenique had nothing like that in her arsenal. People were always waiting for her to fail. Late and a no-show was a disaster. Unassailable was all she had, her only Black-girl magic.

"What?" Zsuzsu wheeled close and nudged her. "You're muttering. I can't hear."

“I feel like I’m stuck in a horror VR that my evil ex designed, and there’s no way to switch off and get the hell out.”

“Es ist nicht so schlimm.” *It’s not so bad.* Zsuzsu chattered on in German about *the lovely stroll with Oona through the State Forest to her house.* Exactly what An’qwenique wanted to believe. Indeed, normal Real Life had never appealed to her so much. She resolved to quit the VR rig for however long it took to get herself right.

The poodle wolf nosed Ralph’s armpits and wagged her tail. She sparkled with dew, as if sequins or lightning had gotten caught in her tight curls.

“Sniffing out good news, huh?” An’qwenique hoped the dog was right.

“We didn’t realize what was happening.” Two medical technicians tiptoed close. Their blond bangs and purple *Star Trek* scrubs were quite fetching. “We were down by the water. Is he out of danger?” They tag-talked like one voice in two bodies. Cute.

“I think so,” An’qwenique said. “We should get him to a doctor soon though.”

“Jawohl!” Zsuzsu snapped her fingers.

“Do English,” the techs whispered. “People think you’re talking crap about them.”

“No problem,” An’qwenique replied before Zsuzsu sniped. “Help us shift Ralph onto his side. Better for breathing, right?”

After the techs turned Ralph and put a cushion under his cheek, Zsuzsu waved them away. “Thanks.” They hesitated, looking butch and feisty with neon buzz cuts in the back. “We’re good.” Zsuzsu deployed ballistic-missile voice. They scurried off.

The poodle wolf sat behind Ralph on guard duty, a paw on his shoulder.

“They were hoping to help,” An’qwenique murmured.

“Sorry,” Zsuzsu grunted, not sorry at all. “When Belle returns with Gwen, she’ll help. Even tripping on shrooms, the librarian’s our best asset.”

"Is everyone high?"

"How would I know? Maybe they're messed up all the time. This ain't my party."

"Whose fuckin' party is it?" An'qwenique matched Zsuzsu's tone.

"People in flip-flops and T-shirts stranded in a blizzard on a mountaintop want to blame their frostbitten asses on the weather, but es gibt kein schlechtes Wetter, gibt nur falsche Kleidung." *No such thing as bad weather, just the wrong clothes.*

"We got caught in a May blizzard near here with Paula," An'qwenique declared. "Don't you remember?"

Zsuzsu scrunched her face. "I guess."

"We almost froze to death. You forgot?" An'qwenique sucked her teeth like Paula, disgusted Bajan style. "You can't blame people for random bad luck, for the world coming apart around them." Or for a detour that took you to *the other side of reality.*

"Yes, I can!" A petulant, unreasonable response.

"What's wrong with you?"

"Sorry." Zsuzsu sounded genuine this time. "I'm not who I used to be, but I don't know how to be who I am now."

An'qwenique sputtered at this raw truth, offered up as if they were great buddies. "What do you mean? A, a . . ." A straight, professional woman hitting fifty without a man or close friends? An athlete stuck in a wheelchair with mystery condition? An environmentalist staring into the abyss?

"Forget it," Zsuzsu muttered. "I don't know why I said that."

"You can't take it back." An'qwenique forced a smile. "Hey, I'm struggling to find the new me too."

Zsuzsu scowled. "Yeah, but do you push everyone away? Make them hate you? Most of the time, I can't stand myself. I'm as bad as Melody. Amazing no one has stuffed me in an old Audi."

An'qwenique didn't know what to say.

Zsuzsu chuckled. "It's true. You're too nice to agree, but—"

The poodle wolf barked and the porch lights flickered. An'qwenique jumped. Maybe it was getting a little darker or maybe time seemed to stall because she was so lost.

"We're in *BIG TROUBLE*," An'qwenique declared. "Solving that is the priority at the moment. We'll deal with the rest later."

Zsuzsu trembled. Terror streaked across her face. "Is that a threat?"

PAULA—*Nobody Home*

Entangled in miracles and mysteries, Paula hesitated before opening An'qwenique's exquisitely carved Dogon door. She shoved the microwave door key into its metal mesh sleeve and turned her back on friendly aliens landing in West Africa centuries ago. Everything felt wrong, off, *ill.* Even the sunlight was too shimmery. *You see what you expect to see. Make it* strange. *You'll see more.* Who told her this? Triple-E? No, someone else, perhaps during that snowstorm last spring. Unusual for Paula to forget a face, a voice, an entire encounter yet recall what was said. She groaned at another freaky puzzle, like the St. Berdoodle.

It *was* the May blizzard! Around Memorial Day, at the crack of dawn, An'qwenique drove her out to clean Zsuzsu Hönig's house and barn, a $500 cash job. The day started warm and sunny. Zsuzsu and An'qwenique sat on the back porch arguing about personal responsibility versus systemic oppression (really, girls!) while Paula worked her butt off in the barn. Crows had trashed the hay loft. Bat guano fell from the rafters. A funky mess. The house was easier. After Paula finished, Zsuzsu made Kaffee und Kuchen—the German version of afternoon tea with coffee and cake.

An'qwenique insisted they walk/roll into the State Forest to a hidden marsh—for the dragonfly dances and frog concert—a marvel Paula should experience. Zsuzsu wasn't thrilled. Maybe not keen on palling around with the help? Or not a bug enthusiast? Nature-lover An'qwenique pressured Zsuzsu. Paula needed a shower and real food, but also agreed, for the dragonfly dances, for An'qwenique really.

Fifteen minutes in, Zsuzsu was scared they'd get hopelessly lost without her dog, a rescue pup, off doing her own adventure. Paula was about to ask for more on adventure dog when the blizzard blew in. Lurching through a whiteout, they stumbled across a hiker or park ranger in rugged boots headed for the Appalachian Trail. Almost too tall to be real, the hiker/ranger had a cascade of faces like the gnarly, silver-haired ladies glowering on the bus today. Paula had chalked this up to snowstorm daze. Lame! The hiker/ranger pulled three lightweight, climate-control blankets from a pack. A burst of neon colors in the snow squall. What were the odds? She traded the blankets for two empty water bottles and a rain poncho.

Tune into the weird. Make it strange and you'll find what you're looking for, the hiker said, then vanished.

Paula's heart had thundered in her ears, too loud to hear anything. Zsuzsu rolled ahead, tuning in to what they usually tuned out. Paula and An'qwenique slogged behind her, following the fluorescent blanket tucked around her shoulders. According to Zsuzsu, the hemlock, birch, and red oaks along the boardwalk were whispering a tree song map to her house. What was in that Kaffee und Kuchen?

Whenever Paula chased this memory down, details blurred, the way a vivid dream dissolved as you woke. Or she made excuses for the impossible bits—like with the St. B. Tree song? She never asked An'qwenique or Zsuzsu what they saw or heard, what they recalled. Coward. And whatever happened to those fluorescent blankets?

Perhaps she had muddled two memories. Belle wanted her to mount a library exhibit on forest spirits from New England and around the world. Paula tapped Gwen to interview Gwen's Nipmuc/Black grandfather at the nursing home. That was right before Gwen and little brother Lance slipped off the radar. Grandpa said, *Trees talk, but we don't know how to tune in anymore*. Lance made Bagwajiwinini or Pukwudgie puppets to stash around the library with other gnomes and sprites. Gwen threatened to have forest spirits tattooed on her inner thighs or hips for her seventeenth birthday, to enchant future lovers. Naturally, Lance wanted this too. Would they ever get to do all that?

Paula startled and almost dropped her HEPA onto the asters by An'qwenique's door. Right here, right now, the neighbors hooted at each other on their porch. Their turkeys cackled. A serious party going on, and Paula had missed it. And what else? *Make it strange* was good advice, no matter who said it. *Notice what you're not noticing.* She slowly retraced her steps on the flagstone path. Speed was a false god, a demon trickster. Triple-E would be proud of her.

Moving in slow motion, she noted everything that was off. Her socks were in shreds. The trail of her blood on the stones made her feet throb. She halted. Muddy ground from two stormy days was helping her out. Yesterday, most likely, some big body with hefty clompers stomped the button blazing stars in An'qwenique's front meadow, as if angry at the wildflowers.

"That's what I'm talking about," Paula declared. "Tune in to the weird."

Hail had melted in two footprints, men's size twelve or thirteen. A dead monarch butterfly floated in the muck. Ironweed and red maple branches beaten down by this morning's hail concealed more tracks leading to Charlize's. The tank girl who took care of the grounds, the mail person, and any neighbors or friends knew better than to decimate An'qwenique's pollinator paradise. Who then?

Paula closed her eyes and felt the heavy footsteps shaking up ants and worms, causing fungi to release spores. She opened her eyes, blinked in the sun, and trembled. With so few story details, trying to read someone she couldn't see, hear, smell, or touch was rough. Detectives spent their lives honing their skills. *Well, bitch, you the one claiming superpowers!* She glanced up at Tomás's cameras, impatient to watch Sunday's events on video. Who knew if she'd ever have access to that? *Trust where the clues take you.* Upstairs Karl always said that to her, and An'qwenique agreed.

The perp was a hefty dude, like Karl and Big Foot. He favored his left leg. Ralph was light on his feet, careful of wildlife, and balanced. A knot in Paula's stomach released. She didn't believe for a second Ralph killed Charlize, and now she had proof.

The perp stomped from An'qwenique's driveway across ironweed to Charlize and Tomás's medieval side door. The sculpted glass window was missing. No shards of glass anywhere, too noisy, too destructive. He'd carefully removed the glass with special tools—a souvenir for his collection, same as Melody's drums, shakers, and bells.

Paula gasped. He'd cased the joint and decided what precious bit of Charlize to steal: La Llorona, the wailing woman ghost. Like Paula, he loved the spiderweb veil hovering over a skeletal face, the pale yellow eyes glowing in hollow sockets, and a flowing white dress with flecks of mud/blood at the hem.

La Llorona was an unreasonable woman refusing what life dished out, even refusing death. In some versions of her story, she drowned her children and then herself, because her husband cheated, the way Tomás cheated on Charlize with multiple lovers. Maybe the perp appreciated these mythic connections to real life. Was it cheating if you had an open relationship?

Charlize flirted with everyone, even An'qwenique. Paula was a little jealous. Perhaps the perp was jealous of Tomás and Charlize for living and loving out loud, for wanting to bring a child into their world. They wrote their own story and also celebrated La Llorona: she came back from the dead to scare us to a better life.

Paula smirked. She was reading the perp's what just fine and speculating on the why! She'd check her theories with An'qwenique. "I'm onto you, dude. Watch out."

Someone else had tiptoed along the edge of the neighbor's yard. A lightweight with smaller feet who walked as if drunk—uncertain, erratic. An unhappy or reluctant partner? Paula squinted at a few dog tracks on the esplanade: big, devil-may-care feet plopping anywhere, unafraid, not the cautious wolf on the prowl, saving energy to take down a threat or a meal. The St. Berdoodle bounded into her mind and wagged her tail. She was Charlize's friend, visiting when the perp snatched her. A witness. The St. B tracked the perp to the Cloud Heights parking lot. No superpower needed, just a willful nose.

The pavement and driveway were almost dry. The fancy German EV, designed by a friend (old lover?) of An'qwenique's engineer mom, was not all the way out of the garage to maximize sunlight exposure or all the way in, charging up with the door locked. This wasn't An'qwenique's style. Random parking done by who? Hail had dented the solar-panel roof. Paula stroked the pockmarks, glad she hadn't been under that cloud.

New waterproof trail runners stood on the EV hood, dry inside except for sweat and splotches of blood. Someone set them here after the hailstorm. These shoes lived in the front hall closet or on the passenger seat. They were never anywhere else, except on An'qwenique's feet.

A bin from yesterday's recycling trip sat under the mailbox. A *New York Times Magazine* dissolved in the bottom. A soggy letter from President Obama (a friend of An'qwenique's dad!), requesting donations for his library, was plastered against the composter. A miracle-weight-loss flyer was stuck in the fence. An'qwenique might have been in a hurry getting the recycling to the car, but on return she would have tidied up.

Wrong, off, ill!

Paula returned to the front door and eased it open. Her heart pounded in her mouth. The air conditioning rattled; a few analog clocks ticked; the monster Algerian ivy hanging by the window caught a draft. The marbled leaves scraped the window. Otherwise quiet, as if nobody was home. Four empty recycling bins were strewn around the giant purple calathea, a prayer plant. Out of place. An'qwenique hated anything out of place. Half the calathea leaves drooped, in the prayer position, as if it was night, as if the sun wasn't beaming in the skylight. A puzzle for later.

Paula set her pack and equipment on the welcome mat noiselessly. Miscreants might still be lurking about the house, holding An'qwenique hostage. (Paula had never had an opportunity to use miscreant before.) Or they might have taken An'qwenique off the premises. But why unload the car and dump the bins in the driveway and the hall? Why set bloody running shoes on the hood? Nothing added up because availability bias had Paula conjuring the absolute worst scenarios. What was she missing?

An'qwenique's vanishing act might have nothing to do with Charlize's murder. Reality never came as a single storyline. Entangled strands always confused the issues. The perp needed to focus on the St. B, no time to kidnap Charlize's neighbor. Yet. And An'qwenique slept like a baby, through jets roaring, sirens screaming, or hail battering the roof. If writing, the world could come to an end and she wouldn't notice.

Paula peeled off her bloody socks, wiped battered feet on a utility towel from her pack, then slipped on the house shoes she left in the hall closet. She tiptoed up the carpeted stairs and peeked in the bedroom. Empty. The bed was as neat as a soldier's bunk in basic training.

An'qwenique usually made a sweaty mess, thrashing in intense dreams. These sheets were crisp and smelled like the dryer, as if she'd done laundry and made the bed up fresh early this morning. Early was for running, writing, or thinking, not making the bed. Paula opened the office door. Also empty. No dead body, no signs of struggle. Her laptop, big journal, and knapsack were missing.

"Huh." Paula gasped. She'd been holding her breath. "An'qwenique, where are you? Out for a solo hike without your shoes? There was a murder next door!"

Every room on the second floor was empty. The shower was bone dry. Paula took two steps at a time up to the attic, then raced downstairs and searched the first floor then the basement.

Nobody. Back on the first floor, she checked the sideboard in the front hall. An'qwenique often left a list of special tasks with her cash payment under a lapis lazuli paperweight next to the landline message machine.

Today was an envelope decorated with hearts, smiley faces, and hummingbirds. Inside were eighteen crisp twenty-dollar bills and a note with gold foil trim.

To the esteemed Ms. Paula B. Queenie,

An'qwenique Robinson requests the pleasure of your company for High Tea in the Gazebo.

Afterward, as the dark descends, we can watch the stars rise and talk up a storm.

Our Gumbo-Yaya magic! Unless of course, you have other plans already.

No pressure, but it would be my absolute delight to spoil you.

Your An'qwenique

AN'QWENIQUE—*Back from the Brink*

An'qwenique needed to pee sooner rather than later but didn't abandon Zsuzsu for the bushes by the gothic mansion. Zsuzsu spewed German curses, teetering at the edge, so vulnerable and in public. Unbelievable. Sharp features looked more angular than usual. Living alone, was she eating enough? The poodle wolf pawed the wheelchair, whimpering.

"That hound should be on a leash," the CEO muttered. "Probably a carrier." He was pissed at Ralph for indefinitely delaying their departure/escape. He hit a battered sign hanging on rusty chains: THE REDEMPTION CENTER IS CLOSED ON SUNDAYS. "Closed Sundays makes zero sense. What kind of park is this?" He kept his distance from everyone, droning on about people catching whatever the murder suspect had. His anxiety sweat was pungent at thirty feet. His word salad was equally unappealing. The tall Change Ganger snarled anti-vax goop at him. They almost agreed, but fussed on, alpha male to alpha male, power playing. An attentive man and woman (couple?) kept score at the picnic tables. Pink umbrellas looked like psychedelic mushrooms.

"I feel so disappointed in humanity, in myself," Zsuzsu whispered. "Belle needs to hurry her ass back here. She knows how to defuse macho bubbleheads without shit blowing up. A librarian thing, not in my wheelhouse."

"You with the handy needles." The CEO loosened his tie to shout. "You hear me?"

An'qwenique had heard every word. "Me, a government spy doctor? Wrong! Not a doctor at all. You're confusing me with a TV action series."

"Contagion is the big risk. We might catch what the murder suspect has and die out here." The CEO repeated himself. Tourists eyed Ralph, fearful now. Repetition = Truth.

"What about you," An'qwenique said. "Got an alibi beside your suit and tie?"

"Great costume to get away with murder," Zsuzsu declared. The med techs snickered. The dog barked, on their team. Other tourists nodded, afraid of the CEO too.

"What do you know?" He scowled at the marsh behind the gothic mansion as if any moment the Loch Ness monster would charge out of the ooze and infect them. Abruptly, he fixed his face to indulgent but in charge. Slick. "Mr. Carter is very ill."

"Anaphylaxis." An'qwenique used the medical term to shut him down. "Allergy, not a virus or bacteria. Probably from a bug bite or prickly plant, believe me."

"You're not even a doctor. So, no," he replied. "I don't believe you."

"You think I'm making shit up?"

"Hell no!" A robust woman dressed to survive the apocalypse marched between them. She was pale with freckled, sunburnt cheeks and sharp blue eyes that were a normal size. "He'd find an excuse not to believe a doctor. He's mad as hell and can't take it anymore!" The CEO glowered at her like she knew his dark secrets.

"That's from an old movie, right?" An'qwenique said.

"Isn't all our dialogue?" The woman's backpack was the same careful leaf, grass, and shadow pattern as her clothes and much bigger than An'qwenique's. Not a fashion statement; this lady could vanish in the bushes and, deploying goodies from the ginormous go-bag, make it through the end times to the next times. "I trust you. You trust me, right?" She pointed at An'qwenique's go-bag. "Ready for anything. Me too."

"My friend Paula's fault." An'qwenique slipped into her hiking sandals. The new trail runners had disappeared from the sundial without her noticing. Really, people?

"Props to Paula." The survivalist pulled her away from Zsuzsu, Ralph, and the poodle wolf.

An'qwenique took a few steps and halted. "What?

The survivalist narrowed icy eyes. "See any strange characters on your way here?"

The strange characters had congregated around the sundial. "What do you mean?"

"Flimsy figures, ghosts lurking in shadows, pretending to be hikers?"

"Wouldn't ghosts be up-front with their spectral nature?" Almost snark! Zsuzsu was rubbing off on An'qwenique.

"You'd think," the survivalist replied, serious as a stroke. "These days, everyone's fronting, lying through their teeth while doing whatever evil crap they can get away with, because," she shifted her hefty backpack, "we're so damned gullible by nature." She sounded ashamed, as if human nature was a personal failing. "So we're pissed."

"Uhm . . ." An'qwenique fronted German, a minor infraction. She probably remembered more German than she realized. "People mostly do small-scale lies. Mutual trust is a major part of our survival kit."

"So is deception. Why should ghosts be any different?"

An'qwenique scratched her neck, a fiery itch. "I guess."

"So, did you see anyone?" The survivalist peered through tiny binoculars. "Think before you say no. We're never all by ourselves. *The Lone Individual is an Illusion*."

The title of one of An'qwenique's eco-podcasts. "Where'd you hear that?"

"I'm walking the world on a mission for truth. I listen and I remember."

"Right, the Appalachian Trail is close."

The survivalist pursed her lips. "*Always running in the background, almost unnoticeable in the spectacle of nature unbound, but I still feel it—at the bottom of my breath, in the tumult my eyes ignore, a symbiotic planet holds us. We are, each one and all, nodes in the web of life. Maybe lonely, but never alone. Trust that.*" An exact quote, even mimicking An'qwenique's cheesy, self-righteous delivery. Damn.

"That's from the *Great Escape* podcast." An'qwenique felt strange meeting a fan in this horror VR. "A little overblown, melodramatic, but I agree."

"*Escape* saved my life a couple times." The survivalist pocketed the binoculars. "*Surprise got woven up in the cloth of the universe along with cosmic rhythms and routines, rituals and romance.*" She extended her fist. "You listen too?"

An'qwenique bumped her knuckles. "Yeah. I've heard 'em all."

She admired An'qwenique's silk camo pedal pushers. "We have a lot in common."

"Oh?" An'qwenique resisted going that far. "I'm—"

"Better at passing for normal," she whispered, then pointed at the birch trees. "A pioneer species, taking root after ecological collapse, when the soil's almost dead."

An'qwenique nodded. "Birches are short-lived for trees, but they can bring an ecosystem back from the brink."

"A fellow tree nerd! I knew it." The survivalist grinned, then shivered. "We tell lies on and to each other, but believe me, these woods are haunted. Acres of hungry, restless ghosts waiting for us to take responsibility."

An'qwenique gulped. "You mean that literally, not just metaphorically?"

"No real difference. You felt weird walking here. In the wrong skin, in an alien place, surrounded by unseen spectators who wanted to bleed you, suck you dry."

"Well, I was lost and—"

"Our hearts have been poisoned. Ghosts wait till dark to drive us out of our limited little minds. Women hardly ever roam the night or venture into the unknown as free beings." The truth muddled in her words was compelling. "So, tell me, what do you have to say for yourself? How'd you end up here?"

"I don't know." An'qwenique resisted bizarre memories. "I . . . After . . ."

After marching across the marsh, she'd halted. The boardwalk branched in several shadowy directions. Garter snakes slithered over her new trail runners, which weren't broken in yet, so blisters. Jewel-toned fungi exploded out of leaf muck. A horned owl scattered songbirds who'd accompanied her from the sandpit. The cello/mandolin music turned into static. Suddenly, she was a hummingbird, hovering in too many places at once. The damn maze of mazes again, with no center of gravity to organize her. She shrieked and flailed, 1200 heartbeats a minute, a cosmic freakout.

The wild turkeys paraded by, cackling and spitting, blasé. Even the chicks were unimpressed. They startled An'qwenique back onto solid ground, back into her arms, backbone, and feet. She clomped behind the birds into a grove of spindly, ash-white forms swaying in the wind. These specters yammered, *We know you hear us. What the hell are you doing?* then metamorphosized into silent birch trees. Beyond them the Redemption Center loomed.

"I was alone till you guys, except for the trees, birds." She saved mysterious truth for tomorrow in the gazebo with Paula. Monday couldn't come soon enough!

"I bet trees can haunt us," the survivalist murmured. "Ghost bears and crows too."

Zsuzsu wheeled close and gripped An'qwenique's hand. "Should we check Ralph?"

"Not just ghosts, a murderer on the loose. I felt him, nearby." The survivalist nodded at the Change Ganger and the CEO. "Watch your step." She drifted off.

"Ralph's looking better," An'qwenique said loud, then whispered, "Thanks."

"Anytime." Zsuzsu grimaced. "Isn't the *Great Escape* podcast your baby?" An'qwenique shushed her. Zsuzsu snorted. "Forty percent of Americans believe in ghosts and UFOs. Women go more for the specters; men are waiting on ET."

"No way." An'qwenique wanted to argue, and with zero proof. She slipped behind a hydrangea bush to relieve her agitated bladder. "That can't be right."

"It's a stable statistic." Zsuzsu, like Paula, was a quantiholic. They both nailed the numbers before speaking. Zsuzsu offered up a tissue and positioned her chair in front of the showy blossoms for additional cover. "People spin wild State Forest tales too. But this crew today. Let me tell you." She did. Belle and her Change Gangers were tripping in Wonderland. The survivalist lady thought Pocumtuc ghosts did soul-sucking payback after sundown, à la *The Haunted*. The CEO was an invaluable asset trapped in a *Mission: Impossible*, Jason Bourne, Jack Ryan spy thriller. The med tech twins (lovers like Zsuzsu said?) decided today was *The Day the Earth Stood Still*. They hoped to meet our alien overlords and zip around the galaxy. She chuckled. "But it's not funny."

"Yes it is." An'qwenique emerged from the bushes, grateful she got to wipe her butt. "Everyone's stuck in a different movie. Kopfkino, *mind cinema*. I'm in horror VR."

Zsuzsu scoffed. "Du? Nein. Unsinn." *You? No. Nonsense.* The poodle wolf whined agreement.

"Does your dog speak German?"

"Bullshit is the same in every language. Oona's got a nose for that."

"Swelling's way down." An'qwenique checked Ralph's pulse. "I love the heartbeat."

"You're an ace at bringing 'em *back from the brink*."

"Shut up."

"I'm serious! You are."

"But a killer on the loose?" An'qwenique shuddered.

"Some people just heard about Melody today. Living on Mars, right?" She wiped Ralph's face. "He found another murdered woman before coming here with Oona."

"Fuck! No!" An'qwenique hugged herself. "Who was she?"

"He didn't say. And yeah, she could be someone we know." Zsuzsu pressed Ralph's hand to her heart. "Calling nine-one-one didn't go so well, but he found Melody's dumbek near poison berries in the State Forest."

"Ah, so our survivalist thinks the killer is lurking in these woods, coming after her."

Zsuzsu gripped her wheels and growled, ready to charge into battle. "I feel her." She admitted empathy! "That creep could be after any of us, anywhere, anytime."

"He was at Crossroads for Melody's last concert. I'm sure."

"Oh hell, you know something, don't you?" Zsuzsu quivered. "Do I want to hear it? I knew most of those people, or I'd seen them around."

"Doesn't that break your heart?" An'qwenique murmured. "He probably showed up at the Haven too for her celebration of life to sneer at us."

"Like a firebug, torching your life then sticking around to see you freak out."

An'qwenique nodded. "Half the people doing testimonies never liked Melody. I mean, she said *recycling is against my religion* and *the climate crisis is a hoax*, to me."

"OK, she voted for the wrong guy, never smiled, but just give me what you know."

An'qwenique sighed. "A Haven regular rode his studded-tire bike in the ice storm to her last Crossroads concert, then rode back to the Haven. He was out back in the alleyway, acting holier-than-thou, yelling about Melody's drumming. She told him to fuck off. I mentioned this to Oshun Jackson and Blue Rosenthal. Nothing came of it."

"Jackson and Rosenthal are busy, suspended on corruption charges."

"What?" Oshun and Blue claimed to be An'qwenique's friends and never mentioned this. Because An'qwenique was a terrible friend. "That's awful."

Zsuzsu scoffed. "You expect justice, closure, peace of mind. Even if they catch the wanker, what changes? He's not the only predator out there."

"So we should do nothing?" An'qwenique shook her head. "Catch him and there's one less psychopath running free, around here at least."

"We admire psychopaths, put them in charge." Zsuzsu sounded defeated. "We worship them."

An'qwenique snorted. "We take them down too!" The poodle wolf licked her trembling hand, a rough, cool tongue. An'qwenique shook slobber in the dirt. "Does that mean you like me?" The dog nuzzled An'qwenique's knee and thumped a bushy tail. "I'm not used to puppy love."

"Oona is a promiscuous hussy." Zsuzsu was jealous.

"She loves you with all her heart." An'qwenique ruffled Oona's sparkly curls.

"How do you know?"

Oona put dirty paws in Zsuzsu's lap and nuzzled her neck.

An'qwenique smiled. "You don't really doubt your dog. She'll lead us to your farmhouse, right?"

"Jawohl." Zsuzsu affirmed the rescue plan and hugged Oona.

An'qwenique nodded. "That's what we all want to hear, leash or no leash."

PAULA—*Landline Follies*

It would be my absolute delight to spoil you.

Paula read An'qwenique's invitation several times. Her breath fluttered and her skin prickled, more than when they danced barefoot on the clean kitchen tiles. Was this for real? Romance or what? Paula had no friggin' idea how to do romance, how to get vulnerable, naked to her soul. How was she supposed to be real and true with a rich lady, her most solid $360-a-week client? An'qwenique (twenty-nine) was too young for Paula (forty-one)! What about on-again, off-again lover babe, Kitty Richards? Paula was much better at science fiction and fantasy or mystery. The umpteen ways she might mess up a romance terrified her, made her ignore the romance clues. Even friendship was a stretch. OK, Triple-E was almost a friend, Ralph and Belle too, and the St. Berdoodle for sure. She told the dog everything. Dogs were easy. Maybe a dog didn't count.

Clutching An'qwenique's note, Paula's hand shook. Wasn't romance and adventure what she wanted? Truth be told, romance seemed as impossible as a disappearing dog.

The light on the message machine jolted her back on task. Even if not the perp's next target, An'qwenique shouldn't be out hiking with her phone off, feet barely touching the ground, mind on the stars. She never thought anything bad would happen to her. Upper-class fog. Paula pushed Play, hoping for clues to track Ms. Oblivious down.

The first message was Sunday at 2:46 PM. "This is Kitty. Are you punishing me? Did you block my number? Call me. Let me apologize."

Tomás called at 3:03, looking for Charlize. Paula wanted to

skip his heartbreaking message, but listened to the full three minutes (longer, really). She flinched hearing how he considered An'qwenique Charlize's best friend. Wow. Maybe Charlize was bad at friends too.

There were thirteen more messages. Should Paula be spying like this?

"Hey, this is Azul Mendes. I'm at the reservoir. The biscuits are warm; the hibiscus tea is chill. There's a good breeze blowing off the water. Cedar air. What happened to you? OK, I was forty minutes late, sorry, but you know me, up in the Cloud Heights, solving shit. I know I should take the whole day off, Faulenzen. I brought German chocolate from Zsuzsu. German beer too. Oh, but you don't do much alcohol. You're also never late. I tried your cell and it said OUT OF SERVICE. Since when? Call me."

"Azul again. It's almost five PM. I've been waiting longer than I was late. Damn, woman, I drank the beers and ate the whole basket, whole picnic myself, so forge it, I mean forget it." Sounding tipsy there, Azul. "Actually, I fed the vegan shrimp to the squirrels and a cheeky crow. Don't scold. I know I'm not supposed to, but not my fault. The crow barged in on my squirrel party. I have video proof.

"I'm heading out, so if you ain't gonna show in five minutes, let's reschedule. I don't want to be pissed, but not a single fuckin' word from you? That's not very nice. I know I was forty-five, fifty minutes late, but just ghosting me? I'll be early from now on. I promise. No further torture necessary. Communicate! You know, I don't usually give interviews. Ciao."

"Sweetie, this is Mom. Does this old contraption tell you it's six PM? Did you get my other message? Probably not. I can't get through to your cell. I guess I'll just say it. Your brother is in the hospital. I hate leaving you a message, but your father insisted you'd rather know something than worry. But if you knew nothing, you wouldn't worry. The doctors are optimistic, so don't worry anyhow, just call as soon as you get this."

"Azul checking in. It's eight PM. Where are you? OK, I was an hour late. Sorry for the whiny blip before. Radio silence is unnerving. Have you ever been late for anything? I'm crazy worried and, honey, I never worry. I pay other people a lot of money to do that for me. I texted your inner posse. They said you had VR fun in the jungle Saturday night to dawn. Today was supposed to be straight Real Life. I even reached out to Tomás and Charlize. No answer, and they never unplug. What are you guys up to? Taking the Faulenzen-do-nothing joint on Sunday to the nth degree! Let me know you're OK. You're one of my people, so whatever. CALL!"

Paula's heart was pounding in her mouth again as she erased a gimme-your-money-or-else robocall. Something bad besides murder could have happened to An'qwenique.

"Mom calling again. Did you smash your cell in an anti-capitalist rage and lose our numbers? Your brother took a bad turn. Your father wants you to drive here immediately. St. Mary's Hospital, you know the one. I told him you probably weren't listening to messages. He insisted I call one more time. I didn't want to. He has a phone, but you never call or even text him. Frankly, I don't want to hear you're also in trouble, so send *him* that message. I'll give you our numbers again."

Her quick mumble was too quiet for Paula to catch.

"Hey, babe! It's Kitty Richards. You recognize the voice, right? Did you block me? Seriously? Your cell also refused to take a text from the nice gentleman on the train in front of me. Have you blocked the whole damn world? I got a bad feeling, you know? Are you OK? I went to that stupid Native, Indian, Indigenous, whatever Museum. It wasn't half bad. They say Indian, you know. But I should have gone there with you, 'cause stupid people can ruin anything, like great food, dreamy atmosphere, classy dancing. I'm talking fuck up Broadway front row for Alice Childress. I can't believe Ms. Childress wrote that script in 1950 whenever, another Black woman way ahead of her time. She died before the rest of us even came close!

"The tips from your cleaning service lady are stellar! And I was worried because it wasn't a musical. Big thanks for getting us into the cast party. They all love your dad. He can write them a movie anytime. Retreating to your country estate, you're missing so much, missing everything. What good are your golden connections?" Kitty took a few breaths. "Uhm, just trying to talk my way back in your heart . . ."

Paula felt as if someone poured acid in her veins. Jealousy this fierce was a shock.

Kitty found her words again. "At your age, you still have a stupid landline? Even my throwback parents have dumped their landline. I'm glad you still have it though. So, what, you're writing and you turned the cell off? Banished it to a distant room, so you can work yourself to death in peace? Does that make you feel superior to us phone sluts and slackers? Or did you go to the lake without me? Running through empty woods with the wolves or some shit? No Wi-Fi up there, no dependable towers. Nobody can reach you. That's why you love it.

"OK, Tracy is a loser. She and I are over before we even started. Last night she found the perfect slut. Muscle, sinew, big booty, and big tits—the bitch must live at the gym and eat only diet protein packs and chia seeds. They can have each other. I'm on the night train home.

"How do you put up with me? I should erase this, but I don't think I can. You're so old school. Damn. See why texting is superior? You can correct your shit before sending it. Perfect it! I hope you're doing OK. I am sorry for my part. Just text me you're alive and don't laugh at my bad feeling thing. I don't want tragic crap to happen to you. You are still my favorite person." Ha! That was a fantasy from afar, in person Kitty and An'qwenique worked each other's nerves.

"Hey there, tying up loose ends," a distorted, breathy voice muttered at 10:32 PM. Not the usual robocall recording—too late in the day and no caller ID or spam alert. "Your cell is OUT OF SERVICE, but you left an urgent message this afternoon. Stroke of luck, your landline is also in this directory. Catch you later." Who was that, leaving no name, calling from a hidden number, and maybe not their own phone? Random. Except, An'qwenique had left an urgent message. A few details, please.

"Mission Control to An'qwenique! It's your mother calling at six ten AM Monday morning. We were up all night, hanging by a thread, life and death. YOU NEED TO CALL! Oh god, this is pointless. What am I doing? Are you truly so selfish?" Why didn't Mom wonder if An'qwenique was OK?

Paula skipped the messages she left, or she might have erased them. That would be cheating. An'qwenique should hear Paula's invitation to the Haven for vegan cheese buns with soy bacon bits, Paula's treat. They could spoil each other and tell all. Romance or whatever, work the dog problem. Although if Big Bro was dying, An'qwenique might have to drive to Saint Mary's. Was it terrible to hope he got better quick so An'qwenique didn't have to go anywhere?

"Hey lady, Azul bugging you. Monday and nobody's heard blah blah from you, but the cops say you're not a missing person just 'cause you blew me off or your neighbor was—Wait. You know about Charlize, right? I'm next door. Tomás is wasted. He and I broke up six months ago. Very messy. I was hurt, but, uh, he called this morning going to fuckin' pieces, so I called back then raced right down here.

"I was in the house five minutes and he started trashing the torture chamber front hall. Then he curled up on the Persian prayer rug. So I got down and held him. Wow, sorry, TMI. Hey, I'm rattled.

"Zsuzsu never showed for work. She's like you, never late. Ralph Carter has gone walkabout too, and the police would like to talk to him. Belle missed the Change Gang breakfast meeting for tonight's Tech Up Your Skills and Literacy Project shindig. All the dependable people are MIA! Eerie, you know? Random, coincidence, or . . .

"You're Charlize's BFF. Call or come over. It'd help Tomás deal. He's sitting on the back porch with the turtle you gave Charlize, Adele or Aretha, in his lap, crying about his lady and worrying about you. Not the only one. I watched our security tapes. This perp is sick! He hacked our feed, a clever asshole working special effects. Straight-up horror. We're worried. You mean a lot to everyone."

"That's the truth," Paula muttered.

In the middle of a message from the police complaining about the OUT OF SERVICE cell and asking An'qwenique to contact them immediately, the phone rang. Paula jumped three feet. An'qwenique's bright voice greeted the current caller, then a beep.

"Hey you, it's Kitty. Remember me?" She spoke softly, plaintively, live. "Why won't you answer the damn phone or call me or . . . Somebody offed your next-door neighbor. You didn't like the pop diva that much or anything, but did you want her dead? I don't think so. That hunky husband must be a mess. Right next door. How are you doing? I'm a wreck. You know I love you, right?"

Paula picked up. "Hello."

"Who is this?" Kitty gulped. "What's going on? Where's An'qwenique?"

"She isn't here," Paula replied.

"Why are you answering the phone?"

"I'm Paula, I clean on—"

"Mondays. She told me about you."

"I've heard stories about you too." Paula regretted saying this. She clamped her mouth shut. She hated how Kitty ditched An'qwenique and then came crawling back with *You're the one I really love.* This was the fourth time. Shameless. Telling her all this would only be fun for a minute.

"Don't believe everything you hear." Kitty's voice cracked.

Luckily, Paula didn't have to watch her squirm. "I can hang up and let you finish leaving a message."

"No, that's all right. I've already left a few. Landline Follies! Shit, did you listen?"

"An'qwenique likes long messages. That's why you have over three minutes."

"Right. Did she stay at the lake then, by herself?"

"By herself?"

"I bagged on her." Kitty cleared her throat. "Maybe she invited someone else."

"She never invites people to the cabin, except you."

"Oh. OK." Kitty sounded relieved. "So I messed up the plan, but maybe she's there alone writing her hummingbird piece. It's due today. She hadn't started on Wednesday. She's not telling me anything, not answering her cell."

"*Beginnings are a bear,*" Paula quoted An'qwenique, fronting casual.

"And can you believe someone did that to Charlize? I'm worried, you know."

"Understandable." Paula wished she had perfected alternate nostril breathing. "I don't think An'qwenique is punishing you." Oops—that was from Kitty's first message.

"I can't help myself. I'm a mean bitch sometimes. You don't know!"

Paula did know. "Torture is not An'qwenique's mode."

"So true." Kitty sounded like she might cry.

Paula wanted to avoid that. "An'qwenique is tied up. A hard day. She had to cut her run short because of blisters. Her brother is in the hospital. She has a bunch of deadlines. Her car got battered by the hail. She's off somewhere in her own world."

"Right. I didn't think of all that."

Of course not. "I'll have her call you as soon as she can."

"I appreciate that. But maybe she and I should do whatever we do face-to-face, live."

"Live is good, for relationships particularly."

"OK. That's what I'll do. Thank you for having my back."

"Don't thank me. Thank Jigonhsasee and Harriet."

"Who?"

"They help me offer free passes for the Underground Railroad of the Spirit. That's so anybody can find the Peace Path to their best self. Goodbye."

Paula hung up before Kitty had a chance to react or before Paula snapped. Kitty squandered more resources in one day than Paula had in a lifetime. Shaking, Paula pulled a mint cough drop from her utility vest pocket and stuck it under her tongue.

Careless, reckless people like Kitty shoved Paula onto the wrong track. They blasted tons of CO_2 into the atmosphere and wasted food, water, and love. Paula bit the cough drop and shattered it into several pieces. She saw herself outside Kitty's real estate window screaming for her blood. Not an image she needed to entertain.

AN'QWENIQUE—*Spirit Jamboree*

Stranded on the other side of nowhere (for what felt like forever!), An'qwenique was running short of patience, grace, and reasonable or unreasonable explanations for their predicament. That must have happened to these other lost souls. They'd been stuck at the Redemption Center much longer. She gripped the lizard railing to the big house.

"Which one of you rogues nicked my new trail runners?" An'qwenique used a fake British/Caribbean accent to cover fury.

Oona wagged her tail, acting *who me* innocent. Oona might be able to lead them out of the maze, however the Change Gang insisted on waiting for the librarian and the snake kid, Guinevere. Worse, Ralph was still unconscious, and Zsuzsu was counting on the second shot to wake him up and make him right. Slim odds for that.

"Whether an alien poison, ghost allergy, or engineered superbug, Mr. Carter won't be walking anytime soon." The CEO stormed around a bee balm garden and sneered at exuberant purple blossoms. "Even if the shots save his life, who among us can carry two hundred fifty pounds of dead weight?" A good point that no one wanted to hear from him. "Better idea: the dog leads us to cell phone service. We send a helicopter back."

"You believe in my dog now." Zsuzsu scanned from the gothic mansion to the marsh. "Where would they land?" The sundial gnomon was a mountain. Stone benches crowded around the timepiece. Ice-age boulders and garden sheds were scattered in the gardens. The forest beyond was dense and visibility spotty in twilight mist.

The CEO looped his tie around his forehead. "We leave now, any help would arrive sooner, by whatever means. You can remain with Mr. Carter." He smirked at Zsuzsu.

"Reasonable," An'qwenique said. "But I bet Oona won't leave either one behind."

"Shit." This had not occurred to him. Oona licked her nose, catching a scent. She trotted close to the CEO and paused under a heavy purple blossom nodding in the mist. Her tail was erect, her ears forward, on high alert. The CEO muttered smack about a leash. Other tourists groaned and grumbled. Everyone was still fighting mad yet stupid with exhaustion. "Call your dog!" the CEO demanded.

Zsuzsu kissed her teeth. Dog owners were so entitled, not helping their case.

Oona raced through the bee balm to a shed with a steep roof resembling a witch's hat. A thread of white drifted from a crooked smokestack. Raised beds under two round windows featured doll's eye shrubs. Five hundred white eyes with purple pupils peered at them from bloodred stalks. Next to the horror blossoms, a black straw broom leaned against the shed. The witch was at home, not out riding the wind. The door was slightly ajar. An invitation. Fearless Oona squeezed inside. A minute ticked by on the *Star Trek* watch as the tourists exchanged fearful glances.

An'qwenique laughed. "You think the Wicked Witch of the West nabbed the dog?"

They looked to be imagining something worse. Zsuzsu wheeled to the edge of the bee balm bed. The leggy blossoms were over four feet and abuzz with greedy pollinators, including hummingbirds and hefty bumblebees. The ground was sloppy mud, from the storm earlier. Not quite wheelchair accessible.

"Oona? What are you doing?" Zsuzsu heaved herself up, lurched behind her chair, and gripped the handles. The tourists were amazed and horrified behind her back. Warrior woman, ready to mow down tough flower stalks and plow through muck to save her dog from a witch.

"Wait, I'll go check." An'qwenique raced by Zsuzsu. The bumblebees were too busy getting drunk on bee balm nectar to sting anybody. She breezed past the lethal beasties and threw open the shed door. Oona was nowhere to be seen.

Tools, pots, and bags of mulch were piled all over. A log smoldered in the fireplace under a black cauldron. Puppets and masks from around the world dangled from hooks on almost invisible wires. Dragons, sprites, and hungry ghosts twisted in the air, grinning and grimacing, a spirit jamboree.

Fish-bodied aliens swished raffia skirts. These aliens visited the Dogon of Mali long ago and were carved on An'qwenique's front door. Iyami Aje, wise women witches from West Africa, cut lightning eyes at An'qwenique's surprise. They had breasts like blades and a firestorm of henna-red hair. One hook had a scrap of felt and a strand of beads, as if one little wise woman had escaped. An'qwenique fingered the beads.

Coyote crouched at a back door that opened onto a sculpture garden. Perhaps an Aje had torn free and escaped to the garden. Strange, otherworldly figurines frolicked among even stranger plants. Definitely a shed for a garden witch!

Oona yip-yapped from behind several towers of clay pots. An'qwenique startled at the agitated tone. "What have you found back there?" She banished an image of a naked, murdered woman stuffed in a bag of mulch and peered around the corner. Oona stood in a red wagon, identical to the childhood classic, except it was adult-sized and the handlebar was suited for two. She offered a look-what-I-found grin.

"Good girl." An'qwenique patted her head. Oona collapsed onto the wagon bed and lay motionless. "Are you playing dead?"

Oona exploded out of the wagon and sent several pots flying. The sturdy vessels landed in the mulch without shattering.

Oona offered a muddy paw to shake. An'qwenique squeezed her toes.

"You're turning me into a dog lover. No mean feat."

Barking and snuffling, on the trail of something good, Oona darted into the backyard, raced past the uncanny gargoyles, humanoids, or djinn, and headed for the marsh. What An'qwenique wouldn't give for a working camera.

The tourists were grumbling in the courtyard. An'qwenique hurried out the front door, pulling the wagon. "Look what Oona found! We can borrow this and wheel Ralph down the boardwalk."

"Oona to the rescue!" Zsuzsu's voice cracked as she sat down. "Was that shed there all along? Looks like part of a steampunk rocket ship. How did I miss that?"

An'qwenique wondered what else they'd missed. "Yeah . . . Steampunk and witchy."

"Let's take turns pulling the wagon. We'll do the first shift." The med techs riffed on Michael and Janet Jackson moonwalking, ready for their social media reel.

The mandolin player plucked an eerie version of Jackson's "Beat It." Strands of frizzy hair resembled static electricity in the mist. She looked more mad scientist than Joni Mitchell as she muttered, "Who is going to believe any of this!"

"I don't believe it myself," An'qwenique replied. "And I'm here with you."

The med techs gripped the wagon's handle and pranced onto the sundial. Neon-blue buzz cuts and golden bangs sparkled. "We have an announcement. No more waiting for the right omen to be absolutely certain. We've decided to tie the knot."

"What? Just now?" the survivalist marveled. "Wow!"

The med techs pulled the wagon toward the ramp to the porch. "You are all invited to our wedding."

Lovers! An'qwenique smiled. That felt like a good omen indeed. "I'm there."

Oona charged from the marsh and jumped into the wagon,

wagging her butt, a happy pup. The survivalist hugged her backpack and twirled. Even the unassuming het couple jumped up and got rowdy. Change Gangers blocked the med techs. They yelled about Belle in the woods tracking Guinevere. The CEO cursed out the librarian for tripping and wandering off the map.

Before everyone went there, Zsuzsu declared, "We wait for Belle. No one left behind. You'd want us to wait for you, right?"

"What was I thinking?" The CEO wobbled on shaky feet. "The Feds won't let us walk out of here alive, even following a wonder dog. That's why every chance we get turns hollow, every road brings us back to the Redemption Center."

"Not the Feds or the Deep State," the Change Gang alpha said. "It's 5G plus messing with our brains." Maybe he heard the static drowning out the cello and mandolin music. "The dog is immune. Her senses are tuned to a different frequency."

The med techs hooted. "The Redemption Center is beyond regular Earth technology. Oona tunes in to alien science." Perhaps they noted the shadow stuck on the sundial.

"Idiots distracted by nonsense." The CEO tripped over that truth.

Before he fell on his ass, the survivalist caught him. "Ghosts yearn to drive us sane, so we'll notice the terrible mess we've been taking for granted."

"Yes." An'qwenique bent down to Zsuzsu. "*Make it strange*. A hiker told us something like that near here, right?"

Zsuzsu snorted, refusing strange.

"You lot won't see a penny of the blood money they promised you." The CEO rubbed red eyes. "The cutthroats who hired you to gaslight me don't leave loose ends."

"Why are you so sure?" An'qwenique probed.

He grunted. "They savaged me, a brutal, take-no-prisoners plot."

Zsuzsu sneered. "Oh? I'm so surprised."

"I'm the architect of their money and power," he boomed.

"I was loyal, a rock, not just hired hacks like you people. The other board members, including my best friend and my wife, called a secret meeting without me. Fuckers left me zilch except jail time."

An'qwenique flinched. The man hung with folks who had iffy ethics (no ethics) and yet was shocked when they burned him. "My brother's so-called best friends stole his shit too, all the profits, then set him up to take the fall for their bad business." And Big Bro still admired and defended them. Damn!

"I bet you didn't betray your brother." The CEO glowered. "But my wife, how could she use the kid against me? Who does that?" He blubbered. "I know secrets the Feds or the competition are dying to know. I have dirt on everyone, even my traitor wife and the kid. Fuck 'em!" Angry tears streaked his stubbly cheeks.

Zsuzsu scoffed. "Aber Sie gehen auch über Leichen." *But you also stomp over dead bodies*—German for *you're a cutthroat too.* "I refuse to feel sorry for you. You were fine with the whole shitshow till your crew turned on you, till they came after your assets." She prodded An'qwenique. "It's been more than twenty minutes."

"Crap!" An'qwenique should have jabbed Ralph again after *fifteen* minutes, not *twenty.* "Please wake up," she whispered, and pressed a second autoinjector against his thigh. He flinched, surfing the edge of consciousness. Indeed, it felt as if she, Ralph, and the entire sundial gang hovered at the border between dreaming and waking, confusion and clarity.

She gazed a moment in each person's bleary face, ending at Oona: black masks over bright eyes, floppy ears alert. She licked her chops, happy about Ralph getting better, about the big red wagon, about everything.

"Oona is at home in everyone's version of reality," An'qwenique murmured. "Probably why she knows her way around these parts." Paula's entangled multiverse wasn't just a metaphor to Oona. She had the map.

Zsuzsu snatched the librarian's empty water bottle and the snake kid's sunglasses from a purple chokeberry bush. She waved at Oona, who leapt out of the wagon and sniffed eagerly. Zsuzsu kissed the dog's nose. "Bring Belle and Gwen back quick, so we don't lose our minds and start eating each other." The dog dashed into the woods. Several tourists grumbled at Zsuzsu, murder in their eyes. She shrugged. "I suspect Oona was trained for search and rescue in another life."

An'qwenique glanced at the black straw broom and almost squealed. "We all have a bead on the Redemption Center. Even if it's a different place, a different *reality* for each of us: black ops site, steampunk rocket ship, haunted house, whatever. We're in a multiverse insisting it's one world." She blurted Paula's nerd nonsense before she lost faith. "The witch's trick is to break that spell, inadvertently or on purpose." Everyone glared at her then each other. Understanding was one or two scowls away.

The survivalist jabbed the CEO. "Admit it. She sounds reasonable."

"No." He scoffed. "We need objective analysis, a neutral weighing of evidence."

"Neutrality is a mirage. Bias is a way to navigate infinity. Cognition is always emotional." A rehearsed speech from Zsuzsu, who helped Cloud Heights counter disinformation. She tugged An'qwenique's pants. "How'd you figure that?"

"Paula. I've been—" Crazy in love with her for months without admitting it. "Our spring blizzard walk with Paula was near here. Remember? That hiker said, *Tune in to the weird. Make it strange*! to find what we need. Everybody's making it strange."

"That hiker gave us the neon blankets." Zsuzsu raked a hand through cinnamon curls, a power gesture from a fairy queen, an African witch, definite friend material.

"When did Blue and Oshun tell you about corruption charges?" An'qwenique asked.

"They didn't, so don't pout. Geek lord Azul told me. Allegedly, a corporate scumwad paid Blue to lose evidence. He and partner Oshun are tight, so she's also suspect." Zsuzsu sighed. "Azul claims to have found proof they were framed. I don't know what to believe. My big question: Why did this particular crowd show up at the Redemption Center today? What's your witch up to?"

An'qwenique shrugged. "Hard to know what's random, what's part of the pattern."

"Don't you hate that?" Zsuzsu smacked the rims on her wheels.

The tourists mumbled agreement.

"We're talking like the witch is real." An'qwenique suddenly felt as if she'd pulled several all-nighters. She'd been dizzy, muffled-brained, *wrong* since an angry voice and Oona's barking woke her out of a nightmare. She sank onto a portable chair from her bag, then jumped up. "Who put this together?" Shrugs and grunts but no one came clean. "While I was in the shed?"

"I didn't see a thing," Zsuzsu said. "Not who snatched your trail runners either." She gripped Ralph's hand and pressed it against her heart. An'qwenique marveled at Zsuzsu's public display of sentiment.

A purple-throated hummingbird with metallic blue/green wings and tail flitted by An'qwenique's nose. She startled at the Caribbean species breezing through New England. A green violet-ear from Central America hovered at her cheek. Her favorite birds to do on the VR rig. Tiny claws grasped a wisp of her hair. Violet-ears spent their lives in the air, rarely landing on vestigial feet except—"You can't build a nest with my hair. It will break apart on you. Go find a spiderweb, much sturdier."

OONA—*Go Everywhere, Just Come Back!*

Delighted to do search and rescue, Oona raced through whispering trees along the moon boardwalk. This path shrank to nothing during a new moon and was broadest when the moon was full. Oona's nose tingled with the aroma of fried plantains. She huffed, conflicted. The musician, magician, and clown had been in the witch's shed, briefly, a flicker of them, TODAY. Although, since An'qwenique arrived at the Center, YESTERDAY, TODAY, and TOMORROW were a muddle in Oona's nose. She ignored temporal confusion, waggled her butt, and yip-yapped. Her carnival crew had been eating plantains smothered in peanut sauce and having fun times with a dog friend, a frisky young male, RECENTLY.

Oona loved her new life and the friends she'd found, quite a lively pack including singer Charlize, who was probably never stepping out of that recycling bin. Losing a member of her new pack was awful. How would she leave Paula, Zsuzsu, the crows, Ralph, Melody, and the next-door mutt behind to head out with her carnival crew?

Oona snarled then whimpered, mad, sad, but also glad. This was the closest she'd come to finding her carnival family or to being found. Their trail was spotty, *neither here nor there*, and dead-ended at the marsh. Still, they left the wagon squeezed between the mulch and water cans for Oona to find! A reunion and a wagon trip could be SOON!

Oona had slept in that wagon—a dream shuttle—under the moon and stars while her crew snored in sleeping bags on the ground. During shows, the musician blew a wooden flute and the magician and clown wheeled Oona through the audience.

She *played dead* then jumped up to let someone squeeze her paw. She loved this game, especially when the whole audience *played dead* too and burst back to life singing. Oona was a sucker for a good tune, a real music hound.

The clown loved to pick sad or sick people from the audience for a special *follow your nose* ride. The musician sang a traveling song while the magician pulled the wagon with Oona and their special guest into a closet, dim back hall, or cloak room. In the dark, Oona jumped out to lead the way. *Follow your nose* was even better than *playing dead.* Crossing the border to another side was a surprise the first time, but then Oona got good. She crossed many borders to reach a waterfall, rocky beach, cloud forest, or a wind-swept desert.

An audience passenger could go anywhere in the wagon with her. They squealed and giggled the whole journey, but when their hearts kept time with a place, they got quiet and still, and Oona halted, thrilled. The musician always said, *Good vibes are contagious.* There was never enough time to investigate intriguing smells or strange new creatures. As soon as everyone's heartbeats were in sync (in the audience and on the road), the musician switched from voice and wooden flute to the cello. The clown sang a recent favorite to call them back to the front hall, lab, or bathroom, *Sing me a song that breaks the curse*, and the magician answered, *Plant a garden to save the Earth.*

What Oona never realized: staying away too long caused problems for people, discontinuities hard to correct or explain, and worst of all, a body might get stranded. Her carnival crew wasn't exactly sure how long was too long, so they tried to play it safe. On return, the sad or sick person smelled better, a fresh wind in their smile, a touch of the sea in their voice. The audience always went wild, stomping and cheering.

Oona wished the magician, clown, and musician were here right now. She was almost too distracted by their recent aromas in the witch's shed to track anyone else. Most dogs weren't big on deferred gratification. Something good right in front of their noses usually took precedence over fond memories or future possibilities. Oona wasn't most dogs—Who was?—and her carnival crew had trained her well. Yet without encouragement, she slipped toward a grab-the-now-and-let-tomorrow-take-care-of-itself life. Without regular reinforcement, she might forget who she meant to be.

Oona whined. She was a leader, ready to sacrifice her own moments, the food in her belly, the breath and blood in her body for the good of the pack. Whenever she stuck to a search, no matter what else she longed to do, that turned into the best times with the carnival crew, with everybody. And didn't Oona want the gang back together more than anything? She woofed relief. Because, maybe if she rescued the librarian and the kid, she'd find her family or they'd find her. The two searches were one.

You can go everywhere, the clown always said. *Just Come Back!*

Tracking Gwen and Belle was easy. They'd wandered in circles, not getting far, and they were very happy to see Oona. Her rescue problem was how to turn them in the right direction. Gwen smelled desperate. Skinny braids unraveled against her sweaty back. She flapped bony arms like the red-tailed hawks darting through treetops. She still carried the bad man's scent on her bloody raincoat.

Oona wanted to hunt him down and rip him apart. She growled at such an unsettling, novel desire. The bad man was worse than the raccoons who tried to eat Aretha the turtle, worse than the coyotes who went after the groundhog under Zsuzsu's porch and the bobcat who snuck into the barn to eat baby crows. The bad man acted like a good friend when he just wanted to eat somebody.

Belle stopped under an elderly oak tree. She hunched her shoulders and panted sour breath. A butterfly flailed in her hair. She was unaware of or ignored the creature. Oona paced between her and Gwen, tracking their ratchety energy. The oak tree was a good choice for a rest before they tromped back to the Center. The oak off-gassed comforting air and exchanged high-pitched chatter with distant trees. Oona liked this tree song, but couldn't tell if Belle or Gwen tuned in to the good scents or music.

"You can't give me anything specific about him?" Belle pleaded.

"I'm in such deep shit." Gwen clutched Belle's arm. "Don't tell on me."

Belle pulled away. "How can you ask me that?"

Gwen stumbled around, sad, talking fast—a fuzzy jumble of words, spit, and high anxiety. She drifted the wrong direction toward the hemlocks.

"Willing or unwilling, you're an accomplice." Belle undid her topknot and shook out her hair. The butterfly escaped. "We're talking murder. Fuck! *Don't tell on me . . .*" Oona had heard these last few words many times. Belle never let her roam the stacks of dusty books, but in the mushroom glass house behind the library, they often danced together. Belle snuck Oona watermelon or cheese or popcorn and said, *Don't tell on me.* A happy tone and good-time scents, not like right now.

"Just till we rescue Lance," Gwen pleaded.

Belle moaned. "How are we supposed to *rescue Lance*?" Oona woofed. She wanted to *rescue Lance* too. People were always losing each other. She'd hunt for Lance later. Two searches at once was her limit. "You said Dragon Dude killed Melody too."

"Right."

Belle sputtered. "See, I know this creep, how he moves, a dancer, an athlete. He stomps around the library, so full of himself. He barged through a STAFF ONLY door and spied on me this morning in the greenhouse, when I was collecting mushrooms. Sunglasses, purple scarf, skeleton suit, and a dragon coat on top, but I recognized him." She narrowed her eyes. "Last week, he crashed a Change Gang meeting, sneering: *Isabelle Shamiram Roberts, I bet there's a tall tale for that name.* I said, *There's a story for every name. I'm not telling you my story till I know you better.* I didn't ask his name. An awful show-off, why encourage him?" She strangled a shriek and staggered the wrong direction. Oona blocked her. "He knows all about me." A wheeze turned into a cough.

"Everybody knows you," Gwen said. "You're a local hero."

"You must remember something that can help us locate him. Any detail?"

"He blindfolds me, but," Gwen spoke slowly, "he plays Nicki Minaj and old-school gangsta rap way too loud and drives in circles, from our first trip. Getting out of the car I hear nothing. A nowhere place, it smells swampy and like chemicals. It's a storage unit or some shit. Maybe two connected units. He takes off the blindfold after I'm inside with Lance, who is going bat booby.

"The kid curls up in my lap. He's ten but so scared, he pees himself. I'm scared too. I tell Lance lies about what Dragon Dude and I do outside. But he knows whatever we're up to, it's awful. Every time I leave, he freaks out, like I'm never coming back. He throws granola around the twenty-by-twenty cell. I have to clean it up, every day. And . . . And I never know if I'm coming back either."

"That's, that's . . . horrible."

Gwen growled, sounding tough but smelling freaked out. "For lunch and dinner, Dragon Dude shoves in pizza, french fries, candy bars, and diet soda. I hate diet. No better than sugar sodas. Paula says we're guzzling carbonated slave labor, like gag me. Months, the same nasty food and my stomach's always a mess.

"He gives us stupid games and an old TV. No Wi-Fi or phones, *they rot your brains anyhow.* He brought us a stationary bike and tons of books. We're reading demons! Dragon Dude quizzes us—bio, math, music, English, history—all the meanest teachers in one. Freaky. I act tough for Lance. I tell him some King Arthur fanfic and Pukwudgie tales Grandpa told me, then we act out the good parts. We're too scared to figure an escape."

"Of course." Belle reached for Gwen, who shied away. Belle sank down in springy hemlock needles. "Sorry," she murmured. "Nothing feels real. I can't think." Oona set her head on Belle's shoulder and whimpered. "Why expose himself to me?"

Gwen shrugged and stomped around them. Oona licked Belle's face. She tasted funny recently. Before, whenever Oona visited her at the library, Belle tasted calm, even spread calm to other people. Like the guy screaming and peeing in the library foyer. She sang soothing sounds, and he quieted down. She gave him a bucket, and he mopped the stairs. During a Friday-afternoon open mike, the woman who lived under the bridge walked out of the fourth-floor window and teetertottered on a ledge. Belle sat on that ledge laughing with her while the rest of the audience trembled. Eventually they both came inside, talking and almost singing.

"Stop pacing." Belle jumped up and grabbed Gwen. "You're making me dizzy."

"Not my fault," Gwen snapped. "You're tripping your brains out."

"Yeah, well, a forest labyrinth, a haunted house, and now this kidnapping/murder mess—not exactly the trip I had in mind."

"Plans don't always work out." Gwen sniffled and yanked ratty braids.

She and Belle were both terrified, yet Oona smelled nothing dangerous nearby. Beavers scurried through mud by the marsh; deer feasted on crabapples; an Eastern coyote had a belly full of blueberries and took a nap in a rock cave. Safe every direction.

"Lance and I wanted to run away from the foster jerks. Grandpa said that was a stupid idea. *Worse folks out there than your foster parents*. See, I didn't want to get in Dragon Dude's BMW. I mean, a freak dressed up like a Day of the Dead skeleton in February?" Gwen gulped. "Lance jumped in the back seat and wouldn't come out, so I had to hop in too." She unwrapped a candy bar, chomped a piece then offered Oona a bite. Chocolate, on the poison list—food never to eat even if tempted. Oona hated being tempted. This day had been too sad and too long. In fact today was already tomorrow in her tummy. She licked her chops, famished again. Eyeing the poison food, she panted out some heat and looked up at Belle for help.

"Whoa. No. Don't give her that." Belle snatched Gwen's hand from Oona's nose. "Chocolate is toxic for dogs. It can be lethal."

"Sorry." Gwen stuffed the rest of the giant bar in her mouth, crying and gagging. She probably shouldn't eat chocolate either.

"Sorry too. I've not been myself recently," Belle said. "So what're we doing?"

"You asking me?" Gwen's (and Belle's) stomach rumbled. The Center had plenty of safe food. They should stop yapping at each other and start walking back. The foyer was cool and dry with a comfy couch. People needed less sleep than dogs, but they could take their time eating while Oona napped. She butted Belle, who took a few steps the right direction.

"I can't go back." Gwen was ready to run down the trail to a dead end. Oona blocked her, snarling.

"Oona is right. Bless her! That direction goes nowhere. Believe me. We have to return to the Center. The tourists need her to lead them out of this labyrinth. So do we."

"You don't understand." Gwen hissed like a snake. "I can't go back to *him*."

"No way! We'll go to the police."

"He promised to kill Lance if I do that. He said he'd know if I told anybody."

"An old trick. How would he know? Is he a cop? He's a liar."

"No. He has an inside track. Maybe he killed Lance already, 'cause I disappeared."

"So you might as well turn yourself in. He's going to kill you both eventually." Belle sighed. "Sorry. But it's the truth, the horrible truth."

"I try to stay, uhm, useful. I drove his fuckin' Ford wreck, and he made me turn on a nasty torture machine. They'll throw me in jail." Gwen stumbled over a boulder. "I did warn that rich woman rocking camo silk who charged in here after Ralph—"

"An'qwenique Robinson. Paula wants her to join the Change Gang."

Gwen smacked the boulder. "He tortured her neighbor to death, then dumped the body in the Cloud Heights parking lot. I was behind the wheel, an accomplice. He pointed that out too. If he's holding Lance hostage, am I really an accomplice?"

"I'm sorry I said that. Accomplice is the wrong word. Dragon Dude likes—"

"Doing awful shit in front of me." Gwen almost fell. Oona braced her.

Belle pawed her face. "I saw him with Blue Rosenthal and Oshun Jackson."

Oona knew the people who went with those names. They chatted Paula up at Haven Bagels and drove a car with painful sirens.

"Blue who?" Gwen frowned and rubbed Oona's head.

"Blue and Oshun are nobody, some friends," Belle said quickly.

"I flirted with Dragon Dude, but I never planned to get in that BMW." Gwen staggered away from Oona. "Lance thought I wanted to. He jumped in the car to help out." She let the oak tree hold her up. "I am so fucked! Everyone will say it's my fault."

"No way."

"You don't understand!" Gwen shrieked. Oona flinched and Belle bit her lip as Gwen spewed. "My stepfather wanted a son, not a daughter. After Grandpa went to the stupid nursing home, step-asshole kicked me out. My foster parents hate me too. I stole three hundred bucks from them, for me and Lance on the run and for a Pukwudgie tattoo." Gwen pulled down her pants and displayed a recent wound on a bony hip. Oona wanted to lick it. "The foster jerks will say I wanted to drive the getaway car. They'll blame me for Melody, Charlize G, and Lance, and they hated him too."

"Charlize Giddens, the singer, that's who he killed?" Belle shuddered. She and Gwen needed a ride in the go-anywhere wagon to their heartbeat place. The wind shifted, and Oona caught a familiar odor. She tugged Belle's sleeves. "What?" Belle snapped, as if Oona had stepped on her tail or eaten her bowl of treats. Like most humans, she didn't taste what rode the breeze. Oona ran down the boardwalk toward Melody's scent in the doll's eye patch.

"Where are you going? Oh my god!" Belle pointed. "Ralph said Oona found Melody's dumbek in a poison patch."

"I'll get it." Gwen darted past Belle right behind Oona, a fast runner like Ralph. She plunged into the doll's eyes, protected from sharp leaves by long sleeves and pants. She slung the dumbek across her back and handed the double bell to Belle.

"*Weave me a way that leads to why*," Belle pressed the bell to her bosom. "Did Dragon Dude hide these instruments here?"

"He locks trophies in a closet by the toilet somewhere." Gwen gulped breath. "Can I tell you something weird?" Belle nodded and Gwen sank onto a stump, relieved. "In the parking lot, dude was two feet from my nose, but didn't *see* where I went. He couldn't get *in here*, wherever *here* is." She held up a fanny pack that reeked of the bad man.

"His burglar tools fell in the bushes. I nabbed the pack and scooted away. He reached for them, clutched air, and freaked. His electric voice got muffled, like he was a faint signal, a ghost of himself. I kept backing the fuck up, and the parking lot vanished or turned into sumac trees. Nowhere I'd been before, but forget going back through the portal or whatever. I sat there, thinking I was going bat booby, till Oona bounded in, like no big deal. She led me to the sundial."

"Eight Change Gangers started this morning's hike, only six ended up lost at the Center." Belle blinked and sighed. "Some people can't go everywhere."

"You mean to a different dimension?"

"I'm not sure. Time and space are wild in these woods, but we can manage with Oona, I think. That's what we have on Dragon Dude."

"Really?" Gwen twirled around, muttering and hissing. Oona jumped up and nipped at her braids, ready to move too.

"Plus evidence!" Belle pointed at the bad man's pack. "Let's not worry. Worry is a waste. An old bat on the bus told me that. She's right. We'll figure something out."

Gwen stiffened. "No. If I run or hide, even in another dimension, Dragon Dude says he'll torture Lance to death. He could be doing that right now. My fault."

Belle hugged Gwen. The kid leaned down to the tiny woman and sobbed in her poufy hair. Oona whined too. "He won't kill Lance yet. He needs him to reel you in." Belle wiped Gwen's cheeks. "What a genius move, nabbing his pack. He needs you and these tools to get away with murder."

"You're just saying that."

Belle poked Gwen. "Why haven't you made a break for it before?"

"Lance. You're right." Gwen held up the bad man's pack. "You think he'd trade Lance for the burglar works?" Oona snatched it and dashed across the marsh toward the Center. "No! Fuck! Give that back!" Oona looked back as Gwen sank to the ground.

Belle chased after Oona, pumping short legs and clanging Melody's bell. Oona slowed to let her catch up, a familiar game. Gwen groused but jumped up and sprinted toward them. The drum banged her ribs, how Melody sounded in a bad mood. Someone at the Center played cello—long, sustained notes, the *come back* song. The musician? The Center was upwind and Oona couldn't smell for sure. She bounced on her toes, hopeful. Even if a stranger was playing, the familiar music made each step easier. Oona howled joy. No matter what, she planned to explore the gothic mansion for a trail to her carnival crew. Heavy storms might have dulled their scents outside, but inside was a different story.

PAULA—*The Cracks*

In the distance, a dog barked and one of An'qwenique's fancy neighbors played cello, a call-and-response duet. Why so mad at fickle Kitty? Paula jerked out of the echo chamber of outrage and back to An'qwenique's front hall. Tentacles from the Algerian ivy were crawling everywhere, trying to take over the entryway. One sucker snagged her hair. She pulled it loose with too much force and broke off a lengthy vine. "Sorry."

Her third violent fantasy today. Kitty was a minor league wastrel, a bit player in Environmental Armageddon. Why so jealous, actually. Paula never let herself want much. Her secret desire for adventure and romance with An'qwenique was dangerous. Violent outbursts were yesterday's Paula. Today-and-tomorrow's Paula was Peace Path all the way, Harriet and Jigonhsasee! No *blood in her mouth.*

The ancient phone machine blared. A torture device. The police were leaving a second message, almost unintelligible. Detectives yelled on top of each other, as if loud would conjure An'qwenique back from wherever she'd gone, from beyond their technological reach. How dare Ms. Robinson refuse instant access. The situation was life-and-death urgent. They hung up in the middle of a bass, voice-of-authority rant about tracking suspects while the trail was hot, fresh.

Paula ground her teeth, a bad habit. The perp had the jump on them all, a very clever fellow, and not working solo. The police might miss the accomplice clues: an unwilling partner or someone suffering stage fright had tiptoed around the deed down to the street. They were careful of wildflowers, side-stepped anthills, and probably drove the getaway car while the perp subdued Charlize. Risky working with an uncommitted or skittish sidekick, so why do it? What held this duo together?

Electric insight jolted Paula. Blue and Oshun fought about Melody's crime scene being a horror science experiment or a terror art exhibition. In either case, the perp was a performance artist. The unwilling partner/protégé was a live audience providing immediate gratification. The horror and admiration of a wider, after-the-fact audience was cheese on that burger.

Paula forced herself to call up the scene. The St. B arrived too late to stop the perp and reluctant sidekick from dragging Charlize away. Whenever thugs went after Paula, the big furball turned into a fanged demon and chased them off. She must have bounded onto the esplanade as the perp stuffed Charlize into the car and the sidekick sped away. The St. B tracked them with that relentless nose and got caught doing magic (alien science?) with Ralph (or other burly Black man) on the Cloud Heights security cameras. Paula shivered. This perp liked doing it for the cameras.

He and/or the disinfo-teers leaked crime scene footage, not the cops. Detectives were probably scrambling to keep a lid on the investigation. The perp hoped to frame Ralph, go viral, and collect a million followers, anonymously. Internet trolls would help him locate the St. B. He'd kill the dog on camera, then hunt other bold women, living out loud, making up their own rules, like Charlize and Melody. Soulful music and a this-is-my-universe attitude were what they had in common. If he was jealous, Paula understood that. At least An'qwenique wasn't his type. So far.

"Wait." Paula reined in her runaway imagination. "How can you know all that?"

She needed access to the videos and Triple-E's February journal plus the June book with Melody's celebration of life. Stupid not to set up a rendezvous with Triple-E today. Tomorrow on the bus might be too late. Paula had to get her head straight. Each minute wasted checking herself (jealous of Kitty, really?)

or searching the wrong direction meant he/they had a better chance of getting away with murder again.

Paula had to persuade the police to take her intel seriously. Short of that, she should have detectives stumble over clues and do the profiling themselves. If they felt on top of her, the perp, and the dog, they'd be more effective. She also had to concoct a good dog story, not: *The St. Berdoodle regularly slipped out of our world/dimension/universe to other realms then slipped back*. The police didn't want to believe in extra dimensions, alien science, or canine wizards. (Did Paula? Did the perp?) If she presented a plausible, non SF and F fabrication to (almost) explain *unreal* phenomena, the police and the Feds (Were they really involved?) might let the St. B slide under the radar and get away with miracles in secret.

A scary thought: A good dog story, even if not quite true, would make Paula feel better too. Big Problem: She was terrible at lies, at fictions period. An'qwenique was the story spinner, tall-tale teller, griot. She was classy and smart and knew the perfect wise word, metaphor, snark to dish out. Plus, she always looked good and smelled nice. People took her seriously, respected what she had to say, including the police.

Paula smelled like Dr. Bronner's soap, baking soda, and vinegar. Her hands were wrinkly, her nails jagged. Her afro was going wild, and after the hailstorm, she was a shoeless, raggedy mess. Worst of all, she couldn't help blurting her nerd nonsense. Except for batty losers like Upstairs Karl and Triple-E, men and women looked right through Paula. Nobody took her big booty, thunder thighs, and muscular arms seriously. People chatted her up on the way to someone better.

Debonair Ralph was chasing Zsuzsu, dapper Duke wanted to get next to Belle, and silver fox Azul had the hots for An'qwenique. Dimples was the exception that proved the rule. Who knew what that hunky white boy was after? Worse, An'qwenique might be doing authentic content research for a *Great Escape* podcast on the underclass. Ms. Robinson sweetened the deal with big tips and fancy tea in the gazebo. Paula winced at this possibility as the phone rang. Insistent yet calm, Detective Blue Rosenthal needed to talk to An'qwenique ASAP. Didn't everyone?

"We're next door for god's sake," Oshun Jackson yelled. "We can just walk over."

"We did that already," somebody complained, "nobody home." They hung up.

Blue and Oshun had been reinstated! So sipping teas together at the Haven meant they were back on the job. Paula shrugged off nasty suspicions about middle-class white folks getting away with anything, because Blue and Oshun were decent if flawed people and they would take her intel seriously. She just needed a good dog story.

Sudden darkness made her jump. Inky clouds raced across the sun. Through the living room windows, she spied police cars parked around Tomás's and Charlize's house. She vaguely remembered lights flashing when she first arrived. The yellow tape marking off the crime scene broke loose, smacked the cop cars on their butts, and whirled away on the storm wind. Duke's whole bus route was the crime scene anyhow. Everyone was involved.

The phone shrieked again. Paula grabbed the lapis lazuli paperweight, ready to smash the damn thing. Tomás's raw voice stopped her. "He made her suffer." Tomás whispered a river of sorrow in Spanish, ending with, "Mi vida." Paula should pick up. Coward. Tomás continued, "There was more footage. The shithead thought she was flailing, but my lady switched on the *indoor* cameras and signed *te amo*."

Paula made a fist, lifted her pinkie, then her pointer and thumb to sign *te amo*.

"She also signed *gym rat*." Tomás choked. "That can't be Ralph Carter."

"Not a rat," Paula replied out loud. "Ralph's more of an otter or a hawk, and he walks steady." She refused to believe

Ralph was the killer, because, well, he took her seriously. They only talked about Zsuzsu a few times, when Paula put marmalade on a soft pretzel and honey in mint tea. They joked about fierce German ladies—like Marmalade Dietrich, or Marlene. Paula and Ralph were definitely friends. They'd shared painful secrets even. Both were on the Peace Path, **DUMPING IT ALL** and **DOING BETTER**. If Ralph was the killer, Paula would be shaken to the core.

"Ralph fits the description outside, not inside." Tomás agreed with Paula. "Charlize never let me call animal control. That dog loved my lady and would never make friends with the man who—"

"Stop!" Blue shouted. "We don't know who's listening." The phone disconnected.

Ralph and Upstairs Karl had talked to Paula about gym rats. Nothing specific, stupid stunts they pulled, buying the same fanny packs and watermelon-sherbet shoes for big feet on sale. Last year Ralph broke his nose and celebrity Tomás crunched a finger, showing off. After that, Tomás was an honorary gym rat. He bought the sherbet shoes. So did College Bro #42, and probably Dimples, Big Foot, and the whole gym. Perfect cover for the perp. Perhaps Charlize wasn't fingering anybody, just saying she loved her gym rat. Paula swallowed a curse. **Pump It Up! Be The Best You!** was either a dead end or a starting point. Triple-E nailed it: *For every clue, many possible stories.*

"Yeah, and infinity has no center." Paula's head throbbed. Thoughts struggled to rocket out of a gravity well, but hefty g's of force flattened them against her skull.

Filtered light from the high windows shimmered, the same weird glow as when she arrived—like a portal to another dimension opening again? The portal notion had been random musing as she walked to the front door and the light was strange, but right now . . . She tried to blink the air clear and stay on her old, trusty map. That didn't work.

She stumbled away from the sideboard into an empty recycling bin—not empty. An African puppet/mask stood in the corner, what An'qwenique called Iyami Aje, a wise woman wielding elemental power. This figure had erect breasts, purple bug eyes, and a riot of red-orange hair. Hummingbirds (An'qwenique's favorites) hovered above a narrow headband, bobbing up and down on tiny golden springs. She wore a bracelet of gears. Goggles hung around her neck, a steampunk necklace. The Aje clawed at the rim of the bin, as if scrambling to escape the plastic wasteland.

"I was on high alert for clues. You weren't there when I came in. I'm sure of it." Paula wasn't sure. She could bullshit herself later, when this was an outrageous memory she'd survived, like that hike through a May blizzard. "Who are you? Where do you come from? What are you doing in there?" A wide mouth with full lips was shaped into what might have been a scream. Ditching caution, Paula bent down close to the Aje's face. "Tell me what's going on?"

Paula's ears rang, a high-pitched squeal then static. This sort of phantom noise was happening more and more. She worried about the tiny sensor hairs in her ears getting smacked down by all the loud in the world. Instead of fading like usual, this static turned into a creepy feeling that An'qwenique was here, behind her back or in the corner of her eye.

Paula whirled and caught a ghostly figure flickering at the top of the stairs, singing a familiar tune but coming in faint. Hard to say if it was An'qwenique, too little to go on, although, no, the afro cloudburst was a dead giveaway. The stairs looked wrong—from a different house?

Paula wobbled on achy feet and gave in to panic. Who could blame her? She blinked and lost the signal. A white curtain in the landing window fluttered in air conditioning, but no, she hadn't mistaken gauzy fabric for a ghost. Outside, the sky was an unsettling, dark shimmer, a tornado brewing.

Paula turned to the puppet mask. "An'qwenique needs my help, right?"

The Aje had managed to climb halfway up the smooth blue plastic.

"Ms. Oblivious is lost somewhere. Perhaps where you come from. Where the St. B goes." Paula's wild thoughts had reached escape velocity. Nothing to do but test the insights. "I have to make it weird to find her, don't I? Like that blizzard hike."

She plucked the witchy puppet out of the bin. No electric jolt—cozy felt and velvet, smooth wood, and a fresh, walk-in-the-trees smell. She set the Aje on the sideboard next to the lapis lazuli paperweight. "Better?" The same face looked like a triumphant grin now. The Aje clutched a broken strand of beads in a velvet fist. A patch of felt hair was missing from her neckline. Paula had no idea what to make of these details.

"Why can't there be one freaky mystery at a time? Solve that then on to the next, like serial monogamy." She was whining. She rarely let herself do that. "So what now?"

Demanding help of elemental spirits without being generous first could backfire. This was true all over the world. Trusting tricksters was dodgy, even after plying them with gifts. They always had their own agendas. Paula looked around for worthy offerings, a meaningful sacrifice.

She opened up the envelope An'qwenique decorated with hearts, smiley faces, and hummingbirds to make an altar under the Aje's belly and breasts. On the hearts she set a clutch of Algerian ivy blossoms from the branch she broke. That plant bloomed almost never. She added the lapis lazuli paperweight and her midmorning nut-and-dried-fruit snack. No appetite anyhow. A respectful offering, even if she didn't quite believe. The Aje's eyes bulged, bright and fluorescent, nothing else.

"What am I doing?" Paula backed away from her offering. "No time for this."

Time was nobody's friend today. Luckily, the killer was also scrambling to regroup. The dog had thrown a wrench in his carefully crafted plans. The St. B would be at the Haven tonight. Paula had till then to find An'qwenique. Together, the terrific trio might be able to solve the crime. Holding forth on the *Great Escape* podcast, Ms. Investigative Journalist insisted the mind was a community joint, not confined to our skulls, but networked to the entire universe. *Never alone, trust that.*

Paula shrugged off doubt as lightning streaked the dark sky—backlighting for a messy spiderweb undulating between the window jamb and the sill. Spiders loved fresh air. You found them where there were drafts: cracks in the walls, windows, or the foundation. A speckled arachnid raced along a thread from the edge to the center, a raggedy crossroads. Chasing vibrations, it disappeared into the shadows.

Paula had to search the house again, look in weird places where you wouldn't expect a person to be. "I have to find the cracks between here and somewhere else. Right?"

Extending her mind with spiders, puppets, drafty old buildings, or anything available was exhilarating, even if later she'd worry about going bat booby—Gwen's phrase. Paula's breath hitched. Gwen would understand about feeding the tricksters. The kid planned to tattoo a Pukwudgie on her hip.

Paula whispered thanks to the Aje, spider, and Gwen, wherever she was, hopefully alive and well with Lance—alive at least. She ran upstairs to search the attic again. On the tip of her tongue, she tasted the tune ghost An'qwenique was singing, and wild ideas filled her mind. Since the stupid loans were paid off, she'd soon have enough extra cash for the criminal justice and detective courses at the community college. Why not hone/refine her superpowers? Despite a bad AI profile and other skeletons in her closet (She beat up a Mercedes-Benz, not a person!), somebody might eventually hire her to do police work.

"Who you kidding?" She knew better than to want anything amazing from such a messed-up world. Still the detective prospect thrilled her, almost but not quite as much as the hope of finding An'qwenique in the chimney crawlspace or the sweetgrass laundry basket from the Georgia Sea Islands that was never sullied with dirty clothes.

AN'QWENIQUE—*Duck and/or Rabbit*

Ralph's temperature was normal, his heartbeat like a djembe drum, and both thighs normal-sized. He just wouldn't wake up. The med techs told An'qwenique, *Don't sweat this.* Still she worried he was stuck in a coma, *never* waking up, because of her. They were all stuck, but that couldn't be her fault, right? Acting chill, she put tiny baskets of nuts, beads, feathers, and seeds wherever Zsuzsu pointed: under the doll's eye bushes, in the roots of a mulberry tree, on the stone steps to the big house. Something to do besides freak out while waiting for Oona and company to return.

"Who am I to rank on magical thinking?" Zsuzsu confessed to doing two offerings to honor the spirits of the forest every Sunday without fail. She almost forgot the second one today. Guinevere mentioning Pukwudgies jolted her on track. One offering was to ensure a good visit, another was for a safe return. No courting disaster. An'qwenique hid shock at this serious spiritual streak in Zsuzsu, because, well, wasn't everyone full of surprises? Paula would love this ritual. According to her, acting humble, appreciating the tumult, chaos, and creativity of the cosmos was good for the mind and body.

In love with Paula, what's that about?

An'qwenique ignored the nightmare voice and set a basket at the edge of the moon boardwalk. The tourist, immigrant, or errant hummingbirds dive-bombed her afro-puff. Aggressive little fiends. She tried to ignore them too. Fingers of chilly fog itched her bare arms and chased the fluorescent creatures into the witch's shed.

Are you really doing English costume drama/romance slop with Paula? In camouflage silk?

An'qwenique cringed. Paula was the most observant person she'd ever met. It was spooky how well Paula read people from almost nothing. Did Paula suspect or know that An'qwenique had fallen hard for her? Pining for an unattainable crush was such a cliché. Wasn't An'qwenique better than that, better than average, better than most people? She snickered at herself. What did "better than most people" even mean?

The daughter, granddaughter, and great-granddaughter of strivers, nobody worked harder. A perfect record till today, and followers extolled her humor and brilliance on the *Great Escape* podcast. Yet her family and love relationships were crap. Another cliché. Egged on by Mom and Dad, she and Big Bro picked at each other. Plus she had no real friends.

Charlize claimed they were besties, a social media mirage. Her inner posse used avatars online and never did live sessions. She wouldn't recognize them face-to-face. She and Kitty had nada in common, like her last two girlfriends. Geek lord Azul was cool, but one-way lust might hamper friendship. One-way lust might ruin her and Paula. What would Ms. SuperNerd think of the Redemption Center?

An image of Paula poking around, running thought experiments, and collecting clues made her chuckle, made her want to kiss Paula's sweet-berry lips and dance barefoot on the boardwalk. Paula seemed like the kind of woman who could stomp up a storm! The Mi'kmaq birchbark canoe glided through An'qwenique's mind. She and Paula paddled furiously in sync. It was after a storm, and the mountain lake was a white-water deluge, carrying them toward . . . A raging waterfall?

You're terrible at romance, babe.

"Fuck!" An'qwenique almost spilled the final spirit offering in the gravel.

"Watch it." Zsuzsu chastised her. "The offerings are about

setting your mind right! About getting back to what you really want."

"Really want?" Besides recording more *Great Escape* podcasts, An'qwenique wanted to join the Change Gang and do actual good in the world. She'd like to break up with Kitty live. She'd love to make peace with her family and help older brother with *BIG TROUBLE*. But if they couldn't find a way back home, her biggest regret, her tragic regret would be never doing gumbo-yaya in the gazebo with Paula again. No matter how their romance/drama turned out, that's what she wanted. Was that love?

An'qwenique's hand trembled as she set the last offering where the sundial gnomon plunged into gravel. Static electricity made her skin crawl. She scurried back to the gothic mansion. Tourists shook their heads at her, slack-jawed. Not fighting each other was a triumph, yet no denying the horror special effects: they looked as gray, drained, and insubstantial as she felt. The red tie and pool-blue buzz cuts had gone sooty. The survivalist and her ginormous go-bag were little more than moon shadow. The survivalist nailed it. Stumbling around the Center too long, a person might slip out of sync with their previous life, become ghost, zombie, or some shadow figure.

An'qwenique huffed at dire thoughts. Mapping a route back to your old self was a tricky prospect. A map to *who you were going to be before a rude, cataclysmic interruption* might be impossible. She was thinking metaphorically, not literally, but—*How much difference, really?* What she didn't realize: Their prolonged presence at the Center meant things leaked across the borders or got stranded, neither here nor anywhere. What she knew for sure: This crew was nearing a point of no return, exactly what the CEO feared. *Leave soon or never leave.* She gulped a breath of wildfire smoke and marsh gas that made her throat itch. All she needed was an allergy attack.

"Fuckin' A!" The med techs cursed alien overlords for abandoning them to a cruel fate. An'qwenique snorted irritation at the aliens too. The gnomon spit an electric bolt at a lightning rod on the mansion's roof. Dragon weathervanes spun into a blur.

Suddenly An'qwenique wobbled on the deck of an otherworldly vessel that had crash-landed by the marsh. The command module was cleverly disguised as the Redemption Center. The wheelchair ramp was a gangplank onto a ghostly space-galleon. Porches and turrets were shuttles and rocket modules. Boulders, sheds, and the gnomon were part of the navigation system. Umbrellas shading picnic tables were dials for life support. The tourists wobbled and sputtered, also in an extra-dimensional space opera or some weird reality, but too whupped for awe.

"Fuckin' A is right!" An'qwenique shouted. The alien ship phased again into the haunted house, but only for a blink, then the rocket modules came roaring back. They rattled and flashed as if gearing for takeoff. An'qwenique's thundering heart drowned out the engines, and the haunted house reasserted itself. Lights glimmered in every window. Ghostly curtains flailed against broken glass, getting ripped to tatters.

Zsuzsu rolled close, effervescent green and cucumber cool. "Ralph is doing great, but you look terrible, like someone drank half your blood. You OK?"

"Not really." An'qwenique scowled at the creepy house, daring it to shift again. "Did you feel that? *See* that?"

"What? The heat lightning? That happens here a lot."

"No," An'qwenique grumbled. "The back and forth and back and forth." Wobbly tourists gaped at her. They'd definitely seen something odd, but were too zombified to yell at Zsuzsu. "Everyone picked it up! You had to notice."

Zsuzsu sighed. "The Redemption Center, das ist nicht dein Bier, oder?" Literally: *This is not your beer, huh?*

"Not my beer at all," An'qwenique muttered. "It stopped flipflopping now."

"Well, that's good then." Zsuzsu was truly unfazed. Was it just heat lightning?

"The Center went from haunted house to steampunk spaceship, like from the rabbit to the duck in that famous optical illusion." This sounded random, but was the best An'qwenique could do. "The rabbit's ears are the duck's bill. One head, but a different face in opposite directions. They have the same eye. One eye between them."

Zsuzsu smirked at this lame explanation, however her eyes darted about as if searching a file of images. She glowered at the house, resisting the weird, or girlfriend didn't fucking mind: Rabbit and Duck! After all, in the May blizzard, it was Zsuzsu who followed tree song and guided them home. And now, instead of zombie gray, she was iridescent greens and cinnamon sparkle. How was she managing that?

"Wait." Zsuzsu nodded slowly. "I know what you mean. A flipflop thing happens sometimes at twilight, magic hours . . . I don't always believe it later or even remember."

"You and Oona come every week. Maybe you're immune."

"To what?" Zsuzsu was baffled.

"The chems in the mist, alien static from the gnomon, angry tree ghosts. I don't know, the Pukwudgies who eat spirit offerings? You aren't grayed out or stressing."

"Überhaupt nicht." *Not at all.* Zsuzsu scanned the zombie tourists. "They *are* looking dull. But trust me. Oona is on her way." Zsuzsu glanced at Ralph, love for sure. "I've only met one person as reliable as the St. Berdoodle. Isn't that pathetic?"

"No." An'qwenique thought of Paula.

Zsuzsu leaned out of her chair. "The house shape-shifting, that's connected to Paula's multiverse thing, right?" The tourists held their breath, waiting for an answer.

"Well . . ." What could An'qwenique say? "I don't know. My nerves are shot."

"Don't walk this back. Trust yourself and Paula." Zsuzsu grinned. "I hear Oona."

An'qwenique's ears were full of static, zero dog noises. "You do?"

"A rumble she does, when she's happy, when she has a whiff of something good." Zsuzsu barked commands at everyone. "You all are wasting daylight, moping around, losing hope. Let's not defeat ourselves. Let's be ready to boogie on out of here when Belle returns." Throwback slang, like An'qwenique's Wild Bunch neighbors. OK, fifty-something Zsuzsu was serious friend material in or out of conservative-bitch lane.

The med techs, grateful for some good thing to do, pulled the wagon up the ramp to the porch. Lifting Ralph was a trick. The survivalist and mandolin player helped. Gently, they set him into the bed on two super blankets. Zsuzsu covered him with the third. As they pulled the wagon down the ramp to the boardwalk, Ralph's neon orange/pink sneakers glowed in the fog. An'qwenique gasped. The dragon cosplay dude, up to no good in her wildflowers, wore the same shoes. More than a coincidence.

Oona barked, loud and clear, coming their direction. "What'd I tell you?" Zsuzsu beamed as everyone cheered. "That's my girl."

The mandolin player gathered spaced-out Change Gangers as Zsuzsu wheeled over to the CEO. He sulked on a boulder. She plucked his jacket from the gravel and thrust it in his face. "Nobody left behind, not even you." He grumbled, took the jacket, and joined the others. Zsuzsu rolled her eyes and turned to An'qwenique. "I'm glad you and Belle got lost today." She looked vulnerable again. "Not just for Ralph's sake."

"Friends then." An'qwenique shivered, thrilled and vulnerable too. "Let's meet at the Haven next time, or Crossroads for dinner."

"Is that a threat?"

"A promise." An'qwenique sneezed and fell against the boulder by the steps.

"Gesundheit." Zsuzsu shoved the portable chair at her butt. "Sit. While we wait."

"I'm fine," An'qwenique lied, but sat anyhow. Song lyrics for Melody's anthem were carved on the boulder's face. She traced the words. Incipient hives deflated, her throat opened, and her stomach relaxed. "This song guided me here."

"I'm the only one who doesn't know Melody's community ditty by heart."

"Did Melody come to the Redemption Center?"

"She told me about this place or I told her. I forget which. I don't think she wrote the music or the lyrics. But I remember this." Zsuzsu signed the first line. An'qwenique's fingers echoed her: *Draw me a map that sets us free.* A bell and dumbek sounded from the woods, as if they'd conjured Melody's ghost. Cello music drifted from the circular attic window. The mandolin player plucked counterpoint.

"Who's playing cello up there?" An'qwenique murmured.

Zsuzsu frowned at frayed curtains caught on broken glass. "Has someone been in the attic all along?"

PAULA—*Music from Another Dimension*

Paula had checked An'qwenique's elegant study twice. This third time, she tripped on the colorful ellipse of designer silks that graced the bamboo floor. The fancy rag rug cushioned her landing on a bad knee. The Iyami Aje slipped from her grasp and smirked. A lot of attitude for a puppet/mask.

"What? You know what I'm missing? So just tell me!"

This cavernous chamber had once been a master bedroom for robber baron rich people. Half of Paula's apartment could fit in the closet; the other half would go in the spa bathroom. Curtains on the bay windows were sumptuous maps of the cosmos. Paula smacked a few galaxies and sent ripples from right now back to the Big Bang.

"Where are you?" As Paula struggled up to standing, her heart ached. Worse than clumsy, she felt ridiculous, totally outclassed. Romance? On what planet?

The sun was already hiding behind the western hills, about to set. How did it get so late? She was sweaty and covered in cobwebs and dust doggies. She was desperate and hungry. The spirits ate her snack. The entire offering, including the lapis lazuli paperweight, had disappeared, while she searched the attic. A trade, but Paula didn't know that yet.

She burped up acid from an empty stomach and set the Aje on An'qwenique's desk, a vast, nineteenth-century library table from Oxford or Cambridge or somewhere British and grand. Maybe a conference table, it filled the bay windows and looked so desolate without An'qwenique's computer, journals, and drawing materials, without her supplies to survive the apocalypse.

"How far did you go, girl?"

Paula dropped onto the ergonomic desk chair. She wanted to slump. The chair insisted on good posture, which supposedly aided cognition. Ha! Chasing will-o'-wisps, Paula had searched every *weird* place an An'qwenique-sized person would fit, if she curled into a ball and didn't need to breathe or pee or . . .

What if Paula had jumped to the wrong conclusions? What if she was as bad at mystery as she was at romance, and the murderer was torturing An'qwenique right now, offsite in an abandoned building, garage, or storage unit? That's where Paula needed to search because—

Welcome to the Great Escape *podcast. Let's shuttle ourselves to the other side of surprise.*

Ms. Robinson did live out loud, writing her own rules like Charlize and Melody. Definitely the murderer's type. Paula groaned, spun in the chair, and scanned the room for less aggravating clues. The flat-screen over the mantel had a crack. Hardback books were piled everywhere, but other decorations were sparse: musical instruments, a few antique telescopes and astrolabes. One lone shelf featured tricksters collected on An'qwenique's travels around the world: monkey kings, spiders, coyotes, foxes, ravens, and various little people, imps, fairies, and trolls. Paula set the Aje next to her international kin. They looked ready to jump Paula.

"Wherever An'qwenique has gone and lost herself, not my fault." She huffed. "Why is everything always my fault?" Time to stuff the self-pity and work the problem.

The tune that phantom-An'qwenique sang tingled on the tip of Paula's tongue. It kept running away, making her chase after it. The St. B did this too. How was a stupid melody or random lyrics going to help her find a missing person? She wanted to cuss out the mystery song, but she'd given up cussing along with doomscrolling and violent fantasies. Of course, this song might be some sort of spell, but she dismissed that thought almost before it formed. So many of us, Paula included, took the power of music for granted, for nothing. Dragon Man would make the same mistake.

A life-size Rihanna poster/banner rippled as the air conditioning cut out. Paula glared at the Bajan diva as if mystery song was her fault, as if stratospheric success and pouty lips were responsible for the pissy mood blunting Paula's detective sensibility.

"I'm not built for romance," she admitted to the Monkey King. He and Rihanna glowered at her. "Not everybody is, you know?"

Paula squashed pointless jealousy at a billionaire celebrity. Was Rihanna even singing anymore? In fact, Paula's thinking was fine. Passion made her hyper alert, relentless. Passion made giving up, giving in, or giving out impossible. Hormones shifted unconscious neural nets into overdrive to SOLVE THIS FRIGGIN' MYSTERY.

Paula shook tension from her hands and rolled to the center of the rag rug. She closed her eyes and blotted out visual distractions for meditation mode. Not just what she wanted to believe or what she thought she already knew—Paula had to get herself to *the other side of surprise.*

The previous owners had soundproofed the master bedroom. An'qwenique proclaimed this to be cover for rowdy, rough sex. Whatever. No noise leaked in or out, a balm for agitated nerves. Paula's grumpy gut bacteria didn't care. Her intestines cramped and her tummy growled.

"I'll raid the kitchen after I find An'qwenique," Paula reassured her pesky flora and fauna, and burped acid again. The mystery song was a spicy taste of fried plantains and pickled onions on her tongue. Crossroads treats. Were the little buggers trying to help?

Perhaps Melody and the donsó ngoni player, a griot, tall-tale teller from Mali, had played the song at Crossroads. What was his name? She'd remember that later. SOLVE THIS MYSTERY FIRST! The griot and Melody did umpteen songs from all over

West Africa, Wales, Zululand, and Ireland. Paula liked music OK, but it was not her strong suit. Melody, however, lived up to her name. That made Paula smile. Bittersweet.

April or May of last year, Melody was afraid her first Crossroads gig—an *old lady debut*—would be a bust. Paula barely knew the Haven's star waitperson, but promised to go, even if Crossroads was très chère like Triple-E said. A cranberry seltzer with lime cost $8.75 plus tax and tip. No budget for that, and forget the $18.00 designer cocktails. Still Paula and Triple-E showed up.

A hot climate-change wind blew across the very large and exuberant crowd. People milled around the outdoor terrace because nobody wanted to go inside, even for air conditioning. Covid angst, but folks were juiced for Melody's performance, so the musicians set up outside.

Some guy told a joke that made no sense about gas prices, a busted economy, and half-deaf singers going off key. A laughing woman jostled Paula, who spilled ice water down the joker's neck. Oops. "She bumped me," Paula blurted. "If you weren't expecting a good time, why come? To enjoy someone flopping? Who does that?"

The whole crowd tuned in. Too embarrassed to jump bad, Joker Man muttered nonsense about funning around. He was half drunk and unsteady. He wanted to punch Paula bloody then leave. Easy to read, well, the what not the why of him. His lady wanted to punch Paula too. Maybe they came looking for somebody else to blame for their misery. Paula understood that. In fact, she had to watch jumping on the blame freight train too.

Luckily, the donsó ngoni player stroked a rhythmic riff from his African harp, eerie modal music. Melody drummed and sang nonsense syllables, more in key than Paula would ever be. People clapped and stomped. Joker Man and his lady friend slipped away.

Melody claimed she was having trouble finding words for a

tune from another dimension. She insisted the audience come up with their own lyrics, create a community anthem. Fear ripped through the audience, through Paula too. Her singing voice was unreliable, and who wanted to come off as a corny fool or sentimental no-talent?

Triple-E nudged Paula with a you're-holding-out-on-us grin. Melody issued her plea again, and Paula blurted two lines about maps and stories, what came to mind with the rhythm and also rhymed. Melody's velvet voice and elegant fingers signing made the little couplet seem grand, thrilling. So did the crowd's raucous applause. The chef brought Paula a free plate of fried plantains and pickled onions, dodo. Triple-E ate half.

Not long after this evening, Paula started hanging with An'qwenique in the gazebo, then working for Cloud Heights and the Pet Rescue. She joined Belle's Change Gang and did exhibits for the Iris Library and for a home inspiration gallery. Correlation not causation, still Paula attended Melody's concerts and sat with Triple-E whenever possible. They nursed glasses of ice water, even in winter, and had a grand time—even if Triple-E forgot later.

Whenever somebody came up with another verse for the map song, Paula got a free plate of plantains. Once the St. B appeared out of nowhere. The usually exuberant furball acted hangdog. She put her big head in Paula's lap and whined for some love. Paula obliged, hugging her close, but never figured out what made the dog so sad. How could she know Oona missed her carnival family? Licking peanut sauce, rice, and plantain from Paula's fingers always cheered her up a bit.

Melody taught the audience to sign the new verses. The St. B enjoyed that too. Eventually the regulars could sign the whole song with donsó ngoni accompaniment. In fact, people signed along with all the songs Melody did. Hand dance. The St. B would do a doggy trot.

Paula missed Melody's last concert for some stupid reason. Since the funeral, she hadn't gone to Crossroads even for good causes. Too sad—she hated admitting this. However, she remembered how to sign the community anthem better than how to sing it. Her eyes popped open as the verses slid off her fingers.

"Bet you can't do that," Paula said to Rihanna's sultry smirk.

AN'QWENIQUE—*The Other Side of Surprise*

The cello music crescendoed. Melody's community ditty poured from the Center's attic window. The lightning rod on the highest roof shivered, but dragon weathervanes were stock-still. Haunted house mode prevailed, no twitch or glitch to something else. Zsuzsu rolled up the porch ramp to see if the witch was in. An'qwenique quashed an urge to grab the handles on the wheelchair and stop her. The green elf grinned and pounded the metal knocker against the door on the beat. Her cinnamon curls sparkled.

Whatever happened next was unclear, disputed.

The door creaked or whooshed open. A womanly figure strolled, strode, or stomped onto the porch. She introduced herself as Beryl, the collector of maps and a concierge of dreams, the captain of this ship, a witch, host, ghost, alien, trickster agent. No good human words—a seeker of life at play in the universe. A trickster, all the tourists agreed on that, although eventually specific memories blurred or dissolved.

An'qwenique always stashed a mini-journal and a couple pens in her pockets. Freaky luck! Writing at the speed of thought, she took furious notes and made sketches. Hooray for that $500,000 liberal arts education which included Drawing I, II, and III.

She drew Beryl as an old Black woman wearing steampunk goggles over craggy features. A stream flowed across the lenses, obscuring her eyes. Bee balm and doll's eye grew on the right side of a gargantuan silver afro. Hummingbirds landed on pearl eggs in teacup nests perched on the left. At Beryl's crown, a starfish wriggled barnacled arms and inched toward the wildflowers. Beetles and caterpillars frolicked on bone earrings. Beryl's tunic and midi skirt looked like the night sky tucked around muscular shoulders and thunder thighs. An occasional shooting star streaked down the tunic to the skirt. A constellation exploded. Beryl interrupted a hummingbird duel with a flick of her wrist.

Later Zsuzsu remembered more than anyone and praised An'qwenique's drawings, yet swore she'd seen a different Beryl, who she called Oona's friend. There might have been a belt of gears grinding away, goggles, and shooting stars. Both agreed, Beryl was a giant old woman with swamp breath. Bare feet were roots gathering nutrients from the dirt. Beryl sat down in An'qwenique's other portable chair, that nobody had put together.

Oona bounded out of the oaks. She dropped a fanny pack at Zsuzsu's feet, jumped into Beryl's lap, and curled up asleep.

"How do you both fit on such a small chair?" An'qwenique said, dumbfounded.

Everyone assaulted Beryl with stupid questions. She snapped her fingers like drag queens of old and answered with riddles. Half her words were arcs of electricity, not sound waves. An'qwenique scribbled what she could. *It was tomorrow already*, and the trail runners had *slipped back in space* and *ahead in time*. The lightbulbs in the attic were flickering and *what will keep the bats from flying downstream* (downstairs?) *and perishing?* Oona was born at the Center, *in between here and there, now and then*, or *between here and everywhere*. And although *nobody goes everywhere on their own steam*, Oona might use the wagon/shuttle *to help find what you need*. The dog was a *border crosser*.

"I know that's true!" Zsuzsu proclaimed.

Beryl touched her broad forehead to An'qwenique's, and the starfish tugged her afro-puff. After this skin-to-skin contact, what Beryl said came in clearer although An'qwenique sounded funny to herself. "I don't know who built the Redemption Center," Beryl remarked. "*Surprise got woven up in the cloth of the universe along with cosmic rhythms and routines, rituals and romance.*"

An'qwenique sputtered at an exact quote from her *Great Escape* podcast.

Beryl stroked Oona, who seemed to be running in a dream. "A friend of yours says, *Infinity has no center.* She offers sacrifice to a wise woman on your side."

"Paula?" An'qwenique frowned. "I don't understand how you know that or—"

"I can hear, yes? Iyami Aje."

"You're a witch, wielding elemental power?" An'qwenique's heart thudded, matching a pulse under her feet. "Is that a metaphor? You gotta tell me more than that."

"The Redemption Center was one of Melody's heartbeat places. Same as you, same as everyone here now." Beryl gurgled, a creepy sound. "You've figured us out: Visits should be brief. Lingering too long, most of you tend to slip out of sync."

"How long is too long?" An'qwenique whined.

"We can stay longer than you, but not forever. More and more dead-end maps."

"What does any of that even mean?"

Murky water sloshed across Beryl's goggles. "The Redemption Center closes on Sundays. So, the honor system. We take the empties and you make the change."

"We have to redeem ourselves?"

"Don't look so panicked. You can do better than random luck, can't you? You're alive! Make some meaning. *Not just who you happen to be, who you mean to be.*"

"That sounds like something Paula says. How are you doing that?"

Beryl cackled, witch persona. "I'm waiting on three wayward mates. They must say their goodbyes and hurry back. Can you help them return to me? Navigators, yet lost."

"I'd like to help, but I've been feeling lost myself. And I don't even know them." An'qwenique and Zsuzsu said these words together, acting like the med techs.

"Surprise yourself. *What's it all about?*" Beryl shook Oona and spoke gently, nose to nose. "Nobody stays forever, and I'm not sure we can take you with us. No good trade."

Oona slid to the ground, wagging her butt. Beryl stood up, as if unfolding new layers of herself, more giant than before. The night-sky tunic crept up over her face and wildlife afro, a literal spacesuit, leaving only watery goggles bare. She gestured at awestruck tourists and old-growth trees, then at hawks flying in spirals, and a spider swaying on a thin strand from the porch railing. Oona woofed, eager, excited.

"They need you. You need them," Beryl told the dog. "I need my mates. We are this big houseboat on a sacred quest." She poked An'qwenique. "At night, it's cold enough 'round here to freeze the nuts off a bridge. The doll's eyes are a potent hybrid, maybe lethal, so not that shortcut. Take the sundial posse down the hall to the backyard. Step carefully. Time is stacked up. Space folds in on itself." Beryl snapped her fingers at Guinevere, who slouched in a stupor on the swing. When had she returned? And where was the librarian? "Take her too. Oona hates to leave a soul behind, even in Avalon."

"Right. You said that!" Zsuzsu shouted. "And also: *Just head toward sunset.*"

"Someone singing would help, with everything." Beryl ambled up the stone stairs across a flickering doorsill into a dim hallway. "Sacrifice is necessary, an offering, trade." She paused under a skylight (porthole? portal?). Crickets and tree frogs hushed their racket. Beryl dissolved into a meteor shower streaking across the sky. An'qwenique's hand throbbed as she finished this last sketch, in black and white and bold technicolor. WTF?

"Your friend never lasts long." Zsuzsu hugged Oona. The dog nosed the spot on the steps where a spirit basket should have been. Every offering had disappeared! "They always vanish with Beryl," Zsuzsu said quickly. "Don't freak." Oona was chill, but Zsuzsu failed to reassure An'qwenique or the tourists who stomped their feet and scowled as *what just happened* slipped from their minds.

An'qwenique clutched her journal. Memories on paper were an anchor, but her head throbbed. She'd captured impossible details of a cosmic encounter in colors she didn't possess and usually didn't even see. *What the hell is it all about?* She should have asked better questions. Who cared about the damn trail runners? *How do you find where you are on a map if you don't know where you are?* She held up her journal, displaying images of Beryl. Only Zsuzsu dared to look. An'qwenique shouted at addled tourists. "Beryl said the Center was one of Melody's heartbeat places. What's a heartbeat place?"

"You ask like we should know," Zsuzsu replied. Oona woofed and waved her tail.

An'qwenique laughed at the dog. "Of course you'd know."

"Oona could help Beryl find her mates." Zsuzsu rolled toward the marsh. "I hear Belle singing, coming this way, keeping time with a bell." After a bit everyone heard her. "Time to move. Dämmerung hat Silber im Mund." *Dusk has silver in her mouth.*

An'qwenique packed the chairs with trembling hands. Her muscles twitched, out of sync, like her thoughts. What just happened kept slipping from her mind. Glancing at her journal, she almost remembered. She heaved the backpack over a shoulder and nearly fell. Zsuzsu steadied her. Oona snarled at the fanny pack hanging on the wheelchair.

"I need that." Guinevere jumped from the swing. A dumbek banged her shoulder.

"Oona took you and Belle to Melody's instruments," Zsuzsu murmured.

An'qwenique blocked Guinevere's lunge at Zsuzsu. "What's in the fanny pack?"

Zsuzsu peeked inside. "Did Oona steal this from you or someone else?"

"Just give it back." Guinevere hissed, a petulant teenager full of dark secrets that grown-ups would never appreciate. "It's fuckin' life and death! I need it."

"For what?" Zsuzsu held up wrenches and picks. "Breaking and entering?"

"For Lancelot, my brother. A trade," Guinevere shouted.

"Why were you skulking around my yard?" An'qwenique demanded.

"I told that drag queen spirit-being, you lame bitches would never get where she was coming from," Guinevere snarled. "You ain't been through what I have."

"I'll buy that," Zsuzsu replied. "You think you know who you are, what you'll do when awful crap slams down on you, but then—"

"Horror shit is happening and you're nowhere near who you mean to be." An'qwenique blocked Guinevere's second lunge at Zsuzsu. "Who was the dragon stomping my button blazing stars? A boxer or no, somebody up to bad business?"

"You know this dragon person too?" Zsuzsu shuddered. "He gets around."

Guinevere thrust the dumbek at An'qwenique. "Belle knows who he really is, not me. I'll trade for his fanny pack and the go-anywhere wagon. Beryl said I need that."

"Ralph needs the wagon right now. You tell us what's going on, how we can help." Zsuzsu was gentle, a wonderful surprise. "Is Dragon Man the burglar?" Guinevere went slack. The drum slipped from her fingers. Zsuzsu caught it as the kid crumpled.

Sober and clear as glass, Belle paraded into the courtyard clanging Melody's bell. Her hair was a snow squall, her streaky face radiant. The survivalist cheered the return of the hero librarian. Guinevere scrambled over to her. Belle hugged the trembling wraith close and whispered, "I got you." Guinevere pointed at the pack. Oona snatched it from Zsuzsu's lap and bounded up to the Center door. Fearless or clueless, the dog trotted inside. She paused where Beryl had vanished, then looked back at everyone.

"Oona's always snatching things." Zsuzsu chuckled. "She'll give it back. Eventually." Oona shook the pack, snarling like it was prey or an enemy to subdue. "She wants us to chase her through the house and OUT OF HERE."

Everyone groaned. Nobody except Zsuzsu wanted to set foot in the haunted house, black ops site, alien ship, or whatever, even to escape. Oona took off down the endless hallway and jumped against a back door. It creaked open onto the alien sculpture garden. Belle clapped her hands at the med techs till they pulled Ralph back up the ramp. Zsuzsu rolled beside him. The med techs hesitated at the door.

"Go on. We follow the dog," Belle said sweetly. "I met a ranger in the woods. She told me for now that's the only way out of the maze. She was a sharp old Girl Scout, tall and straight, and didn't need a map to navigate these woods." Beryl? Yeah. Beryl.

The wagon bumped over the doorsill and Ralph sat up, eyes wide. He mumbled something to Zsuzsu. She patted his cheek and he leaned into her touch. The tourists cheered. Tears caught in An'qwenique's throat. Maybe they'd all be OK.

Belle thought so. "We didn't eat each other. The fog is lifting, and Mr. Carter is still with us." Short, but fierce, she clomped onto the sundial. The gnomon sizzled behind her. Shadows wavered between 2:30 PM and 8:00 PM. "Listen up, people! I know you don't want to stay here forever." As if dealing with sixth-graders on tour, she ushered the shy het couple, the mandolin player, Change Gangers, and the CEO up the ramp to the haunted houseboat. "Sing with me!" After a few beats, the tourists crooned Melody's community ditty like their lives depended on the next notes. The cello helped with wayward pitches.

"What is this, camp?" Guinevere sneered. "With Yo-Yo Mania?"

"Yo-Yo Ma. I was a Scout leader. I love camp. Still." Belle put her arm through Guinevere's. "Plus I have a plan to deal with dragons." An'qwenique was glad to hear it. Belle grinned over her shoulder, looking devilish like Oona. "You two coming?"

The survivalist grabbed An'qwenique. They charged up the fieldstone stairs, bellowing together. Their hefty go-bags pounded an up beat. Inside the Center, shadowy corners, musty furniture, and faded maps on the walls were unremarkable. A gothic stairway spiraled up and down. Without thinking, An'qwenique stumbled up a step. The survivalist pulled her down. She'd check it out next time, if there was one.

HELP YOURSELF! Everyone guzzled sweet water and grabbed fruit, nuts, and biscuits from a sideboard. A plush rug ran to the back exit, a tapestry storyboard of people, plants, and creatures tramping down this very hall.

An'qwenique halted under the skylight/porthole/portal. An image of their tourist parade emerged on the carpet under her hiking sandals. Zombie gray turned into fluorescent blues, reds, and greens. Ralph's wagon became a hovercraft flying on lightning bolts. Oona was glitter threads, streaking across a boardwalk through birch trees. Red-tailed hawks circled above her. The tapestry-An'qwenique had spiral galaxies for eyes and a half-moon grin as she drew in a journal. Not the ragged-out chick who'd stared at her from Dragon Man's sunglasses, but who she used to be? Who she meant to be? A cosmic swirl on the journal's cover pulsed. HELP YOURSELF!

The front door slammed, sucking air from her lungs. She glanced to the backyard. The tourists looked vibrant, full of spirit, zombies no more.

"We got this!" Belle told Guinevere as they tromped by the weird sculptures.

A sign, EXIT THIS WAY, hung from a birch tree limb over the boardwalk. (Was that there earlier?) They'd fuckin' made it! The back door hinges screeched. *Leave now or never leave.* An'qwenique sprinted out a narrow opening. The portable chair

Beryl sat in fell out of her go-bag and back into the hallway, just as the door banged shut.

Belle shook her head. "Why didn't we look behind here before?"

"I did," An'qwenique declared. "There was no sign then."

Up ahead, someone belted the community ditty. "That sounds like Paula." Zsuzsu leered at An'qwenique. "Girlfriend is tracking you, sweet thing."

"No way," An'qwenique replied, embarrassed. Were she and Paula so obvious?

Oona, the fanny pack clutched in her maw, charged at them, grumble-growling. When she had everyone's attention, she raced down the sunset boardwalk only to halt again under a rusty-leafed red oak. As Zsuzsu, Belle, and the troops sped her direction, Oona dashed off toward—*Someone singing on the other side*. Paula for sure.

An'qwenique halted. She'd catch up to the others easily, even wearing sandals and lugging a thirty-five-pound go-bag. She stole a moment to jot down the lyrics on the last empty page of her pocket journal, because, well, forgetting a single line would be a shame.

PAULA—*Studio Magic*

While Oona lured ornery humans through the haunted houseboat back to where they needed to go, the air conditioning in An'qwenique's study blew on. The Monkey King and Aje puppet/mask gaped at Paula's hand dance. Her signing was rusty, still . . .

"This is what phantom-An'qwenique was humming," she explained. The tricksters scowled. "What? Farts and Fleas!" Grandma Junebug's almost-curse gave her courage. She should call Junebug. They hadn't talked much since covid, since their big fight over nothing. *Stop stumbling through your life, going arse over tea kettle.* The tricksters pouted. "I gotta do the melody too?" Paula jumped up and belted the lyrics. Cello music snuck in from somewhere (near the Aje?) and kept her on key. Music from another dimension.

Draw me a map that sets us free
Tell me a story I could be
Sing me a song that breaks the curse
Plant a garden to save the Earth
Write a formula for good sense
Build us a bridge over that fence

Ask me to lose bomb, match, and fuse
Ask me to find what'll change my mind

Conjure a spell to feel the sky
Weave me a way that leads to why
Holler the truth before we break
Dream the next move we need to take

Tell me a story I could be
Draw me a map that sets us free

"It may be corny, but—" Paula signed *free/freedom,* twisting her wrists and shoving palms in Rihanna's face. The Bajan diva undulated over the entrance to the walk-in closet. This served as An'qwenique's podcast and VR studio, and was soundproofed too. Paula couldn't hear inside and nobody inside could hear out.

A self-cleaning ventilation system in the closet maintained a pristine atmosphere for finicky equipment. Paula never went in the studio, except to help An'qwenique carry heavy new gadgets. This was a private realm with a no-trespassing vibe. The autographed Rihanna banner was a gift from Charlize and camouflaged the treasure vault from burglars or any unwanted intruders. Singing the song again, Paula slipped behind Rihanna and opened the door to pitch black. As she groped for a light switch, raffia streamers engulfed her. She smacked the prickly fabric away from her face.

Hanging above the doorway, attached to the raffia, was a mask with two heads facing opposite directions. A fearsome bird perched on the crown, wings as sharp as the dagger beak. In the faint light filtering through Rihanna, Paula recognized the West African deity of thresholds and crossroads, of the borders and cracks between this world and other worlds. The Guardian at the Gate . . . to the multiverse?

Set in motion by her flailing, the double-headed mask spun from a cunning half smile to a face with an indulgent smirk. When the first face rotated back, it displayed a quizzical grin, which was followed by a flirtatious sneer. For the third go-round, Paula caught a challenging scowl then a welcoming leer. "OK, I get it." Dizzy, she flicked on the lights. "Damn." She forgave herself for cussing because—

In the far reaches of the closet, An'qwenique was all trussed up in the VR rig!

Cords from the command chair to the surge protector were looped around her feet and ankles. The chest harness and the VR helmet were on backward. The earphones and visor dangled over a shoulder. Straps to the helmet cut across her collarbone, throat, chin, and lips, constricting movement.

Wires encircled a knapsack on her back, which contained computer, journal, medical supplies, and the survival paperback Paula loaned her two Mondays ago. Stuffed in with all this was a dumbek drum (Melody's?) two fluorescent blankets, enormous steampunk goggles (for a giant?), and one of An'qwenique's beloved portable chairs. Everything almost spilling out, yet held in place by a single bungee cord. Packing magic, but the goggles were half the size of the chair.

Why take all that on a virtual trip?

An'qwenique grunted and thrashed against her precious VR contraption like a trapped wild animal, ready to sacrifice a paw, a whole limb, for freedom.

"No, wait." Paula bumped by the water dispenser and the podcast table to reach her. "You don't want to hurt yourself or ruin expensive equipment." She'd seen $3000 price tags on replacement components. "How long have you been in here?"

Spit and jibber-jabber burst from An'qwenique's lips as her struggle intensified.

"Stop! You're making it worse." Paula stroked An'qwenique's shoulder till the wild look in her eyes faded. "Just hold on. I'll get you out."

Paula traced jumbled cords and straps with trembling fingers. Working on a solution that didn't require cutting and hacking, she leaned close and caught the scent of a tropical forest after a downpour. A sweet, muddy smell that recalled Paula's childhood stay in Barbados with Grandma Junebug, when her parents were in jail.

"You been running in a VR jungle? Sorry. Bad joke." Paula's heart raced. This tangled mess was not a horror sci-fi art exhibit, so probably not the work of the perp who took out Melody and Charlize. Still—"Who did this to you?"

An'qwenique groaned and slumped against Paula. Her tongue wasn't working with words. A strap across her lips to the VR helmet didn't help either.

"The recycling bins were scattered all over, and your car was half in and half out of the garage. Not how you roll! I was scared the killer had snatched you. Availability bias," Paula admitted. An'qwenique recoiled at killer. "But he didn't. Triple-E says worry is a waste of good energy. I mean you just had a weird VR adventure, right?" No need to mention Charlize right away. Belle had already told An'qwenique, but Paula didn't know this.

An'qwenique blinked. Her lips trembled with frustration and relief, with desire and dread, quite a complex brew, yet easy for Paula to read.

"I looked for you all over the house, three times." Paula chattered on. "Nothing but secret dust-doggie strongholds. I should have looked here hours ago. Sorry."

An'qwenique jiggled her head violently, trying to fling the VR helmet off.

"Whoa. Wait." Paula detached the input plug from the chest harness, undid the chin straps, earphone jacks, and power cord before easing the helmet off. The earphones, visor, and padding smelled swampy. "Wow! Where have you been?"

An'qwenique scrunched her face, yet failed to get a word or even a sound out.

"Sorry, you don't have to answer any questions yet." Paula set the VR helmet in its station at the edge of the podcast table. She filled a cup with water from the fancy dispenser and held it to An'qwenique's lips. She guzzled three cups then threw back her head, worked face and jaw muscles, and wiggled her tongue—warm-up exercises for a podcast, an in-person speech, or a good wolf howl. Paula untangled the hefty go-bag and set it on the floor without anything falling out. The last snarl of cords and straps from An'qwenique's waist to her ankles came undone practically on its own.

"Et voilà." Quoting Triple-E, Paula backed up, as if releasing a volatile wild thing.

An'qwenique sucked a deep breath and gurgled—almost words. She jumped up from the command chair, took a wide stance, and stretched her arms. Rumpled clothes hung from her frame like she'd lost weight while wearing this outfit. She stomped, shook her booty, and howled. An exhilarating release. Paula joined her.

They pranced around the studio growling and snuffling, possessed by jubilant wolf spirits. They snarled at the VR rig then bayed into podcast microphones and at the giant goggles, which also smelled swampy. They collided under the Guardian mask that was still whirling in the doorway. The streamers were silky, a caress on feverish skin.

"No way," Paula murmured. "These were scratchy before."

"Oh?" An'qwenique whispered also. "It's been that kind of day." Words finally.

They fell into each other's arms and squeezed for dear life: cheek to cheek, bosom to bosom, thighbones entwined, grateful for the miracle of breath together. Eternity in a moment. They'd soon be taking it all for granted again, but not right now.

"I'm in my house, talking words," An'qwenique rasped. "And you understand me?"

Paula nodded then blinked back tears. She suddenly felt shy and stepped away from their intimate embrace. An'qwenique heaved the knapsack on her back and gripped Paula's hand. She pushed the Rihanna banner aside then marched them out into her study. The sun left a faint trail of fiery clouds in a purple sky. Ceiling lights on automatic dimmers offered a romantic, film noire glow.

An'qwenique halted in the center of the designer rag rug. "I'm actually here?"

"Where else?" Paula replied. "Were you in the closet all this time?"

"Not really." An'qwenique strode to the desk and set the knapsack down. She turned to Paula. Shock radiated from every pore. "Oh my god, you're here to clean."

Paula shrugged. "It's Monday."

An'qwenique flung the curtains wide, revealing evening stars. "How long was I gone?" Accusation colored her voice. Unclear who it was directed at. "My watch stopped again." She held out her wrist. The starship *Enterprise* stuttered at 2:45.

"Yeah, time has been funny. Your prayer plant couldn't decide if it was day or night." Paula braced herself. "I don't exactly know when you went missing."

"Sunday afternoon, after recycling duty, I planned to hook up with Azul Mendes, for a tech interview, not a date. I took a detour, and the car died. I never got anywhere."

"A first for you, and Azul freaked out." No mentioning lover girl Kitty or the family drama just yet. "It's Monday night."

"I lost a day. Get the fuck out of here!" An'qwenique looked around as if her study might disappear or a monster might leap from the shelves. She backed away from the trickster crowd. "Oona took everyone back. I don't know how I got tangled in the VR rig. Oona scrambled to deliver me here before it was too late—"

"I know that name." Paula reached out to steady her. "Who is Oona again?"

"Very good question," An'qwenique replied, and they were hugging again.

BOOK III

BACK IN TIME TO MAKE IT STRANGE

JOURNAL ENTRY:

*It's impossible to say in advance who might make it all the way there, all the way anywhere.**

STORM MUSINGS:

*Mucking it up is easy. But can you put it back right? Back better? Those are the questions to ask.**

* Captions from the Iris Library's International Trickster Exhibition

MONDAY

OONA—*The Between Place*

Before An'qwenique returned to her studio and before Oona found another body, there were several challenges. Taking folks from the Redemption Center to where they wanted/needed to go was more difficult than usual, even with the go-anywhere wagon and Paula singing. What Oona didn't realize: These intrepid souls had almost stayed too long. No return to who they used to be. What Oona did know: Backtracking was a bust. She did the best she could, but the old trails were tangled and confused, ghost trails leading nowhere.

Multiple times Oona and her sundial posse came to a dead end: a collapsed bridge, treacherous ravine, or now this muddy river and a waterfall nobody remembered. Something similar had happened to her carnival crew. New maps were required. Trudging behind Oona, the tourists smelled bleary and exhausted, ready to sit down in the mud and stay down. Even Oona's endless energy was running low. She whined and put her head in Zsuzsu's lap.

An'qwenique stroked Oona's back. "Do you hear that?"

Cool spray from the waterfall cleared Oona's nose. Beyond the waterfall, a familiar voice belted the *come back* song a second time. Paula! Everyone perked up. The right direction was near. Oona also caught a whiff of the musician, magician, and clown. Search and rescue with her carnival crew was always reach the destination or else, even if you were dog-tired. The music and sweet memory spurred Oona to ignore scent static from obsolete maps and rush through the wall of water. Surprise! She found a new path, a map for this moment. As reluctant tourists followed her, their heartbeats synched, and home territory came into view. Nobody got soaking wet.

Oona led the tourists not back to where they started but to where they belonged, for now. Joyful people hugged her. She licked salty tears. They shook hands, kissed cheeks, and breathed deep, collecting scents for future recognition. They promised to be in touch, yet, except for Zsuzsu, no one asked for contact info. How would they find one another? Still, success! Each arrival and farewell recharged Oona enough to carry on.

Once home, the sundial posse offered reasonable explanations for what the hell happened at the Center, for why they returned a day later than expected. Poorly marked trails, a psychedelic mushroom trip, or an endless VR escapade were to blame. They also spoke of top-secret interrogations and experiments at a clandestine research center. These accounts went unchallenged. Only vague mention of aliens, ghosts, or witches. A giant park ranger and her(?) trusty mutt figured in every story. Memories of Beryl were contradictory, muddled, impossible, yet what good was rooting through anomalies and discrepancies? Eventually, the sundial posse believed the stories they concocted.

The clown liked to say: *We forget in order to survive an infinite cosmos.* Yet—

Drifting toward sleep, walking among whispering trees, or staring at a dragonfly dance over a misty pond, the truth was impossible to deny. They'd survived an extraordinary experience, even if the facts remained elusive, disputed. Wandering the giant sundial together, parading through the haunted houseboat / black ops site, and riding in the go-anywhere wagon changed who they were and also who they meant to be. This was neither a fearful nor distressing revelation. It was the naughty delight of their secret society. And they were waiting on someone to call them out of hiding.

Zsuzsu had collected as many cell numbers as possible. She and An'qwenique were the last to arrive home. They'd helped the others return first. They clutched each other and babbled.

Who is going to believe any of this? They insisted on unreasonable stories. An'qwenique planned to use the VR escapade as cover. She trusted her drawings and journal notes. Zsuzsu did too, despite slightly different images in her head. Most likely Zsuzsu was more acclimated, as Beryl said. Zsuzsu parked the go-anywhere wagon on her porch. She suspected the classic red wonder was more than mere transport. It helped save Ralph from the allergy mess.

Oona loved the wagon. The magician called it a dream shuttle, what you took instead of the big houseboat for special, tricky trips. Zsuzsu planned to return it to Beryl next Sunday. She and An'qwenique wished Oona could describe Beryl, tell them her Beryl stories. They cursed themselves for not asking Beryl more about Oona, more about everything.

Oona met Beryl as a puppy. The trickster captain, agent from the beyond, was a friend of the magician, musician, and clown. They were all related; Oona smelled this. She'd encountered Beryl only a few times since she lost the go-anywhere wagon and her crew. That fateful afternoon, the Cosmic Campers Carnival Band did a free show at the library. (All their shows were free.) Kids from the audience read favorite books, sang or beat drums, then played *follow your nose* all over Oona's maps. Belle and her Change Gang were thrilled. She slipped Oona popcorn treats.

When the show was over, when the props and instruments were packed and it was time to go, somebody lost the wagon or it vanished on its own. No trail to follow. The wagon went beyond where Oona's nose would take her. As the Cosmic Campers raced out of the library, the fussing and fighting began. They wanted someone (or something) else to blame. Didn't everyone? Even navigators got lost or stranded. Lingering so long out of place, anyone could slip out of sync. And who wanted to say goodbye?

This Sunday, Oona found the go-anywhere wagon or the wagon found her. She'd been running in circles, getting nowhere, chasing scent static from jollof rice and fried plantains. How long before she forgot who she used to be?

There was no fresh trace of her crew in the big houseboat. Recent spoor was only in the witch's garden shed and down near the marsh. The trio hadn't been gone from the Center long according to the musician's reckoning, just enough time to sync back up with themselves and gather energy to return and find Oona. To Oona, it smelled like months since they'd set foot on the Center's carpeted hallways, since they walked through control rooms upstairs and cargo bays down below. Time was like that—different for everybody. Oona never argued with her nose, about time or anything.

After An'qwenique's tangled return, after Zsuzsu drove off in her van to meet Ralph at Crossroads, Oona lapped cold water from the stream near Zsuzsu's barn. It was Monday evening and the big-hearted St. Berdoodle was exhausted, overheated, and beyond thirsty. She tried to drink enough for two days. She managed a short trot upstream to the old tollbooth at the covered bridge. This secret refuge was where she stashed treasures to smell, gnaw, or pounce on. Even during heat waves, it was cool inside on the weathered wood.

Oona dropped the bad man's pack by his sunglasses under the window. Outside, a waterfall spilled down a hillside into the stream. She loved waterfalls, the wet, soothing rush and the gurgle on the rocks. Too tired for a shower, she snuffled around her treasure room then plopped a bloated butt on the rag rug and panted out heat.

The tollbooth was a *between place* where many maps overlapped, like the doll's eye patch behind Haven Bagels and the Redemption Center sundial. The tollbooth was harder to reach. Crows, hawks, and owls followed Oona here (a skyway thing), but not the next-door mutt or Zsuzsu. Those two tramped more places with Oona than anyone, except Paula and Melody, her oldest friends in this second life.

Paula was a border crosser like Oona, gliding onto any

map. Oona woofed delight at Paula singing them back on track. Musicians touched hearts, fueled spirits, never knowing how many lives they changed. Running through neighborhoods earlier, Oona found one of Paula's shoes. The battered sneaker now sat in a pile of bottle caps a few feet from her nose. Sweet comfort. The bottle caps came from the crows. They stole small toys from Oona but also brought presents. She had quite a collection of shiny buttons, earrings, and bottle caps. Oona was famous. Crows all over knew her—a savior of chicks and an eager playmate, frequently generous with food and always ready to chase danger away. Crows visited Oona at the barn and the tollbooth.

An old friend landed by Paula's shoe with foil wrapping from a pepperoni pizza slice. The bird flapped wings at Oona's snout. Unlike turkeys, crows were ready to play anytime. Oona's paws throbbed. She was too sore, too exhausted for crow games, too overwhelmed. So much had gone wrong.

She whimpered as Charlize's fear filled her nose, then her death aroma. Oona howled. Charlize was never stepping out of Ralph's recycling bin. Part of Oona was stuck in that bin with her. Oona was everyone she loved. After misplacing the magician, musician, and clown, it took a while, but she'd formed a loose-knit pack. When Zsuzsu brought Oona home from the Pet and Wild Animal Rescue, Oona had to create a new routine, a different rhythm for her days. One beat followed another, like the music in a show.

The Sunday trip to the Center with Zsuzsu meant a run at sunset with Ralph. The next morning was a search for her carnival crew while Zsuzsu worked too hard at Cloud Heights. Monday afternoon, Oona stopped by the library for greenhouse patrol with Belle then swung home to check on Zsuzsu. Monday night, Paula and Oona shared a cheesy, crunchy bun at the Haven and an adventure walk in the dodgy sections, crisscrossing several maps. They tracked promising scent trails, checked on folks living under the bridge, and often caught Gwen climbing out the second-floor window of her foster home to smoke marijuana.

Each day had a shape. One adventure led to the next, with room for improvisation: mysterious fun odors to track or a lost soul reeking of panic or someone new pissing on the hydrants. The crows were always up to no good, pranking the neighbor mutt or harassing an enemy. You didn't want to get on the crows' bad side. Sturdy but flexible routines had carried Oona along for months. The last couple days were a terrible muddle. Not just Melody AWOL or Charlize lifeless in that bin or Ralph swelling up, there were too many misplaced people, too many dead ends and threats to defuse.

Oona curled around a sweetgrass basket, a cello bow, and a striped knee sock from her carnival family. Finding what they left behind was easier than finding them. Their old aromas lulled her. She dozed off. Her tail thumped a rhythm with the waterfall. The pizza crow settled in the rafters, watching over the only furry member of the flock as Oona yipped then snored in a good dream: running around the multiverse, doing a show with everyone. Nobody lost or left behind.

The bad man's pong woke Oona up. His fanny pack and mirror sunglasses reeked under the window. The wind blowing through the tollbooth was filled with his menace. She snarled, and friend crow sounded an alert in case danger was near. Oona had no idea where the bad man was. What would she do if she smelled him close? Lunge? Rip his throat? She had zero practice with these urges. Snarls and lips curled over fangs were usually enough to chase threats away.

The crow scolded Oona for a false alarm. She wagged her tail and woofed reassurance. The bird marched out of the tollbooth and squatted on a Frisbee from Lance and Gwen. Oona stood up and trotted into inky dark. Although the throb in her toes had faded, she felt almost hangdog, not like herself at all. Friend crow scolded again and flew to a nightly roost, hidden from owls, hawks, and other hungry mouths. Oona growled for good measure and swished her tail, spreading a big-dog scent to discourage predators downwind from coming this way.

Someone was attacking Oona's pack. She was pack leader, the guide to all the maps. If she couldn't figure what direction to do next, were they all lost? The bad man's sunglasses and fanny pack didn't belong with her other treasures. Since Zsuzsu hated his smell too, forget leaving his funk in her farmhouse. Luckily, Zsuzsu had parked the go-anywhere wagon on the porch. Oona would sleep on Captain Beryl's cozy blanket in the wagon tonight and recharge her heart. She wagged her butt at this prospect.

Audiences at Cosmic Camper shows assumed you had to pull the wagon one direction or the other to get somewhere. Actually, the wagon/shuttle amplified your heartbeat sensor and let you map a route through the static to where you needed or wanted to go, asleep or awake. Oona mostly wanted to go wherever audience passengers wanted to go or where lost people might find themselves. That was how she got folks from the Redemption Center to their driveway, parking lot, hospital emergency room, back porch, library, restaurant, or podcast studio.

Oona should deliver the bad man's things to her carnival crew. The magician was as good with the wagon as she was. Maybe better. Together they would hunt him down. The clown would know what to do when they caught him. The clown always did crowd control. The musician had created the melody for the *come back* song and would bring them all home, safe and sound.

Two problems: Oona didn't want to leave her new pack, and her carnival family was still lost. She was about to be too sad when the pizza crow and a buddy dive-bombed her. She chased them back to Zsuzsu's barn. The crows raided the food from the chute. It smelled wrong: not to be eaten. Crows never minded eating rotten, poisoned food. They ate chocolate without getting sick or being scolded. Oona let them feast.

Her nose tingled. Troubling aromas rode the wind. Once she started tracking trouble, she had to finish the job. If you didn't clear out trouble, it came back to ambush you. You had to hound trouble, wear it out . . . Oona ran back to the tollbooth, grabbed the fanny pack, and headed for the Haven. It was time to check in on Paula at the bus stop. Paula liked tracking trouble almost as much as the Cosmic Campers.

MONDAY

PAULA—*Making Sense*

An'qwenique scowled at her master-bedroom office like she'd walked into the Twilight Zone or the Sunken Place. Paula longed to see what she saw.

"Oona is not who she seems to be," An'qwenique said, as if that explained anything.

"Uh-huh." Paula kicked off her ratty house shoes and danced from foot to foot on the silk rag rug. She kept her back to the trickster shelf. "Oona is . . . who?"

"What happened at the Center is hard to explain." An'qwenique lifted the Rihanna banner, pushed aside the raffia streamers dangling from the Guardian mask, and stared into the podcast/VR studio. "Maybe I tangled myself up, coming home this way." She scrunched her face and blinked away strange memories or visions. "I was worried sick that I'd never get back, that we . . ."

"That we might not see each other again," Paula blurted.

"You too?" An'qwenique leaned closer. Her breath was warm, moist. Flirting, despite the high danger quotient and a world gone loopy. "You sang me home."

"I did?" Paula's skin tingled. She enjoyed the romance despite her better judgment.

"You sang us all home," An'qwenique replied, beyond grateful. Dazzled by Paula! "Doing the song twice was—"

"Wait, you heard me, in that soundproof closet? I was out here with the door shut."

"Magic, right? That ain't the half of it." Words tangled on An'qwenique's tongue.

"Take your time. I believe you. We're in this together." Paula gulped a shaky breath. "You promise to believe me too?"

An'qwenique tilted her head, taking full measure of this request. "People usually doubt you, don't they? But some wild shit happened here that maybe you don't believe yourself." Her amber eyes had flecks of red brown, very red-tailed hawk. Dusky purple lips were hummingbird fierce. Had she always looked so, what? Beautiful? Precious?

"Hell yeah, I'll believe you." An'qwenique beamed at Paula. The what was clear but not the why. Ms. Celebrity Podcaster was as hard to read as Dimples on the bus this morning. Paula still suspected, or no, still feared that rich lady might be indulging in cross-class high fantasy. Dimples too. "I'll believe you anytime." An'qwenique used a fierce wolf voice, very sexy. "What are these bruises on your face?"

"Fairies firing ice missiles today at the bus stop." Paula pointed at a mark on An'qwenique's collarbone from a helmet strap. "Does that hurt?"

An'qwenique shook her head no and studied Paula with evident delight, the way Dimples had, and Paula was a worse rumpled mess. They were both raggedy-assed.

Paula tugged An'qwenique's silk camo pedal pushers. "What are you wearing? Survivalist chic from Needless Mark-Up?"

An'qwenique snorted. "I never shop at Neiman Marcus."

"Welcome back." Paula kissed both cheeks the way Triple-E did.

An'qwenique pressed Paula's fingers into the cleft between her collarbones and kissed her full on. Paula's insides twisted, her thoughts tangled, desire and terror. What about Kitty? What about $360 a week, cash guaranteed, but really, what about Kitty? Paula pulled away. "Kitty left messages too, as worried as boss man Azul, boss person."

"Kitty's not worrying about me. She and I were barely a thing." An'qwenique winced. "I'm not a fickle, two-timing bitch. That's her."

"I'm not a card-carrying dyke, a card-carrying anything," Paula confessed.

"We carry cards?" An'qwenique chuckled. "I don't care. Do you care? Plus no rush."

"Wow." Paula shivered. "I'm new at this, but that was too easy, wasn't it?"

"Hey, I'm a changed person, not the coward I was yesterday."

"Me neither. I left you a message about us. We're magic, what you said, on the same wavelength. Oh, shoot, messages, right! Your mom called. Big Brother—"

"You played my messages?" An'qwenique seemed to be annoyed and thrilled. "You were worried, so—" She and Paula jolted as murky water streamed across the giant goggles sticking out of her knapsack and dribbled onto the rug. A brown splotch sizzled on the designer fabrics. An'qwenique set a wastebasket under the ooze. "A fan, Trash Art Fart, gave me this rug. Will that stain come out?"

"Amodex works wonders." Paula was too matter-of-fact. They should keep it weird, strange. "Did somebody wear those goggles where you were?" She glared at the Aje puppet/mask sitting placidly on the shelf, like butter wouldn't melt on her sizzling trickster behind. Wet-looking goggles hung over her torpedo bosom.

An'qwenique pulled a journal from her pocket and flipped past grayscale and full-color drawings. She talked too fast about being trapped in a time-warp maze of ghost trees with Zsuzsu, Ralph, a few tourists, a fan, and a killer on the loose. *The* killer?

"Wait, ghost trees? What?" Paula muttered. "Slow down, so I can see."

An'qwenique paused at zombies, pale birch trees, and ghouls dancing around a misty sundial. The gnomon resembled the knob on an old-fashioned timer or a '50s sci-fi weapon. She pressed the drawing against her belly. "Zsuzsu was airy-fairy chill, yet it felt like that horror movie where the monster picks the characters off one by one or they do each other in. Luckily, this didn't happen to us. Captain Beryl happened to us." She shuddered, a wolf in that trap again, about to gnaw both paws off.

Paula hugged her. "Tell me about Beryl."

"I keep forgetting her. Everybody did, like she didn't happen." An'qwenique's lips trembled. "The memories kept blurring, dissolving."

"Did you draw Beryl?" Paula stroked the journal's spine. "Show me?"

"Beryl helped Oona get us home. There was a go-anywhere wagon." An'qwenique flipped pages, muttering about a haunted houseboat with rocket engines and an agent from the beyond. "Zsuzsu, you, and I met her last spring in that freak snowstorm." She tapped an image. Beryl towered over a derelict mansion with rocket towers on the roof. She had cliff-high cheekbones and a warm smile like the ranger who gave them fluorescent blankets. Her monster afro was silver, not the Aje's fire-hydrant orange. They both had hummingbirds in their hair and muddy steampunk goggles. "I'm not telling this right." An'qwenique groaned. "We each saw a *different* Beryl, a *different* houseboat. What you say, we're living in a multiverse, only literally."

"Beryl's rocket houseboat is where the detour took you?"

"No, after the detour, I walked to the Redemption Center through a maze of ghost trees whispering curses, or questions, really. OK, I know ghost trees sounds crazy. Birch trees, more shadow than substance." She rubbed her forehead. "I was off all Sunday, ignoring the signs. Too long on the VR rig." She slammed the journal shut.

"Don't." Paula shook An'qwenique's shoulders, rougher than intended. "You and Zsuzsu always do this."

"What? I do not. I'm nothing like Zsuzsu."

"You brought her up." Paula pouted.

"Because she was at the Center with me. Acting like it wasn't weird at all."

"When it's hard, you both push people away and shut the door."

"You do that too."

"No, I don't have anybody close to push away." Paula swallowed a shriek.

"Zsuzsu's not so bad. What are we going on about?"

"Just tell me what you think went down with Beryl."

"It doesn't make any fuckin' sense."

Paula shrugged. "Why should an alien encounter make sense? Right off, I mean."

"Oh, so it'll make sense later." An'qwenique almost giggled.

"Make a good story, at least. You love good stories." Paula giggled full out, then pointed at the Aje. She sat, not where Paula put her, but on top of Coyote with an arm around the Monkey King. He reached for the strand of beads in the Aje's velvet fist.

"Not mine. Some masks like her were hanging in the witch's hut, I mean Beryl's garden shed." An'qwenique did a wolf-girl growl. "I remember an empty hook. Like a puppet/mask ran off, leaving half a strand of beads and a patch of felt behind. Where did she come from?"

"The recycling bin?" Paula peered at the beads in the Aje's fist and the patch of felt hair missing from her neckline—ripped from a hook? "She wasn't in the bin when I first arrived. The bins were empty. She appeared later. I brought her upstairs so we could keep an eye on each other. Too many unsolved mysteries lying around."

"I never made it to recycling. One of Beryl's babes, a trade for my recycling maybe."

"Trade?"

"Beryl traded her goggles for one of my chairs," An'qwenique explained.

"OK, but . . ." Paula gaped out the window at evening stars

glinting in blue-violet clouds. "Oh shoot, I gotta hustle! I'm—" Still in a race with the killer. No time for romance or gumbo-yaya on the weird from another dimension. Involving An'qwenique in the murder mystery was a selfish fantasy. Panic propelled Paula back into her ratty slides and toward the hall.

"Where are you going?" An'qwenique blocked her.

"Can I hold on to my pay and clean later this week? I was counting on that cash."

"No. No. Talk to me."

"No? Wow. The money's downstairs." Paula tried not to feel burned, not to feel anything. "You're home safe. You can figure out the rest later." Disappointment over short-lived adventure-romance was a luxury. "I have a life-and-death mission."

"Life-and-death is today's cliché excuse." A wolf-girl whine. "You're shutting the door now. Just hit me with it. I won't shatter. *We're in this together*—your words."

"OK. I have to meet a dog friend at Haven about a murder investigation."

"Let me guess. A St. Berdoodle?" An'qwenique displayed an image of the St. B racing through birch trees—a bolt of lightning in an enchanted forest. The drawing was clearer than any photo Paula had seen. "Zsuzsu's dog, a border crosser. Oona."

"The Oona who brought you back to the closet, who brought everybody back, Zsuzsu's dog, wow." Jealous, Paula touched Oona's nose in the drawing and got a mild shock. "A Houdini dog, boldly going wherever she wants. The cops are on her tail, maybe government agents too."

"Ralph told us about the cops, but government agents after Oona? Why?"

"That could just be disinfo-teer slop. But somebody did catch her magic or alien science on video. She can ID the killer for sure, so he'd like to take her out." Paula resisted grinding her teeth. "Life-and-death clichés can be true."

"I know."

"So maybe not government agents, but Oona doesn't realize the danger she's in."

"Holy shit! You mean the dog can ID Melody's and Charlize's killer, don't you?"

"Who told you about Charlize?"

"Belle and Gwen told me on the way back, a horror story. I didn't want to believe them. The kid said I better believe it. And, and . . ." An'qwenique sank onto the rag rug. She lost words and tears drizzled. Paula hugged her as she sputtered and blubbered.

"Dragon Man stomped my wildflowers." An'qwenique scrubbed away tears. "I almost ran him over. I texted Charlize, tried to warn her." She shook her head, like she was trapped again. "Everyone thinks Charlize and I are best friends."

Paula squeezed her hand. "It's not your fault."

"Yesterday, I would have said BFF is social media hype. Today, there's a hole in my heart." She gasped. "Shit! You think the killer is after Oona?"

"Yeah. I'm following the clues. I'm meeting her at the Haven." Paula sighed. "You said you'd believe me."

"I do. We have a lot to tell each other. I'm going with you." An'qwenique heaved her monster go-bag over a shoulder as if it weighed nothing. The giant goggles clanged against a dumbek like Melody's. Before Paula could ask about this, An'qwenique jetted down the stairs. "You said my car came back, right? All on its own."

Paula grabbed the Aje (no leaving the little witch behind) and followed. She grabbed her pay off the front hall sideboard and thrust the bills in An'qwenique's face. "All there."

"No, that's not what I meant." An'qwenique pushed the bills aside. "Keep the money. You earned it, girl, searching all day, singing me and everybody home."

Paula rolled her eyes. "You don't have to pay for that."

"Would you take the three sixty as a gift?"

Paula pocketed the cash. Arguing once was righteous; twice was stupid. "You know I came up with the first verse of Melody's community anthem."

"That's the last verse too, my favorite. *Tell me a story I could be.*" An'qwenique moved close. "I've been losing faith five times a day. You can sing to me any time." She kissed Paula, a weak-in-the-knees, breathtaking kiss.

Paula licked her lips. "I never understood why people in TV shows and movies were always sucking face with bullets and bombs flying." Embarrassed for blurting this, she collected her HEPA and cleaning supplies.

An'qwenique snatched up a flyer that fell from Paula's knapsack. "Whoa! The Cosmic Campers Carnival Band is doing a farewell concert at Iris Library? Are they breaking up? Heading out with their captain?"

"Somebody gave me that on the bus. Who cares?"

"Beryl. 'Property of the Cosmic Campers' is painted on the bed of Oona's red wagon."

"Damn!" Paula couldn't help cursing. "I saw the Cosmic Campers today. A drag king, River, and Benjie, a golden retriever who didn't like riding the bus. They met the rest of their troupe at the Crossroads bus stop—two tall drag queens. Big coincidence. Oona has some explaining to do." As they hustled out the Dogon door to the garage, Paula grumbled like Grandma Junebug, "De sea ain't got nuh back door."

"Say what?"

"The ocean doesn't have an escape hatch. I mean, is risking us both a good idea?"

"Leaving me home alone is not an option." An'qwenique held up a key fob. Her hands shook. "I'm totaled. You drive. Don't argue. We all want to catch the shitbooby."

"Shitbooby? This is serious."

"A murderous shitbooby, but no glamour or glory for him, no hero-villain. We have to find Oona before he does." An'qwenique fingered the hailstorm dents in the car roof then dumped her go-bag on the back seat, a tight fit with Paula's kit. "I'd be a cat person, but allergies." Her voice caught in her throat. Sweet lips trembled again. "I'd do anything for Oona."

Paula stomped agreement. "Me too."

"What are you wearing on your feet?"

Paula cringed at the beat-up house slides. They were slime green, and the ratty fur could pass for fungi. "My other shoes fell apart in the hailstorm."

"You're a size ten, ten and a half, like me, big feet." An'qwenique seized the trail runners from the hood. "Wear these. They're already broken in. Adventure shoes." She grinned. "So, what's the plan?"

"Treating you and the St. B to vegan bacon buns at the Haven. Coming up with an action plot, a good story, that's your superpower, not mine." Paula admitted this as they jumped into the car.

An'qwenique kissed Paula a third time, an electric echo of their miracle moments.

"Passion is fuel," Paula murmured, and stroked An'qwenique's collarbone cleft.

"Yeah. So drive and I'll tell you my whole weird tale, then you can tell me about these clues you've been collecting on Oona and the murderous shitbooby."

Luckily, the fancy solar EV was charged up and roaring to hit the road.

MONDAY

ON CAMERA—*What the Hell Happened #2*

Iris Library event center and video conference cameras, remote activation, 7:36 PM

A high-ceilinged open space on the library fourth floor is dim. Cold blue street light ghosts through two large windows. Fluorescent strips in the hallway sputter on and off, eerie. Shadows dance on the walls, an imp jamboree. A poster by the door proclaims:

COSMIC CAMPERS CARNIVAL BAND
GALA FAREWELL CONCERT 2:00 PM SUNDAY
ALL WELCOME! FREE!

A blurry photo displays a drag trio and a goofy mutt (practically a ball of static and yarn with floppy ears) in a big red wagon.

A mound of junk sits on a podium at one end of the event center. Tables are lined up at the other. The snake person slouches against a table. Bug-eyed sunglasses are bright blue, not green. The man in the dragon raincoat and fire-breathing hat strides into the frame. He does exaggerated bravado, a superhero villain making an entrance, wishing for slow motion in real life. Overacting, too many comic book movies. His mirror sunglasses are also blue. He wears the skeleton jumpsuit, skeleton gloves, and fluorescent orange/pink athletic shoes as in previous video appearances.

Dragon Man halts at an open closet by the windows. Two

hundred folding chairs, plus boxes and music stands, have been stacked haphazardly. One wrong move, false breath, and an avalanche. "What are you two plotting?" His voice is still altered at the source. He now sounds like a raspy Darth Vader.

"Why tell you that?" Snake Person's electronic voice isn't working.

"Because," he deftly pulls a pistol from under the raincoat, "I'm quick on the draw and I have Lance." He holsters the gun and holds up a phone. "You're on camera. I'm not. This is your show." He seems unaware of tiny video cameras mounted in the shadows above him on the molding. He addresses someone who is opposite snake person yet unseen. "Tell me a good story for your name and—"

Snake Person grumbles. Dragon Man hisses her direction. She startles and knocks several mythic figures onto the floor. Muttering, she picks up the Pukwudgie, a Wampanoag forest imp with spiky hair down to a fat butt, a definite porcupine riff.

"Tell me the secret of your name and I'll . . ." Dragon Man hesitates. "I don't know, let you—"

"Let me live? Ha!" A strangled voice interrupts him.

The junk pile on the podium turns into Belle Roberts—Isabelle Shamiram Roberts. The head librarian was crumpled behind a stack of books, magazines, remote controls, a double cowbell, and a Change Gang mug. As she stands up, pale skin sparkles in the streetlights. Her silvery mane shimmers around her face. A short, intense woman, tears glisten in slitted eyes. She wears bedraggled jogging pants and tunic, a paisley riot.

"Don't bullshit me." Belle looks away from him, disgusted. She talks right to a conference camera. "I know your face." Eyes shift back to him. "I know what you do."

"Is that so?" Dragon Man scoffs. "Why didn't you call the police?"

"Her phone is dead." Snake Person yells. "Or else she—"

"No use calling nine-one-one." Belle slams the video remote

several times on the pile of books. "I told you. He's got an in with the cops. Oshun Jackson and Blue Rosenthal at least."

"Corrupt cops all right." Dragon Man dances, practiced, athletic moves.

He executes a flashy whirl. The dragon head bobs, and a tail swishes under his coat. On his second go-round, Belle slips the remote into her pants pocket. Her hands shake, but she nods at a conference camera, working him as much as he is playing her.

He halts and gloats, "Blue and Oshun are not what or who you think they are."

Belle curls her lips. "You don't know what I think."

"I've watched you play the hero librarian for the public—generous, thoughtful, a spirited change-maker." He laughs, a nasty sound. "Afraid of nothing, working tirelessly for the people, for the trees and the fungi, for the whole damn planet."

Belle shakes her head. "You've been watching me, planning this?"

"A pop-up event." He is pleased with himself. "Tying up a few loose ends tonight."

"Ahh, you're off your game." Her voice cracks. "You're—"

"Everyone loves the Change Gang act." He talks over her. "Even the people you piss off secretly admire and fear you. Angel Belle." He laughs. "Too good to be true."

"Oh? Well—"

"You lost faith forever ago. Who can blame you? This is a shitty world. Lately, you've been wondering what's the fuckin' point. You're shining everybody on."

Belle shudders. She looks about to lose it, then tries to pull herself together.

Energized, Dragon Man circles her. "The good causes are cover for an empty spirit."

"You sound disappointed."

"Corruption, atrocities, genocide, and where's the outrage? Fungi are better people than people. OK, empathy may be slightly overrated, but these dumb shits *believe* empathy makes you a wimp, a loser." He sighs and spins to Snake Person, a live audience for this show. "Humanity has let her down."

"They let you down. You're describing yourself, not me," Belle declares.

"The suicide notes you threw in recycling, I rescued them. Preserving your legacy."

"A fake garbageman. Wow." Belle blinks rapidly. "So, that's how you get in."

"I'm a mirror, throwing ugly back at you." He nods to Snake Person. "Ask her why she, the Change Gang's crown head, isn't at Crossroads tonight for the Tech Up Your Skills shindig."

Snake Person shrugs. She doesn't want to play. "I already know."

"No, you don't," Dragon Man booms. "Shall I tell the kid?"

Belle hugs herself. "A full-tilt diva, you're not asking my permission."

"Belle can't front for a big crowd anymore. She's been researching how to do herself in." He does a second athletic dance, leaping onto a metal table—agile for a big guy. "She has a deadly end all figured out, a good plan, I think. But, I'm no mushroom expert." He does, however, know how to do a soft-shoe. "A coward."

"Wrong." Snake Person shakes her fanged head. "You know shit." The Pukwudgie peers out of her raincoat pocket, smirking. "Going down the boardwalk to the Redemption Center was a trip. You had to be there."

"Your magic place?" Dragon Man snorts, almost falls off the table, then recovers.

"I thought we were just tripping at first, lost . . ." Belle murmurs.

"Beyond lost, like in another dimension." Snake Person is excited. "The dog led us out of this maze of trails in the State Forest. A map in her nose to everywhere."

Dragon Man roars. "You told me tall tales about a magic red wagon, not a dog."

Belle glares as Snake Person blabs on: "The dog brought us back to the library."

"Where I got the drop on you." He jumps to the floor. "Wait, whose dog?"

"Hush," Belle shouts. "He won't believe the truth."

"Is that the plan? Drop tantalizing secrets and keep me talking. Then what?"

"That dog can take you anywhere with the wagon. Magic," Snake Person declares.

"Liar. Where'd you go yesterday?" Dragon Man's wings unfurl. The tail pokes out of his raincoat. Fake fire spews from the hat. "You weren't supposed to *actually* vanish."

Snake Person sneers. "Shit like that didn't work on me before I met the drag royalty spirit-being. They're the real deal, a park ranger from another dimension."

"The Ranger's dream shuttle allegedly goes anywhere. You'll tell me about this spirit-being, and the dog, later." His coat swings open. The skeleton suit glows in the dark. Street light glints off the pistol in a shoulder holster. "You can tell me and Lance."

Snake person quivers as Belle distracts dragon man. "You give up on people too easily. Negativity bias has us believe bad is mostly what there is. A good friend says, *One tragedy trumps five triumphs.*"

Dragon Man turns on her. "A hope junkie, full of clichés right to the end."

Belle taps the bell. "My friend insists, *Clichés are often true.*"

He cocks his head. "Who might this mythical good friend be?"

"Did you talk this way to Melody?" Belle does a polyrhythm on the double bell.

"Is that her bell? A gankogui, right? Where'd you find it?" He almost sounds eager.

Belle sets the bell on her book pile. "Last spring, after Melody . . ."

"Distraction," he sneers. "I know tomorrow terrifies you. Why keep that secret?"

"I told this old bat on the bus. *The future ain't what it used to be.*" Belle chatters as Snake Person edges toward the exit. Part of their plan? "The old bird said, *So do right now!* She scribbled in her journal: *Later, something kills me. In the meantime, I live happy.*"

"I know that old bat," Dragon Man replies.

"Were you snooping on us? A cold, rainy day last spring. Jam-packed bus."

"I hate riding the bus."

"Too bad." Belle sighs. "I didn't know what she meant till . . . Crap, I missed the bus this morning and I won't see—"

"Stop." He waves the phone. Snake Person freezes as he talks on. "Always useless whining and wheedling about a life you were never going to achieve. I've heard it all."

Belle snorts. "So, why are you videoing?"

"You're a better show than the last two. Hanging on to your last minutes. Keeping me engaged." He jumps high, his raincoat fluttering about him. "But if you're not gonna tell me your name story or where you two disappeared to—Let's hit the best part."

"The Center looks different to everyone. Beryl says nobody is ever in the same place." Belle blinks. "The Iris might be next door to the Underground Railroad."

"Wishful thinking. Guilty white people indulging fantasies."

"Some people can't go everywhere, can't walk themselves to another perspective, ride a legend."

"Quit stalling." He pats the gun. "Drink."

Snake Person is stricken. Belle sticks her nose in the Change Gang mug, grimaces. Snake Person yells, "Don't. You said he'll kill me anyhow. Why help?"

"Gwen doesn't know my face. She can't ID me," he murmurs. "Gwen is useful. Lance misses her."

Belle studies him. "Is Lance really alive?"

He stamps his feet, mock indignation. "I don't need to lie. The truth's a killer."

"I believe you." Belle fingers the Change Gang mug. "Poison and what else?"

"Lethal mushrooms from the garden. Your end-of-life recipe. Perfect for loose ends."

"Ends? More than me?" Belle shakes her head, eyeing the conference camera.

"No," Gwen sobs. "Please. Don't."

"It's OK." Belle taps the bell. "Remember. We have an ace in the hole."

Dragon Man sniggers. "Melody's double bell? That's your plan? You have nothing."

"What do you have? My fake suicide?" Belle picks up the books, bell, and Change Gang mug then teetertotters toward him. "OK, exposing me, trashing the hope junkies, and also killing me. Well played."

Watching his phone screen, he backs up. "I added psychedelic shrooms, a helluva high to go out on. Quicker than waiting to broil alive in climate crisis hell."

Belle stops at the window nearest the closet. She sets her pile on the sill and opens the window. "Sunset is stellar tonight. Pun intended." She looks insubstantial in the streetlight glare, a will-o'-wisp. "The air is clean. No forest-fire breath." She takes a deep one. As she talks and moves in on him, Gwen inches toward the door behind his back. "Most people can probably reach the Center. But I don't know about you. Getting back is the trick. My mythical friend sang us home. She says anyone can sit in the Longhouse of the Mind, take a ride on the Underground Railroad of the Spirit, with Harriet and Jigonhsasee, and tell a different story on this world."

"Shut up and drink!" He backs into the closet for a better camera angle.

Two grinning Belles are reflected in his mirror sunglasses. "On the way back, I decided not to do myself in. I'd picked up recruits for the Gang and even new friends." She glances at Gwen, who strokes the Cosmic Campers poster near the exit door. Belle is talking fast now, a definite distraction. "I was excited because the trickster exhibit was still a go. I had a wild adventure to tell my mythical friend. Feeling back on my game, despite deadly mysteries."

He moans. "Ah, the lamentations of the condemned."

"Old friends threatened a surprise at Crossroads tonight. Characters I haven't seen in forever." A bittersweet smile breaks across her face. "The Gang will do Melody's anthem, catch any new verses. There's a handsome devil who drives his accordion bus like a band master riffing on the blues. Duke, we call him. He flirts on the regular, always shaking me out of a funk, making me laugh out loud. He's coming tonight too."

Dragon Man sneers, "So it *is* a wonderful life after all."

"Since losing Melody . . ." Belle talks and signs, awkward but clear, "Melody is my heart beating on, for as long as I can." She rams his solar plexus, a small woman, yet forceful. He falls back into the chairs, boxes, and music stands. She slams the door as everything crashes down on him. She holds it shut and barks at Gwen, "Get out of here. Avoid the cops for now, but find Paula. Tell her everything and do what she says."

Gwen hesitates, whimpers.

"Go now. Take the trickster route out. Don't argue."

Gwen wants to argue. She runs to Belle. Banging and cursing come from the closet. Gwen stumbles, and the Pukwudgie almost falls from her raincoat pocket.

Belle shoves the trickster in deep. "The avalanche of chairs did not take him out. Do the plan. RUN!"

Gwen kisses Belle's cheek. Racing down the hall, she turns the lights off. Her footsteps fade into definitive dark. Belle looks to the camera and mouths: *Find Gwen. Rescue Lance.* More cursing and crashing in the closet. She braces herself. Dragon Man rams the door twice, yet she holds it shut. He rams again, almost knocking her away. On the next attempt he smashes it open. She crashes onto the floor and yelps. One leg is crumpled under her. He looms. She looks tiny under him.

"Gwen is gone," Belle declares. "She's fast. You won't catch her."

He walks to the dark hall, hand on the gun, tail undulating. "I could have shot you."

She struggles up. "A bullet death is loud, messy. You want to film me dying, the best part. Can't do that and chase Gwen." She limps to the window ledge, dragging a leg.

He whirls on her. "Your plan: Talk shit, get me in the closet then sacrifice."

"You see right through me." Belle stares out the window.

"So drink up." He holds camera high. "Kid won't get far, won't tell anyone. I let her talk to Lance."

"People aren't always as weak or terrible or fake as they seem." She grabs the poison mug. "That's what you're hoping to find. Someone to prove you wrong."

"Glad you have me all figured out." He rubs a shoulder. Injured too?

Belle caresses the mug. "A search-and-rescue dog brought us back from the beyond. She nabbed your fanny pack of burglary tools from Gwen and wouldn't give it back. Do you pose as a garbageman *and* a locksmith?"

He lowers the phone. "What do you know about that?"

"The dog and how many loose ends dangling in the wind?"

"The dog is nothing," he snarls. "Not your concern much longer, is it?"

"You were certain I'd lost faith, so how'd you know I'd follow your plan?"

"I have Lance and Gwen. Stalling to give her a head start won't matter. It's you or them tonight. You don't want their blood on your image. You want to believe you're a marvelous person, depressed, but still a lay-down-your-life-for-little-nobodies hero." He taps the phone. "I'm giving you a star opportunity."

"You do have faith in me."

He looks up from the camera and pats the gun. "I guess I do. Drink now or—"

"Fine." Belle trembles, closes her eyes. "My own poison instead of your bullet. To Gwen, Lance, and everyone I love." She gulps the nasty brew, gags, but slurps the last drop. "What about you? A lonely dragon sitting on a useless treasure dump, burning up inside, or is there anyone you care about more than your weasel dick self?" She licks poison brew from her lips. "What don't people know or understand about you?"

"You're really asking." He shakes his head, can't resist answering. "Most people are for shit, beyond stupid. Cowards. They actually think mean is strong. Ready to rationalize, no, celebrate any sick shit they or somebody on their side can get away with. We don't feel each other. Nobody is wild or free. Domesticated cows, trashing our only world. You're the Change Gang Public Librarian. You know this better than me."

"Do I? So much bad crap going down, you better seize the good moments."

"OK, every so often I meet someone almost special, like you. It never pans out."

"We're shit, so you torture and kill folks? Lame." She sets the mug on the book pile by Melody's bell. "Before Sunday, I might've said, *You're right. Don't count on me. The Change Gang is all an act.* Turns out, *acting is believing.*" She slumps onto the window ledge. "Dizzy, and my feet feel numb."

"Whoa! Your recipe works faster than I thought. Should get painful soon."

"*Blue* not *Lou* Rosenthal has a great story for his name. He'll buddy up and tell anybody. Blue's a good cop who maybe took a wrong turn. Oshun has a wild tale too, but the lady detective never blabs. Now, my name." Her smile is radiant, astonishing.

Dragon Man perks up and leans in to his cell phone screen.

"Here's my mom's advice, what I tell everyone. Talk to the elders. Look it up. Find multiple sources. Face your biases.

Check lies and hallucinations, especially bullshitting algorithms on social media. *Work the clues!*" She winces and grabs her stomach. "My mom loved the libraries of Timbuktu. They saved a world. I'm a link in that chain."

He snaps his fingers, fake applause. "Grandiose to the end. They will all miss you. Your funeral will be something." He bounces on his toes, barely containing himself.

Belle points out the window. "An elm tree, a real old lady, survived Dutch elm. What's her secret?" Twitching, she breathes deep, gathers the books, bell, and mug to her bosom, then jumps onto the ledge. An elegant move, she's not off balance or dizzy. Her leg is fine. She was acting before. "These are my good moments. Living well, ad astra or beyond!" Singing a haunting melody, she leaps headfirst out of the window.

Stunned, Dragon Man sprints to the ledge and leans over the edge as—

The mug shatters and the bell clangs.

Event center and video conference camera, abrupt remote deactivation, 7:52 PM

M O N D A Y

RALPH—*Secrets and Lies*

Ralph Carter's eyes drooped. His nose was headed for a plate of jollof rice and dodo—fried plantains. Snorting hot sauce, Ralph jerked upright, and banged his no-longer-swollen thigh on a marble tabletop. He gasped for air, as if he'd been underwater, drowning. No, as if, riding a big red wagon, he'd gone through a waterfall and, well, somehow made it back from where his compass was all jacked up.

Ralph peered at blacked-out windows and dazzling stage lights. A dark wood interior was filled with masks, shields, baskets, and instruments from across the African continent—a festival, carnival decor. Several double-headed masks were looking spooky. Animate, sentient. No, Ralph was spooking himself. Too many twenty-hour days, appeasing clients, pushing himself to work miracles with garbage. That was as bad as blackout drinking. He blinked and tried to shake himself clear.

The Crossroads Pan-African Restaurant was hopping. He'd almost nodded off in a front-row seat at the evening gala. A full house, the audience was sitting in each other's laps and hanging from the rafters. Literally. Or the yahoos perched on the beams were part of the show. Ralph sat close enough to see sweat beaded on the performers' faces. He felt breath and heartbeats syncing up for the show. How the hell did he get here?

Nobody onstage or off acted like Ralph had materialized from the beyond. They laughed, slurped frothy drinks, and roared at each other. Performers, waitstaff, and audience were dressed to impress and/or seduce. Ralph rocked a dazzling rayon ensemble that he didn't recall buying. Deep purple jacket and pants hugged his muscular form. A lilac silk shirt caressed slightly aggravated skin. A kente cloth tie was loose at his neck. He strained to remember when he put on such fancy clothes. Purple was Darlene's favorite color and she gave him the tie.

That woman had to stop haunting him.

His thigh burned for a second, a phantom sensation. He blinked at a banner for the *Monday* dinner-concert to benefit the Literacy Project and Tech Up Your Skills, a Change Gang gig. Poets, musicians, storytellers, and dancers—local celebrities—had come to share their work for a good cause. Saturday, after Ralph emptied the shredded paper bins at Cloud Heights, Chief Nerd Azul Mendes gave him two tickets. Sunday, coming back from the beyond, Ralph offered Zsuzsu one. She was more than happy to accept.

What the hell happened to the rest of Sunday?

Losing a day was as bad as losing north and east! He cursed softly as a waitperson handed him a cloth napkin for the goop dripping from his nose.

"How we doing? Missed you last night." They swung a cascade of bronze braids and offered a sexy gap-tooth grin, like Darlene. "Where's the rest of your party?"

"I don't know. Zsuzsu should be here already." Ralph wiped his face. A miracle there were no tomato-red splotches on his fancy pants. An image of the blood-splotched woman in rainbow confetti strafed his mind. He winced.

"Don't worry." The waitperson leaned close. They smelled of cloves and cumin. "Your crew has time. We're not starting at eight thirty. The Cosmic Campers want to hold the show for Belle. The audience will wait. The Campers are magic." A frown. "You look janky, like you've seen a ghost. I'd try the rum special. It'll warm your heart."

Ralph recoiled. "I don't drink. Too much brain fog already."

"Right," they said quickly. "I *do* know that."

"Sorry," Ralph sputtered. The usual **DUMP IT ALL** charm eluded him. He'd been stupid drunk when he punched Darlene. Total cliché. "Alcohol doesn't agree with me."

The waitperson brightened. "You're the room-temperature ginger beer man! Warm soda coming up." They sashayed to the bar, flirting with everyone on the way.

Ralph marveled. The waitperson was half his age, half naked in the Nordic air conditioning, and wide open for adventure in this dangerous, cruel world. Wow. The dark mood startled him. He felt like crying. He had to choke down a blubbering, raging fit. Finding the murdered lady had done a number on his spirit.

"No shit, Sherlock." Stupid to rank on himself. Instead, he should—"Get a grip." Not like he'd gone to war, into actual battle or anything, just a witness, and after the fact. What was a person supposed to do with horror flashbacks? Ralph wanted to vomit. Resisting that impulse made the room swirl until—

The bus driver Paula and everyone called Duke slapped Ralph's back. They bumped fists then snapped and popped their fingers. "Love the hand jive," Duke said.

He wore a cutaway jacket, fat white tie, and a jaunty top hat in homage to his namesake. He was fifty-three and old school, a race man. Not a transactional bone in his body and generous to a fault. Of course he'd come out tonight, despite a hailstorm messing with his route today. A lumber truck skidded on slush and spilled tree trunks onto a main drag. Accidents were off the charts and traffic had yet to recover. A lot of pissed off tourists going nowhere.

"Didn't want to ruin my good mood so I walked over." Duke beamed, in a grand mood. "You bike in those threads?"

"Probably. I bike everywhere." Ralph cracked a smile, feeling better. "Join me. Always two free chairs at Azul's table."

"I have a hot date, meetup, or whatever they call it now." Duke held up a fancy envelope. "Dispatch handed me Belle's VIP invite when I finished the worst shift of the decade." He grinned. "She sent a special delivery to the bus depot. Threatened to hook up with me at the gym Wednesday, if I came. Hey, every Girl Scout can use weight training." He sat down at

Belle's table under a double-headed Guardian mask, best seats in the house. "I gave my tickets to a couple gym rats. Spread the love."

Ralph snickered at him. "You and Belle, since when?"

Duke bragged about her flirting during last spring's blackout. They were stuck on an elevator between the library's third and fourth floor. He'd joined the cleanup effort after a Change Gang gathering. They ate leftover falafel and baklava while trading raunchy jokes. Belle was good company in an emergency, good company anytime. They hadn't gotten quite that cozy since. Maybe tonight was their night.

"Belle and I agreed. So much bad shit going down, better seize our good moments." He and Ralph bumped fists again. "What's up with you?"

"Same old same old," Ralph lied. Like it was no big deal he was upright. Like he hadn't run from horror and gotten lost in the woods with the cops on his ass. He didn't recall ever getting lost before, not once his whole life. Couldn't recall this time either. His mind was a mess, foggy patches and gaping black holes, like he'd gone on a bender. Except, his thigh *had* been on fire—bitten by a poison doll with green leafy hair and razor teeth. A thousand beady eyes on bloodred stems tracked him, straight out of a horror movie. He felt those eyes still. Not much to say about any of that.

Duke rambled on about wacky passengers and crazy detours. Ralph hardly listened. He was chasing his memories, straining to find as many of the lost moments as possible.

Oona *did* lead him through a waterfall, then the doll-bite ache faded. And boom, he was high and dry in the emergency room. An'qwenique fussed over a dead phone. Zsuzsu squeezed his hand, charging him up with snarky fairy energy. *I got you,* she whispered. Ralph felt guilty, but he couldn't hear her say that enough.

Two med techs with pool-blue buzz cuts tested his vital rhythms and fluids. Satisfied with the numbers, they invited him to their wedding. They claimed Ralph was *out of the woods* and *good to go party.* An'qwenique and Zsuzsu agreed. But Zsuzsu didn't know who Ralph Carter truly was, who she was getting herself mixed up with.

Everyone in the emergency room had murky secrets. This made triage difficult. The med techs confessed to fantasizing political assassinations at 3:00 AM. An'qwenique had never been late for anything till Azul yesterday. Zsuzsu had squandered a law degree on scumbag clients. However, she'd maintained her license. In trial-lawyer mode, she used the hospital phone to call the Cloud Heights Chief Nerd and the cops. She intended to sort things out for An'qwenique and Ralph. Because no way was he the perp.

In like five minutes, Azul blasted in with Oshun Jackson and Blue Rosenthal. The hotshot detectives pummeled Ralph about suspicious behavior caught on video in the Crown Heights parking lot. Blue kept scratching his bald spot. Did that help him think? Oshun towered over him, over everyone, an amazon pressing Ralph for truth and insisting on justice. She could wrestle anybody to the ground. Ralph felt guilty. He'd been a drunken asshole with Darlene. He mumbled some delirious crap.

"Darlene?" Blue halted his note-taking and frowned at Ralph. "Who is she?"

Oshun had a squall on her freckled face that fit the thunderstorm hair. "Another victim?"

"No." Azul to the rescue. The premature gray mane was slicked down for serious business. Who knew the Chief Nerd was consulting on this case?

According to Azul, Ralph had the good sense to get caught on video taking cash from an ATM and ambling into the Haven while Dragon Dude was kidnapping his victim. Not a deepfake. Azul was at the Haven, ordering gluten-free brownies and the vegan shrimp and deviled eggs special. (Vegan shrimp tasted better than you thought.) Even the **DUMP IT ALL** miracle man couldn't manage to be in two places at once.

Tomás de la Cruz blew into the Haven after Azul left. He bought dark chocolate croissants and peaches and cream. Tight leather jacket and pants accentuated his muscular physique. Serious silver bling hung from his neck and one ear. Eyeing him on the sly, other regulars pretended celeb Tomás was no big deal. He didn't notice Ralph and Paula huddled in the corner trading terrible secrets. Not their usual Saturday rendezvous; a chance encounter.

Tomás was in too big a hurry to notice anyone. He had to get the croissants to his lady while they were warm and gooey. Ralph didn't holler at him because they'd both hit the gym Monday, and Paula was blurting a confession. Good friends shared hard truths. Ralph worried he had no really good friends, so no missing this chance.

Paula once took a sledgehammer to a vintage Mercedes-Benz. The glam couple who owned the car lied, claimed they paid their $678 lunch bill with cash. (They'd ordered a bottle of rare wine from the vault.) When busgirl Paula refused a strip search, the owner fired her. As security escorted her out, she took off *all* her work clothes. No cash anywhere. Afterward, Paula wandered the streets in a daze for several hours.

The glam couple or a reasonable facsimile jumped out of the old Benz and waltzed by her into Needless Markup. No hint of recognition. The street was a construction site. Paula threw a slab of sidewalk at the hood of their car then whaled on the windshield. She wanted to whale on the smug con artists too. A cop arrested her before she did that. Luck, man, because what if she hurt somebody? Nobody deserved the hammer, and what if they were the wrong glam couple?

Ralph had to laugh. Paula did too. *Living too long in an echo chamber of outrage.* She never wanted to be that mad at fools again. *You a storm child. Gotta bottle that lightning.* Her Grandma Junebug's words. *Why you want their blood in your mouth?*

Ralph's fuckup wasn't so righteous. He was unworthy of

friends like Paula. Unredeemable. Forget getting cozy with Zsuzsu. The worst day of his life was a bad dream, always loaded and ready to go off in his mind. Except, he couldn't remember what he and Darlene fought about: his working too much, drinking too hard, or spouting bullshit lies and excuses. He regretted throwing that punch before his fist hit her cheek. He tried to take it back. Too late. His second thought—*what the fuck am I doing*—came too slow. Momentum over mind. And alcohol. Ralph fell back rather than into the punch or he might have shattered her jaw.

Darlene never told a soul. She moved into her art studio and, when the bruised blood dispersed, filed for divorce. Ralph tried to give her more than she asked for. *Just my share of our life. You can't buy forgiveness or redemption.*

Ralph hadn't told anyone the whole story. Azul knew he'd smashed up his marriage, but no details. The Chief Nerd hired Ralph because who didn't need to **DUMP IT ALL** and **START DOING BETTER**? Ralph was grateful for the chance but secretly suspected Azul had made a mistake.

Paula agreed with Ralph's drunken-asshole assessment, but thought the unworthy, unredeemable bit was grandiose, an excuse not to work on change. She made this same mistake. Ralph was worthy of the gut bacteria counting on the next bite of a three-grain muffin. He was worthy of the *Trichophyton rubrum* fungus on his toenails, the eight-legged demodex mites on his eyelids, and the good friends who liked and loved him.

Who do we mean to be now? That was Paula's question. *'Cause Zsuzsu deserves romance. She does that bulletproof diva act, but you're perfect, a rock for an airy-fairy spirit.* Ralph tried to argue. Paula refused to hear any bullshit, the definition of a good friend. She insisted he come to the next Change Gang meeting. Plus, Paula was Ralph's second solid alibi.

Zsuzsu worked her diva lawyer persona in the emergency room. She told Blue and Oshun: *You have zilch on Ralph.* After he'd spewed what he knew to cops, *they* forced him to chase the dog (not his) into sketchy underbrush. Was that normal protocol? Ralph then survived a deadly allergy attack (at a haunted houseboat in a marsh, a detail she omitted) only because An'qwenique showed up with an EpiPen. Saving Ralph was an excellent excuse for Ms. Robinson missing Azul's high tea, for Zsuzsu missing a day at Cloud Heights. And how exactly was a semiconscious Ralph supposed to contact the cops? It was a wonder An'qwenique and Zsuzsu stumbled into the emergency room with him still breathing. The med techs corroborated this. Zsuzsu rested her case.

Azul threw grateful arms around An'qwenique, a teddy-bear hug—all was forgiven. Azul also worried about having real friends. The detectives looked discouraged, lost in the maze. The med techs gave Blue ointment for his sunburnt bald spot. Oshun applied the greenish goop, fluffing his blond fringe. Blue smeared a dab on her freckled cheeks then over the angry red blotch in the cleft of her collarbones. After this buddy action, they explained: Ralph was never really a person of interest, just wanted for questioning.

Slipping that noose felt too easy—free-floating guilt over Darlene. What was he capable of? What if he'd been home alone, sulking, so no alibis? When the detectives pressed Ralph about orange/pink sneakers, gym rats, and the dog, the med techs declared their patient was in no condition for more murder interrogation. A dodge. The detectives had too many questions about the dog.

Zsuzsu said nothing about the magical mystery pooch being her dog. The med techs also feigned ignorance. An'qwenique made vague reference to the tall park ranger and her service mutt. Behind the detectives' backs, she mouthed: *Oona is in BIG TROUBLE*. It went without saying that nobody from the sundial posse would ever rat out the St. Berdoodle to the cops. She'd saved their booties.

Blue and Oshun scowled, Azul too, probably picking up the stonewalling vibe. Azul looked forward to a thorough debrief with Zsuzsu and Ralph later. The detectives handed out cards and begged folks to call with any info they had on the St. B, her whereabouts, owner, whatever. Ralph, An'qwenique, and Zsuzsu made lame promises. The med techs didn't bother lying. They just ushered the detectives and Azul out.

When the coast was clear, the med techs threw open a utility closet door. Oona was asleep in the big red wagon. Nobody could blame her for being wasted. She still had to take An'qwenique and Zsuzsu back to where they belonged. Ralph too. The emergency room was a pit stop. That's what the park ranger said.

The sundial posse laughed, cried, and clutched each other. Oona poked crotches and licked hands while the med techs helped Ralph into the wagon. As An'qwenique made sure folks had their Redemption Center stories straight, Zsuzsu whispered in Ralph's ear, *See you at Crossroads*. Everyone pledged to stay in touch, then the med techs shut the closet door as if nothing unusual was about to happen.

The tall park ranger (part of their sundial posse?) had explained how the wagon transport-system worked when they were in the waterfall. (Did anybody get wet or understand?) The park ranger said *back to where they belonged* was a poor translation. At the Center, folks existed in many stories, many maps at once. Hard to wrap your mind around the multiverse. The frothy space-time maps the park ranger drew in the air seemed to make sense, but two minutes later who could believe what she drew or said? Who could even remember it?

"Earth to Ralph!" Duke shook his shoulder, still Monday night in Crossroads. "Nodding off, 'bout to crash land in your plate." The double-headed Guardian mask over Duke spun from a sulk to a grin back to a sulk. "Melody gave Jabril that mask." Duke drooped. He signed lines from Melody's anthem.

Holler the truth before we break
Dream the next move we need to take

The rest of the Crossroads crowd was looking janky, except a couple in the corner—the med techs. Their pool-blue buzz cuts were filled with sparkles, like the sun reflected in a choppy sea. They wore identical tartan kilts and caps, deep purple, like Ralph's suit. "We want to do our reception here," they squealed, and waved. Ralph nodded at them.

The frizzy-haired mandolin player winked as she plucked a chord for the Change Gang choir. At the waterfall, An'qwenique insisted she looked like Joni Mitchell. Her face crinkled into a devilish grin, because she, Ralph, and the med techs were in on a naughty secret together—the sundial posse ready to ride into action. Ralph planned to nail the woman about that after the show.

"She's doing music for our wedding." The med techs were thrilled.

"All kinds here tonight. That's Belle." Duke chuckled then turned serious. "Nodding off, dude? You said you were taking Sundays off, catching some rest, doing nothing."

"Faulenzen." Ralph loved Zsuzsu's German word. "What were you saying before?"

Duke scratched his pencil mustache and peered at the door to the street. The mandolin player jumped up mid-strum and raced out through latecomers streaming in. The mandolin banged her back and emitted a plaintive twang. Where was she rushing to right before the show?

"Belle is never late," Duke said. "She comes early to meet and greet."

Ralph nodded. "She likes soaking up the backstage excitement."

Worry skittered across Duke's face. "I wonder what's holding her up?"

And where were Oona, An'qwenique, and lawyer Zsuzsu now?

MONDAY

AN'QWENIQUE—*On the Case*

"Unbelievable! Traffic has been a disaster all day!" Paula screeched.

She wanted to haul ass and save the dog before the shitbooby or the Feds caught her. An'qwenique appreciated the sexy dimples that only broke out in Paula's cheek when she concentrated, a delight in the midst of horror. Headlights showcased her dark smooth skin, long eyelashes, and plum lips.

Paula shot sideways glances at An'qwenique. "What are you looking at?"

"What? No. Sorry." An'qwenique was avoiding the terror.

Get serious. The alien witch-doll glared bug eyes at An'qwenique from the EV armrest. The goggle-necklace streamed(?) videos of exploding stars, otherworldly cityscapes, and alien flora and fauna. Unnerving. Did Paula notice? The EV banged through a canyon pothole, and the Aje brandished her bracelet of gears like a weapon.

"That's you, not the potholes," An'qwenique muttered at the trickster.

Action-adventure romance with Paula was tricky enough, but horror sci-fi with zombies and aliens was definitely not An'qwenique's genre. Sirens blared near and far. She startled and bumped the headrest. Paula gripped the steering wheel. She was on alert yet unfazed by all the cow paths and state highways merging into Main Street. Traffic every direction was almost at a standstill.

An'qwenique smacked the EV's smoky side window. "Sorry," she said in a full voice. "My fault." She'd told Paula no detours. She might never risk another detour again At least the traffic jams meant they had time to tell all. Nobody (except the sundial posse) would believe the weird tales they exchanged.

"Gwen and Lance are still with us." Paula was thrilled to tears.

"You were right. The murder and disappearing-kids cases are connected." An'qwenique trembled. *How could she be working this case?*

"Don't worry." Paula tried to reassure her. "We can find the perp, rescue Lance, and spin a good disappearing-dog story for the cops. You're the tall-tale-teller, griot."

"Griot?" An'qwenique knew actual griots. "Wrong." She was a marginally successful podcaster with a trust fund. Weak sauce. "Jabril is—"

"Who?"

"The donsó ngoni player from Mali who does shows at Crossroads. He's the real deal, from a family of griots."

"Jabril, right. OK, but you're a great story spinner. Quit lowballing yourself."

"I'm not." An'qwenique had felt wrong since she woke up Sunday afternoon, then she lost a day plus a night of sleep. She barely recalled who she was before the detour. The An'qwenique who came back from the beyond was a mystery. "It's just—"

"Everybody listens to what you have to say, even the cops. I call that griot chops."

An'qwenique shook an achy head. The fog behind her eyes refused to clear. "You think I can conjure a plausible story for the magical mystery dog to hide in?" She held up her pocket journal, a sketchbook of the impossible. Oona was the pivotal character. She flipped it open to the Redemption Center shapeshifting from haunted houseboat to steampunk spaceship. "No way can I explain away all this."

Paula snorted. "We're not going to tell them what they don't want to believe." She honked at an Amazon delivery van cutting across their lane to get basically nowhere. "You freak out before coming up with a brilliant piece. That's part of your process."

"Maybe not this time." Acid in An'qwenique's stomach roiled. The last time she ate was fuzzy. "Plus, I'm so far behind I will never catch up."

Paula scrunched her face. "You said you'd do anything for Oona."

That bold, courageous babe was who An'qwenique wanted to be. However, according to Paula, their save-Oona-and-catch-the-killer mission had a very high danger quotient. In fact, in the lethal range. You didn't need to be a quanti-holic to figure that.

An'qwenique mumbled, "I did mean that."

"You don't mean it anymore?"

"I don't know how to do what I mean."

"Who does? I sure don't."

Emergency lights streaked the windshield and a rash crept down An'qwenique's neck. Scratching would only make it worse. "Tell you the truth—"

She wanted to collapse in bed with Paula, watch a good English costume drama, then fall asleep in each other's arms. Sex could wait till they had more energy, till it wasn't life and death. Paula smoldered beside her, on the case, ready to save the dog from the Feds and take the shitbooby down with her bare hands. Why was such a badass falling for a pampered wimp, who was allergic to bad news for fuck's sake?

"You deserve a better partner," An'qwenique murmured.

"You're joking, right?" Paula laid on the horn again at the Amazon van trying to ditch her lane and butt in front of them. Not happening. The driver cussed out an open window. Paula powered the right window down, leaned over An'qwenique, and spoke calmly. "They've done studies. Cutting from one lane to another ain't getting you there any faster. It just slows everyone down and increases your chances of a lethal accident."

"What, bitch?" the harried driver bellowed.

"Hey, my friend, don't I know you?" An'qwenique smiled, her *Great Escape* persona making a surprise appearance. "You carried my giant screen to the second floor."

"Did I?" the driver sputtered. It could have been her. She was built like a brick house, to weather any storm. "Yeah, maybe," she allowed.

"I know you're on a wicked clock, crunching every move down to the nanoseconds. That's messed up." An'qwenique shook her head at this injustice till the driver and Paula shook their heads too. "Everyone has somewhere important to be: a friend to find before something truly awful happens to her; a big brother in the hospital on life support—" Her voice cracked. She glanced at Paula and carried on. "The love of your life is counting on you, and maybe you can't measure up." Paula gasped.

The driver's mouth hung open, then she swallowed carefully. Truth had landed.

An'qwenique sighed. "We feel golden opportunities ticking away, a time bomb. We're driving ourselves silly, as if everything is life or death, as if we're living on a doomsday clock." Flashing on the Amazon van smashed against a pole yesterday, she reached out the window to the driver. "We don't want you dying for a stupid delivery."

Paula sucked her teeth, Bajan style, endless breath and sass. "'Cause we know they ain't paying you enough. Am I right?"

"No they aren't," the driver proclaimed.

"Hear those sirens?" An'qwenique quivered at the doppler shift. "Can't afford to lose good people. Somebody's counting on you walking in the front door tonight in one glorious piece. So please, be safe with yourself."

"Right," the driver sputtered. "I've lost too many people already. Sorry about—" She gestured at the other cars crossing lanes, jamming each other up.

"It's all good. That kinda night, right? But we got this." Paula waved, closed the window, and they inched forward. "So who is this better partner?"

An'qwenique shook her head.

"Come on, girl, that speech with the delivery woman is what I call griot chops."

"It doesn't work unless I mean what I say."

"So speak Oona's truth but do metaphors and poetry stuff." Emergency lights from far away reflected off the Aje's goggles. Paula gripped the wheel. "We've been doing gumbo-yaya magic since we first met. You wrote that to me, no taking it back now."

Embarrassed, An'qwenique pulled out her colored pencils. She started sketching the Aje on the inside back cover of her pocket journal, right next to the song lyrics. *Tell me a story I could be.* Who knew when the alien puppet/mask might vanish back to wherever? The hummingbirds in the Aje's afro had sharp needle beaks and were poised for attack. An'qwenique squinted at the fierce buggers. Static filled her ears.

We take the empties and you make the change.

Galaxy-hopping Captain Beryl expected too much of An'qwenique. Everyone always expected too much of her, even Paula. Especially Paula. Talking the delivery woman to her better self was nothing. The cops, federal agents, and the killer were professional skeptics and cynics. An'qwenique had no clue how to access what they wanted to believe. That was her only griot-interviewer trick.

Lightning crackled above oak and elm trees. A monster wind bellowed and chased clouds across a sickle moon. Branches ripped loose and thumped several cars around them. Another wild storm brewing. Tree missiles missed the EV, still the Fates were weaving crappy luck for An'qwenique Robinson. She pouted, and the Aje was unimpressed. Her bracelet of gears was grinding, revving up to something. A rebuke? "What do you know? You just met me," An'qwenique muttered.

Paula chuckled. "You must be talking to the doll. 'Cause I been knowing you, way before we officially met. Although tonight is our first date."

An'qwenique's skin prickled and not from hives. In fact, the earlier rash had faded. "You were checking me out on the sly?"

"Guilty as charged." Paula nudged her. "What do you say on the *Great Escape* about brave people?"

"*There's no courage without fear.*"

"That's what I'm talking about." Paula bobbed her head. "And courage is contagious."

"A lot of people say that, but I don't know." An'qwenique groaned. "You listen to my show? I'm not all that. It's a, a performance."

"Everybody be performing all the time." Paula glanced at the Aje sketch. Colored pencil nubs littered the EV floor. "How can you be drawing? In the dark, girl."

"Streetlights shining through the sunroof provide—"

"Cruising a bumpy road with danger up ahead, and you making art. Wow."

The sketch was electric, sparking off the page, full of the Aje's power.

"I draw to calm down, to think," An'qwenique admitted.

"No way could I make my fingers to do that right now. This steering wheel is holding me together." Paula lifted trembling hands for a beat. "Who do we think we are?"

An'qwenique kissed Paula's cheek, scanned stormy streets, and giggled. "We can't turn back, babe, not with that monster wind, not in this traffic." They laughed too hard.

"You know what scares me?" Paula murmured. "I get what the perp is doing, but not why. Why do such evil shit?"

"Zsuzsu and Belle argued over why evil at the waterfall. They got nowhere." An'qwenique sighed, frustrated. "Are we asking the right questions?"

"Probably not. Now, Oona I understand." Paula snickered. "Isn't that weird?"

An'qwenique glanced from the Aje's goggles to the giant ones in her go-bag. The images on Beryl's lenses were less alien: oceans pounding mountain cliffs, space stations lumbering in inky dark, and microscopic creatures feasting. "Tardigrades, one of your tiny critters, radiation-proof." An'qwenique sat up out of a slump. "Who trusts video anymore?" She squealed. "We claim Oona's disappearing act is *like* a SF/Fantasy special effect, a deepfake engineered to throw everyone off. No better distraction than a Houdini dog doing alien science that's like magic. Fodder for the steal-your-attention algorithms. While detectives scramble over YouTube sensations, shitbooby gets away with murder."

Paula bounced in her seat. "The truth as a special effect. That'll fly if we back it up with tech-magic talk from Azul."

"Azul's not in the sundial posse."

"Boss nerd would do anything for you." Paula froze. "The perp's trail *is* getting cold, and unlike the cops, he knows what's what with the St. B."

"No. He worries that Oona disappears, and he can't figure how to go where she goes. That's how Gwen escaped him."

"Right, he's not thinking alien science or hoodoo dog."

"He doesn't know what to think or where to find Oona. Storm/tourist gridlock means he's stuck somewhere too, improvising, on a time-bomb clock." An'qwenique glanced at the *Enterprise* ticking off seconds on her wrist. "He thinks he's a big genius, smarter than everyone, smarter than god."

"So he low rates other people," Paula murmured.

"That's our advantage. He doesn't realize what or how much we know." An'qwenique shuddered at what they knew. Paula insisted they make a list:

1. The shitbooby was a familiar face, perhaps even a friend. He fronted as an unremarkable, upstanding citizen. He rode his bike everywhere, even in snow, to stalk Melody, Charlize, or anybody.
2. A gym rat, he collected La Llorona and other wailing women.
3. The shitbooby won't miss Charlize's celebration of life. He'd do a big show of grief—tears dripping from puffy

eyes, a catch in his breath, a stumble to his gait. He was a wannabe performer with a horror backstory.

4. The shitbooby has been educating Gwen in murderous cynicism. Consciously or unconsciously, he groomed the aggravating teenager (and Lance too) to follow in his footsteps. Progeny was better than killing the kids.
5. Belle worried that he'd somehow corrupted Blue and Oshun. Although Paula's theory was that Oshun and Blue were close to figuring how Melody's case and the foster kids kidnapping were connected. But corruption blew up in their faces. Not a coincidence. Someone, like the shitbooby, didn't want them connecting the dots.
6. Gwen said he was a *Star Wars* fan same as An'qwenique, although Darth Vader wasn't An'qwenique's guy. A purist, he'd never wear his grandmother's lucky *Star Trek* watch, but maybe he carried a light saber.

An'qwenique cringed at the goofy saber in her go-bag, a sorry-I-forgot-your-birthday present from Big Brother. Her stomach dropped. She felt terrible for ignoring Big Bro at death's door. She plugged in her zombie phone, willing it to charge up, because: What good was avoidance? If, god forbid, Big Bro was no longer with us, Mom would leave another message on the landline to guilt-trip bad daughter for not rushing to his bedside. If Big Bro had pulled through, Mom would guilt-trip bad daughter for not attending the miracle comeback rally. In either case, Dad would be terribly disappointed in her, but say zip. Yeah, An'qwenique was screwed no matter what.

Paula snorted. "Chegh-chew jaj-vam jaj-kak."

"Say what?"

"Klingon. *Today is a good day to die.*"

"No, it is not. Are you a Trekkie?"

Paula shrugged. "The perp's just profiling as Vader. He ain't a fan of nobody but himself. He got feeling beat out of him."

"You're still on *why evil*! I don't care about the nasty someone did to him when he was ten, the women who dissed him, the men who crushed his fragile ego, or any trauma he turns into abuse. I could give a crap if the internet ruined his mind or if God told him to sacrifice immigrant turkeys and torture wild women to death. Fuck him and his god! I'm in our story, not his."

"OK." Paula scowled at the road. "But we don't know where to find him."

"We need to find Oona first. And we know where he'll be eventually." An'qwenique smacked the EV roof. "Damn, he still has Lance."

"Oona can find Lance. She found this kid's lost Frisbee and didn't know what she was looking for. She licked the kid's tears, took off for some high grass, came back with the Frisbee."

"Impressive, but—"

"Two weeks ago Triple-E forgot herself, medication mix jacking her up. Oona found the old lady wandering by the river. Tussling with the dog, she came back to herself." Paula's dimples twitched. "The dragon's lair is near the river. Gwen told you a fifteen-minute drive in circles from Cloud Heights parking lot. Oona will find Lance."

An'qwenique's cell vibrated. The battery was finally over 20 percent; enough for a text notification. "Zsuzsu was at Crossroads to meet Ralph and realized leaving Oona home alone was an awful idea. She rushed back but Oona was gone."

"The St. B lives for search and rescue. She's going where we're going. The Haven."

"Are you sure?" An'qwenique's voice fluttered.

"I don't know anybody as dependable as Oona, except maybe you."

An'qwenique flushed again. "But a dog detective? How is that going to work?"

"Lance made Tikbalangs for our library exhibit, Filipino forest and mountain tricksters. We'll give them to Oona to sniff." Paula licked her lips. "When I work late, Oona snoozes in the Viking boat by the Haven bus stop, her head in Elaine, Eleanor, Edith's lap. That old lady always be taking notes on her life. Drawings and poems, like you, in a leather-bound journal. Triple-E is a friend, and on this case too. They'll keep each other company, waiting even if the last bus rolls in without me."

"I hope you're right." An'qwenique's voice shook. "Sorry for being so mushy." She swallowed tears.

Paula patted her thigh. "Sentiment ain't cheap, a precious resource in the universe. Think how long it took to evolve from a rock to a cockatoo. Compassion is never wasted, always good medicine for your soul."

"From a rock to a cockatoo—that's an image."

An emergency vehicle cut in front of the EV then breached the sidewalk. Paula followed them. An'qwenique pressed her right foot on a phantom brake. With a spin of the wheel, Paula shifted from conductor on the Underground Railroad of the Spirit to Pam Grier, Angela Bassett, or Viola Davis burning rubber in an action-adventure car chase.

The EMTs sped half a block before bumping off the sidewalk onto a side street the wrong way. Paula hung close as they broke the speed limit and careened around corners. After all that talk about staying safe. The emergency vehicle turned in to the bus depot. Paula also turned, regretting her error too late. The EMTs halted at a double bendy bus. Paula braked.

Streetlights illuminated an accordion keyboard and buttons painted around the bus's bendy middle section. A giant's hand reached from a window to play the keyboard. Ominous. A crowd kept their distance from a limp man wedged in the bus's bike rack. The EMTs swarmed the body. Fluorescent-orange-and-pink sneakers—what Ralph wore—glowed on his feet.

"Duke's ride," Paula said. "And I know those shoes."

"Me too. Gym rat shoes, right?" An'qwenique ventured.

"The shitbooby could also show up at **Pump It Up! Be The Best You!**"

"He's a regular I bet."

"Upstairs Karl says everyone serious trains with him at **Pump It Up!**" Paula's throat tightened. "See that guy's shirt? That is College Bro #42." He looked dead, or close to it. For the first time this night Paula seemed truly rattled.

"Jackie Robinson's number," An'qwenique said. "You know him?"

"Sort of. He rode the bus this morning." Paula clenched the steering wheel. "Is he breathing?" Too far to tell. "We argued. He claimed altruism is bullshit and sacrifice is irrational, 'cause we're all just out for ourselves. Projecting. I wanted to stick my HEPA up his nose and suck the stupidness out. Big Foot posted something about him not being the murderer's type."

"Yeah, wow." An'qwenique grimaced. "I have to check messages. Big Bro is in BIG TROUBLE. I'm a terrible daughter who ignores Mom's urgent messages. I'll work that catastrophe while you see what's up with your friend."

"Friend?" Paula choked. "Sitting here, not knowing, he's dead and not dead."

"Yeah." An'qwenique beat back tears for her brother.

"Your plan, good plan. Oona will wait." Paula jumped from the EV and volleyed questions at the crowd. Nobody said much. Grim faces and tense bodies were eloquent. The rent-a-bum who worked the mall parking lot mumbled about *a mushroom overdose* and College Bro #42 being chased by *dragons and skeletons*. Tripping? Paula approached the EMTs.

An'qwenique tore her eyes from this distressing drama and called into her landline. There were seven new messages, starting with Mom.

M O N D A Y

OONA—*Don't Tell On Us*

Trouble smelled like death on a storm wind. After Oona found another body (at the bus depot this time), there were many disappointments. She gripped the bad man's fanny pack in her fangs and raced along a cobblestone alley to meet Paula at the Haven. She'd tasted traces of the bad man, Paula, and Mexican turkeys on the dead stranger at the bus depot. She whimpered, afraid for Paula, for all the friends she loved. Three turkeys were never flapping up out of Ralph's recycling bin. Nobody was safe.

Fat raindrops splattered on the ground. The wind whipped through branches and lightning cracked overhead. Oona paused mid-step. Thunder shrieked and the scary sounds rattled her. Heavy rainfall would make tracking much harder. Too many bad things were happening at once. Too many scent trails she should not ignore.

The rain petered out. The single cloudburst dried quickly in the heat, leaving thick air and hard choices in its wake. For the first time in her life, Oona didn't know what direction to take. A fresh whiff of the magician, clown, and musician tingled in her nose, but from the wrong direction. She whimpered.

The bad man threatened the world Oona loved. She was pack leader. Abandoning the search for him was impossible, even to find her old family. Her instinct was to hound him till his muscles burned and his breath was bloody, till he had no energy to run. Then she'd make sure he never got up again, no matter the cost. No matter that she ached to give up before starting.

Crows cawed a greeting and flew ahead toward the Haven, the right direction. The crows knew how to hound someone to death. Oona shook the fanny pack in her snout, defiant. She'd trained from a puppy with her carnival crew for difficult nights like this. Her spirit well was always full. Giving up or giving out wasn't an option.

Oona zoomed off, faster than before. Folks in their backyards thought she was lightning zigzagging down the alley. They groaned about weather getting weird. Oona resisted feeling helpless. She needed reinforcements to take the bad man down. Impossible for a pack leader to know or do everything. She had friends scattered all over who might help. Although, if they didn't smell danger, how would she persuade them to join the hunt? Paula followed Oona across any map with little prompting. Paula might have a better nose than other humans; she'd definitely have food. They'd chow down before the hunt. And Paula might convince others to join them. Energized, Oona careened around a corner to the Viking ship beached on the Haven's terrace.

The scent record was disappointing. Paula hadn't been here since the morning. Paula's friend, Triple-E, sat in the ship hunched over her journals. Vegan cheese buns with soy bacon bits (Oona's and Paula's favorite) were piled on a plate beside her.

"Hey you! We were worried." Triple-E offered Oona a greasy hand to lick. Oona dropped the fanny pack and obliged. The old lady smelled excited to see her, a great prospect. "I'm not always here on Mondays." She held up a journal. "Yesterday's memory vision: you almost run over by an old Ford. A snake was behind the wheel, a dragon in the back seat." She scratched the itchy spot behind Oona's ear. "Tourists are ruining the world. Traffic is a horror tonight. Anyone could be gone in a heartbeat."

Oona eyed the vegan cheese buns. One was much bigger than the others.

"I wake up aching for people dead ten, twelve, forty years. They took pieces of me . . . Left bits of themselves . . ." Oona cocked her head at the sadness on Triple-E's breath. "I liked who I was, who we all were together." She sighed, nose to nose with Oona. "What I miss the most is my mind." Haven regulars at a nearby table glared at them.

"They think I'm batty," Triple-E whispered, "talking to a stray-hound. Don't I tell you everything? Danger might be coming for you, me, them too." She shook a pill bottle that smelled salty and bitter. "New medication. I was taking this, that, and the other pill. Muddled up my short term. Paula wrote me this note."

She held it up. Oona wagged her tail at Paula's name and scent. "*Check the Combination of Meds*. Paula's fault I remember better." She ate a pill. "Paula's up to dangerous business. I have clues, memory visions: you chasing the car and that dead singer scrambling to get out the back seat. Dragon shut the door on her fingers." Triple-E winced. "Don't tell Paula I was whining."

Triple-E tapped another journal. "Guys from the bus got pissed because Melody let me sit on one chamomile tea half the night. Melody and I loved arguing." She poked her chest twice with the tip of her middle finger, *heart* in sign language. "They never liked her. So why go to her last concert and memorial service? That's suspicious, right?"

Oona barked. They needed to leave soon. She licked her chops—troubling scents rode the wind.

"Hungry?" Triple-E offered Oona the two biggest buns. "You feel me. I feel you. I bought the last four. We'll save the other two for Paula."

Oona wolfed the buns then nosed the bad man's pack toward Triple-E.

"What you got there?" Triple-E bent down.

Oona snatched up the pack, dashed to the curb.

"You do that with Paula. You want me to follow you. But can't we wait for her?"

Oona shook the pack and growled.

"Crap!" Triple-E smelled uncertain. "So the mission's that urgent, huh?"

Oona lifted her nose into the wind and snarled.

"OK. Hold up a second." Triple-E put the remaining buns in a string bag and nabbed a waitperson toting a bin of dishes. "You know Paula?"

"Paula Queenie?" The waitperson still smelled of Melody. Her scarf held down his hair. He also reeked of black ash trees, a basket weaver. Zsuzsu bought tiny ones for offerings at the Center. "Paula's good people. I slept on her couch when . . . Sorry, TMI."

"Tell Paula, me and the stray-hound were here, and I did find clues in my current journal and February's. One of these clues was on the bus this morning. I bought the stray-hound our favorite bun, and two for her. No popcorn, that's Wednesday. The stray-hound caught a scent. We're gonna answer a distress signal. OK?"

He smelled confused. "Do you need help?"

"I'll call nine-one-one if I do. Paula says the St. B's search and rescue trained."

He peered at Oona. "I'll see Paula if she comes tonight. I have the graveyard shift."

Triple-E held the heavy Haven door for him. "Write down what I said. All of it."

"OK." The waitperson slipped inside. Triple-E watched till he scribbled on a napkin.

"Look out for dragons and snakes," she yelled, then turned to Oona. "Where to?"

The doll's eye patch behind the Haven was a *between place* where many, many maps overlapped, almost impossible to navigate. Despite the hot night, Triple-E wore long sleeves, long pants, and sneakers. No bare flesh. "People think these plants are creepy. I love the eyes. This beauty is a hybrid I haven't seen before. Ha! Alien invasion."

The storm wind had knocked a trash can on top of several

plants. Oona pranced across the slippery surface, avoiding razor-sharp leaves and ripe white berries. She wagged her butt from the other side.

"What's over there?" A good sign that Triple-E and Oona didn't disappear on each other. "I'm coming." Tiptoeing across the cans, Triple-E traversed several borders then stepped off at the old tollbooth. She gaped at the waterfall. "Has this always been back here? It looks like the State Forest, but that's too far . . . I never know where I am, how the big-picture map fits together. Which is not the same as being lost."

She turned and gasped. The alley had vanished. Instead, old hemlock and oak trees waved in the last of the storm wind. They scented the air with calm. What Triple-E didn't realize: so many borders at a *between place*, you needed someone with map sense to anchor the vision.

"Paula says you break out of anywhere, and you know the best shortcuts. I'm following you." Oona trotted downstream to Zsuzsu's. Triple-E kept pace with her. "You're a bright bulb, like these fireflies." The fields were a carpet of flickering lights. Triple-E halted as Oona loped up the ramp to Zsuzsu's porch. "You live here?"

The pizza-foil crow swooped at Oona's tail and cawed to other crows in the dark. The neighbor mutt barked a greeting. Oona jumped into the go-anywhere wagon. She spit out the bad man's pack and burrowed into Beryl's blanket. Drinking in the rich funk of countless lifetimes, she was dizzy a moment, on a doggie high. Fortification.

"Why are we here?" Triple-E scanned Zsuzsu's dark house. "Is anyone home? Your owner might mistake me for a burglar." She tiptoed up the steps and stroked the wagon's handle. "I drew you in this wagon doing a show. A drag king had a shooting-star top hat and a chainmail vest. Cello player. No trouble remembering that."

Oona pawed Triple-E's arm, wagged her tail, and batted the handle.

"You want to do like in the show?" Triple-E scrunched her face. "You all took me on a ride into a closet amusement park. The walls turned into a meteor shower. The Earth was a blue marble under the floor. It felt like we were zooming in outer space." Oona licked Triple-E's nose. "I can't figure how your crew did that. We wheeled out of the closet, and Belle said, *Don't tell on us*." Belle's scent rode the wind.

Oona whined and nudged Triple-E. Her heart pounded with Oona's.

"Why not?" She tugged the wagon down the ramp. "Practically locomotes on its own." They glided past Zsuzsu's favorite mulberry, then gravel morphed into concrete and the State Forest dissolved. Streetlights blazed—foggy domes of light. "Like an old black-and-white mystery." Triple-E was dazzled. "I wish you could explain this to me."

A few more steps and they arrived at the bus stop near the Iris Library. Oona stood up in the wagon, ears erect, tail like a blade. She licked the scent spoor across her nose.

"That was definitely too quick." Triple-E headed for the library gardens and greenhouse. "I know where we are, even if I don't know what's going on." She stopped and panted. Belle was crumpled, face down in the bushes, her neck at an impossible angle. "I know those paisley pants. She rides the bus." Triple-E sank to the ground. "Is she dead? This is what me and Paula were worried about. No. No. No."

Oona wanted to argue with her nose too, but that never worked. She snuffled the same scents that Charlize, the man at the bus depot, and other lifeless bodies gave off. Oona tiptoed toward the librarian. No breath, no heartbeat. Oona whimpered and backed up. Belle wasn't getting up out of the bushes. No more rainy-day hide-and-seek in the greenhouse. Oona always ignored the tiny popcorn treat in the orchid room—carnival training. She ran right to Belle and got popcorn, cheese cubes, and watermelon.

Don't tell on me.

"Not an accident, not a coincidence." Triple-E gulped thick air. "Always reading another book on the bus. She loved books." Triple-E repeated this several times and wiped tears from her cheeks. Oona leaned against her thighs. They howled together, a plaintive song.

Isabelle Shamiram Roberts had fallen into hydrangea bushes below the window ledge she'd stepped out on to talk a homeless woman into singing instead of jumping. Belle said Shamiram was a legendary Assyrian queen who secured peace for her people during uncertain times. Triple-E had written that in her February journal.

Later tonight, Oshun and Blue will find a stack of suicide novels in the far corner of the window ledge on pigeon poo. The books' main characters are about to jump. Unlike Belle, they hook up with some other desperate body on a rooftop, bridge, or balcony. Or an angel. Instead of splatting on the ground and embracing oblivion, these characters save one another. They demonstrate that even a difficult life is worth living.

The book covers are slashed and the spines peeled away from the pages. Someone scrawled *HA!* with a blue Sharpie on the title pages. Uncharacteristic behavior toward books for head librarian Belle. Face down in the bushes, she clutched a Change Gang mug and a double bell. Oona knew the bell belonged to Melody. Scattered around Belle was a collection of fiction and nonfiction books about imagining a future you want while in the dragon's mouth. Belle was a fan of Audre Lorde according to a Post-it in one book.

Tomorrow, the toxicologist will report that Belle ingested mind-altering and lethal mushrooms from her private greenhouse room. Oona smelled this instantly. It will be hard to determine whether Belle was tripping or not when she died. Some folks will insist the fall was a drug-induced tragedy, not murder.

Eventually a different story will emerge, but Monday night, cagey detectives will claim it was doubtful that someone pushed her. Everybody liked Belle Roberts. She was beloved by people who couldn't stand each other. There were no witnesses or signs of struggle, and nobody with a motive to push her off of that window ledge.

At the last Change Gang meeting she ever attended, Belle yelled, *We've been fighting the same stupid battles, over and over, my whole life. Like pissing in the wind and getting wet, as my uncle used to say. Sometimes I wonder.* Melody's murder hit Belle very hard. Nobody realized how depressed she was.

Yesterday, high on mushrooms, Belle and her Change Gang wandered in the State Forest, hallucinating superspies, ghosts, aliens, and witches. This morning she was AWOL for meetings and her library shift. Tonight she ghosted a hookup with Duke at the fundraising gala she organized at Crossroads. Despair, it would seem, and personal demons, hounded her off the fourth-floor ledge. The news will report that she stumbled or jumped to her death. A good story. Detectives will let this narrative float to throw off disinfo-teers and the perp. Right now, Oona howled at six dead bodies (including the turkeys) who smelled like the bad man.

Triple-E patted Oona. "We were too late to help." She dug her phone out of the string bag and muttered the endless password. It took four tries to type it right:

Ask me to lose bomb, match, and fuse
Ask me to find what'll change my mind

Typing errors meant Gwen and the Change Gang mandolin player had time to charge down the side staircase and stop her from dialing 911. "We heard the howling." Gwen snatched the phone. "No cops." Triple-E gripped Gwen's empty hand so tight she yelped. Oona stepped between them before somebody got bitten.

"You have to watch the video." The mandolin player covered Belle with a tarp. "Should have done this right away. Belle had a plan."

"Give me my phone!" Triple-E yelled. "Paula said we'd turn over whatever we found to the pros."

Gwen was startled. "Right. You know Paula *and* the dog." Oona licked Gwen's phone hand. "We're the good guys, doing what Belle wanted . . ." Gwen and the mandolin player choked up. "Call Paula and we'll do what she says." Gwen returned the phone.

Triple-E tapped her password verse in one go. "Paula B. Queenie's in my directory. It's ringing."

"Not a good time." Paula's voice was in Triple-E's hand. Oona barked a greeting, relieved. "Is that the St. B with you? I'll call back in a sec."

Oona cocked her head. Always weird to hear someone so close and yet not smell them. The mandolin player ushered them up the side stairs to the fourth floor. Oona hated leaving Belle alone in the bushes, even dead to the world.

M O N D A Y

RALPH—*Suspects*

"Yo, Ralph! They're letting you run the streets?" Two gym rats from **Pump It Up! Be The Best You!** sniggered. "What's America coming to?" The meathead powerlifter and his running buddy sat at a table behind and to the left of Duke. White dudes, mega serious about their workouts. When did they arrive? "Guess you made bail."

"Something like that." Ralph hoped his run-in with the cops hadn't gone viral.

"Is that all you got for us?" Meathead was big like Ralph and obnoxious, online and off. He thought not using deodorant and wearing funky drawers was manly. "Come on. You can tell us." Meathead thrived online, calling folks out for everything, for nothing. Clickbait King. No feeding that monster.

"Ain't much to tell," Ralph replied.

"You made bail. Garbagemen can count on a paycheck. AI won't steal your business or any of those shoveling-shit jobs."

Meathead cried poormouth but made out like a bandit. He ran a successful security enterprise—locks, cameras, alarms—more cash, more status than trash and recycling. "Missed you this evening at the gym." He could bench-press Ralph, or that's what he wanted folks to think. Ralph didn't know what to think. Meathead pressured everyone to buy the sherbet, Kool-Aid shoes, on sale, SUPER savings. Actually, he had his buddy buy them first, then everyone else followed suit. Even Ralph and Tomás. Go figure.

"You clean up good." Crossroads wasn't Meathead's kind of joint. He and his best bud looked out of place in their fluorescent sneakers and funky workout gear. Recent bruises discolored his cheek and forehead. His right arm was bandaged. Gym accident or fight? Car wreck? Falling on his stupid ass? Yeah, Ralph never liked Meathead.

"Don't sit there alone, crying in your stew." Meathead pounded the table.

Duke rolled his eyes and whispered to Ralph, "My bad." He'd given them his other tickets because Meathead was going off on the bus company for highway robbery. "He did a big scene this morning about a bus pass expiring before he used it, held up the line. Paula charmed him. He told her diet secrets for building muscles and blasting fat."

"What's the big huddle?" Meathead was loud. "Join us."

Meathead's buddy punched the uninjured left arm. "Leave them alone, Frank." Frank Ferguson. And Albert or Arthur, no, it was Andrew Evans. Andrew had dimples like Josh Holloway or some old movie star. **Pump It Up!** trainer Karl said Andrew was famous like Tomás. But then Karl was starstruck.

"Sitting with us is better than sitting alone," Frank insisted. "Andy agrees."

"I'm waiting on someone," Ralph said. That must be true. Zsuzsu said she'd be back in ten, right before he nodded off. Something about Oona going walkabout.

"Oh yeah, the buff wheelchair chick. I saw her rolling around. Figures." Frank ranted at Andrew for dragging him to such a boring dump.

Andrew interrupted him. "You were passed out on the couch, streaming static. You rolled off the couch into the coffee table. Knocked yourself awake. Farting and drooling and flailing. You hit me in the mouth." Andrew had a split lip. He always made excuses for Frank. How he put up with the man was a mystery. "Admit you're enjoying yourself. Crossroads has to be better than static."

"Naw." Frank dissed the food, décor, and big-butt, stuck-up

ladies slinging dishes and flirting with everyone except him. He sure loved the sound of his own voice. He was so loud, they heard his BS on the street. Looking pained, Andrew insisted that Crossroads was a five-star jewel. Frank laughed. "I'm joking. You're too sensitive." He glowered at two women inching their table away from him. "Nothing's funny anymore. Everybody's prickly. I hate touchy people who can't take jokes."

Ralph refrained from shouting: *Go somewhere else and laugh. Have some respect for . . .*

Charlize. She was the murdered woman in his recycling bin. Ralph shuddered.

After the waterfall washed away the burning itch, Ralph was feeling grand in the big red wagon. An'qwenique liked his heartbeat action. The med techs still wanted him to get checked out when they arrived somewhere. Ralph promised to stand at their wedding with the whole sundial posse. Oona pounced on him, wagging her butt and licking his chin. Zsuzsu stroked his cheek, as thrilled as Oona, but restrained. She hid her heart in German whispers. A glorious moment.

Then Belle said the murder victim was An'qwenique's neighbor, Charlize, Tomás's wife. *I know who killed her and Melody. Not his name, but you might know him. He's at Change Gang meetings. I don't know what to do. The cops could be compromised.*

Why tell Ralph this? He refused to believe it. Nobody he knew would torture Charlize, a sweetheart who loved plantains, oolong tea, and chocolate croissants. Actually, Ralph didn't really know her. He and Tomás were almost tight, but she was elusive. Ralph's heart ached even so. And what could he do?

Charlize, like Melody, was a prickly diva with serious pipes. Well, Melody was more than prickly. She smacked down fools on the regular. Both ladies took no shit. Ralph appreciated them, egged them on, flirted—with Charlize more than Melody. They both flirted back. Charlize flirted with everyone, default mode. It was fun.

Ralph's heart pounded. Some dirtbag was fucking with his gym crew. That, and the cops coming after him for a crime he didn't commit, pissed him off. Belle should talk to the cop with a broken nose and big muscles who treated him right when Oona found the body. Officer Wang, she'd understand. There had to be better suspects.

What about Karl, the survivalist trainer with Norse gods tattooed on his ass? What about Frank or Andrew? They were always ticked off at Melody for the funky vets who got free coffee at the Haven and the homeless old woman nursing a chamomile tea all night. They were pissy about Charlize too, Frank mostly. He thought Charlize was *a world champion cock tease, so stuck up, she made you want to knock her on her big tits.*

Detectives should go after the meathead white dudes.

Ralph's suspicions bubbled, frothed, then fizzled out. He had no hard evidence, just—what did Paula call it—availability bias? Frank was aggravating. Stuck on himself, didn't know when to shut up and sit down, but a killer? Ralph resisted thinking the perp was a gym rat. Who would that make Ralph? He rubbed his knuckles, a phantom ache. Skunk drunk, he'd punched Darlene. What else was he capable of?

Tripping over your own shadow 'cause you don't want to tell Zsuzsu the truth.

He groaned. Darlene was still calling his shit. Performers and audience eyed Ralph, like they heard Darlene shouting in his head. He hated sitting alone at the Chief Nerd's table. The second-best seats in the house and always two empty chairs for the unexpected. Where was everyone? Azul promised to buy the first round, and Zsuzsu should have been back. Did she drive all the way home?

Ralph took out his phone. It was dead to the world. He plugged in to a socket at his feet. What would the phone tell him? Not what to do about anything. Not how the hell he got here or who dusted Charlize and Melody. Certainly not how to tell Zsuzsu terrible secrets. And Belle might know the killer. They all might—somebody had to.

What would the phone have to say to that?

M O N D A Y

AN'QWENIQUE—*Landline Follies #2*

An'qwenique squirmed in the tiny EV. She wanted Paula to hurry back. The bus depot in the dark was always eerie. Tonight, the giant hand busting out the window was too spooky. The EMTs weren't resuscitating Paula's friend, so dead then. Paula pushed past gawkers and shuffled toward the EV. She halted to talk on her phone, then dragged on. An'qwenique ached to wipe the shadow off of Paula's spirit.

"I'm the worst partner," An'qwenique sputtered out the window. "Didn't make it through one message. They'd never make a buddy film with me as your number two."

Paula furrowed her brow at this feeble joke. "We'd have to be a ten-episode TV series. More time to develop the characters and also feature good chase scenes." Deadpan, not trying for funny, surviving. Paula slipped into the driver's seat.

An'qwenique leaned close. "What's the scoop?"

"I hate my phone." Paula clutched the device in quivering hands.

"I meant with your friend over there." An'qwenique pointed at the EMTs conferring over College Bro. One disaster at a time.

"A big poodle dog found him in the bike rack, wouldn't stop yapping till they called nine-one-one, and then she disappeared."

"Oona?"

"Who else? Triple-E and Gwen called from Iris Library. Oona's with them now."

"That dog gets around."

"Word is, the guy OD'd, but . . ." Paula shook her head.

"Oona's tracking the shitbooby. I think he murdered the kid, doing a horror spectacle. All this, a big show."

An'qwenique tried not to freak. "All what?" She touched Paula's shoulder but Paula flinched away from her.

A distant siren screeched, coming their way. Paula buckled up. "We gotta boogie. Finish your messages. Seven, right? It'll take that long to reach the library."

"What're you keeping from me?" An'qwenique pressed. "You were on your phone."

"I can't talk and drive fast. I'll get too mad." A grim tone with little explanation, but trust was their deal.

"I'm not fragile. I won't shatter." An'qwenique insisted. "But I can wait." She buckled up and called in to her landline again.

Paula drove off like a bat out of hell. Good thing traffic had calmed down.

"It's Mom. How many messages have I left you?" Mom sounded as grim as Paula. "I don't know what time it is— the sun is low. Your brother is out of the woods. A difficult thirty-six hours, but tomorrow is looking good. I told your father, we don't need to worry about you. But, you're still Daddy's girl, so he's concerned. Have some mercy and call. Or . . ." She hung up on herself.

"Mom again, eight PM. Don't you care? How did I raise a child like you? They almost put your brother on a ventilator. He never got the vaccines. Running around like a wild man, doing god knows what, breathing contaminated air to prove what? He said he might as well go on out after a good time! Both of you, careless with other people's feelings. You can't even pick up the phone. I don't know what to say. I don't."

Mom sputtered, choked, and avoided asking if there was a reason for radio silence. She couldn't imagine daughter in BIG TROUBLE. To be fair, nobody would imagine or believe the truth.

"Not just Oona, I need a good story," An'qwenique muttered.

"Everybody needs a good story," Paula replied. "Even the—"

"You'll have excuses." Mom was back. "Missing a big deadline by five minutes. Or your girlfriend turned out to be a slut and ditched you for somebody with more booty. Or wait, you can't figure how to save this messed-up world from itself."

Dad yelled in the background, word salad, yet relieved that Big Bro was out of the woods. "Let's be happy," he proclaimed.

"I guess we'll keep you posted." Mom hung up.

"So predictable. Mad at me no matter what," An'qwenique grumped.

"Text her something," Paula commanded.

An'qwenique sighed and typed: *Sorry for keeping you all in the dark. Glad to hear about Big Bro's recovery.*

I know you don't want to hear this, but I've been hanging by a thread myself.

Life and death, and not quite out of the woods yet. I'll keep you posted.

This seemed snarky, cruel. She sent it anyway and let the next message roll.

"Hey you, Azul here. How's Ralph?" He was relieved to get the skinny at the ER and hoped for more details later. "When all the shit blows over." Whenever that would be. "OUT OF SERVICE? What was that? And the time sequence is wonky. Where were you, Ralph, and Belle for so long? I hate not knowing what's random, what's the plot."

"Don't we all," An'qwenique muttered.

The next caller had blocked their number and was an unfamiliar, breathy voice, distorted. "Are you home yet? Still tying up a few loose ends."

Paula jerked. "The strange voice dude called twice, about loose ends."

"Coincidence. It doesn't have to be Dragon Man's loose ends." An'qwenique needed to believe that.

"I hope you're hanging in." Her editor, sounding solicitous. "I talked to Azul, so don't sweat the VR review. How about two weeks from now? You have a lot going on. The **DUMP IT ALL** guy and your neighbor, poor woman. We'll chat next week."

The sixth message was Kitty. "It's your ex! Remember me? It's only eight eighteen PM, but going dark already. Stupid answering machine records and records, but won't tell me anything, won't answer my questions. Your cell is BACK IN SERVICE, but you aren't picking up, plus there's no real message time and you hate texts, so . . . I'm doing the landline thing." Kitty sounded drunk, slurred yet speedy, words falling over each other.

"So I was leaning against your African front door, my cheek against the Dogon fish aliens, watching the sundown light show, and this creep in dragon cosplay tiptoes out of a bush, whispering *An'qwenique Robinson,* like he's been after you his whole life."

An'qwenique's heart thrummed in her mouth. While she and Paula were in the soundproof closet or master bedroom, the shitbooby was at her house again, about to be all over Kitty. Paula clenched the wheel and glowered. If Dragon Man was standing in the street, she'd have run him down with the EV.

Kitty chattered on. "His voice is jacked up, a James Earl Jones wannabe. That tail is nasty. I'm like, why would my girl know this loser? I say, I'm not An'qwenique. You're not here. You're avoiding me and everybody. Nobody knows where the fuck you are. OK, I've had a few cocktails, designer drinks. I spent a fortune on this pukey high.

"The creep's wearing mirror sunglasses, and the sun is a glow from underground. Fire shoots from his left ear. Dragon head is on sideways. While he straightens himself out, I remember your Wild Bunch neighbors: vegan lawyers and dirt-farmer activists who do community theatre, right? He must be a stray from next door.

"*Not An'qwenique?* Dude is so disappointed. Acting like this was a hookup and you ghosted him. I'm jealous. Why should

I be jealous? I left you for a big-city slut. Dude doesn't even know what you look like, if he thinks I'm you. We both have big hair, but—Are you into guys now? He's worried or pissed, 'cause I have no idea when you'll be back. Or where your dog is. What dog? You said you were a cat person, but allergic. Don't you know who you are anymore? Who is making shit up here? Him or you?

"I complain about you never answering the phone, a diva. Your cell was OUT OF SERVICE for over twenty-four hours! Like a fool, I kept checking. OUT OF SERVICE? You closed up shop and moved to Mars? You found some other babe or this neighbor dude on a dating app? Payback for how badly I've treated you? I deserve it, but this is so unlike you. He says I'm funny, does a canned laugh. Creepy is an understatement. I would not be showing him empty houses all by myself. Who is he to you anyway?

"I talked to Paula. She cheered me on, gave me hope. In fact, coming to face you live was Paula's idea. My courage is her fault. Where'd you find this girl? She sounded cute, in a freaky duck kind of way. You like ducks. Cosplay creep says he hates ducks and turkeys, shitting on the lawn, even if they are iridescent purple. Aren't those his turkeys? He asks if you and the librarian are tight. I ask for a definition of tight, and bam! He is nowhere. Vapor. Sorta walked into that big bush you love. I ain't looking in there.

"I don't want to spook you, but he gives off a stalker vibe, like he's watching the house, waiting for you to come back so he can nab you. Maybe that's me, projecting my shit on him. I thought about camping out on your flagstone doorstep till you came back from whatever. You better have a great story. You better be all right.

"OK. I don't want to get anybody in trouble. I'm drunk, confused. Be nice to the neighbor dragon if he's worth it. Maybe just a donation hound? The next-door Wild Bunch is save-the-whales-and-the-bees righteous, right? Still, I say watch out.

This is not just Kitty being negative and suspicious. He did a jump scare in real life and enjoyed the hell out of my heart skipping beats. Eyeballs ready to burst, bladder about to let go and let flow like your phone greeting. I am a horror fan, but it is absolutely false that adrenaline sobers you up. You're just drunk with a jagged edge.

"Why am I running on? Took four cocktails on an empty stomach to get my shit together for this live appearance, and you're a no-show. I mean, what time is it? Maybe it's not that late. Neighbor guy, or whoever, said I was a lucky girl. Very lucky. *Just wait and see.* That sounds like a threat. Watch out for trolls gone live. I mean, Charlize, right?

"I'm trying to sneak back into your heart and warn you at the same time. That's how I am, complicated. That's why you had a thing for me. Sorry I messed us up. You weren't perfect, but you tried harder than I did. Weird cosplay dude is wrong. I'm not lucky. Sure, I ain't been run over by a train, but I don't step on board and go somewhere grand either. That's you. That's lucky. Wow, here he is again. How does he do that? Is that three minutes—"

6.5 minutes before the machine cut you off. Why tell anyone that? An'qwenique exchanged desperate glances with Paula as the next message played.

"Boo!"

An'qwenique pumped the phantom brake as Paula almost drove into the gutter.

Kitty laughed, drunk out of her gourd. "Sick of me yet? Sorry to keep bothering you. You have another visitor. She looks like a bush or—no, she's correcting me—like bittersweet attacking forsythia near garbage cans. Urban camouflage. She scared Dragon Dude off with a flashlight that sends the beam miles into the darkness, to the moon or some shit. A real light saber, you need one like this. The Mexican turkeys scared him off too. The Big Bird Beasties are mad at him about something. Stingy with the turkey feed?

"Camo-Lady is a big fan of your *Great Escape* podcast. She says you went camping in the State Forest yesterday. No cell towers, just ghosts, static from another dimension, and a seven-foot-tall park ranger." Kitty chuckled. "You left your water bottle at the falls in the State Forest. Have I been to those falls? She drove back before you, wanted to leave the bottle on your doorstep while she still remembered. I was so glad you weren't dead or kidnapped, I hugged her. No, seriously, Urban Camo-Lady saved me. I am thrilled you're all right.

"So . . . I'm wrong for you. Still, I was freaked. Too much evil crap going down. I'm heading to Crossroads with the camo lady. She seems nice. Out there, but who isn't? A big feel-good show is what the doctor ordered. You'll probably do a run to the Haven if you get in late. That's how we met. Me mainlining espresso, you grabbing a mango smoothie before running home. Do we want to bump into each other? Tell Paula I tried. My face-to-face courage is used up. Glad you're OK. We were fun sometimes."

The robot voice declared, *End of messages.*

"Wow. Camo-Lady is part of your sundial posse, right?" Paula said.

An'qwenique shuddered. "He stormed my house a second time and with the police next door."

The library loomed ahead. "Yeah. He's been all over."

"What are you not telling me?"

Bumping through potholes, Paula squeezed into a tight parking space. The Aje fell in her lap or jumped. Paula stuffed the trickster in her utility vest pocket and stepped out of the EV. The shadow had not lifted from her spirit, but spread to An'qwenique.

"It's Belle," Paula said.

"What?" An'qwenique froze in her seat. "Tell me now."

"All right." Paula came around the side, opened the door, and held out a hand.

M O N D A Y

PAULA—*Passion Fuel*

On the library event center screen, Belle saluted her beloved elm tree and reached for the stars. Paula, An'qwenique, and the mandolin player gasped, tears drizzling. Even Azul and the detectives seemed stirred by the video from hidden cameras. Outside the window, the placid elm towered over the greenhouse. The colonial garden center beside it was rumored to be a stop on the Underground Railroad. Belle never found definitive proof. Maybe somebody would.

The screen went to static, and Paula's ears rang. *To Gwen, Lance, and everyone I love!*

A hormone stew made Paula dizzy, made the spit in her mouth dry up. Her stomach dropped to her knees. Oshun and Blue were sweat-stained and rumpled, running on empty like An'qwenique. Hardly any sleep and only a few bites of bad food since Sunday afternoon. Oshun's usually defiant blond curls hung limp. A muscle in Blue's neck twitched. Otherwise they looked chill. How the heck did they manage that?

Paula was terrified and cussing-mad, worse than when she beat up the Benz. *Work the clues.* Belle spoke from the grave. Who did she think they were? While Paula worked the clues and tried to save the dog, the perp got to Belle, College Bro #42, and trolled An'qwenique's front door, again. *Tying up loose ends.*

Despite deep breaths, Paula's stomach refused to settle. She wobbled. Rage, fury, and disgust were a terrible mix, and exactly what Dragon Man wanted from his audience. *Full-tilt diva*, like Belle said. Good chance he was hooked into disinfoteer social media, a hellscape. The ringing in Paula's ears gave her a headache. She leaned into An'qwenique, who leaned back into her. They held each other up.

"*Ad astra or beyond!*" An'qwenique insisted.

"Right," Paula replied. No feeling gutted.

Belle talked to hidden cameras asking her and everyone to take the killer down. But how could they? Paula clutched An'qwenique's hand. Azul noted this intimacy. Jealous? What about Tomás? Azul was a tech consultant on Charlize's case and had promised Tomás to use Cloud Heights's genius power to solve this mystery.

"Why didn't Belle fight him?" Azul asked.

Blue snorted. "She's tiny. He's a bruiser with a gun. Where would that get her?"

"It's amazing she didn't freeze up completely," Oshun remarked. "That's what usually happens. Belle figured, I'm dead anyhow, so—give the woman some props."

An'qwenique nodded. "She did fight him, her way."

"And we're part of Belle's plan," Paula said. "Right?"

"Right." Azul turned to the mandolin player, Belle's right-hand Change Ganger. "Gwen is a victim turned accomplice, on the run. Are you the mythical friend?"

"No." The poor woman crumpled on the floor. Her ragged breath resonated in the mandolin on her back. She clutched a paisley scrunchie in her fist—Belle's?

"This friend might be in danger," Azul pressed her. "They might need—"

"Stop." Oshun helped the mandolin player stand up. Danger was where Oshun lived, the mandolin player not so much. Azul was a cloud dweller.

"So what are we doing now? Letting Mendes run interrogations?" Officer Judy Wang, the cop guarding the door, grumbled about janky protocol. Wang had spiky black hair and a once-broken nose. As fierce as Oshun, she glared around the room, unhappy with the proceedings. Was any of this standard detective protocol?

Not going by the book was probably how Blue and Oshun

landed in big trouble. Dragon Man could have exploited some misstep and had them sidelined, then after they beat that, he bent the truth to mess with Belle and control Gwen. What if the perp was a policeperson, a detective? Paula shivered and peered at Oshun and Blue. Actually, they were rattled, off their game, but covering this well. Who could they trust? The perp had jacked everyone up.

"You're the mythical friend," An'qwenique whispered in Paula's ear. Paula shushed her. Nobody needed to know that. Yet. The detectives needed to focus on finding him.

"Who else has seen that damn video?" Blue itched his bald spot.

"Just this room." Oshun poked Blue and he stopped scratching. "Nobody else sees it, for now." Oshun glowered at the podcast journalist. "Nobody talks about this."

"College Man #42 and Belle will be considered unrelated incidents, a terrible coincidence," Blue added. "Don't tell Tomás or Belle's friends or anyone about more murders."

"We're not stupid," Azul scoffed.

The mandolin player nodded. She secured scraggly wisps with Belle's hair scrunchie then curled into a ball on a chair.

Blue looked pained. "We'll let you all leave in a minute."

"Controlling the flow of information around this case has been a challenge." Oshun seemed to be reprimanding Blue and everyone. "Let's do better."

"Social media disinfo-teers, man," Paula muttered.

"I'm on your team." An'qwenique sounded innocent, all sweetness and light.

"You'll have an exclusive after we catch him," Oshun promised.

"We're all on your team," Paula said. Someone else might have suspected a cover-up, but Paula called Blue and Oshun for College Bro and Belle in the hydrangea without hesitation. They were grateful. She should have called sooner. "You can count on us."

"Just no leaks," Officer Wang repeated. "That's how we catch him." Through the whole corruption mess, Wang had stayed loyal to Oshun and Blue. Who'd dare step out of line, now or later? Wang would hunt you down. "And don't touch anything."

Regrettably, Dragon Man wore gloves and a costume that covered his hair and skin, so no fingerprints, no shedding DNA. He'd watched that show.

"Is this the only copy, hon?" Oshun spoke gently to the mandolin player. They wanted to secure the video before the legion of evidence collectors arrived. What if the perp was one of them? A provisionary cover-up—a few hours to get ahead of him.

"The only one," the mandolin player croaked, then cleared her throat, hoarse from not screaming, from swallowing down too much bile. "If we turn the system off, we'll need Belle's password to turn it on."

"I bet you have that," Paula blurted. The mandolin player nodded.

"So we turn the system off?" Blue asked, and Oshun concurred.

"Belle played him. He was unaware of conference cameras." An'qwenique sidled up to Azul, shifting fully to her *Great Escape* persona. "Nothing supernatural in this video." Officer Wang tuned in. "He knew Tomás's outdoor system and performed for that. Nothing supernatural there either. He hacked Cloud Heights cameras for special effects."

"What are you saying?" Blue strode close.

"The dog and kid disappearing in the parking lot video is like, I don't know, a science fiction/fantasy special effect," An'qwenique mused. "The perp even said the kid wasn't supposed to actually vanish."

"So my theory is—" Azul repeated exactly what An'qwenique said with techno babble spice, taking full credit for her insights on the video evidence. Azul seemed angrier at detectives for ignoring genius theories than at the perp for hacking the Cloud Heights cameras. "He's messing with us, sowing doubt." Azul waved at Blue and Oshun. "He's afraid you two will figure him out and end his bullshit reign of terror."

An'qwenique agreed. "He diverts your energy with high-tech smoke and mirrors."

Officer Wang raised a skeptical eyebrow. She was at the scene when Ralph and the St. B walked into the brush and could not be found. A stubborn eyewitness.

"Belle told me about secret Underground Railroad passageways in the garden center." Paula offered Wang truth as special effect. "Tunnels leading to the river trails near Cloud Heights."

"Huh." Wang scrunched her face.

"It's poetic." An'qwenique snapped her fingers, on a roll. "Ralph Carter is lost in that maze of trails, out of his mind, about to die from anaphylactic shock. The dog takes him along the Underground Railroad to me and Zsuzsu. This saves him."

Wang blinked at vague memories. "Right. Ralph said the dog knew secret paths."

"Yes, the Railroad is still running," the mandolin player murmured. "Oona and the sundial posse to the rescue."

An'qwenique talked over her. "This shitbooby twists a feel-good rescue story to his advantage. He loves cosplay, putting on a horror show, and while you're chasing a magical mystery dog, he's cracking up and getting away with murder."

"Shitbooby?" Wang chuckled and her shoulders dropped. "Tunnels, huh?"

"People have been running and hiding since colonial days," An'qwenique replied.

"You make more sense than anything." Wang liked this story.

"We'll check that out," Blue said.

"He won't get us chasing the dog," Oshun declared

Azul gripped An'qwenique. "The perp is a tech wizard, but an awful storyteller. He can't do a credible deepfake. Facile and arrogant, he adds his signature style to the code, a fantasy element. He's quick but not deep. Can break shit, but no real vision. Too much melodrama. I mean, the dog is always blurry."

"Oh yeah?" An'qwenique acted impressed. "I'd like to see those videos."

"I can arrange that, eventually. I'd love to pick your brain." Azul grinned.

"Are you two working up a tech profile?" Oshun and Blue were relieved to be off the magical mystery dog and on to the perp's horror science and terror art. Success. This spirited confab took place ten steps from a Cosmic Campers poster for a farewell concert. Oona was a blur in a big red wagon. *The* wagon?

The ringing in Paula's ears turned into a giggle. The cosmic drag trio cut their eyes at her. *Girl, it's on you now! Work those clues!* The Aje hung by one arm from the vest collar. Purple bug eyes were luminescent. The felt afro shocked Paula's chin. The Aje pointed at her trickster crew on the floor. Azul had claimed Wang's attention. Ignoring the don't-touch admonition, Paula plucked Coyote, the Monkey King, and Anansi off the floor and set them on a table with other tricksters.

Make it strange. Tune in to the weird.

Wooden boxes, chairs, and music stands spilled out of the closet. This avalanche could have done real damage, broken the shitbooby's neck. Luck, man! He must have cuts and bruises. She smelled disinfectant. He'd cleaned up any traces of blood.

Bracing herself, she approached the window ledge. At the far end, the cheesy cover of a come-back-from-tragedy romantasy glowed in street light. Books in bird shit were a good frame for Belle's "suicide." The perp blamed a shitty world for driving her over the edge. Paula snorted at a winged, bare-chested hunk who clutched the hand of a buxom woman dangling from a bridge over the abyss. Both were honey blondes with nut-brown suntans. The book had to be better than the cover.

"Tacky romance is An'qwenique, not Belle," Paula murmured. She clutched the Aje before leaning out of the window. Staring at the hydrangea bushes below, her stomach flipflopped. She jerked back. Five-foot-one Belle could never have set the books so far down the ledge without falling. Over six feet, a stranger in the world of short beings, the perp hadn't thought of that. Nobody thought of everything. This was reassuring.

What wasn't Paula thinking of?

The perp could have ridden the bus this morning: that dude hunched over his phone blending into the seats, doomscrolling, or one of the guys making fun of Paula with College Bro #42. The perp was an athlete, hefty and agile like Paula's new neighbor, Big Foot, Dimples, and Duke. Not Ralph though, wrong moves. Actually, nobody from the bus talked, moved, or felt like the dragon man in Belle's video. The shitbooby was a consummate performer in real life. A master of disguise and maybe not passing for normal, but still fooling everyone. He could have cosplayed one of the guys and fooled Paula today. That shook her. Reading people was supposedly her superpower.

Her cell phone vibrated with two notifications and interrupted her slow thinking. Naturally, phones were verboten. Good thing Paula had her back to Officer Wang. Upstairs Karl was frantic, imagining the worst: Paula dead in a shopping cart at the dump. His gruesome but heartfelt concern touched her, then he almost spoiled it:

The cops let the real (burly Black) culprit and his dog walk.
If they haul you in, don't resist.
You might end up arraigned in front of an activist judge.

She replied with a smiling alien emoji.

Triple-E sent a Signal because Paula liked encryption: *Can't talk! Help! Gwen thinks we're keeping stuff from her.* She was typing something that hadn't come through.

When Paula first arrived at the library, she had no time to reconnect with Gwen or hash out a plan with Triple-E. Oona kept trying to lick Paula's face off and roughhouse in the grass.

No time for that either. The cops were closing in, and the kid refused to talk to the detectives Belle warned her about. Even if they were honest and true—which Gwen seriously doubted—they might inadvertently tip off Dragon Man (a cop? tech nerd?). No arguing that, so Triple-E and Paula hustled Gwen and Oona into the greenhouse. Paula had keys for special cleaning jobs. Temporary sanctuary.

More Signals from Triple-E landed:

Oona broke into the garden center. Gwen went with her. Me too.
Gwen says we can use the wagon to find Lance and why didn't I tell her I had it.
I don't have it. It's nowhere. Disappeared.
We're headed for the secret stairwell room. Gwen says you know where that is.
She wants to head out NOW with Oona. No more waiting around.
Oona is restless too.
Rescue Lance is risky, right? Help!

Paula replied: *On my way.* Using the wagon was risky. Even An'qwenique might have a hard time explaining that weird away. Could they trust the wagon? Did Paula believe the wagon? She wanted Oona to find Lance with her nose, then call in the professionals, a simple story. She had no idea what to do about Gwen.

Paula had to get to the garden center. Since magic dog had been put to rest, An'qwenique let Azul take the lead. She hit the water fountain and slurped like a kid. Paula strode over and, acting kissy face for Azul's benefit, whispered, "Time for Operation Nose Job."

"Yeah, I'm hanging in." An'qwenique covered for their spy action. She nuzzled Paula's neck and blew in her ear. Who knew that really was sexy. "Are you good?"

"Yeah." Murder and mayhem receded. They were cheek to

cheek, bosom to bosom. Paula's breath fluttered; her skin tingled and sparked. An electric connection, like dancing barefoot on a clean floor to Brittany Howard and the Alabama Shakes: *I don't wanna fight no more*. Paula gasped. Officer Wang rolled her eyes at the lovebirds. Could everyone tell Paula was a novice? So what? Passion was fuel. Cheesy romances nailed this. Paula just had to get used to occasional jolts.

"I'm firing on all thrusters." She defiantly kissed the hollow of An'qwenique's collarbone.

"True love, don't knock it." An'qwenique spoke to the room. "You all look like you could use some." Angels never let you fall off yourself into the abyss.

"See you on the other side of surprise," Paula murmured, then shouted, "I gotta pee."

"The ladies' room nearby is locked. The one beyond the special collections is open." Wang pointed at darkness and snickered. "Six stalls if you both need to go."

"I'm good." An'qwenique laughed with her.

Paula raced beyond tall bookshelves to the back stairs. Wang trusted her, listened to what she had to say. Paula hated betraying trust even for a good cause.

The side emergency exit was not visible to the police detail posted at the library front door and by the hydrangea. As Paula slipped through shadows past the greenhouse, what she didn't know: Oona had come out of the garden center to check on Belle in the bushes. The dog smelled Paula and heard her creeping in the asters. The police were oblivious to them both. Oona leaned into carnival training and refrained from barking at Paula. The clown, musician, and magician would have been proud.

M O N D A Y

RALPH—*Aliens*

"Here you go." The waitperson set a ginger beer and a glass next to Ralph's plate of dodo. "Sorry for the wait. Everything was icy. You go for the warm burn, so I had to hit the basement." Ralph guzzled straight from the bottle and ordered a second one. The waitperson admired his thirst. "Good thing I lugged up the whole case."

"It's late. We paid for a meal and a show." No, Meathead Frank, you got free tickets. "Americans are pathetic." Frank went from dissing the restaurant to slamming the whole USA. The janky crowd tuned in, even the waitperson. The Guardian masks displayed their evil-clown smirks. Frank launched into a monologue Ralph had heard several times already. Wouldn't the murderer keep a lower profile?

"Like this old movie I watched. Alien spaceship crashes to nowhere South Africa. The ship's wrecked, but not totaled. Lobster aliens have no clue how their ship runs or how to fix whatever broke. This miracle tech brought them light-years across the galaxy, the universe, but it might as well be magic."

Ralph thought of Beryl, the freakishly tall park ranger from the beyond, stranded in the woods without her navigators.

"The dumbshit lobsters can barely piss upside a wall. They fight over junkyard crap, wear bras on their heads, and have no clue what they're doing on Earth: invasion, exploration, sightseeing, wrong turn. Totally lost in space. Sound familiar?"

"Like AI wrecking our lives," someone muttered.

Frank pounded the table. "Lobster aliens are not wild, free beings, getting the fuck out of Dodge, risking all to explore a new world. Naw, they're domesticated, worker widgets, mopping floors, taking out the trash, cleaning toilets."

"Like you know anything about aliens," Duke muttered, and Andrew chuckled.

Frank didn't notice. "After the crash, the aliens are wasting away in a refugee camp. I'm telling you, that is America, five minutes from now. No, five years ago."

Andrew rolled his eyes and the med techs groaned.

"One genius alien has the right stuff. But here's the kicker, if a wounded human is contaminated with alien goop—bodily fluids—he turns into a dumbshit lobster. Naturally, our Afrikaner hero gets alien shit in an arm wound and starts morphing. Savage Nigerian gangsters want to eat his infected body part to acquire alien super voodoo juju." Frank jumped up. "High-tech ooga-booga-wooga gunpower."

Frank brandished a light saber in a fake voodoo dance. Sudden quiet. Andrew put his head on the table. Ralph exchanged glances with Duke, who mouthed, *Really sorry.*

The med techs shook their heads, disgusted. Sitting at their table, Camouflage Lady and a woman with big hair sucked their teeth. When did Camo Queen arrive?

"Shut up and sit down, man!" the techs yelled.

Frank loomed over them, brandishing the light saber and flexing his gym physique.

Ralph jumped in his face. "When the fuck are we, 1955? 1838?"

"I don't know." Frank blinked at him. "The movie was twenty-first century." They were eye to eye. He waved the saber above their heads. "You tell me when."

"The wrong time." Ralph glanced at the med techs then back at Frank. "What're you so mad about?" Frank was thrown by a genuine question. He lowered the light saber.

"Hey guys, we're not the show." Andrew pulled Frank into his seat. "Don't set yourselves on fire."

Duke snorted and shook his head. "A good friend of ours says that." Paula.

Andrew saluted Duke and Ralph. "Umuntu ngumuntu ngabantu: *A person is a person through other people.* My friends call me Drew." A charmer, he dropped Zulu wisdom then punched Frank's uninjured shoulder. "Don't sulk. If the real show doesn't start soon, we'll leave. I thought you were hungry. Your food is getting cold."

"Andy, my guardian angel." Frank tugged Drew's hair (wig?) then crammed his mouth with stewed flesh and the gravy drizzled down his chin. Jesus, talk about a cliché. What about Ralph? Losing track of himself, as Darlene predicted. Did he almost fight Frank over a bullshit movie and an ooga booga dance? To stand up for aliens?

Ralph hated bully crap, but—"Sorry," he murmured to himself and the med techs.

"You're great." They always talked on top of one another, cute and also annoying.

"Yeah, man." Duke nodded. "You could survive driving a bus."

"Or waiting tables." The waitperson hovered with ginger beer number two. "On the house. You have way more self-restraint than me."

"Not really." Ralph almost punched Meathead Frank. He sipped the ginger beer, relishing the burn. Coming close and not losing it was control. *Wanting a drink ain't drinking.* Cliché aphorisms. Any bum could get over as Ralph the stellar garbageman. What was he doing on Earth: invasion, exploration, sightseeing, wrong turn? Sunday he told Paula the whole sordid Darlene story. She hugged him and asked the same questions Frank did. Frank was just an asshole about it. *Who do we mean to be right now?*

Shit had gotten serious, and not only with Zsuzsu. How was Ralph going to handle himself? He'd been avoiding this question since Darlene left him and he **DUMPED IT ALL.** He closed his eyes, felt southwest at his back, and pointed his nose toward sunrise. His internal magnets had realigned. So where was he going?

"You finished with your meal?" the waitperson asked.

Ralph forked a plantain. "Barely begun."

"The show will be starting soon."

"Great." He hoped Zsuzsu and Azul were heading this way.

"Some people are demanding refunds." The waitperson glared at Frank, who hadn't paid a cent. "It's a benefit, and they ate their dinners already plus the special dessert. Can you beat that?" A theatrical pout. "Everyone needs to tech up their skills. If you don't want the machine to use you, you better learn how to use it."

"Or create another world," Ralph countered. "Redesign the machine to your terms."

"A revolutionary." The waitperson bumped Ralph's fist. "Thinking out of the box."

"Or stuck in a different box."

"No, you're busting out, man."

Lightning cracked outside and wind slammed debris on the windows. Ralph startled. The double-headed masks whirled too fast, hurling accusations and recriminations: **START DOING BETTER NOW!** What if the perp was a gym rat?

Ralph's phone was finally at 20 percent. He texted Zsuzsu: *Where are you?* Despite Belle's warnings, he should call the cops, tell what he suspected, let them worry about biases skewing his logic. No reason to mention Oona. She hadn't killed anyone as far as he knew. If they caught the killer, maybe they'd forget about weird dog syndrome. Zsuzsu and the sundial posse could breathe easy. They could get on with whatever they meant to do with their lives. They could come back from those wrong turns.

What if Ms. Hönig also wanted to take their thing to another level? He should have told her his terrible secrets. Too chickenshit. He was glad she had yet to return.

"I don't know where Belle is," Duke explained to an agitated Jabril, the griot from Mali, a co-owner of Crossroads. He'd organized tonight's performance lineup for Belle. "She was supposed to meet me here a few hours ago."

Jabril frowned. 10:00 PM was the latest show time, and all over by midnight. "We have a big surprise for her." He tuned his donsó ngoni, hunter's harp.

Ralph loved the sculptural instrument. You wanted to hug the giant gourd resonator to your heart, feel the rattles vibrate your bones, let the strings catch your breath and turn it to song. The other musicians coalesced around Jabril's soulful plucking. The whole restaurant settled down *inside* Jabril's music.

"Good to see you here." Change Gang musicians patted Ralph's back as they paraded by him to the elevated stage. More sundial posse folks!

A drag king / drag queen act sashayed through the audience for a grand entrance. They carried a cello, wooden flute, and juggling pins. A golden retriever wound between their legs. Ralph saw them last fall at the library—the dog was sick. Two big glam girls wore Milky Way gowns that blurred in and out of focus. (Really?) Galaxy fascinators perched on bouffant hair. Solar-system earrings whirled. A dapper fellow rocked a nebula tuxedo jacket and a shooting-star top hat. Ralph beamed good vibes their way. They waved, as if they knew him.

"The Cosmic Campers Carnival Band are our surprise guests." Jabril bowed to them.

The Campers danced into the storage closet that doubled as backstage and green room. Ralph jerked at something about them he should remember but couldn't.

"Don't worry," Jabril reassured him. "We're saving that act for the end."

"Let's get this show on the road!" Frank yelled. "What the fuck time is it?"

Upstaging him, Zsuzsu, a mischievous fairy, a dangerous fairy, wheeled in Ralph's direction. Vine earrings matched a leaf belt and the airy scarves at her neck. A night-sky jumpsuit, black velvet sprinkled with crystals, hugged her sharp angles. She needed to eat more. The hummingbird fascinator in cinnamon curls was homage to Beryl. Zsuzsu danced to Jabril's donsó ngoni music, scarves rippling as she bopped and whirled.

Ralph downed a third ginger beer, bubbly courage for speaking truth.

Zsuzsu glided close. "Jeder weiß, wieviel Uhr es ist. Wie spät es ist, begreift keiner. *Everyone knows what time it is. How late it is, no one knows.* My Oma—grandma."

Ralph leaned in. "Let's seize our good moments. Belle's advice."

Zsuzsu kissed him. "You taste like ginger."

"You taste like more." He tickled her lips with his tongue. Duke leered at them. Ralph chuckled and whispered to her. "I got something hard to tell you after the show."

Zsuzsu stroked his jawline then turned serious. "Paula says clues are everywhere."

"No shit. That's it. What I couldn't remember." Ralph peered at performers jammed in the green room closet. "'Property of the Cosmic Campers' is painted on the wagon bed."

"Oona has taken it somewhere. That dog lives another life behind my back." Jealous, or vulnerable, actually.

"Don't worry." Ralph shook his head. "We're on her map, in her story."

"Yeah." Zsuzsu rubbed her forehead. "I'm thinking the Cosmic Campers are the navigators Beryl is looking for."

"I'm still foggy on that bit," Ralph admitted. "Foggy on a lot."

She pursed her lips, narrowed her eyes. "You're still up for the mission?"

Ralph almost said *murder mystery or sci-fi adventure*, but decided it wasn't an either/or situation. "Hell yeah. What're you cooking up?"

"Belle says no police. You might like that, but—"

"No, I don't like that. The cops aren't all corrupt, plus dealing with murderous fools is their gig!" Ralph flashed on Charlize's soprano lilt and Melody's alto chuckle. "Belle's hooking up with Duke here tonight."

"He's cute." Zsuzsu and the bus driver exchanged smiles. Ralph beat back a jealous ripple. "After the show," she whispered, "we corral the Cosmic Campers, secure Oona and the wagon, then call in the cavalry. The sundial posse will have Belle's back."

"Sounds good to me." Ralph kissed her again, long, lingering.

Jabril brought the opening jam to a rousing conclusion. The whirling masks halted, suspended in an upbeat, faces unclear. The audience clapped, stamped their feet, and whistled.

Ralph glared at the door. "You know, Belle is never late."

Zsuzsu gripped his arm. "What are you thinking?"

He scanned the audience, ending with Frank and Drew, gym rats, suspects, even Duke. "Belle can ID him, right?" So not Duke. "He might have realized that."

Zsuzsu pulled out her phone. "I wrote down everyone's number."

MONDAY

PAULA—*Rescue Gwen*

Paula hated skulking around shadows, her feet not quite on the ground. Action adventure interfered with slow thinking. She desperately wanted to organize the clues, study Triple-E's journals, and make a list of options. Tough beans! She had to focus on the task at hand: juggling a petulant teenager, a magic hound, and a lost boy. Thank you Jesus for Triple-E.

The three-hundred-year-old garden center, despite housing rich history and sparking legends, was unremarkable: a sturdy wooden box with a curved roof to let ice slide away. Paula had a kitchen door key. She and Gwen worked here on library exhibits, Lance too. They made a mess where nobody minded. As Paula tiptoed toward the front staircase, Gwen and Triple-E fussed at each other about who you should or could trust.

During the colonial onslaught, British immigrants hid under the staircase from Pocumtuc or Nipmuc folks looking to recover stolen land. In the nineteenth century, Black folks on the Underground Railroad might have hidden in the same spot. Supposedly Nipmuc women, free Blacks, and abolitionist white women from a nearby church sheltered and guided them north to Canada. Triple-E saw no harm believing this. Gwen worried the legends were feel-good white lies, like Dragon Man said.

"Plenty of those for sure," Triple-E agreed. "Still, Black people running to freedom took refuge somewhere around here. Not all the legends are white lies."

"Fuck! I lost Lance's favorite one." Gwen scrambled on the floor, looking for something in the dark. "Where's your damn light?"

"I can't see to type the password," Triple-E muttered.

Paula flicked on the fluorescent strips under the stairs.

"Turn it off." Gwen stomped through the remains of a trickster display. "You want to put a target on us?" Her eyes were dangerous, unnerving, like the blood caked on her snake raincoat. She groped for the light switch.

Paula blocked her. "Nobody can see us inside here under the stairs."

"She nixed my phone light, but then wanted it," Triple-E grumbled, "because it's pitch-dark under here."

"What the fuck have you stupid bitches been doing over there?" Gwen hissed. "You were gone forever." She wanted to bray or just explode. "We don't have forever."

"Low blood sugar." Triple-E shook her head. "I gave her your two vegan cheese buns. I said you'd be here as soon as you could. She scraped off the soy bacon bits."

"I don't eat that soy shit." Gwen was in Paula's face, her chest heaving, her breath a spray of spit. She'd been Dragon Man's prisoner, his assistant and captive audience. How was she holding it together at all? "We have to move now and find Lance before . . ."

Paula wanted to scoop the kid up and run somewhere safe, forget everything else. "I wasn't planning to leave you out here forever."

"Me and Lance were gone a long fuckin' time. Did you even look for us?"

"Paula pestered the cops and everybody, put up posters." Triple-E wanted Gwen to be grateful. "I drew that in my journal."

Gwen sneered. "A lot of good dumb-ass posters did."

"I didn't know where to look." Paula hugged herself instead of Gwen. "The note said you and Lance ran away."

"And you believed that? He made us write bullshit." Gwen wanted to pummel somebody, herself actually.

"I thought it might be fake, but there was nothing else to go on."

"No more talk. We go save Lance now. He's in the shit!" She

bumped her forehead on the stairway underside and stomped on a Tikbalang, the Filipino forest and mountain trickster Lance made. She snatched it up. "We're farting around, wasting time, and he'll kill Lance, and that'll be my fault."

"Not your fault," Triple-E declared. "None of this is your fault."

"If Lance is dead, who the fuck cares?" Gwen snarled.

Paula ignored Gwen's bluster and read the panic-guilt. She stepped close to her. "What are you keeping from us?"

Gwen stuttered then shrugged, on overload. She set the Tikbalang on a stool.

Triple-E pointed at the snake raincoat. "That must be hot." Good move.

"Stifling," Paula agreed.

"And the snake-head hat. Let us get you out of that fanged foolishness, all right?" Triple-E reached for it, but let her hand hover. "OK?" Gwen nodded, and Triple-E gently tugged the hat off. Terror rippled through Gwen's skinny braids. Several had unraveled. "Let us get you out of the coat too, OK?"

"Yeah." Gwen was ready to crumble.

"Don't lose these." Triple-E set Gwen's Pukwudgie next to Lance's Tikbalang. She and Paula eased the coat off of bony shoulders and down stick arms. The tank top and pencil jeans underneath were sweat-soaked and funky. Gwen's skin looked raw. Triple-E hustled into the hall with the coat and hat. Paula wished for fresh clothes. Gwen sank onto a wooden box and hid behind her braids.

"Talk to me. Aren't we friends?" Paula's breath hitched. "I've heard your wild tales. You say anything to me. The time you boosted gadgets from those bullies. That cute boy who kissed you in the ice fort, snow on your lips, you stuck together." Gwen's expression wavered between *Who the fuck cares, bitch?* and *That was funny.* Losing it, but not lost. "I missed you." More than Paula had realized. "I have a backlog of wild tales, and nobody to tell them to."

"Me too." Gwen shuddered. Maybe she wanted to escape the horror stories, not relive them. She clawed at a braid tangled in her tank top.

Paula murmured, "Can I fix your hair?" Gwen nodded. Paula gathered her braids into a tail. She wrapped one sturdy braid around the whole bundle, looping it twice.

Triple-E returned with a bowl of water and dish towels from the kitchenette. "Can we?" she asked. Gwen shrugged. Paula lifted Gwen's ponytail, and Triple-E dabbed Gwen's feverish neck and face, then pressed cool towels on sweaty arms. "Better than air conditioning," Triple-E declared. "Put these under your arms."

Gwen complied, shivered, and sighed.

"I found this READ THE WORLD T-shirt in the kitchen, brand new." Triple-E held up a cotton tee with a goofy design: the blue marble Earth coming out of a big book. "We'll turn around, let you put it on." Triple-E and Paula swiveled and the funky tank top flew into the hall. They turned back.

"I called Dragon Dude." Gwen flinched, waiting for an attack.

"Where'd you get his number?" Paula asked, unfazed.

Gwen blinked. "He has burner phones, endless passwords, and he disabled the emergency call function. I couldn't crack his firewall, and I'm good with tech shit."

"I know," Paula said. "You schooled me, several times."

"Lance snuck me the number when Dragon Dude let us talk. I called back on the old lady's phone, while she was in the bathroom. She chants her password when she types. It rhymes, easy to remember."

"Let me guess. The verse she wrote for Melody's anthem." Paula sang:

Ask me to lose bomb, match, and fuse
Ask me to find what'll change my mind

"You know it too! Well, Dragon picks right up. I say, *I give you the fanny pack and you let Lance go.* He says *Deal.* No bargaining, and he sounds happy, like this is *his* plan. I say *We do it at Crossroads after the last show. I see Lance walk in and I put the pack on a table.* Then he says, *So you're going back to someone who wants you to be Glen?* Like I would ever stay with him and be Gwen the psycho killer!"

"The trade is a reasonable plan," Paula remarked. For professionals maybe . . .

"But," Gwen sniveled, "it won't work. It's getting too late, and the fanny pack was in the stupid-ass wagon, which disappeared."

"The wagon isn't where I left it," Triple-E grumbled.

"Beryl told me the wagon has a mind of its own. So does Oona. Fuck!" Gwen cursed too much. "The wagon would help Oona find Lance fast, since we all know him."

"Do I?" Triple-E asked.

"I think so." Paula wasn't sure she believed in the wagon.

A deep, big-dog bark made them jump. The St. B crowded into the hideaway. Tail-and booty-wagging interfered with locomotion and knocked over boxes of bric-a-brac. She launched herself full force at Paula's chest as if they hadn't seen each other an hour ago. Together, they toppled Gwen. The St. B danced from Paula's belly to Gwen's bony hip, a total goofball—in the middle of murder and mayhem.

"Where have you been? I thought you ran out on us." Gwen burst into tears, for Oona coming back, for everything. Oona licked her cheeks. Gwen buried her face in the sparkly ringlets. Oona barked.

"Quiet," Triple-E said. Oona's ears shot up and she tipped her nose at the doorway. She wagged her tail and licked Triple-E's hand. The coast was clear. "They can't see or smell us, but they might hear you. We're still on mission."

For the second time tonight, Paula allowed too many doggy

kisses. "I love you too." Paula stood up. "The gang's all here from the midnight patrol."

Oona licked her chops, ready for whatever was coming.

"Right, I did a midnight run with you guys once." Triple-E patted the journal in her shoulder bag. "I drew you three. Early in February."

"I remember that, back when . . . Before." Gwen sounded like this was ancient history.

"Your plan is good." Paula smiled. "We just need to refine it a little."

"How?" Gwen let Paula pull her up into a hug, then backed off. "I'm not talking to the badges or going back to someone who wants Glen."

"Dragon Man knows what you look like, but you can't ID him. He'll double-cross you, leave Lance back in storage, then wait at Crossroads to nab you plus retrieve his fanny pack. That's what I'd do."

Gwen perked up. "So you think he's sitting at Crossroads, and here's our chance?"

"Exactly." Paula held the Tikbalang to Oona's snout. "We have to rescue Lance."

Oona nosed the trickster figure, wagged her tail, and yip-yapped. Gwen stuffed the Tikbalang and Pukwudgie in her pants pockets. Tight fit. Oona pushed past her and jumped against shelves built into the wall. Rubber bands, glue, cardboard, paper clips, and construction paper spilled on the floor. Gwen leapt over the junk and joined Oona's effort. The shelf unit shifted backward—a hidden doorway? Triple-E and Paula also pushed, and it swung open. Paula didn't bother with shock, just peered into the dark.

She murmured, "Belle claimed there was a secret passageway in the garden house, but I never quite believed her."

Triple-E had her phone light on in a flash. Oona and Gwen bounded down rickety stairs to the basement. Paula and Triple-E descended with caution. The big red wagon was waiting. It glowed in the shadows, far from prying eyes. Gwen held up the fanny pack, triumphant. Oona knocked her onto the fluorescent blankets. The Pukwudgie and Tikbalang fell out of her pockets into the wagon bed. At a door to the outside, Oona turned to Paula with a *Let's go!* doggy grin. This was the best fun ever.

Paula ground her teeth. "What if I'm reading him wrong? Long-distance ain't as good as face-to-face. What if he's in the dragon lair chilling with Lance?"

"He doesn't know we're in the mix," Triple-E reassured her. "Or Oona."

Paula licked dry lips. "And he's sure lone-wolf Gwen won't find Lance." The Aje fell (jumped?) from Paula's vest pocket onto the fluorescent blankets to join the other tricksters. "With Oona's nose, do we need the wagon?"

"It's quick. We're in and out, faster than thoughts." Triple-E thrust the handle in Paula's hand. "The last Crossroads show ends at midnight. We have time, but not forever. Gwen is right. Speed is our good friend tonight." She patted Paula. "You know Lance. That's how the wagon rolls, spirit tech. Gwen told me all about it."

Everyone stared at Paula. "OK." She tucked Gwen in the blanket. "But once we nab Lance, we're calling Oshun and Blue."

"I'm never going back to any foster farts," Gwen declared.

"Of course not." Triple-E talked like she had a plan. Good, 'cause Paula didn't.

Hauling the wagon out of the basement was easy. Outside, a mucky river smell smacked them. Fiendish clouds raced across the moon. Tall grass and skinny bushes bent over in a monster wind that blew itself out after a minute.

"Rescue Lance," Paula repeated.

Oona pranced off into the dark down a wide, well-worn dirt path. Her tail was a sparkly torch, easy for Paula to follow. Gwen fell asleep in the blankets. Triple-E brought up the rear, singing Melody's anthem softly.

Unlike Paula's other late-night Oona-adventures, they crisscrossed many borders, but they sidestepped the storm. Paula felt queasy if she looked around. Too dark to tell, but it felt as if they marched along several different riverbanks at once. Or maybe her empty stomach was acting up. Paula focused on Oona, who grinned back at them and barked encouragement. They walked five minutes or ten, hard to tell. Time was wonky.

The dirt pathway turned into a gravel road. They found themselves in the old mill district, somewhere behind Cloud Heights, a serious hike from the library no matter what shortcut you took. A couple brick piles had been turned into storage facilities. The rent was cheaper than the classy new ones near the mall. Probably because it smelled like river rot and stale marijuana. Oona pawed a weathered door below a sign:

UNIT ONE ENTRANCE ONLY
FOR UNIT TWO ENTRANCE: GO DOWN THE ALLEY
AND AROUND BACK

Gwen pulled out the dragon man's tools and attacked the door. "I watched him pick locks a hundred times."

"Since February? You're exaggerating, right?" Paula expected any moment to be caught breaking and entering.

The door clicked open. Gwen switched on the lights and deflated.

Metal shelves reached almost to the ceiling and were neatly packed with canned food, inflatable rafts, gas masks, camping stoves, and tents. One shelf featured paper maps and books on surviving after the world ended. Beans and canned fruit were in alphabetical order and so was a wall of toilet paper, by brand. Seed bags alternated with ammunition: bullets, arrows, and BBs. No wasted space, like someone playing Tetris, reminiscent of Upstairs Karl's apartment—on steroids.

Bows, swords, spears, guns, and other weapons from ancient cultures to the future hung from the ceiling above the Tetris shelves. Phasers and light sabers dangled in the center. This tenant was a fan of *Star Trek* and *Star Wars*.

"This isn't where he kept us," Gwen moaned. No sign or sound of Lance.

"We're close." Paula pointed.

Oona sniffed Melody's big drum in a back corner. She pawed a metal pear-shaped contraption next to it—a medieval torture device from Charlize's collection? Purple turkey feathers were stuffed in a vase on a table. A silky robe was draped on a chair. A rack of monster coats and hats hugged the wall: vampires, aliens, zombies, and ghosts. A stained-glass window of the wailing woman, La Llorona, leaned against the wall.

"Where is Lance?" Triple-E asked Oona. "Rescue Lance."

Oona nosed the door by the feathers. Triple-E unlocked it from the inside, and Oona shot across a hall to **Unit Two**. A sign hung on a big sliding door:

UNIT TWO: FRANK FERGUSON—SECURITY
WE GOT YOU COVERED.

Gwen picked Frank Ferguson's secure locks with Dragon Man's tools, slid the heavy door open a few feet, then hesitated. "What if Lance is not here either?"

Oona barged past her. Paula and Triple-E stepped inside, pulling Gwen with them. They switched on the lights. Old cameras, computers, and ancient TVs were scattered haphazardly. An oversized shopping cart was parked next to a DUMP IT ALL bin of sparkly rainbow confetti. A dragon hat and light saber were in the cart. Gwen gagged on too many words then clutched Paula and Triple-E. This was where she'd been a prisoner since February. A small person dressed in an astronaut suit was curled against a stationary bicycle, a helmet at their feet. Oona licked the tiny astronaut awake.

"Lance!" Gwen stumbled around a busted screen.

"Gwen?" Lance fell into her arms. They cried and shrieked.

Paula and Triple-E followed suit and hugged them close.

"He said you were gone for good," Lance blubbered. "I ate your pizza slices, sorry, but I knew you'd come back with reinforcements! I knew you'd save me."

"Of course, spaceshot! What is Guinevere without her Lancelot?" They hugged and cried too long. Dragon Man might return, yet who could move?

Oona darted off and returned with a flying saucer Frisbee. Lance's no doubt, he was always losing it. The Tikbalang hung from the lip. Oona dropped these treasures at everyone's feet. Outside the storm came roaring back down the alley, knocking a few trees to their knees. Everyone jolted except Oona, who wagged her tail and barked, ready for fun right now, 'cause they had *rescued Lance.*

Paula ruffled Oona's ears. "Not in this weather. Frisbee tomorrow."

MONDAY

ZSUZSU—*Arrest*

"Das ist doch alles Scheiße!" *This is all shit!* Zsuzsu cursed her phone in German.

Midnight approached, and Crossroads was still rocking. Patrons were pleasantly potted on the rum special. Luckily, Ralph was only on a ginger beer high.

Today's second storm-of-the-century battered the windows and doors. Worse, it interrupted cell service during life-and-death communiqués with Paula and An'qwenique. Zsuzsu lost Paula's Signal. The cavalry was on the way, but battling golf-ball hail and gale-force winds. Capture and arrest delayed.

Zsuzsu's heart fluttered. According to An'qwenique and Paula, the killer (most likely Frank Ferguson) cosplayed normal and posed no immediate danger—mass shooting not his style. Cold comfort. Frank kept souvenirs from his victims in a storage unit! How could Zsuzsu just sit across from the murderer, or rather shitbooby, as An'qwenique called him, and hold Belle's ghost all by herself? She sucked a lemon slice. Impossible to tear her eyes from him. Dude was a gym rat and had to show off sleek muscles in his funky workout togs. She could almost smell him or maybe she'd gotten rank herself. Terror sweat. The cops were taking too fucking long!

She nodded at the med techs and the camouflage lady. Belle had probably signed them up for the Change Gang. They were going to be devastated. Not telling anybody was torture. Her phone vibrated and An'qwenique's text came through:

Sorry. Service in the storm is iffy!
A lot of siren action, coming from every direction. Accidents. Cars don't know what to do.

Almost to the restaurant. Any minute now.
Thank Ralph for the Frank Ferguson tip.
Paula loves the Avalon plan for Gwen and Lance—tell all to a judge, stay anonymous.
Triple-E is thrilled to be their magic witch grandmother.
Glad you know the folks who can make that happen.
Hang in there. We got this!

People only said *We got this!* when their shit was raggedy! Faux bravado. Zsuzsu's head throbbed. The doctors insisted she avoid excitement; calm was the best she could do for mystery condition. Her joints, muscles, and nerves always rioted a day or two after even trivial stress. Blowback from the last forty-eight hours would be epic. Steampunk aliens and murder madness was too much, and they weren't done yet.

A Guardian mask spun over Belle's VIP table. Motorized or what? "Can you believe Belle's a no-show?" The nosy/gossip crowd and the waitstaff wondered (out loud) if the Change Gang head honcho had dissed her own crew and ghosted Duke.

"I doubt it." The med techs defended Belle, but Camouflage Lady looked worried.

The gossips would feel like crap when the murder-truth came out. Zsuzsu probably felt like crap already, but she resisted feeling. Bad habit, and not working so well. Her heart ached. The shitbooby sneered at Belle's empty chair. Zsuzsu wanted to put her fork in his eye, or grab Ralph, run away, and hide. Who could blame her? No juju left to persuade the Cosmic Campers (Beryl's navigators) to say their goodbyes and hurry back to the steampunk rocket ship.

Ralph smoldered in fine purple threads, ready for romance. Terrible timing. His sexy, bedroom voice replayed in her head: *I got something hard to tell you after the show.* Which awful secret should Zsuzsu reveal to him? Shitbooby clients had haunted her for years, but she refused to waste one more minute on them.

"What bomb are you sitting on?" Ralph whispered. "Talk to me."

She shook her head and downed a glass of warm water.

"Why give me VIP tickets and not show?" Duke slurred, feeling the rum.

"I'm sure there's a good explanation," Ralph replied.

"Yeah, but not one you'll like," the shitbooby said, spoiling for a fight. Cold.

Ralph rolled his eyes.

Any minute now was an eternity. Zsuzsu was a coward, aching to do exactly what detectives warned against. "Fuck it!" Under the cover of a neo-funk band, she tugged Ralph close and whispered the Belle horror story Paula and An'qwenique told her. Ralph gripped the table and glowered at the floor, barely containing violent urges.

"I feel you." Zsuzsu sent him to tend to Duke. Ralph could decide whether to tell the poor guy about Belle leaping out a window. The shitbooby slurped his rum special and leered at Zsuzsu, like she'd be easy pickings. He assumed she appreciated his cute muscles and bullish charm. Was it her cinnamon curls and faint freckles? The wheelchair or weight she recently lost? He'd never see her fork coming.

Ralph patted Duke's back and glanced at Zsuzsu. Had he told him?

"How we doing?" The waitperson asked a stupid question they didn't mean.

"You don't want the truth," Zsuzsu muttered.

They flipped bronze braids and set down another glass of hot water. "Naw, I do."

Zsuzsu's ears popped as if she was falling from a great height with nothing to lose. "People can't breathe the air, drink the water, or afford rent on a one-room dump in the wasteland. We're shooting and starving babies. Shit is going extinct, like bananas and chocolate, and we're fussing over drag queens, pronouns, and if Black mermaids are realistic.

While I clean up after an apocalypse, I'm supposed to be *nice* and reach out to the people who keep making the mess. That's my job description, my cultural default setting. I hate *nice*. They don't have to reach out to me. Nobody ever reaches out to me."

"Wow." The waitperson wiped long fingers on an apron, licked quivering lips, then held out their hand. Zsuzsu gripped it. As the waitperson pranced back to the kitchen, Zsuzsu felt fortified.

The shitbooby snorted, unimpressed, how Zsuzsu sometimes responded to rank sentiment, maybe a notch or two worse. Her usual snark and trash talk were on the blink. She set her face to Queens, an evil, die, motherfucker scowl. He looked wounded. *You were flirting too, bitch.* He turned to sneer at the last performers before the Cosmic Campers finale: poets accompanied by a big-mama dancer, a powerhouse who wore seed anklets and bracelets to accent the beats.

Outside police lights sliced up sheets of rain. Zsuzsu almost fainted from relief when the front doors burst open and wind blasted through the restaurant. Napkins, hats, and menus took flight and collided with the Guardian masks. Time went herky-jerky.

One poet valiantly finished their last verse: *No more living in a sealed echo chamber, chanting approved cleverness to ourselves.* Earnest, overwritten, but a good point.

Ralph guided Duke to the back staircase. Nobody noticed their exit. Uniformed officers smelled like wet dogs, hairy and soaked through to the skin, all charged up for the hunt. Just before they gripped Frank Ferguson and read him his rights, Zsuzsu wheeled close, and on a weird impulse stuffed a card in his pocket. He looked ready to resist arrest and bolt into the storm. He gaped at her, dumbfounded.

"Surprise," she said. "Call me. I'm a lawyer."

"Anything you say may be used against you." Officer Wang repeated herself.

"She wants to help you," Drew yelled at his friend, Frank the suspected murderer. "Zip it till you have a lawyer."

"No, but tell them," Frank pleaded as they put him in cuffs.

"I don't know what you did after we worked out." Drew stumbled behind his friend as the police marched him past the poets and dancers.

"I couldn't have done any of this," Frank shouted.

"You lied to me all this time?" Drew almost fell, and Officer Wang caught him.

At the door, other officers held Drew back, and Frank resisted again. "No." Emotions played across his whole body: anguish, disbelief, surprise. An actor? Or was this not how he thought things would go down? "My stuff," he spluttered. Someone held up a backpack, and Frank disappeared in the downpour. Anticlimactic.

Drew stood in the doorway, rain lashing his face. He quivered. "Lying to me."

"What if Frank didn't do it?" Zsuzsu allowed doubt to wash over her.

"Why do you say that?" Drew turned on her, in a rage. He scrubbed away tears. "What do you know?"

"Nothing."

"Tell me. Please." More tears. Big grown man blubbering at betrayal.

"Everyone deserves an innocent-until-proven-guilty defense," Zsuzsu replied, lawyer calm. "I gave Frank my card, if he needs a lawyer."

Drew's lip trembled. "What if he did it?" His best friend; horrible to face up to that.

"Will you be all right?" Zsuzsu kept surprising herself. "You came with him. Do you need a ride?"

Drew jumped away. "I'm fine. Officer Wang is giving me a ride to the police station. They want a statement." He was out the door.

Blue stood over Zsuzsu. He poked his tongue around his cheek. "I don't like this."

Oshun hovered behind Blue, shaking her head. "It's a mess, but it always is."

"You were a hotshot lawyer once," Blue reminisced, "going to set the world on fire."

"Back when you were a hotshot headed for the FBI," Zsuzsu quipped.

"Don't you two start," Oshun muttered. "We know where to find you and Paula."

Zsuzsu snorted. "Paula's the reason you have somebody in custody." And Oona. "I just want to make sure you nabbed the right person."

"This is a dangerous game," Blue warned.

"Zsuzsu knows that. They all do." Oshun ushered Blue out.

The restaurant emptied quickly. The Cosmic Campers had vanished before the cops stepped in the door. Other performers packed up in a flash too. The mood was glum. The med techs mouthed *Call us* to Zsuzsu and hurried onto the patio with the Camo-Lady and a woman with big hair—a friend of An'qwenique's, Kitty somebody.

Ralph dropped down next to Zsuzsu and clasped her hand. "Jabril said we can wait here for An'qwenique and Paula as long as we want. He's hanging with Duke. They're consoling each other." Ralph closed his eyes. Zsuzsu pressed his hand against her cheek. The waitstaff worked around them, clearing dishes away, stacking chairs, and mopping floors. Finally they were alone, even the storm outside was moving on.

"What if Frank didn't do it. What if he's the wrong man?" Zsuzsu murmured.

"Fuck!"

"I gave Frank my card. Strange impulse."

"What if he did it?" Ralph replied. "How can you tell?"

"Murder wasn't my beat. My clients were thieves and cheats, and . . ."

"And you dumped all that."

"Maybe I'll regret the weird impulse tomorrow."

"No. Trust yourself." He rubbed his face, beyond exhausted. "How about I put my bike in the back of your van, if I rode it here. I can't remember. Did I ride over?"

"You're coming home with me. Who cares?"

"I care. I'm not leaving my bike . . ."

"It's out front under the eaves. Locked, with a plastic bag over the seat."

"You'd defend Frank in court? Why?"

"I don't have to like him."

"That's not an answer."

"Frank's not nice. I'm not nice either." Zsuzsu shrugged. "You're a good guy. You don't understand. Everyone loves you. Sure, people think the worst, but not because of you specifically, not because of the person you are. Frank's a ten-carat asshole."

Ralph sat up straight. "I have something hard to tell you, about me."

"No." Zsuzsu surprised herself again. "It's something terrible that you've done, and you want to tell me before we do whatever we do, maybe love each other."

"Going warp speed to that level, damn." Ralph panicked. "I know tonight is an awful time to go that direction, but . . . I was hoping to come clean first."

"You think this bad story is you. You want me to know you before I fall for you. Too late, I've already fallen." She pressed his hand to her heart. "I love that you want to tell me. But you're right, tonight is an awful time for that."

Ralph sputtered.

"You're human. It's been a bumpy road, but that old bad story is not who you are now."

"What if it is?" He sounded frightened.

"You have another story going! I'm in it with you. And the old terrible me, who I didn't really like, she isn't who I am anymore." She laughed. "I hope."

"*Two Zoos, Marmalade, and Honey.*"

"You told Paula, didn't you?" Zsuzsu wasn't jealous. "I told her my crap too. We were walking in the State Forest in a May blizzard. Paula says listening is her superpower." They chuckled over Paula. "You can wait to hear my horror stories, right?" Zsuzsu whispered.

"I trust you," he replied quickly.

"Oona loves you. That's all I need." Zsuzsu tugged him close and they kissed.

Ralph *and* Oona loving her was a thrill.

M O N D A Y

OONA—*Sleep*

The last of a late-summer nor'easter chased Oona across the Crossroads patio and under an awning. After they rescued Lance from the bad man's lair, Oona didn't know how to proceed, but who did? Minutes ago, just before she arrived, Oshun, Blue, and a fleet of cars drove off with the bad man. Oona couldn't track them in a storm. A setback, yet people on the restaurant patio smelled relieved.

Perhaps the detectives had marked this territory to scare the bad man from coming back. Oona had marked Zsuzsu's house, her yard and barn, and the neighbors' place too. The crows and the next-door mutt sounded an alarm if a bold creature ignored Oona's big-dog scent. Who'd warn her at Crossroads or anywhere else if the bad man returned?

Oona shook water from her hair and bounced on tired toes. She yawned, anxious for her humans and everyone to sort themselves out. They reeked of muddled emotions and wandered the patio aimlessly. What Oona didn't realize: They assumed the killer was finally locked up, yet nobody wanted to spend the night alone.

An'qwenique shook Camo-Lady's hand.

Paula stepped into the drizzle, chewing nothing and squinting at the dark. The goggles on the Aje in her pocket sparked and thundered. Oona and An'qwenique startled.

An'qwenique patted a quivering woman. "So good to see you live, Kitty."

"Evil knocking at your door is no joke," Kitty replied and danced away from her.

An'qwenique turned to Camo-Lady, gripped her hand, and spoke softly. "Thanks for saving Kitty."

Camo-Lady drew her close and whispered, "sundial posse," then headed for the parking lot. She smelled calmer than everyone else.

"Take care of our girl." Kitty hugged Paula and swallowed a few tears before hurrying after Camo-Lady. Oona whined at the sadness filling the air.

"What's going on with you?" An'qwenique pulled Paula under an awning. Oona licked Paula's knees.

"Did Frank rent both storage units?" Paula sounded funny and tasted upset.

"I don't know." An'qwenique sighed. "Are you sure it's OK for me to stay with you?"

"I invited you," Paula shouted, mad at somebody. "You told Kitty your drafty old robber baron mansion was creepy, and she could put it on the market tomorrow."

"I know . . ." An'qwenique whimpered.

"Where else you staying? Ralph is at Zsuzsu's. And what if Frank isn't Dragon Man?" Paula sucked her teeth. "You want to be alone with that? I don't."

An'qwenique sat down at a table under a Guardian mask. "Are we going too fast?"

"Of course we are. Everyone is." Paula huffed sad, anxious breath. "I need to check on Gwen and Lance." She stormed off toward the parking lot and Oona followed, sad and anxious too.

Gwen and Lance were curled up in the back seat of the mandolin player's car. Triple-E was slouched against the hood. The old lady jumped up as Paula opened the door. "You're not asleep." Paula dragged Gwen from the car without waking Lance or the mandolin player. "What did you sneak out of **Storage Unit One**?"

"Nothing," Gwen muttered.

"You're a terrible liar."

"What if they have the wrong man?" Gwen wiggled away from Paula.

"What if you shoot the wrong man?" Paula growled. "You're planning to shoot the right one, but hey, shit goes sideways sometimes. Sorry for cursing."

Gwen flinched. "My grandpa took me hunting. He taught me how to use a gun."

"You don't want to shoot anybody." Triple-E spoke softly.

"You're wrong," Gwen bellowed. "I'd love to shoot him."

"Then he wins." Paula stepped close to Gwen. "You want Belle to win, don't you? She got high on the beautiful life you and Lance were going to have."

"Belle flew off to the stars on your possibilities," Triple-E added.

Gwen sagged. "Somebody ought to shoot him." Paula gathered her into a hug.

Who could blame Oona for being distressed when her pack was so unsettled?

Gwen dropped a pistol in Paula's hand. "You weren't looking when I boosted it."

Paula stuffed the gun in her knapsack. "I know a lot, from how someone acts."

"Really?" Gwen shivered. "Clean it before you give it back."

Paula gripped her arm. "I'm counting on you not to do stupidness at Triple-E's."

"That's a big ask." Gwen huffed. "I'm not trusting any badges or officials, no matter how fast Zsuzsu talks or who Blue and Oshun throw under the jail."

"Zsuzsu worked a great deal." Triple-E's tone was soothing. "You tell a judge your story and stay with me, hidden. Perfect hiding place. Word is, since I take a nap in the Viking ship sometimes and ride the bus all day, I'm homeless. But I own a duplex."

"In the borderlands," Paula said.

"Plenty of rooms, even a place for Belle's musician friend and your grandfather."

"That is a happy ending," Paula declared.

"Don't argue." Triple-E pressed Gwen into the car. "We're leaving." She woke the mandolin player and they drove off, singing Joni Mitchell songs and spraying gravel at Paula's feet.

"I lost An'qwenique. Actually, I ran away." She confided in Oona. "I should find her." Paula stepped into the restaurant.

People were always losing each other. Oona trotted around to the patio and put her head in An'qwenique's lap. She was still sitting under the Guardian mask. A voice Oona didn't smell spoke softly in An'qwenique's hand.

"Hey you!" Paula called from the restaurant front door.

"I'm talking to my brother," An'qwenique yelled. "He's on Mom's phone. Good news: still no ventilator. Catastrophe in the rearview."

"Great." Paula retreated inside.

An'qwenique scratched Oona's itchy ear and chuckled. "He wants one of my wild stories, like when we were kids. Should I?"

Oona yapped encouragement, and the whole tale tumbled out. Big Bro laughed for the first time in days at the best wild tale ever. He loved Beryl and the haunted houseboat. He insisted An'qwenique pitch the story to a TV producer friend. "I will, and I'll visit as soon as I can. The parents will be thrilled. I gotta run. Love you." An'qwenique stowed the phone in her giant pack and stood up. "Shall we go face everyone?" Oona wagged her butt.

Inside, Zsuzsu and Ralph were happy to see Oona. She gathered their scent logs quickly and ignored the bowl of treats Jabril offered her because—The musician, magician, and clown had been here less than an hour ago! She avoided the bad man's table and raced to the closet green room. Jabril let her lick the plates they left there. The hint of plantains and goat cheese was yummy. She tripped over her paws, snuffling stools, a napkin, Jabril's donsó ngoni. She nosed every spot her crew had been.

"What is she doing?" Jabril gave Paula and An'qwenique generous plates of food.

Paula shrugged. "Working the clues, getting the story."

"A story better than the chef special?" Jabril laughed. "I'd love to hear her version."

"Me too." Paula and An'qwenique laughed, sounding better.

Oona circled a Guardian mask that occupied center stage.

"That was quite a moment," Jabril said. "The mask came loose when lightning struck a nearby oak tree. The Cosmic Campers stretched out their arms and caught the Guardian before it smashed on the floor. They set the mask down and slipped out the stage door into the storm." Oona nosed this door open right now. Heavy rain had washed their trail away. She scooped up a solar-system earring the musician wore, and dropped it in front of Paula, and barked.

"Shh. Duke is asleep," Jabril said.

Paula held the earring up. Planets danced around a golden sun. "Something for your collection in the tollbooth?" Paula had visited the hidden stash. Oona nosed the earring against Paula's belly. "For me?" Oona jibber-jabbered. Paula put the solar system in the vest pocket below the Aje. "We'll sort this out later. Deal?"

Oona wagged her tail, excited to do search and rescue with Paula.

"Duke wants to drive his route tomorrow." Jabril carried their empty plates to the kitchen before Oona could lick them clean. "Belle will hit him hard. He should take a few days."

"Maybe that's why he wants to drive," Paula said.

"Poor man." Zsuzsu yawned. "We should all take a couple days." Her yawn traveled the room and even claimed Oona.

"I could lie in bed for a year!" An'qwenique leaned into Paula.

"That's my plan," Ralph roared.

"I say we ditch work and drive to my cabin on the lake." An'qwenique poked Paula's frown. "Not tomorrow; as soon as we can. Do nothing. Faulenzen!"

"It's not Sunday," Zsuzsu replied.

Ralph snorted. "Faulenzen works Monday through Saturday too."

"My cabin has two bedrooms, one on the first floor," An'qwenique said. "A boardwalk right out the door. We'll do a run/roll together, like last fall in the State Forest. The lake is clean. People swim and canoe."

"Are you inviting me and Ralph?" Zsuzsu sounded surprised.

"A double-date getaway," Paula blurted. Everyone stared at her. "If we're all still together in a few days. Aren't you two together now? I think we are." She glanced at An'qwenique. "Aren't we?" Everyone laughed. "I'm glad I'm so funny," Paula muttered. An'qwenique squeezed her.

Zsuzsu wheeled up to them. "Can I bring Oona?"

"If she wants to come," Paula replied.

"Two days ago, I'd have sworn I was a cat person with allergies." An'qwenique ruffled Oona's curls. "Amazing how many different people you might be."

Paula and An'qwenique drove off, and Ralph stowed his bike in the back of Zsuzsu's van. Oona attacked the bowl Jabril gave her. Worry over the bad man faded, for now. Ralph pulled the go-anywhere wagon up the ramp. The scent of river rot clung to the wheels. Good odors. A run with Ralph to the otters was always fun . . . Her belly full, Oona stood with a paw in the air, her nose in the wind. She longed to be so many places at once. Even a dream-shuttle was no help with that.

Soon though, she'd find the musician, magician, and clown or they'd find her. This would mean she'd have to decide where and who she wanted to be: pack leader, carnival dog, search-and-rescue maven, in this world or traveling the others. She'd never had such momentous choices before. Not tonight, later . . . Afterward.

Oona scampered up the ramp to the wagon and jumped on Beryl's blanket. She fell asleep in the middle of a sigh.

BOOK IV

TOMORROW AND TOMORROW

JOURNAL ENTRY:

*The journey of discovery is not simply the travel to a new world—which we might just see as an extension of our own world. The real discoverer must gain new eyes, new senses to experience a world that they have never encountered before.**

STORM MUSINGS:

*Some people have a serrated edge to their spirit. So it's a challenge to hold their humanity.**

* Captions from the Iris Library's International Trickster Exhibition

A F T E R W A R D

AN'QWENIQUE—*Picking Up the Pieces*

An'qwenique scanned Paula's 2.5-room abode. The rent per square foot was absurd. The couch resembled a furry mammoth. Handmade posters from solidarity marches hung over the couch: FIGHT TRUTH DECAY; THEY FEAR YOUR MIND; and COURAGE IS CONTAGIOUS. The lava lamp on an end table was hypnotic. A Yoruba stool made An'qwenique sit up out of her slump. She noted three centuries of style and several continents of taste. And yet, somehow, everything fit together. Who was talking Tetris earlier?

"I'm not sure about Frank," Paula muttered and took An'qwenique's breath. "And this looks all wrong." Paula dithered in the tiny galley kitchen, pondering where the cleansers, scrub brushes, disinfectants, rags, and portable HEPA went. "I can't believe I don't remember how to fit everything."

"Can't help you there," An'qwenique murmured. Despite the heat (eighty-four degrees outside and in at 3:00 AM) her skin was cool and damp from a shower. The showerhead spewed mostly air, a water saver and so refreshing. Paula had wrapped her in a cotton bathrobe from the 1950s, a Goodwill treasure. The nubbly weave was reminiscent of a Smithsonian exhibition on mid-twentieth-century American life.

A squeak in the outside hall, and An'qwenique fell off the Yoruba stool. Residual jitters ambushed her every five minutes. She wanted to hit the next chapter of their story. Fuck being stuck in the shitbooby's horror saga. "What do you mean you're not sure?"

Paula hugged the HEPA close and shrugged. Fuck the HEPA too.

"Why aren't you sure?" An'qwenique squirmed.

"I'm just not."

"Is that all you can say?" An'qwenique danced in place, trying to settle her nerves.

"I hate this kitchen. The whole place." Paula scowled. She was the badass, taking crazy horror shit in stride, but nobody's fool. If the clues refused to settle into place for her . . .

An'qwenique stamped around the couch.

Paula flinched. "Don't worry, no resident cockroaches."

"What?" An'qwenique looked at the floor. "Who's talking about cockroaches?"

"Sifting through the whole mess again, for what else I missed . . ." Paula stared off, twitching. The solar-system earring Oona gave her whirled.

"Don't do like with Belle. Tell me everything now! I'm not fragile." An'qwenique ignored a rash trying to creep up her neck. "When will we know for sure it's Frank?"

Paula snatched a vinegar bottle from the top of the skinny refrigerator. "Did I just put this up here? It doesn't go there. Crap! I have to concentrate."

"Right." An'qwenique shook her head. "Stupid question."

Paula squeezed cans, boxes, tubes, and soap bars onto narrow shelves. Plastic wrapping squealed in protest, and joggled An'qwenique's memory: Paula said **Storage Unit One** had Tetris-packed shelves like her kitchen, like her neighbors' tight quarters. The HEPA refused to slide into its charging station. The dust mites had gotten a reprieve today, so the HEPA didn't need a charge. Paula set it by the trash, then jammed towels, masks, and gloves into a drawer and slammed it shut.

"How you doing in there?" An'qwenique murmured. "Tell me something."

"It's hard to believe any of today happened." Paula peered in the refrigerator then closed it quickly. "I hope you're not hungry."

She opened a cupboard, and cloth bags tumbled down on her. "Ignore the mess." She had to be kidding. "How are you doing?"

"I'm petulant," An'qwenique admitted. "Why a twist? Why can't it just be him?"

"It's never just him."

"I do know that." They'd made it to the end of the movie, caught the bad guy, and were both still breathing. "We're living the scenes that come after the credits roll. We should feel grand." Instead, An'qwenique was afraid to be alone and might never do a detour or go home again. After stomping her wildflowers, the shitbooby had come back and desecrated the front steps. At least the Fates had smiled on Kitty. An'qwenique was a refugee, her life in a go-bag: what she packed for the apocalypse.

The dream voice poked her. *Get real, girl! What do you need to make a new life?*

Her backpack squatted on the living room floor. She cringed at the light saber in the side pocket, at what she had left of herself: a computer, journals, drawing pencils, medical supplies, a single portable chair, Paula's survival paperback, Melody's dumbek, and Beryl's goggles. "I'm the mess in here, not you," An'qwenique muttered.

"You're fine," Paula insisted. "I missed something. I know it."

"Should I give Beryl's goggles to Iris Library or the university, so someone can study them or observe them or . . ." An'qwenique faltered. "What if the goggles exude poison slime or give off radiation? What if they're the beacon for an alien invasion?"

"Do you believe any of that?" Paula stood underneath a dead spider plant—an explosion of brown papery leaves, tragic except one baby spider was still green. "Beryl took one of your favorite folding chairs with her. Is that poison?"

"In Beryl's world maybe. Not evil intentions, just unexpected consequences." An'qwenique detached the green baby spider.

Paula held out a glass of water. "I thought the whole plant was dead." She set the spider on the counter to sprout. "Should we inflict Beryl's goggles on anyone else?"

An'qwenique quivered. "What if it's too late already?"

"*No one knows how late it is.*" Paula quoted Zsuzsu and glared at the mammoth couch, Ikea coffee table, and space-is-the-place office chair. "Why make do with trash other people dumped on the street?"

"Recycling's good," An'qwenique ventured.

"Your décor was dumped by nobility last century. Classy, like you."

An'qwenique winced. "I'm not my stupid things. I'm what I do with you. That's who I mean to be."

"Trust, that's the big question." Paula blinked. "Beryl left *you* her goggles. You're a twenty-first-century griot. You'll figure what to do with them."

"Big Bro wants me to turn our wild story into a TV series." An'qwenique jolted as outside a car bumped through a pothole. "I want this to be over. I want to run away to the cabin, the canoe . . ." She hugged herself at the door to Paula's inspiration gallery. A waste-of-space closet, too shallow for furniture, clothes, HEPAs, or supplies, so Paula converted it to a gallery. A bundle of five arrows, a symbol of the Haudenosaunee Confederation, hung on the door. An'qwenique's hand hovered over the knob.

"Go ahead," Paula said.

An'qwenique pulled the door open, switched on a glittery strand of lights, and stepped inside. Life-size images of Harriet Tubman, Mahalia Jackson, and Katherine Johnson swayed around her. Mahalia's voice drifted from tiny speakers. Maps to freedom, music scores, and mathematical proofs adorned the walls. A rocket ship flew past the moon toward the North Star. Previous exhibitions hung above, up to the ceiling. Paula had rigged ropes, pulleys, and sand bags like a theatre fly system.

"Amazing." An'qwenique felt a pleasant rush across her skin.

Paula stepped in with her. "On the *Great Escape* podcast, you say *act who you want to be and the character comes.* That changed my life."

An'qwenique sighed. "You never know who hears you."

"A storyteller's fate," Paula said solemnly. "Strangers be living in the sense you make, the hope you offer. You have no idea."

"I hear that." An'qwenique touched Paula's face. The connection was electric.

Entangled in miracles and mysteries, they felt ancient and yet to be born, and so grateful to have found each other. Eternity in a moment again. They leaned close and celebrated the Fates, the random threads that had woven them together. They couldn't hold on to all that for very long, yet the power of the ancestors and the unborn lingered at the back of their breath and underneath their heartbeats. No way to give up now.

"We should check on Duke first thing tomorrow," An'qwenique murmured.

"On him and Jabril both." Paula stroked the baby spider. "Everybody needs to find another storyline." Anger flickered across her face. "I'd love to quit tomorrow's private clients and Wednesday's. Two out of four owe me back pay."

"Demand your money, then quit. Nothing to lose if they're not paying anyhow."

Paula nodded. "I can take Thursday and Friday off. The Animal Rescue folks will understand. Azul says I have personal days with pay. Cloud Heights policy for regular contract workers."

"Good policy." An'qwenique never knew what to expect from the Chief Nerd.

"Maybe we can go to your cabin sooner." Paula sagged. "It's just so far away."

"We can do Faulenzen right here." An'qwenique bounced on her toes like Oona. "Not my rich-girl trip, but still hook up with Zsuzsu, Ralph, and the dog. Walk the boardwalk in the

State Forest, bring the kids and the grandparents, do a picnic." Her bathrobe came undone.

"Sounds good." Paula's fingers danced across An'qwenique's damp belly.

"I'm ticklish." An'qwenique stopped Paula's wandering hand.

"I've read that orgasms are a wonder drug for the body," Paula said quickly.

"I'm sure that's true." An'qwenique tensed. "But I'm wasted."

"That was a stray thought, nerd nonsense. I didn't mean tonight," Paula mumbled. "I'm wasted too, and I'm not rushing you, us, or—"

An'qwenique hugged her. "I believe you."

A knock on the front door and they both jumped.

"Are you expecting someone?" An'qwenique frowned.

"It's late." Paula scowled at the door. "And nobody drops by on me."

"It's Karl. I heard you come in." He rattled the knob. "I know you're in there. Your shower feels like Niagara Falls under my feet." He knocked again. "I collected clues all day. I thought you were coming up to check in." He banged with both fists and a foot. "Come on, let me in." He wasn't going away, and the whole building knew it.

Paula threw open the door. "What?"

Karl filled the doorframe. He wore shorts and a tank top cut low under his pits and high above his navel. He was ripped, like Tomás, and covered in Norse mythology. His skin was damp from a shower and reeked of tea-tree oil. Bushy, dyed-blond eyebrows were comical. The tank top proclaimed: PUMP IT UP! I'M A BETTER YOU!

An'qwenique hugged her robe tight and waved.

Karl turned red and waved back. He leaned into Paula and whispered, "You never bring anybody home." He continued louder. "You left me hanging all day. Evil dude on the loose, I was worried, couldn't sleep. I heard Niagara Falls and thought you and the dog were hiding out."

"An'qwenique didn't want to be alone tonight," Paula explained.

He gasped, "Your rich lady writer? She lives next door to, you know—"

"This is Karl," Paula talked over him, "a friend from the building. He's a trainer at the gym." Karl basked in the word *friend*.

"Hey Karl." An'qwenique smiled. Paula had talked about her to Karl.

"You can thank me." He walked into the apartment. "I bought new lights for the hall." He pointed to the brightly lit stairwell, then pushed the door almost shut.

"How much?" Paula sucked her teeth, disgusted. "The landlord counts on tenants getting fed up and spending their own money. I'll chip in."

"The landlord should pay for lighting in the stairwell," An'qwenique remarked.

Karl hooted. "He should do a lot of things."

"The landlord's a she," Paula said.

"Fuck no, really?" Karl blundered around the Ikea coffee table several times. "That cold-hearted, cutthroat bastard is a woman? No fuckin' way." He paused at the dead spider plant. "Why keep a corpse hanging over you?" He lifted it from the bracket. "I'll dump this for you." He turned to An'qwenique. "Paula saved my plumbing, keeps my Wi-Fi from glitching. You wouldn't believe the shit she knows."

"Yes, I would," An'qwenique said.

"A landlady? Fuckin' A! Worse than I thought." He rubbed his bald head.

"What clues, Karl?" Paula interrupted his descent into sexist brain.

"Can I ask you something first?" He shoved his phone in

Paula's face. "This is all over social media." He sounded as if the disinfo-teers were her fault.

The image was too small for An'qwenique to see. Paula rolled her eyes.

"Vikings aren't worse than anybody." Karl was livid. "Why am I responsible for crap ancient relatives did back before history? You said everybody has Viking blood, 'cause they were bumping and grinding all over." He glanced at An'qwenique. "I'm butting in on you guys. Sorry." He didn't sound sorry. "Believe it or not, Paula's my only friend in this building."

Paula patted his arm. "Grandma Junebug's people were pirates in Barbados and the Gullah Sea Islands, very well off, up to my father's generation. Stolen goods kept paying interest to the great-great-grandkids. Junebug says: *Maybe the great-grands didn't raid the ships, but they sure be living rich on that pirate booty.*"

"That's a good one." He repeated Junebug's words. "Do I look rich to you?"

"What clues do you have?" Paula shouted.

He pointed at An'qwenique. "She probably told you what I know. It's all over the news. People speculating about trolls going live, dressing up as monsters, doing Charlize and some adjunct prof. I tried to put it together, tried to think like you."

"I wish I could think like me right now." Paula glared at the door. Footsteps echoed in the hall, a crowd going up, fast.

"Who is prowling around?" An'qwenique resisted feeling safer because Karl was a six-foot-something bruiser and had a crush on Paula—which Paula didn't notice.

Karl hugged the dead spider plant. Leaves crumbled into dust. "You say look behind the clues." Footsteps came down the stairs, faster, a stampede. Karl was sheepish. "I tried, but I didn't see anything."

Someone pounded on Paula's door, and it swung open. "Hello?" Oshun and Blue stood in the brightly lit hallway. Officer Wang and other cops flanked them.

"Karl Falkenberg?" Blue asked as they flashed badges.

Karl turned to them. "Yeah. You know me."

"A neighbor said you were at Paula's apartment," Oshun replied.

"That old girl doesn't have a life," Karl griped. "She snoops." The whole building heard where Karl was.

"Do you rent **Storage Unit One** on Mill Alley?" Oshun asked.

An'qwenique held her breath. Paula was ashen, shaking her head, no. The solar-system earring whirred faster.

"Yeah, but nobody knows about that," Karl replied, confused. "My secret stash. I don't go there much. I don't want someone following me."

"We'd like to ask you some questions. Can you come with us?" A command from Blue, not a question.

"What's this about?" Karl let Oshun lead him to the door.

Blue took the dead plant and offered it to Paula. "You take that too," she told him.

Blue handed it to Wang. "You ladies have a good night." He closed the door and they tromped downstairs, talking fast.

An'qwenique turned to Paula. "Karl rents **Unit One**?"

"When Gwen turned the lights on, I thought of Karl's stash. He plans to survive the end times and help other resourceful folks make it right next time." Paula leaned into An'qwenique. "This morning Karl said we were all suspects."

"You told me the shitbooby cosplayed normal, to fool us."

Paula shuddered. "Karl and Frank are in Triple-E's journals—at Melody's last concert and her celebrations of life. But something's wrong."

"No," An'qwenique insisted. Relief flooded her, almost drowned her. "Blue and Oshun caught the suckers! It's over!"

"I know Karl." Paula seemed to blink through visions.

"A con artist." An'qwenique danced a reluctant Paula from the front door, around the narrow kitchen to the coffee table—their spirit wolf dance. "Fuck doubt!" An'qwenique was fierce, growling and nipping till Paula's resistance dissolved. They fell onto the mammoth couch, exhausted.

"Let's go to the cabin now and do nothing for several days," Paula blurted.

An'qwenique howled joy and pulled Paula close. "We'll drive by the hospital on the way out, check on Big Bro." Paula slumped and An'qwenique shook her. "No, stay with me. I refuse to settle for anything less than you and me at our best."

AFTERWARD

PAULA—*Evidence*

Running off to An'qwenique's lakeside cabin at 3:30 AM was a desperate fantasy. Paula knew this as soon as she said *let's go*. An'qwenique was all in. Her go-bag was still packed. Mi'kmaq birchbark canoes glided through her mind. Paradise beckoned.

"Let's throw our shit in the EV and hit the road, Jack." An'qwenique raced out the door and down the warped, uneven stairs. Karl's new lights blasted every crumbling detail.

Something was off, wrong, *ill*, but as far as An'qwenique was concerned, Blue and Oshun were heroes, redeemed from the shadow of corruption. The ace detectives had caught the creeps and were locking them away one day after finding Charlize. Everyone could exhale, grieve, and carry on with good living. Not Paula—her breath came with a hitch. She kept looking behind the clues and, like Upstairs Karl, saw nothing, just Karl's confusion as Blue and Oshun led him away.

Had Paula read Karl wrong all along? Was he smirking behind her back? He cornered her this morning about Oona—exactly what the perp would do. What was she missing? Paula grabbed her knapsack, banged her shin, and drew blood. She pulled out the pistol Gwen stole from **Storage Unit One** and shuddered. Karl's pistol.

An'qwenique stood in the hallway, horrified. "Is that thing loaded?"

"No! Gwen didn't think of ammunition." Paula stuffed it back in her bag. "What are we doing?" Before getting out of Dodge, they needed to make sure Gwen and Lance were all right. Stupid *loose ends* from the dragon man (men?) were live wires, danger, dangling over their lives. "We can't run yet." Paula pulled An'qwenique back into her apartment.

An'qwenique pouted and whined about always being responsible. Eventually she agreed not to disappear and leave friends with a deadly mess. Plus, they were both wasted, unfit to drive. Departure was optimistically planned for Thursday with a return Sunday night. Paula gave An'qwenique the lumpy bed and fell out on the hairy couch. Ms. Celebrity Podcaster had no trouble sleeping till one o'clock Tuesday afternoon. Paula was jealous. Everything was working out for An'qwenique. Her editor was very understanding, a sweetheart. She set an open-ended deadline for the VR review. Despite having been heavily medicated, Big Bro recalled the Redemption Center yarn and hoped to be a part of this TV series project when he was well.

The Cosmic Campers offered to turn their farewell concert into a celebration of Belle. The Iris Library and Change Gang folks were thrilled. They asked Paula to finish the international trickster exhibit by the Sunday after next. An'qwenique proposed a live-stream podcast for *Great Escape*. She intended to grill the Campers about Beryl. Zsuzsu hoped to persuade the navigators to return to their steampunk rocket ship. Of course, the wagon had a mind of its own and might misbehave. Paula wasn't sure she believed in any of this, despite her wagon adventure.

Tuesday Paula jerked awake at 6:00 AM, tiptoed around An'qwenique, and forced herself to make the 7:30 AM bus. Duke was in the driver's seat, looking hollowed out. Paula crossed the yellow line and hugged him. Triple-E's seat was empty except for a purple hydrangea blossom for Belle. Triple-E Signaled Paula that the young people, including the sixty-six-year-old mandolin player, were sleeping like babies.

Paula hoped to use journal entries and Beryl's goggles in the trickster exhibit. Gwen and Lance were psyched to have a good project. Grandpa was coming to Triple-E's on the weekend, a trial run. Except for occasional washes of grief, most everyone was doing better, except Paula.

She regretted going to her Tuesday private-home clients when she wasn't feeling the spirit. They expected miracles for cheap. One guy had no checks or cash and already owed her for two previous deep cleans. According to him, this was Paula's fault, since she avoided electronic pay services. The security on those platforms sucked, and fees ate her earnings. She needed to save money for detective courses.

The guy's house reeked, a man-cave mess. Friends were coming for the weekend. Paula demanded her entire pay, up front. She drove with the entitled creep to an ATM and pocketed the cash. She worked the scheduled four hours then quit for good before cleaning his toilets.

Wednesday went like Tuesday. An'qwenique slept till 12:30 PM; Duke drove the bendy bus looking grim; Triple-E was AWOL; more purple hydrangea for Belle. Paula told one client couple she'd have to take a fancy bike for back pay and suddenly cash appeared. Why did people treat her so badly? Paula felt worse on Wednesday. Even popcorn with Oona and Triple-E didn't cheer her up. Missing Belle, and no denying the truth, her self-esteem had taken a big hit. Reading people was supposedly her superpower, yet she was wrong about Upstairs Karl. **Storage Unit One** had screamed Karl: the seeds, ancient weapons, and light sabers. Paula denied the obvious. She dismissed Big Foot Frank Ferguson because hanging from a bar in the bus wasn't the shitbooby's style.

Karl and Frank were show-off blowhards. They stood out. She was certain the perp was unremarkable. She didn't want to imagine Karl or Frank murdering anyone, even if they were in the dickhead tradition. Perhaps taking criminal justice and detective courses was a stupid idea. Did they offer courses on getting over yourself?

Wednesday after work, An'qwenique made Paula put down

a deposit and register for fall classes. No shame in missing (or refusing) a few in-your-face clues. That's what the courses were for. Paula didn't have to be a great detective already.

An'qwenique pumped her up. "You said: *The shitbooby messes with everybody's head.*"

Paula nodded. "That's how he gets off."

Karl and Frank were Zsuzsu's clients. She'd been an excellent trial lawyer once, but got caught in slime-dog client intrigue and burned out. She felt rusty, and the mountain of circumstantial evidence against them worried her. Their fingerprints were everywhere. The locksmith and gadget repair tools found in their lockers at **Pump It Up!** had traces of the victims' blood. So did their sherbet gym shoes. They had no alibis to speak of.

Upstairs Karl was a loner. He hung online with the disinfoteers. Paula was his only friend anywhere. Other than gym clients, nobody could corroborate Karl's whereabouts on the fatal days. He (and Frank) rarely went to their storage units. Karl feared someone might trail him to his stash—a fortune in *Star Trek* and *Star Wars* memorabilia.

Karl also collected skeleton bodysuits, dragon/reptile raincoats, and monster hats. The mics to alter your voice to the character of your choice were recent additions. Frank borrowed costumes from Karl for Halloween and then claimed he lost them. He paid Karl to buy replacements. Karl's and Frank's DNA was found in the dragon raincoat and hat along with the victims' blood.

Most nights, Frank passed out on his couch streaming old movies. He owned a security business and was a master of locks, cameras, and alarms. He had a computer science background and installed Charlize and Tomás's outdoor system and the Cloud Heights parking lot surveillance, but not Iris Library cameras. He and Melody had several shouting matches. He regularly put down Charlize. Folks at Haven claimed Karl wasn't a big fan of either lady. He claimed they liked to spar with him.

The Ford and BMW were registered in Frank's name—although he alleged the Ford had been a broken-down wreck, unfit to hit the road for years. The BMW kept landing in the shop, a German dud. That's why he took the bus Monday and snarked at Paula. Frank posted a photo of College Bro #42 on social media tagged *Not the Killer's Type*. Upstairs Karl liked and reposted this. It had 3.3K hits before they took it down.

Gwen and Lance were unreliable witnesses. They never saw Dragon Man's face or heard his real voice. Frank and Karl were the right size, but so were Duke, Ralph, and Paula's new neighbor. Paula felt certain Karl and Frank didn't have the right stuff to mount Dragon Man's reign of terror. They were nothing like the menacing figure in Belle's video. Dragon Man was unaware of the conference room cameras. He went *full-tilt diva*, live for Gwen and Belle, a captive, immediate audience. Belle egged him on to warn people. *Work the clues.*

No burner phones had surfaced. So, after registering for detective courses, Paula Signaled Blue and Oshun. "We need to find his phones," she said, "to be sure."

Oshun ignored this suggestion and tried to reassure Paula. Losing friends and neighbors and having a close call with the killer, it was normal to worry that a boogeyman was still out there. Blue referred Paula to an inexpensive social worker who helped people work through traumatic experiences.

Flummoxed, Paula blurted, "How'd you all get your names? I've been dying to ask."

Blue chuckled. "Mom asked Dad, *If it's a boy, what?* Dad said *Lou*. Mom heard *Blue* and loved the name so much that Dad didn't have the heart to correct her. He never told me till Mom died."

Oshun stalled, white girl with African orisha name. "How about I tell you over tea at Haven Bagels?"

"When we come back from the lake," Paula replied. The ace detectives hung up, happy that she and An'qwenique planned to canoe through clear water and birdsong.

An'qwenique was jubilant. She called Zsuzsu. "How about tomorrow?"

Zsuzsu and Ralph were eager to drive up to the cabin anytime. Oona barked in the background, ready as always for an adventure.

"Friday then?" Paula's breath hitched. She dropped onto the Yoruba stool and stared at the lava lamp. "But I know I am missing something."

An'qwenique pulled her onto the furry couch. "What?"

"It's like on the tip of my tongue."

"Be happy, for a moment. This is our time." An'qwenique nibbled her ear.

They ended up sleeping together on the hairy mammoth. This was better for two people than the bed. It was such a comfort to hold someone and be held. Orgasms were great, for the body and the spirit. Paula had proof.

"Like a storm gathering, swirling through me then breaking into a great downpour!" she told An'qwenique, who wrote this in her journal.

Paula slept till 8:30 Thursday morning and 9:00 Friday. They sorted out logistical nightmares and set many good things in motion. Too much to get it all done.

Gwen insisted Paula take the Aje trickster to the cabin and have lots of fun with Zsuzsu, Ralph, and Oona. "You need a break, dude." That cinched it.

At 10:30 AM Friday, Paula and An'qwenique packed up the EV and hit the road.

AFTERWARD

ON CAMERA—*What the Hell Happened #3*

An'qwenique's nature cam and security cameras, at the docks, Sunday

The weather is glorious, sunny with a light breeze. The lake, actually a wide moment in a river, looks like a bowl of jewels jostling each other. Distant hills are a late-summer green, burnished bronze. Paula and An'qwenique drift in a birchbark canoe. Stars and ash leaves are etched on the sides and paddles. The current is gentle. They wear Change Gang T-shirts. Paula also wears her many-pocketed utility vest. The Aje rides in the top pocket, ready to climb out. Underwater images stream across her goggle necklace.

Paula's head is in An'qwenique's lap. The solar-system earring in her right ear catches the low light and sparkles. Crows squawk and fly over their heads. The tranquil mood is broken. Paula jerks upright and scrunches her face.

An'qwenique flinches. "What now?"

Paula grips her paddle. "Let's go back to shore."

An'qwenique groans. "Don't scare yourself for him."

"Oona was acting funny this morning," Paula insists.

"You two have been on alert, all weekend."

"I tried to relax. Sorry." Paula squirms. "I think Karl was set up, Frank too. Zsuzsu agrees."

"Not just that." An'qwenique squirms. "You think he might come here for us."

Paula is grim. "That's what I'd do."

"You wouldn't do any of this."

"OK, but," Paula scans the shoreline, "this *is* a remote location, perfect—"

"For an ambush. You said that yesterday and Friday too, but no ambush."

"Yet. A lucky streak, we could go home early."

"He can ambush us at home." An'qwenique shudders. "At least here, Oona would smell him coming."

Paula narrows her eyes. "He'll take Oona out first. Quietly."

"Good luck with that." An'qwenique smacks her paddle against a log heading for the canoe.

"Ralph thinks the perp is one of Karl's clients."

"They all have alibis, except Frank, according to Zsuzsu." An'qwenique frowns. "Who else was in Triple-E's drawings?"

"Hard to say, other than Karl and Big Foot."

They both jolt at splash sounds. Two athletic women paddling in sync approach in a birchbark canoe. Smiling, they almost glow, happy. The woman in front tosses purple and pink hibiscus flowers as they glide by. An'qwenique catches one and murmurs thanks. Their canoe is quickly a smudge in the distance.

An'qwenique deflates. "I wanted you to love this place."

"I do. I will." Paula grinds her teeth. "Zsuzsu's worried about the case too."

"Not like you, just, reasonable doubt, innocent-till-proven-guilty stuff. Zsuzsu is better at chilling than you."

"You never think anything bad will happen to you."

An'qwenique rolls her eyes. "That's how it looks, but you're wrong. I expect the worst."

"Most of the time you're so focused, on task, not worried."

An'qwenique nodded. "You're hopeful, thinking we can change shit up. I'm not so sure about that."

They startle at the sound of distant barks.

"Oona *was* edgy this morning." An'qwenique makes a funny

face. "I chased crows with her then scooped poop. A dog person now, well, an Oona person."

Paula manages a smile. "You're different since you came back from the beyond."

"Different?" An'qwenique tenses. "Better?"

Paula shrieks. "He told Belle, *Fungi are better people than people.* That's not Karl or Frank."

"You're the fungus fan."

"I'm always on Karl, look behind the clues to figure out what the hell happened." Paula scrambles. Her paddle flies into the lake with a big splash. "Sorry. We have to go ashore. Now."

"Fine." Reluctantly An'qwenique strokes the water. "Let's get your paddle."

"Wrong way. You can do one paddle. Or give it to me." Paula is frantic. "Hurry!" She rocks the boat, reaching for An'qwenique's paddle.

"Stop!" An'qwenique scowls. "Talk to me."

"Umuntu ngumuntu ngabantu. Zulu, *A person is a person through other people.* Dimples is the shitbooby, not Upstairs Karl, not Big Foot Frank."

"Who is Dimples again?" An'qwenique retrieves the paddle.

Paula grabs it. "Frank's buddy, Andrew Evans, Drew." They head for shore, dodging a feathery green cypress tree, felled by a recent storm. "He whispered *Umuntu ngumuntu ngabantu* to me on the bus, a come-on, a distraction. Drew would do a big scene with Belle before poisoning her. He said, *I'm a mirror, throwing ugly back at you.*" Paula's lips tremble. "Why didn't I think of this yesterday?"

An'qwenique paddles faster, a terror pace. "Today, before an ambush, is good!"

"Right." Paula keeps up with An'qwenique. "The odds of figuring it out whenever are random."

An'qwenique squints. "I can't picture Drew."

"Exactly and he's hunky and cute too."

An'qwenique snorts. "I guess."

"Drew fades. He lets Frank take up all the space." Paula groans. "Drew is pals with Blue and Oshun. He's a gym rat, hangs at Haven Bagels, Crossroads. He even rides the bus." They are almost to shore. "I read Drew wrong, not the other guys." Paula's paddle hovers over the water. "He flirted with me. I couldn't figure why."

"I can." An'qwenique guides the canoe to the dock.

"Drew's been coming for us since Monday. Waiting to catch us off guard." Paula swallows a curse. "There's no cell service up here. Crap!"

"Hey, I'm the landline girl." An'qwenique steadies the canoe as Paula steps out, then jumps out too. They heave rucksacks onto their backs. An'qwenique's is a monster, but she runs ahead of Paula as they race into the cypress and oak trees.

An'qwenique's nature cam and security cameras, at the cabin, Sunday.

Cypress trees on each side of An'qwenique's two-story log cabin shiver in a breeze. A boardwalk path comes from the lake and heads into the woods. The sun is low, the shadows long. Idyllic except—after shimmer and static, a big red wagon materializes near the entrance to the forest boardwalk. An FX special effect in real life.

His back to this, oblivious, Andrew "Drew" Evans, dressed in camouflage tank top and gym shorts, parades in front of the cabin. Sparse hair is close cropped. A busted lip is healing. Watermelon-sherbet shoes are covered with muck. Footprints in soft ground lead back to oak and maple trees. An empty shoulder holster dangles under his right arm. He clutches zip-tie handcuffs in his right hand. The gun in his left hand is aimed at Zsuzsu and Ralph. Zsuzsu's shirt and pants resemble silvery mist on delicate moss. Ralph wears the sherbet shoes and a camouflage outfit similar to Drew's, except long pants, long sleeves.

Paula did not figure Drew out before he ambushed Zsuzsu and Ralph.

"Cell service here is zilch." Drew grins. "I cut the landline. Don't waste energy. You're on your own." He smirks at Zsuzsu. "Frank says you always wear green and spout German. He claims you're a fairy godmother who believes he might be innocent."

"What do you think?" Zsuzsu's tone is ice.

"Frank and Karl—innocent of this, guilty of that." Drew shakes his head at Ralph. "You didn't throw away the shoes?"

"The shoes never killed anybody, did they?" Ralph's voice is controlled.

"Don't play hero, big guy." Drew waves the gun. "Secure her to the wheelchair, then do yourself." He tosses Ralph zip ties,

Ralph catches the cuffs, hesitates (to control a swell of rage?), then kneels beside Zsuzsu. He fumbles and bangs the wheelchair arm. The cuffs fall in the dirt. "I don't know how to work these." His hands shake. Drew snorts.

"I do." Zsuzsu leans past Ralph and cuffs him to the chair and then herself.

"They're onto you," Ralph rumbles.

"You're lying. They have nothing." Drew is calm. "Where are the girls?"

"You're not gonna talk smack, ask about our names, rant about jacked-up humanity and magic wagons?" Ralph is defiant.

Drew startles. "How do you know about that?" He recovers quickly. "Gwen. I'm tracking her too. She's a lousy witness though." The wagon wavers, and he gapes at it. "Where did that wagon come from?"

A deep bark makes Drew jump a second time. He points the gun at Zsuzsu. "Call your dog!"

Oona bounds from the forest boardwalk and crouches low. Her tail is like a blade behind her. She clutches mirror sunglasses between her fangs and snarls.

"Oona!" Zsuzsu yells. "Gefahr! Bleibt weg!" *Danger! Stay away!* in German.

"Get out of here, girl!" Ralph yells.

Oona creeps closer. Drew shoots at her, several rounds. Dirt sprays around her, and Oona yelps, dropping the sunglasses. Drew is not a great shot. He fires again. A dirt explosion, and Oona flops into the red wagon. Ralph and Zsuzsu scream. As the dust clears, Drew approaches the wagon, holding the gun on Oona, readying for the kill shot.

A mass of crows descends on Drew. At least twenty angry birds peck his face and head. They claw his arms and back. He tries to ward them off. They keep dive-bombing him. He grips someone's wing, but others attack his hand. He yelps and lets go. Ralph and Zsuzsu observe this spectacle, silently cheering for the birds. Drew flails and staggers in a cloud of dark feathers.

Oona jumps up. Blood drizzles down a leg. Grazed, she was only playing dead.

"Geh Weg!" *Get away,* Zsuzsu commands.

Reluctantly, Oona scoops up the glasses and runs down the boardwalk as:

Drew shoots wildly at the birds then stumbles half into the big red wagon, raising a shower of sparkly dust. Crows fly away from him toward Oona or into nearby trees. Dazed, Drew scowls at Ralph and Zsuzsu zip-tied to the wheelchair. He holsters the gun. Off-screen, Oona barks. Drew glares down the boardwalk. His left knee rests in the wagon on fluorescent blankets. He propels himself with the right leg and speeds after Oona. The remaining crows arrange themselves in branches close to the cabin. Guard duty?

As the wagon sounds fade, Zsuzsu and Ralph gape at one another.

"Did the wagon . . . ?" Ralph asks.

"Yes," Zsuzsu replies. She wiggles the armrest. She almost gives up then it comes loose. "Good ploy, undoing this."

"We'll see." Ralph slips free. He uncuffs her and then she does him. They stare at one another. The crows chatter. Ralph and Zsuzsu look to the birds, marveling. Without a word, they head down the boardwalk behind Drew and Oona.

AFTERWARD

OONA—*Who You Mean to Be*

Anger and fear roiled in Oona's belly. She never wanted to find another dead body in a bush, on a bus bike rack, or in Ralph's recycling bin. Wishing wouldn't make it so. She clutched the bad man's bug-eyed mirror sunglasses in her teeth and drew him away from the humans she loved and the crows too, her pack. She ignored tender paws and a stinging pain where his bullet had grazed her shoulder. Blood was matted in the hair on her left leg. No time to lick herself clean.

Ghostly birch trees sang high-pitched encouragement. Yet, where should Oona take danger? Scrambling from one world to another, she muddled across many maps. Running, no destination. Hounding terror eventually meant wrestling it to the ground. She'd never chomped anyone to death, not a hungry hawk or sneaky racoon, not a bold coyote or aggravating cat. Not even the river bums who tried to mug Paula last spring.

Oona preferred to make friends if possible or threaten and chase danger away if not. Her response to the bad man was different. A whiff of him, and she felt a murderous, go-for-the-jugular urge she'd never practiced. Winded, she found herself careening down a cobblestone alleyway that eventually led to the Haven. In a blink, she'd traveled all the way from the woods around An'qwenique's lakeside cottage. A new mapway she couldn't quite celebrate . . .

The sun dropped below the hills, but the air remained hot, stifling. She looked over her wounded shoulder. The bad man knelt one knee in the wagon bed and used the other leg to propel the dream shuttle. Someone really chasing her was a novel experience. She let him catch up a bit, then forged ahead, her usual game. Everyone was playing, except Oona and the bad man were deadly serious.

Luckily only Gwen's grandpa noticed them racing by Triple-E's backyard. Grandpa nodded at Oona while Gwen and Triple-E laughed at spaceman Lance clowning around the grill. Duke ate a wedge of cornbread at a picnic table with the Change Gang mandolin player. They smelled glum. Triple-E petted them both.

Oona dashed by Charlize's pond. Tomás didn't catch her scent as he scooped Aretha the turtle up before she waddled too far behind the garage, racoon territory. Mexican turkeys clucked and purred approval. Azul hugged Tomás and Aretha close. Azul's silvery hair sparked like Oona's ringlets, a new friend to look forward to tomorrow or the next day, after—

Oona flagged. She hated running from danger. She'd rather turn and meet trouble head on, but she needed a good spot. The safest place on all the maps was the Redemption Center. The doll's eye patch by the Haven dumpsters was the best route to the Center. Oona rallied. Having a good destination recharged her spirit.

Zsuzsu whistled and Ralph shouted her name. They didn't need a go-anywhere wagon to follow Oona. They harmonized: *Sing me a song that breaks the curse*—even though Zsuzsu thought Melody's anthem was cheesy. They were well behind the bad man. In the woods, leaf piles, roots, and rocks slowed Zsuzsu's wheelchair down. Otherwise, the airy fairy would have been faster than anyone. Instead of running ahead, Ralph kept pace with her. They were downwind, so Oona didn't smell their fear.

Paula and An'qwenique had paddled back to shore, perhaps when they heard gunshots and Oona barking. They bellowed her name as the crows fussed, loud enough to be heard anywhere. Who could miss the anguish in their voices? Tracking agitated crows and singing—*Dream the next move we need to take*—Paula and An'qwenique stayed on Oona's trail. They were as stubborn as Zsuzsu and Ralph.

Oona's new pack was no longer just a loose-knit collection of mates. They had become a great team, luring the bad man, corralling him. But Oona was pack leader, the guide to the maps and protector of her territory. Taking him down was her task.

The Haven reeked of delicious food and good times, a welcome bouquet of flavors. Oona halted and huffed. The water bowl Melody put out was always full of fresh water. The basket-weaver waitperson did this now, but he never had tempeh bacon in his pocket. Oona dropped the sunglasses, lapped the bowl dry, then panted. Heat dripped off of her tongue. A hint of Melody lingered on everything. Oona lapped that in too.

Across the alley, the doll's eye patch near the Haven dumpsters seemed thicker than before. Oona hesitated, not only because of sharp leaves. A *between place* was tricky, so many overlapping borders, even she got lost sometimes. Catching sight of the bad man wheeling her way, she reluctantly scooped up his glasses and charged at the creepy plants. She leapt over countless beady white eyes and landed on the moon boardwalk in the State Forest. She wagged her tail at the bridgeway through the marsh.

It was a quarter of a mile to the Redemption Center—where Oona was born, where she met Beryl and her carnival family. They fed her alien science and magic with the puppy chow. Melody first played dumbek for Oona at the Center and the musician bowed a cello: *Draw me a map that sets us free.* The clown juggled sparkling globes that disappeared on the downbeat. The magician danced around the gnomon, snatching the globes from somewhere else on the upbeat. The Center was the best place for a final showdown with the bad man.

The go-anywhere wagon burst into the doll's eye patch where Oona and Ralph found Melody's instruments. The wagon lurched across many borders then anchored to Oona and settled here and now. Suddenly dizzy, the bad man sat down in the wagon bed. Shock flavored his breath, and he almost threw up. Performing Cosmic Camper shows, Oona had learned that whether the dream shuttle was in the lead or bringing up the rear, you still ended up in your heartbeat place. The Redemption Center was where they both wanted to be.

The bad man looked over his shoulder and choked on a horror-movie shriek—like Ralph coming upon Charlize in his recycling bin. Except, no dead body. Two gingko trees leaned into one another, their canopies creating an archway. Fan-shaped leaves were golden in low-angled sun. Stinky orange fruit littered the ground. An'qwenique brought Paula along the route she'd taken to the Center before—the map she knew. Paula labored to keep up with runner An'qwenique, who was toting her heavy go-bag. They smelled of determination more than fear.

Did the bad man hear the singing and panting?

What Oona didn't know: He expected to see the Haven dumpsters and a cobblestone alley. Too many borders interfered and nobody was there to anchor that vision. Like An'qwenique, the bad man denied the evidence of his senses. He resisted inhabiting more than one world at once. Didn't everybody? Even Oona sometimes. He turned from the gingko trees and scowled at the marsh then at Oona on the moon boardwalk.

"This is it, huh?" Panic wafted from his pores. "Gwen said you and the alien wagon could take me to where she vanished. Like magic. The kid wasn't lying." He smacked the wagon bed. "What is that fuckin' music?" Cello floated under the singing. He gulped a deep breath. "So, is there a drag king / drag queen / spirit-being here too?" He tried to laugh and failed. He pulled the pistol from his shoulder holster. It flew out of a shaky hand and landed in the grass. "Fuck!"

Oona should have followed carnival crew training and run from the weapon. Instead, she stood her ground on the boardwalk, snarled, and shook his bug-eyed glasses. He jumped out of the wagon and screeched. Razor-sharp leaves sliced his bare thighs and arms. Thrashing, he crushed berries that smelled like a heart attack. After a thousand cuts, he managed to escape the poisonous shrubs. A bloody mess.

Oona took off down the bridgeway for the Center, glancing back a few times.

He retrieved the gun, holstered it, and tugged the wagon handle. The dream shuttle refused to budge. He'd have to go the rest of the way on his own steam. "Where the hell are you taking me?" Curiosity trumped caution. He chased after Oona.

He was a fast runner, faster perhaps than An'qwenique or Ralph, not as fast as Zsuzsu in her chair. She and Ralph wore long sleeves and pants. Once safely through the doll's eye patch, Zsuzsu would catch up. To prevent that just yet, Oona hit top speed and reached the sundial courtyard in less than thirty seconds. She dropped the bug-eyed sunglasses at **XII** and bounded onto the marble command bench.

The bad man staggered in and halted at the gnomon. The giant stone wing wavered and sparked. Oona's hair stood on end. He squinted through murky fog. "Belle wasn't sure I'd get here. Proved her wrong, didn't I?" He smirked, triumphant as sweat and blood dribbled onto the sundial. The CLOSED ON SUNDAYS sign swayed in the wind. Clanking chains were reminiscent of Melody's favorite bell part. He gawked at the haunted houseboat and the smirk cratered. "What the . . . ?"

Unlike Sundays—Faulenzen, doing nothing—the Redemption Center was hyperactive during the week. It constantly phased here and there, a shimmering specter in many worlds. The dragon weathervanes whirled like the Guardian masks in An'qwenique's closet and at Crossroads Restaurant—impossible for them to make up their minds whose wind to track, even for a moment. That was up to Oona.

She paced along the command bench. Two crows took off from the Center's turrets and dive-bombed the bad man. Oona's pizza-foil friend had spread the description of the enemy far and wide. Never a good idea to piss off a flock of crows. The birds pecked his head and face. Lucky for him there were only two. He batted them off and drew his gun. They circled back to attack again. Oona barked a warning.

The bad man shot wildly and almost lost his balance. He missed the crows, who swerved clear. One bullet shattered a dragon-eye window in the attic. Angry curtains flailed against shards of glass. The gun slipped from swollen fingers. He teetertottered, uncertain on shifting ground. The fog retreated to the marsh and the air went still.

Oona crouched and bared her fangs. The crows flew past the chimney into whispering birch trees to watch her rip his throat. What else to do? She eyed the gun at his feet. No matter the cost, here was her chance.

He clutched his throat and chest. Each breath was a ragged wheeze. His heart jittered off the beat and he stumbled onto the bug-eyed sunglasses. They shattered under his sturdy gym rat sneakers. Gasping, he fell into the gnomon then collapsed at high noon.

Oona swallowed a growl and cocked her head. The bad man twitched from head to toe. She licked her chops to refresh scent readings. He smelled wrong, similar to yet worse than Ralph last Sunday. She jumped from the command bench and crept close. Something terrible was happening. He was barely breathing. She sat down, confused. The haunted houseboat amplified her heartbeat.

A second ago, she wanted to rip his throat to shreds. That would be easy now, and then he'd never get up, never come after her crew. However, reading familiar near-death aromas, she also wanted to run for aid. The two crows scolded her, urging her to attack. They each landed on the head of a whirling dragon and waited for her decision.

Oona never argued with her nose. Why kill him if she could save him?

Search and rescue was in Oona's blood and saving was how

you ended the day. Her people had found one another on the boardwalk by the doll's eye patch. They pulled the go-anywhere wagon across the bridgeway heading for the sundial courtyard. Oona gripped the bad man's gun in her mouth and ran to meet them. They'd know what to do. They would help.

Who knew what she would have become with his *blood in her mouth*?

A F T E R W A R D

PAULA—*A Different Story*

Running. On the bridgeway in soggy air. Two guns were tucked in Paula's knapsack: the one Gwen wanted to shoot somebody with and the one Oona spit at Paula's feet, before the St. B made them chase her into this swamp. How did Oona steal Drew's gun? The weapons were heavier than Paula expected, pressing against her lungs with each labored breath. Actually, the horror vibe made breathing tough.

Static from muttering cedar, red oak, and birch trees gave Paula the willies (where did that word come from?). The trees suspected: *This adventure ain't gonna end well.* They knew Paula wanted to run the other direction. Coward. The Aje in Paula's vest pocket smirked at her, always a lot of attitude for a puppet/mask.

"Kiss my grits!" Paula hissed Junebug's cuss words. Despair was not an option. First chapter of the survival book: *To make it through disaster/catastrophe, get out of your nightmare head; Assess your condition, situation, and resources.* Her whole life, Paula had been aching for romance and adventure. Here she was, exactly where she wanted to be.

Oona's curly silver hair was matted and bloody, her black eyes wild. A murder of crows cruised above her, barely flapping their wings, a death cloud. Two red-tailed hawks hung in the cover of old-growth oak trees. Hoping for stragglers? Not a chance.

Zsuzsu zoomed across the bridgeway with energy to spare. The mad green fairy stayed right on Oona's tail, out for Drew's blood. Behind her, An'qwenique (still carrying that monster go-bag) and Ralph were mad running too. He pulled the go-anywhere wagon.

Drew had ditched that at the doll's eye patch. It looked heavy, but Ralph's sole complaint was losing north and east. An'qwenique snapped at him, too angry/terrified to worry about which fucking direction they went.

"It's like losing up and down," Ralph explained, swallowing irritation. "Or not feeling your own skin, your weight on the ground."

"Right. Sorry." An'qwenique huffed. "Don't mean to be a bitch."

"That's usually me. You're always nice," Zsuzsu yelled over her shoulder. "Drew's getting to you, getting to us all."

"We're headed for the sundial courtyard," An'qwenique explained to Ralph.

"I thought maybe." He looked around. "The first time here, I was out of it."

These stellar athletes jogged and talked, no problem. Paula's lungs burned, but not her feet. An'qwenique's trail runners were like walking on water and running on air—even though slow was Paula's only setting.

Speed-demon Zsuzsu was a speck in the distance.

"Hold up, woman, what's the plan?" Ralph shouted at her. Bless him.

Zsuzsu halted. "I don't know."

"Oona led Drew away from us to this place," Paula said, "*on the other side of surprise.*" Gasping for air made answering hard. "The St. B is laying a trap for him."

An'qwenique stumbled over this realization. "We heard the shooting and—"

"He only nicked her," Ralph said. "Even if you're a great shot, and Drew is not, hard to hit a bolt of lightning."

"Oona ran him down, then came back to us with his gun?" An'qwenique sputtered as she and Ralph reached Zsuzsu and halted. "Now what?"

"Oona wants us to follow her." Paula's heart thundered. She slowed to a walk. "She would not be leading us into an ambush."

"Not intentionally," An'qwenique said.

"There's always danger you miss. What you can't see or smell." Zsuzsu scanned the swamp. Fingers of mist reached for them. "Sneaky danger you don't want to believe in."

"Ugly secrets you keep, even from yourself," Ralph added.

"Does Drew have another gun? That's my question." An'qwenique probably had an answer she didn't like.

Paula stepped over vines breaching the boardwalk. "We have guns too."

"A gun is not a plan," An'qwenique countered.

"I'm saying, Drew should worry about us." Paula wiped sweat from her eyes. "Out for blood."

"No shit, Sherlock." Zsuzsu used Ralph's phrase but with more venom.

Oona dashed back and barked at the doddling humans, *Get moving, fools!* just as Paula caught up.

"The four of us, the dog, and packing heat. We stop the fucker! That's the plan." Zsuzsu charged after Oona. Ralph and An'qwenique sped close behind them.

Paula wanted to curse. In that fantasy run with Jigonhsasee and Harriet (racing through the swamp to save the day), she was brave and buff. *This way to peace and freedom.* Here and now, Paula snagged her foot on nothing. She almost went arse over teakettle into high reeds and bushy foxtail. How she landed on her feet was a mystery. She charged around a big bush and crashed into An'qwenique at the end of the bridgeway. The others had halted at the edge of a fog bank. Paula's muscles quivered.

"You see Drew?" she whispered. "A third gun?" No answer. Paula tromped ahead onto the sundial courtyard, which looked exactly how An'qwenique drew it. The giant gnomon glowed, but no sign of Drew. "Where's Oona?"

Zsuzsu shushed her, sliced the fog, and poked her chest, signing something about knife and heart. Danger! Paula tiptoed beyond Zsuzsu's reach, signing:

Find a knife to cut through pain
A monthly pass on the clue train

Melody loved that line. Nobody else knew it. Paula said this was their secret verse.

"I don't think he's here," Ralph murmured.

The Redemption Center loomed out of the fog, a massive derelict. Paula winced at moss blanketing the roofs and mildew creeping up rickety stairs. Lichen had eaten the faces carved on railings and become wood. Paula had nothing against resourceful algae and fungi jamming together to eat stone—but careless neglect hurt her feelings. The witch's shed seemed like a recent addition, thrown together from a kitschy online kit.

The Center was not what Paula expected, and not quite like An'qwenique's drawings. Was it the house or Paula? She felt zero wonder for a robber baron ruin haunted by old glory. No time to sort herself out. They needed to find Drew before Drew found them.

"I don't see him anywhere," Paula said, full voice.

Excruciating pain made her bite back a wail. Calves, hamstrings, and quads cramped. She crumpled onto hard ground and dropped the knapsack. The guns bounced out. Nothing to do about that, she had turned to stone, and Drew was just two feet away! How had she not noticed him before? Her heart thundered worse than when she was running too fast.

Drew was sprawled over a witch goddess carved into the sundial: a hair-on-fire, take-no-prisoners Iyami Aje. Kin to the one in Paula's vest pocket, and exactly who you'd expect at weird central. Paula's Aje peered at Drew, thrilled, it would seem. Her goggle necklace displayed fireworks, shooting stars, a streak of lightning. Drew had ditched the curly wig. Sparse hair was plastered against his skull. His lips were puffy, his skin the wrong color. Muscular legs and arms were covered in cuts, gouges, and bumps—a swollen mess. That happened to An'qwenique once, sitting outside after Tank Girl mowed somebody's lawn.

Oona dashed around the gnomon and licked Paula's face. Relief flooded Paula and muscle cramps eased. Oona tugged her closer to Drew.

"No. What do you want? Wait." Reluctantly, Paula crawled beside comatose Drew and patted him down. "No third gun or other weapons. We're good," she shouted.

An'qwenique stepped out of the fog. "Is he breathing?" She wanted to rip his throat if he was. Ralph and Zsuzsu grimaced beside her. Actually, they all (Paula included) wanted somebody else to rip Drew's throat. Oona nipped Paula's fingers and nosed Drew's side. She'd shifted from angry killer wolf to search-and-rescue hero.

"You're a swollen mess, boy," Paula muttered.

Drew's immune system was waging war on a phantom threat, allergens cosplaying deadly bacteria/virus. He might die from friendly fire. Oona did her command bark. An'qwenique stepped forward then back, as if hives were contagious, or maybe it was the murderer thing. Ralph scratched his thigh. Anaphylactic echo?

Paula put two fingers on Drew's pulse. "Still with us, not for long if—"

"So, not dead, just incapacitated." Zsuzsu was disappointed. They all were.

Curtains in the Center's broken windows rustled, yet there was no wind. Restless haints?

Ralph scooped up the guns and dumped them in the go-anywhere wagon. The fluorescent blankets glowed in twilight fog.

Zsuzsu grumble-growled. "Melody said: *The spirits of the forest have a wicked streak.* While you all sort him out, I'm going to make sure we can return home." Paula gaped as Zsuzsu wheeled around the sundial courtyard, setting tiny basket offerings on ledges, in crevices and cracks.

Ralph scoped the crooked stovepipe on the witch's shed. "I don't remember this." He pulled the wagon to a box of doll's eye plants under a round window. These same wild-eyed berries spied on folks behind the Haven.

"Yo, Ralph!" Paula resisted scratching an itchy neck. "Did doll's eye leaves get you and maybe Drew too?"

"I guess." Ralph sounded vague, insubstantial, as if his signal was about to fade out. "An angry berry from around here." He strode into the shed. Same as Zsuzsu, anything to escape Drew, helpless on the ground, breath rattling in his chest, dying.

An'qwenique bristled, fierce as an elephant or lioness, ready to stomp or eviscerate Drew. Paula had never seen that look. An'qwenique claimed folks acted funny on the sundial courtyard. Maybe Paula was acting funny too. Maybe they all were.

Drew opened hazel eyes. Recognition flickered, almost a smile. "It's you," he wheezed, and clutched her hand. "Always a surprise. A treasure." She tried to pull away. His grip was strong—unexpected. "Doing search and rescue, Paula B. Queenie?" He sounded pleased, as if talking to a good friend. Hadn't he just shot at them? "Do you believe any of this?"

"Barely." Paula flung his hand away. "You ditched the wig—revealing your true self?"

"People haven't treated you right. Too bad for them." Trying to glamour her for sure.

"Seriously?" Paula snorted.

He glanced up at An'qwenique. Her afro-puff was putting out sparks. Did he notice? "Were you hoping for another dead body?" He managed a smirk. "And now you want my heart to stutter still. Problem solved."

Paula sucked her teeth. "You lucky I didn't bring my sledgehammer."

He choked on a laugh, convulsed. "Not dead yet."

"Unfortunately, that might take a while," An'qwenique said. "Time is freaky here."

Paula looked around. "We're in uncharted territory."

Drew reached for Paula again, but faltered. "Belle claimed the Center looks different to each person. What do you see?"

"Everybody sees a different world." Paula's ears rang, a high-pitched squeal followed by static. "We just pretend it's the same world." She peered at the derelict mansion. "Careless rich people."

"Is that all?" Drew sounded genuinely disappointed. What did he see? Heaving himself up, he brought his bloated face close to hers. "Most people believe what they see is all there is to see." He slumped. "Are you most people?"

"Is anybody?" After the first disappointing glance, Paula had avoided looking at the ruined mansion. Looking now was a different story.

The Center seemed like a cleverly disguised black ops site *fronting* as derelict. Spiderwebs in busted windows were electronic arrays. Picnic-table umbrellas, turned inside out by storm winds, were satellite dishes. Drones masqueraded as nosy crows roosting in ghostly birch trees. They chattered at two compatriots perched on dragon weathervanes, sentinels. The hawks (enemy agents?) hung in the hemlock trees. Very Hitchcock, and so was the lighting. Magic Hours. The sun hung low, tangled in hemlock branches, refusing to set, and barely a shadow on the sundial. Or was this compound actually an observatory? A Data for the Earth outpost gathering precious info on wetlands and old-growth forests. Paula gasped and the mansion phase-shifted to a steampunk rocket ship.

An'qwenique had nailed the weird, shape-shifting thing. Chimney engines belched smoke, readying for blastoff. Under Drew's swollen body, the sundial whirled through a Milky Way star chart. Stone benches shifted up and down and to the sides, orienting to the next destination. A blue marble bench suddenly went transparent then displayed a spiral galaxy. The mansion phased again to the haunted houseboat.

"Are we spinning?" Drew asked.

"All the time, right?" Paula wished she drew like An'qwenique. No way to remember all this.

The haint galleon rode a river of fog that flowed from the stinky marsh to a sweetgrass lawn. A witchy pirate woman (twin sister to the giant park ranger they met in May) wore watery goggles, rocked a mountain afro, and stood in the crow's nest of the haint galleon. Beryl? Spectral figures in the portholes muttered prayers and curses, static that made sense for a second or two. Actually, they weren't vengeful haints or restless souls who hadn't gone on to dance with ancestors. These spirit figures warded off evil and threw out challenges/invitations for a new adventure—as far as Paula could make out—which wasn't very far.

"It's you." She recognized the gnarly, silver-haired ladies who glowered fire on the endless bus ride. They were young and old, from yesterday, tomorrow, and right now. A few carried pine torches, beckoning her to follow them as they slipped deeper into the house. *This way to peace and freedom.*

Captain Beryl stood next to Paula on the Redemption Center porch in a night-sky jumpsuit. Oona plopped down on Beryl's feet. Beryl stroked the St. B and talked too fast, in and out of English and static. Something about *thanking Zsuzsu for the offerings* and *asking Paula to help save Oona and the navigators.*

"Stop." Paula clutched Beryl's tree branch of an arm. "We're on a mission to catch a murderer and I am sick to my stomach just being near him. No juju to puzzle out a big cosmic mystery for you."

"Quit low-balling yourself!" Beryl repeated Paula's words to An'qwenique. Paula glared at the Aje. Spy. "Hold my words for later." Beryl commanded. "Oona must decide for herself. An impossible decision, she is so full of love—which map to follow? This could tear her apart. Oona will need her posse."

"Decide?" Paula gasped. "You mean stay with us or go off with you all?"

"You understand. Good." Beryl smiled. A hummingbird rode a starfish creeping through her forest of hair. Was the bird there before? "Tell everyone. Follow the clues. For the farewell bring something to trade."

"Like the lapis lazuli or the portable chair?"

Beryl was already gone. The Center settled into haunted mansion mode. Paula was back on the sundial courtyard crouched near Drew. "Write this down," she told An'qwenique, then repeated what Beryl said. Drew gripped her hand. "Why?" Paula demanded.

"Why not?" Umuntu . . ." He started the Zulu saying, then his hand went slack as he passed out.

"Trying to drag us into his story." An'qwenique curled her lips.

"Whatever he has, we hope it's not contagious." Zsuzsu rolled next to An'qwenique. They seemed more shadow than substance. Oona barked and batted Paula with her paw. She whined over Drew.

"Right. He's flushed, swollen, and there's a rat-tat-a-tat, machine-gun pulse." Paula squinted at An'qwenique. "I'm betting anaphylaxis."

"For fuck's sake!" An'qwenique grumbled, then emptied the go-bag. Her favorite portable chair, Beryl's giant goggles, Melody's dumbek, and the survival book tumbled out. Drew's fanny pack too. Running with all that. An'qwenique was superstitious about leaving anything behind, and who could blame her?

Zsuzsu wheeled to Drew. "If we save him, if he lives, he might beat the murder rap. No direct evidence, no reliable eyewitnesses."

Oona lay down against Drew and panted.

"I can't find my med kit." An'qwenique searched again, pulling out journals and pens, the light saber.

Paula quivered. "Melody, Charlize, the adjunct professor #42, and Belle. Our friends."

"Throw Frank and Karl in there too." Ralph hauled the wagon from the witch's shed. Several puppet/masks rode in the bed. The guns were gone, a trade. "No good end here." His voice was flat.

"Besser ein Ende mit Schrecken, als Schrecken ohne Ende," Zsuzsu declared.

"*Better an end with horror than horror without end*," An'qwenique translated, and fumbled through the pack a third time.

"Horror isn't our only option." Paula refused despair.

"We put him in the wagon, wrap him in Beryl's blankets, and get him to the med techs," Ralph muttered.

"Good plan, but he'll be dead before we get there, even in the go-anywhere wagon," An'qwenique muttered.

Paula willed her muscles to cooperate and stood up. She paced around Drew. "I'm a conductor on the Underground Railroad of the Spirit, with Harriet and Jigonhsasee."

"I knew you were going to say some Change Gang crap like that. Fuck!" Zsuzsu poked a hidden back pocket in An'qwenique's go-bag. "You haven't looked in there."

An'qwenique found two epinephrine injectors. Oona licked the package and, smelling the good medicine, wagged her tail. An'qwenique tore open the plastic and held up one. Nobody moved. Oona barked encouragement.

"We tell a different story on this world," Paula declared. She grabbed An'qwenique's wrist and they jabbed the EpiPen into Drew's thigh.

AFTERWARD

OONA AND EVERYONE—
If You Trip and Stumble

Sunday morning—a week after rescuing Drew and before Oona rode the go-anywhere wagon to her heartbeat place—started like no other day. She roved across her maps, covering a lot of territory on this side and the others. Feathered friends for the moment and tomorrow too cawed and cooed comfort her way. Furry friends licked her face and bold beings scratched the itchy spot behind her ear, even rubbed her tummy.

Occasionally, she caught a whiff of a dead creature who'd never get up again. Her shoulder wound throbbed and tender paws burned. She tripped over herself and howled. Mostly Oona's nose was haunted by the good times. She collected smelly wonders, *souvenirs to conjure the dead* as Paula said: Belle's scrunchie, Charlize's apron, and Melody's scarf. The basket weaver who worked at Haven Bagels dropped the scarf in the alley by a dumpster. He refused to chase Oona to retrieve it. These treasures joined the stash of memories that Oona kept at the old tollbooth. The waterfall was a disappointing trickle today, but crows left Oona a trail of golden buttons.

In an empty parking lot, the CEO promised to see Oona and the sundial posse later, at the farewell concert. An'qwenique had put out the word on her podcast and social media: Come for Oona!

The bad man was locked in a cage and unable to step onto another map and escape. He told tales of magic wagons and a giantess restarting his heart that nobody believed. Last Sunday, taking the bad man to the emergency room, Oona and the go-anywhere wagon stopped at his locker in the Iris Library. He had a secret stash too. When the med techs discovered him at the emergency room door and saved his life, he was wrapped in a dragon raincoat and wearing mirror sunglasses. He clutched a fanny pack of locksmith and gadget tools. The phone is his pocket was full of incriminating video evidence. His alibis might have been chatbots. Blue and Oshun said Drew was quite a twist.

For Oona and her pack this was a search-and-rescue success.

This morning, after chasing the pizza-foil crow, Oona cuddled up to the sweetgrass basket, cello bow, and striped knee sock. She was still a prisoner of hope—today could be the day! A hint of her carnival crew rode the wind. Oona never argued with her nose. Energized, she raced back from the State Forest, refusing every temptation, even reckless young bears looking for adventure. She dashed to Zsuzsu's for breakfast.

Something big was brewing. The next-door mutt smelled this too. Oona jumped the neighbor's honeysuckle as Ralph set out a dish of chicken, barley, and carrots for her. Zsuzsu turned on the green water dragon and doused them both. Zsuzsu and Ralph had already eaten: blueberry pancakes and soy sausage. Oona hoped for crumbs and the last link still on the platter. Zsuzsu did not disappoint.

For the first time since Zsuzsu brought Oona home from the Pet and Wild Animal Rescue, they missed their Sunday-afternoon roll/walk along the boardwalk to the Redemption Center. Instead Zsuzsu and Ralph drove her and the go-anywhere wagon toward the aroma of jollof rice and dodo, spanakopita, popcorn, beans and rice, baklava, bagels, cream cheese, and lox. A feast! They parked the van beside the garden house and walked through the asters to Iris Library.

Paula and An'qwenique waited in the first-floor foyer. Oona jumped up and licked warm noses. They giggled as she collected their scent logs. Earlier, after eating cheesy buns with soy bacon bits at Haven, An'qwenique ran 10K and Paula stopped by Triple-E's house. She took bagels for Gwen, Lance, and

Grandpa too. Ralph met Duke at Crossroads. Checking on everyone, doing the rounds, like Oona.

Gathering this afternoon with her pack in the library lobby, Oona filled her spirit well.

"Whoa! The suit guy from the Center." Zsuzsu nodded at the CEO.

"Mr. Carter, you look healthy as a horse." The CEO wore a green/brown silk suit with a camouflage tie. "This better be good," he grumbled at Zsuzsu and An'qwenique.

"Why? Are you on borrowed time?" Ralph quipped.

"Bail," the CEO replied, and walked up the stairs away from their surprise.

"Do you think everyone will show?" Zsuzsu's breath fluttered.

"For Oona?" Paula kissed Oona's nose. "They have to."

"Hell yeah!" An'qwenique and Ralph agreed.

Zsuzsu clutched their hands. "I don't want to say goodbye to anyone else."

"Oona gets to do what she wants," Paula said, a dire tone.

Oona licked Zsuzsu's hand, to reassure her. Everyone was suddenly anxious. Maybe later today or tomorrow, they'd do search and rescue together and feel better. People were always losing each other. Searching was a good life.

Zsuzsu and the go-anywhere wagon took the elevator. Oona preferred the stairs. She bounded around library patrons up to the fourth floor. She arrived in time to greet Zsuzsu when the elevator doors whooshed open.

Gwen and Lance's trickster exhibition lined the hallway to the event center. Paula carried the Aje in a crossbody bag that hung open at her hip. The Aje clutched the edge of the bag and cloudy goggles bounced at her neck. An'qwenique stepped onto a stool and hung her closet Guardian mask in the doorway, a gift from Charlize who got it from Melody who found it in Beryl's shed. The Guardian spun in the draft, grimacing and grinning, sneering and smirking. Nobody realized the mask greeted everyone with a different face. Change Gang performers strode into the event center carrying instruments and juggling pins. Oona jumped in the wagon, ready for a show.

According to Jabril, the Cosmic Campers proposed that their farewell concert not only be a celebration for Belle, but for Charlize, Melody, and Dwayne Williams—the adjunct professor in the Jackie Robinson shirt. On her Wednesday podcast, An'qwenique urged everyone to attend the public event, especially the sundial posse, for Oona's sake. "Even a great lead singer prefers to soar over a stellar backup band."

The camouflage woman and the med techs had been the first to arrive. They had front-row seats. Blue, Oshun, and Officer Judy Wang were there unofficially, not to enforce the fire marshal's orders. Gwen rocked a spiderweb dress. Lance came as an astronaut and Triple-E wore paisley hippie wear in honor of Belle. They sat far from the cops and near the door, in case. An'qwenique was live streaming the event for her podcast fans. She roved the audience, capturing memories, the sadness and the good spirits.

Azul persuaded Duke and Tomás to come, even though they felt terrible. They arrived late and might have missed the grand entrance, but tuning the donsó ngoni and cello together was a trick. The quiet couple (who'd hunkered under the satellite umbrellas at the Redemption Center) were the last of the sundial posse to arrive. They sat in the back next to Tomás. Aretha was in his lap and Benjie sat at his feet. The golden retriever service dog spread calm, even though the audience exceeded the 600-person limit.

Oona's big heart could have burst. She bounded in the air and yipped for joy. The Cosmic Campers, dressed in the galaxy gowns and nebula tuxedo they wore at Crossroads, entered from an empty utility closet. Galaxy fascinators hovered over mountains of hair, with no visible attachments. River's shooting-star top hat left a trail of sparkles. The Campers declared themselves to be two drag queens and a drag king from another dimension. "Space is the place!"

"Beam me up!" some members of the audience cheered, ready to be transported. Others groaned and rolled their eyes. Oona missed the references and barely noticed the fabulous costumes. She ran circles around her carnival family, wagging her butt and leaping up to nip their noses. She scented all the places they had been in their hair, on their clothes and skin, in their sweat. She smelled the energy sparks that fueled their jaunts, the otherworldly breath, and food from out of this galaxy. Finally she leapt into the go-anywhere wagon as it rolled in front of the audience.

River, the drag king, sat down beside her and bowed the cello, playing the *come back* song. Jabril joined on the donsó ngoni. The mandolin player plucked counterpoint from the hall. Oona collapsed in a heap, *playing dead.* Half the audience signed and sang Melody's anthem. At the last note Oona jumped up from the wagon to cheers. She zigzagged down the aisles, a bolt of lightning. The audience went wild for special effects in real life.

Paula and An'qwenique beat back worry as she streaked by. Theatre magic was perfect cover. Oona launched herself in the air and the clown caught her. They tumbled about together, doing their show moves again, after almost a year. The clown and the magician juggled their hats and solar-system bling. These disappeared on downbeats and reappeared for an upbeat exactly where Oona could catch them. The audience was dazzled.

"What kind of memorial is this?" Duke groused. "A clown show?"

"And I've seen better drag," Tomás whispered.

"Really?" Azul replied. "Where?"

Oona caught several shooting stars and dropped these at Tomás's feet. She smelled Charlize on him and whimpered. Tomás hugged her. "You loved my lady, I know, I know. She loved you too."

Gwen stepped in front of the musicians and grasped a crumpled piece of paper. Audience and performers quieted, except for the cello, donsó ngoni, and mandolin carrying the mood. Gwen hesitated.

"Go on!" Lance yelled.

Gwen spoke softly. "Belle and Melody were besties. Amazing, huh? What did they agree on? Almost nothing."

Laughter as Oona walked up to Gwen and the wagon followed.

"I didn't know Charlize, but An'qwenique told me about her girl, and guess what, all three loved music, the Cosmic Campers, and St. Berdoodles. Charlize wanted to record Melody's anthem with a choir of everyday folks, singing and signing. That's us today. I'm here talking to you because of Belle. We're her Change Gang." Gwen signed and spoke the next words, "Belle, Melody, and Charlize are *my heart beating on, for as long as I can.*"

The Cosmic Campers signed with Gwen then taught the audience.

"Also, I wouldn't be up here without Paula and Elaine Eleanor Edith either. Triple-E, named for her grandmother and two great-aunts who were also known as Babs, Beanie, and Bug. Just saying. Paula has a new verse for Melody's anthem." Gwen grabbed Paula and pulled her to the cello player.

Paula was as awkward as Gwen. "No speech, here's the verse."

Tell me a story I could be
Draw me a map that sets us free
Do the dance that gives us a chance
Figure the code for vision mode

The Cosmic Campers had the audience signing and singing in four-part harmony.

The drag king musician stepped close to Paula and whispered,

"I love your earring." A solar system dangled from both their right ears. "Connect a moment with someone on a bus, in the woods, on the porch of an abandoned house, and you find the world you've been looking for. Thanks to you and Benjie for saving us, and Oona, of course. Isn't it grand to be entangled in miracles and mysteries?"

Paula hugged the drag king and whispered, "River and Benjie forever!"

"No. We must take our leave," River said. "Navigate the rest of our lives."

Paula and the audience nodded.

"Oona has made a life with you and also one with us," River clutched the wagon's handle. Oona wagged her tail, excited for *follow your nose.* "We need Oona and the wagon to get our haunted houseboat on the road." Only the sundial posse understood what River was saying. "Oona can return with the wagon, if we have enough to balance, a trade for the wagon so to speak. If Oona doesn't want to come back, you'll have the wagon at least."

Without hesitation Paula set a bundle of life-size images from her inspiration gallery in the wagon. Triple-E offered a blank journal yet to be filled. An'qwenique put her new running shoes and a drawing of the sundial posse and Paula. Ralph had brought his bike helmet and gloves from the van. Someone put Change Gang mugs on the pile.

River looked uncertain. "The more meaningful, the better."

Gwen and Lance offered a Pukwudgie and a Tikbalang. Zsuzsu added Melody's dumbek.

"Charlize loved chocolate croissants and I buy too many," Tomás said.

River accepted the greasy bag from him. "Thank you all for believing in us, helping us. Now we play *follow your nose.*" Oona jumped in the wagon, a tight fit. The clown and magician juggled spiral galaxies and River proclaimed, "For Paula!"

Who is that Woman?
Rising up
Dance life, she says
But if you trip and stumble
Then sing life
And if your voice cracks
Let your heart keep time
And if your heart gives out
With your last breath
Leave your story behind
And if you are forgotten
Come to us, in dreams and visions
Shake us from these death-like trances
Haunt us, hound us, like demons
Until we cannot forget
That some slow, shuffling death
is not
the DANCE
that is LIFE

The Cosmic Campers danced into the closet and shut the door. Gwen waited a few seconds, then opened the door. The closet was empty. The audience gasped in unison.

"Theatre magic," Azul declared. Nobody argued with the Chief Nerd, although Officer Wang wanted to. One more anomaly and Azul would have used up all of her grace. The audience broke into applause.

Perhaps it was fast, perhaps it took forever, that's how time works. The audience stomped their feet and demanded an encore. The mandolin player shook her head. She had no more music this night. And then Oona rolled in from the hall in the red wagon. Paula, squealed, gripped the handle, and pulled her center stage. Ralph laughed. Oona tried to crawl in Zsuzsu's lap. The sundial posse crowded around them, cheering and weeping.

No reason to be sad, Oona intended to look for her carnival

crew till she found them again. Searching was a good life. Oona was everything all at once: pack leader, carnival dog, search-and-rescue maven, in this world and traveling the others.

An'qwenique stuck a microphone under Paula's nose. "What do you have to tell the *Great Escape* podcast audience?"

Paula blurted, "I guess, here on the Peace Path with Harriet and Jigonhsasee, we are Oona's heartbeat place."

ACKNOWLEDGMENTS

As always, I pour libation to Eshu and the deities of the crossroads. I am also grateful for the tricksters who shake up my mind and illuminate the multiverse.

Thanks to my editor Lee Harris, and also to Matt Rusin, Giselle Gonzalez, and the folks at Tor who champion my work and make so much possible.

Big thanks to my dog friends—neighbors, running buddies, tricksters, and rescue dogs—Blue, Ellis, Wolfie, Tootsie, Olympia, and Casey. Once when a hulking man got out of his flashy sedan to chastise me for writing a play that shook his world, a very large dog friend jumped a high fence and chased the fellow back into that car.

Thanks especially to Oona, the next-door neighbor St. Berdoodle, who regularly got me to chase after her for a stick or a glove. Blessings on Phil O'Donoghue, Valle Dwight, Aidan, and Tim for letting me tromp around their yard chasing Oona.

I am inspired by the work on animal cognition and emotion done by Frans De Waal, Brian Hare, Vanessa Woods, and Carl Safina. They creep, fly, and wiggle through these pages with my characters.

As I finished *The Redemption Center is Closed on Sundays*, I had the good fortune to be a fellow at the Kahn Liberal Arts Institute at Smith College for "Possible Futures: AI and Human Experience." This semester-long investigation of Artificial Intelligence gathered faculty, students, and visiting artists and scholars to explore questions about AI in a broad interdisciplinary milieu. Ben Baumer, Luca Capogna, R. Jordan Crouser, Kate Flöer, Kiki Gounaridou, Kevin Haung, Regina Hu, Sam Intrator, Susan Levin, Boushilah Mata, Laura Sizer, Lee Spector, Claire Sullivan, Roopa Vasudevan, and Jenny Vogel were wonderful guides through the multiverse.

Wolfgang and Beate Schmidhuber and the entire Schmidhuber clan plied me with good food, beautiful landscapes, and exuberant friendship. They were/are a respite in trying times.

Thanks to my Beta readers who saved me with their fresh perspectives, insightful questions and observations. Bill Oram, Joy Voeth, and Kiki Gounaridou. They encouraged and challenged me to make the novel better. Pan Morigan drew my visions and Ed Check digitized them.

Blessings on Pan Morigan, James Emery, and my agent, Kris O'Higgins, for believing in the stories I tell.